Love Me TOMORROW

MARIA LUIS

LOVE ME TOMORROW

PUT A RING ON IT

MARIA LUIS

ALKMINI BOOKS, LLC

They call her America's Sweetheart.
And me? I'm the so-called "inked god" she dumped on TV.

I've tried to forget her. I've tried to move on.

Until I discover that her family is opening a new restaurant next to my tattoo parlor.

If I were a gentleman, I'd offer my congratulations and go my own way.
If I were a gentleman, I'd let her be . . . *but I'm not.*

Savannah Rose may claim I'm nothing more than a friend, but that slight hitch in her breath whenever I get too close says that **America's sweetheart is nothing but a liar.**

All it takes is one scorching kiss, and I vow in her ear: "You're going to beg. Beg me to touch you, beg me to give you more, and if you're real good, maybe I'll do it all over again before you have to beg for that too."

I'm no gentleman.
But Savannah Rose? She's no one's sweetheart but mine.

Love Me Tomorrow (Put A Ring On It, Book 3)
Maria Luis
Copyright © 2019 by Alkmini Books, LLC
It is illegal to distribute or resale this copy in any form.
All rights reserved.
No part of this book may be reproduced in any form or by any electronic or mechanical means, including information storage and retrieval systems, without written permission from the author, except for the use of brief quotations in a book review.

Cover Photographer: Wander Book Club Photography

Cover Models: Kerry S. and Sam.

Cover Designer: Najla Qamber, Najla Qamber Designs

Editing: Kathy Bosman, Indie Editing Chick

Proofreading: Tandy Proofreads; Horus Proofreading

Created with Vellum

To Mama,
For teaching me what it means to soar, you inspire me more than you will ever know.

Good job, honey.

PLAYLIST

"Another Life" — Afrojack & David Guetta (ft. Ester Dean)
"I'll Be Good" — Jaymes Young
"Waking Up The Ghost" — 10 Years
"Novocaine" — The Unlikely Candidates
"I Will Wait" — Mumford & Sons
"Raining" — Art of Dying (ft. Adam Gontier)
"Easier" — 5 Seconds of Summer
"Too Close" — Next
"Love / Hate Heartbreak" — Halestorm
"Good Rebels" — Kings Dead (ft. Moonflwr)
"Draw the Stars" — Andreya Triana

PROLOGUE

SAVANNAH

Los Angeles, California

There is not enough booze in all the world to help me survive this.

Twenty-seven men. One reality TV dating show.

And me.

The bachelorette.

America's so-called "sweetheart."

The girl most likely to end up face*down* before the night is over, if the contestants I've already met are any indication of how this hot mess express is going to go. First there was the guy dressed in a dinosaur onesie. Then another who dropped to one knee, a Ring Pop clutched in hand, for an impromptu proposal. (I let him down gently, then discreetly threw the cherry-flavored candy in a nearby bush.) And, to round up 'em all up, the last man wheeled out of the limo in a pair of lime-green roller blades . . . only to promptly wipe out on the cobblestoned driveway.

His arms pinwheeled wildly.

I launched to the side but couldn't escape his grasping hands.

One second my red strapless dress was looking modestly sexy, and in the next?

Nip slip, y'all.

Nipple. Slip.

Only two hours in, and I've already managed to surpass every worst-case scenario I've imagined since being told *Put A Ring On It* would be my new reality.

Yay me.

Cheeks burning with the never-to-be-forgotten memory of flashing the production crew, Mr. Roller Blade Man himself and, possibly, even the universe at large—if the editors don't do some major snipping to the final footage, that is—I skip the champagne flute and grab the bottle off the table instead. The red ribbon, wound around the glass neck, tangles with my fingers as I dramatically salute the empty dressing room.

"Bottom's up," I mutter under my breath, then toss back a swig of the bubbly. My eyes water and my chest inflates, and, you know, I'm not much of a drinker, but now seems like a good enough time to start as any.

The good news: as far as first nights go, I'm on the home-stretch.

Only five more guys to meet.

It'll be fine. *I'll* be fine. So what if my heart hasn't fluttered with excitement tonight? Not every relationship kicks off with metaphorical fireworks. Hell, look at my parents; sometimes I'm not even convinced they *like* each other, let alone married for love. And, really, so what if I flashed everyone and their mother within the first few hours of filming?

A nervous giggle bubbles to the surface.

Yeah, I'm not fooling anyone. More champagne is definitely in order.

I guzzle it down, only to freeze mid-gulp when the dressing room door flies open and rebounds off the wall with a heavy *thud*.

Panicked, my gaze tracks the woman storming inside. One of the producers, I think. Rocking an official-looking headset and a pinched expression, she might as well be yanking along the accompanying cameraman by a leash, from the way he trails after her like an obedient puppy.

I sit up tall. "I was told I could have a few minutes before meeting the last group of guys." A few more minutes to remind myself—yet again—that contracts have been signed, promises have been made, and I'm not the sort of person who exits stage right when people are depending on me. Even if I have just managed to flash fifty-or-so people my naked chest.

Never let it be said that I'm not a trooper.

The producer slides me an icy stare. "Your few minutes are up." Her brown hair is a tangled mess on the top of her head, and whereas I'm on dress number two for the night (a gold sequined number that makes me feel like a sausage stuffed into inflexible casing), she's decked out in a T-shirt, ripped jeans, and an old pair of Vans. The plastic ID hanging around her neck reads *Matilda Houghton.* "We need a testimonial."

With dread pricking my skin, I set the champagne down. "Right now?"

"Yup." The *P* pops in time with her smacking a piece of gum in her mouth. "No one hired you to just sit around and look pretty." Jerking a thumb toward the cameraman, she follows up with a *chop-chop* snap of her fingers. "C'mon, first impressions of the contestants you've met so far. Smile big now."

I have approximately two-point-five seconds to prepare myself.

Blinding light beams into my face from the bulb fixed to the top of the camera.

A bead of sweat trickles down my spine.

Like a cornered animal, I dart my gaze from right to left, left to right. *Think. Think!* "The guys are—"

"Specific names, please," she cuts off, somehow managing to look both aggravated and bored, all at once. "Who stood out to you?"

Not. A. Single. Soul.

Is that pathetic? So far, I've met twenty-two guys. Accountants and Hollywood stunt doubles and even a former NFL player, and my stupid heart has not quickened for any of them. Objectively, I know they're a good-looking group of men. *Better* than good-looking, honestly. Half of them could be models, and I . . . I can't recall any of their names.

I'm not the right bachelorette.

It's obvious to me, even if it isn't yet obvious to everyone else, and it's only a matter of time before the guys realize that my heart isn't locked and loaded for this all-too-public journey. Any other woman would be thrilled to be in my position. Any other woman would be dying to spend their days flirting with twenty-seven sexy strangers.

Any other woman but me.

"I, uh . . ." I squint, trying to summon visuals of the men to mind. Dinosaur Onesie. Ring Pop Man. NippleGate Orchestrator. Stiffening my shoulders against a residual shudder of horror, I stare directly into the camera and blurt out, "I've always loved *Jurassic Park*."

Matilda rolls her wrist in a *keep-going* gesture.

I force a strained smile. When Matilda slices a finger across her throat—like she's worried about me terrifying viewers all across America—I shake out the nerves by wiggling my toes in my shoes. Dial the smile down some. "Matthew"—*Richard?* Who the hell knows at this point —"seemed fun. It's, uh, nice to know that we might have something in common." The last time I watched *Jurassic Park*, I was in the seventh grade and still wore a hot-pink mouth guard to bed every night. "That's all I could hope for, coming on the show. To meet someone who matches me, inside and out. Common interests. Shared dreams."

Any hope I have that my answer might satisfy Matilda goes out the window when she nods, then plants a hand on my shoulder to keep me seated when I start to rise. My ass, swathed in Spanx and sequins and skin-clinging fabric, collapses with enough force that the wooden seat protests with a squeal.

Nonplussed, Matilda retreats to the cameraman's side. "If your dream man could step out of that limo tonight, what would he look like?"

It feels like a trick question.

But for the first time all night, my heart gives an erratic *thump-thump-thump.* I despise the excitement currently singing in my veins. Despise it as much as I crave it. Because the truth is: I never wanted to be *Put A Ring On It's* bachelorette. No, the honor was meant to belong to my younger sister, Amelie. *She'd* submitted the first audition tape. *She'd* been on the hunt to live it up on reality TV and date twenty-seven men after breaking up with . . . *him.*

Ruthlessly, I shove the excitement away, sticking it in the Bad Thoughts box that I refuse to dwell on. Because thinking of him—and every tiny tattoo he's inked on my skin in the dead of night over the last year—does nothing but make me wish for something that can never, ever be.

End of the day, it doesn't matter *who* my dream man is.

I'm on this show because the host and creator, Joe Devonsson, came across Amelie's audition, only to stumble across a separate application my mother submitted online for me. A submission, I'd like to add, that she never once told me about until Devonsson's voice was in my ear, hollering through the phone, as he boasted about all the merits of having the Rose sisters battle it out for a suitor on TV. He thought it would make for excellent audience ratings, a way to edge out the longstanding *The Bachelor* franchise. And then there are my parents—both high society New Orleanians—who thought *Put A Ring On It* would be an "utter delight." A way to harken back to the glittering world of debutante balls, various men vying for the affections of a woman, and, as always, a way to get more eyes on the family business.

Except that I didn't come here for any of that. I came here for Amelie.

Because everything I've done in life, I've done for my little sister. I've subjected myself to the special brand of tough love that my parents dole out in spades, all so she could take off to California and then Hawaii and then, finally, to Florida. I've glued myself to the trajectory laid out for me since birth, so that my parents' attention would be otherwise preoccupied when Amelie shaved her dark hair down to her skull and pierced her nose and strutted around wearing clothes that left her bronze skin nearly bare because she's always been one to express her moods through her wardrobe.

I gave my parents all of me so my sister could keep all of her.

Which was great and all—until she backed out of the show two weeks ago, citing a business opportunity in Europe that she could *not* pass up, and now I'm here.

Alone.

Sticky with sweat and nerves.

And dreaming of a man who once belonged to my sister while I'm being courted by twenty-seven other guys.

Not even free champagne can fix this mess.

Clearing my throat, I finally answer: "He'd look like a man who could put up with my family's special brand of crazy."

It's a witty response, a deflective one, too, considering all the heartache that's gone on behind the scenes in the last few weeks, but Matilda and the camera guy must be ready to hit the cocktails themselves because after a few more surface-level questions, I'm being shuffled back down the winding staircase and out through one of the side doors. The crisp air teases my skin with goose bumps.

"Rock 'n' roll time, folks!" Joe Devonsson bellows, off to my right. "Let's do this—no more crazy shit, you hear me? If I see one more man come out of that limo wearing a ridiculous costume, I'm going to fucking lose my mind."

You can say that again.

With feet that feel heavy like iron anvils, I trudge to my marked spot on the circular driveway. The grand mansion is to my back, the waiting limo to my front. I have absolutely zero expectations that the next five guys will rev my engine, so to speak, but Matilda's question continues to nag me: *If your dream man could step out of that limo, what would he look like?*

Temptation. The word slips through my mind and clings fiercely. My dream man would look like temptation.

"Savannah, you ready?"

After a quick thumbs up to Joe, I pin a serene smile in place like the debutante I once was.

Press my shoulders back.

Pray with every bit of my soul that even if the next guy to climb out of that limo isn't my dream man, hopefully he'll be someone I find attractive—or, at the very least, someone who will do a damn good job of convincing me that although I don't *want* to be on a dating show, I made the right decision in honoring my contract by showing up.

The glossy limo door swings open and a pair of black-leather dress shoes hit the stone driveway. One foot, then the other, and maybe I'm crazy or already tipsy on too much champagne, but my stomach dips with anticipation.

Begrudging anticipation, but anticipation nonetheless.

Black slacks appear, and I curse the set director for placing me near the walkway leading up to the mansion. Case in point: my view is nothing but limbs. But yeah, this guy—whoever he is—he's got great legs. Thick thighs that strain the fabric of his pants. Tall-looking, too. Definitely taller than I am.

Wanting a better look, I shift up onto my tiptoes, the rasp of my sequined dress against the cobblestones echoing loudly in my ears.

Tattooed hands are revealed next. Thick, masculine fingers. A palm that could easily span the width of my back, tugging me close for a romantic dance, or a hot kiss, or a gravelly whisper in my ear.

I never cared for tattoos, not before *him*. Not before I watched him work diligently on every person who walked into his parlor. Not before I sat on that flat table, aware that I was rebelling in a way that I never had before, and felt the weight of his big hands coasting over my skin to mark me with black, irreversible ink.

I swallow hard and remind myself that Los Angeles is thousands of miles away from New Orleans.

Pull yourself together, Rose.

And maybe I would have been able to, if the man exiting the limo hadn't stepped into the soft light just then and thrown my already teetering world straight into the abyss of chaos.

My dream man.

In the span of a heartbeat, I soak in his familiar face. The dark, tousled hair. The dark, close-shaven beard. The dark, bottomless eyes that always seem to anticipate my every move—even when I wish he couldn't read me at all. The tattoos that creep up to the collar of his black suit, and cling to the base of his thick throat.

I'm accustomed to seeing him in jeans and flannel shirts but decked out in a tailored, black suit like he is now . . . God, he looks raw.

Savage.

Powerful.

What is he doing *here?*

Instinctively, I step back—off the *X* taped to the stone beneath my feet and away from the man who isn't supposed to be anywhere but in his tattoo shop on Bourbon Street.

Certainly not here. With me.

Amelie.

My sister's face flashes in my mind's eye and I wrangle my rapidly beating heart into submission, pushing the traitorous thing down until the pounding in my ears is nothing but ambivalent white noise.

He doesn't heed the shock that's no doubt kicked my placid smile to the curb.

No.

Without taking those glittering black eyes off me, he

ambles close, all loose limbs and simmering confidence, until we're breathing the same air, taking up the same space, existing in the same moment.

Temptation.

Goddamn temptation.

"Give me your hand."

It's all he says but spoken in that rough New Orleans drawl of his, it's both a request and a command all at once.

Flustered, my gaze shoots over to the crew, to all the cameras trained in our direction. The lights are damn near blinding but there's no mistaking the way Joe sits on the literal edge of his seat, looking enraptured by the scene unfolding before him.

One thing is clear: no one is going to help me out of this.

It didn't occur to me until just now how very public this experience will be. And I'm no idiot: Joe Devonsson will gleefully air this moment all over America in just a few short months, rubbing his hands together in anticipation of skyrocketing ratings. Then everyone will know, just by looking at my face, that I feel like I've been pummeled by an eighteen-wheeler.

I lower my voice, my hands balled into tight fists down by my sides to keep them from visibly trembling. "You shouldn't be here."

His sharp jaw clenches tight. "I'm exactly where I'm supposed to be."

I'm short on breath. I want to blame it on the too-tight dress. I want to blame it on the California weather, but it's late November and the air is cool, for once, without even a hint of humidity. I want to blame my lightheadedness on anything *but* the man standing a hand's width away, looking like the Prince of Darkness.

For a little over a year now, our relationship has been

casual. Friends, no matter how often I found myself looking at him a little too long or secretly admiring the wide breadth of his shoulders or finding reasons to meet up with him that shouldn't have existed after he'd dated Amelie.

And now he's *here*.

Standing less than two feet away and stealing all my damn air.

My chin angles north with false bravado. "You can't stay."

Catching me completely off guard, he steps in close, demolishing the distance between us, and hooks an inked finger under my chin. My chest caves with need, lust, awareness. Although I'll never admit it out loud, my knees quiver, too. *Quiver!* Like I'm some sort of teenage girl faced with her first crush, instead of a thirty-four-year-old woman who knows her own mind and manages thirteen restaurants all over New Orleans.

I should move away. Shove him back. Demand that the producers kick him off the premises.

He doesn't give me the chance to do any of those things.

Moving methodically, like he's expecting me to scramble backward, he lowers his head and grazes his cheek against mine. I feel the bristles of his beard, the softness of his lips as they find the shell of my ear. His hand leaves my chin to clasp the back of my neck with a familiarity that reaches into my soul and twists, hard.

"No more running, Rose." The warmth of his breath elicits a shiver down my spine, my surname sounding like nothing less than a forbidden endearment dripping off his tongue. "Give me a chance. Give *us* a chance."

But there are no chances, not for us.

He lets me go and it's a miracle I remain standing on my own two feet, my legs feel so weak. A small smile plays on his full lips—a mouth I've never once kissed—before he turns away, heading up the walkway to the mansion.

My fingers curl, nails biting sharply into my palm.

He's my kryptonite. My weakness. And the one man who is decidedly off-limits to me—forever.

This . . . *flirtation* that we have going on? It has to end.

Tonight.

Ignoring the cameras and the knowledge that one day this moment will broadcast all over the country, I squeeze my eyes and make a decision: I need to let him go. I need to let him go and move on and let myself fall in love . . .

With someone who isn't Owen Harvey.

1

OWEN

NEW ORLEANS, LOUISIANA

Seven Months Later

"He had a heart attack mid-coitus."

Disregarding the fact that I've asked her to keep still five times now—or face the wrath of my tattoo machine going rogue—Shirley Hamilton glances over her shoulder and gives me the *look*.

One I know way too well.

The lowered brows.

The pursed mouth.

The last time Shirley looked at me like that, I was inking a unicorn on her ankle for her seventy-second birthday. She'd been so invested in her story about her friend from bingo doing "the drugs" that she'd clipped me in the face with her jittery elbow and I came *this* close to screwing up her tattoo.

That was three years ago.

Like she's got a homing beacon tucked away somewhere in that massive purse of hers, Shirley returns every year on her birthday, promptly at noon. And she always comes with a bonkers story that could put even *Jerry Springer* to shame.

At this point, it's almost tradition.

"Don't move," I warn again, returning to the tiny constellation of stars she asked for on her right shoulder blade. One for each one of her grandkids. *Four more to go.*

Either she left her hearing aids at home or Shirley doesn't give a rat's ass that I'm working. She rolls her eyes, shakes out her curly hair, and mutters, "You ever hear of such a thing? Nearly entering the pearly gates of heaven at a critical time like that?"

When I opened Inked on Bourbon almost ten years ago, I never thought that I'd be offering ink with a sprinkle of unsanctioned therapy on the side. I expected the tourists who wander into the parlor, still drunk from the Hand Grenades they slurped down out on Bourbon Street. Hell, I even expected the constant requests for delicate butterfly tattoos and Celtic knot armbands, and yeah, once in a while, I knew I'd get some spectacular pieces done for true ink enthusiasts.

But playing Dr. Phil twenty-four-seven?

Never even occurred to me—which seems somewhat problematic considering that I'm a bit of a broody bastard. I leave the do-good, charismatic vibes to my twin, Gage, and his wife, Lizzie, both of whom work part-time shifts here at Inked whenever they can. Though with Lizzie about to pop out a kid, I'll probably need to start moving my apprentices into more permanent positions sooner rather than later.

Aware that Shirley is waiting for a response, I keep my gaze locked on the second star when I answer, "Can't say that I have."

"Of course not. You're a strapping young man, Owen. Big and tall and brawny—*anyway*." She blows out a heavy breath. "The way Peggy told the story, there he was, carrying out God's work, when *bam!* Couldn't breathe."

I cock a brow. "You sure he was havin' a heart attack? Might've just came."

Shirley giggles like I'm some kind of womanizer, which couldn't be further from the truth. "His lips turned blue."

"Ah. Definitely a heart attack, then." I pause for effect, just because I know Shirley gets her rocks off on a spot of crazy gossip. At the end of the day, Inked on Bourbon is a business—if the woman wants to talk smack about her friends, I can definitely scrape together my bedside manners for another thirty minutes and make it happen. Customer satisfaction guaranteed. I offer her a teasing grin. "You think he got her off first? One last hurrah before he bit the bullet?"

"Oh, Owen. You are *so* bad."

Shirley's thin shoulders shake with silent laughter, and I raise the needle off her skin before she ends up looking like she's undergone a Magic Marker experiment at the local pre-school.

Leaning back on my stool, I snag a fresh paper towel off my workstation and run it over her shoulder blade. Halfway done. Six little stars shouldn't even take more than twenty or thirty minutes, but I do what I can to make Shirley's birthday somewhat memorable, like always booking her appointment for an hour and a half, so she has plenty of time to talk my ear off.

Last year I picked up red velvet cake—her favorite.

Today, I grabbed a few cannoli from my favorite bakery over on Royal Street, just a block away. Shirley's a widow, her kids have fled the roost and live in different states, and maybe it makes me a total sap, but I hate the idea of the woman sitting alone in her house while the world around her continues on without a second glance.

In that, Shirley and I might as well be soul mates.

Difference is, of course, Shirley's alone because her offspring are doing their own thing and I'm alone by choice.

Only because you let her push you away.

My fingers flex around the towel, which I sharply fling into the nearby trashcan.

Nah, there was no *letting* involved when it came to Savannah Rose sending me packing from California. She made her decision. I walked away. She opted to pursue other interests, and I sure as fuck don't beg anyone for anything. Not even when being sent home from that ridiculous TV show meant staggering into the airport so wasted that I'd been forced to wait another twenty-four hours before any of the flight attendants even let me *look* at a plane ticket.

So, yeah, it was rough.

Painful, my brain supplies helpfully like the asshole it is, *it was brutally painful.*

If I have to guess, I'm hedging my bets that Savannah is engaged by now. Which is good. I hope some douchebag actually put a ring on it because then I can move on. No more hoping she might waltz into my parlor, grief written all over her face when she begs me for another chance after all these months of radio silence. No more purposely skipping over Channel 6 whenever *Put A Ring On It* airs on Wednesday evenings. No more pining for a woman who—

Crack!

My head snaps to the left, to the shared wall between Inked and the kitschy souvenir shop next door, just as the antique barge board gives way and a sledgehammer bursts through.

Bursts *through*. As in, I'm staring at a set of fingers

currently trying to wrangle the massive tool back through the concave hole about four feet off the ground.

Christ.

"*Shit*!" shouts a panicked voice from the other side of the wall. "I'm *so* getting fired for this."

Shirley darts a concerned look my way. "Maybe I should come back tomorrow?"

"And miss the present I bought you? Not happening." I push off the stool, letting it roll to the side as I rise to my full height. I strip off my latex gloves and toss them in the garbage. "Plus, don't think I'm lettin' you leave without filling me in on whether or not Peggy's husband died by orgasm."

"He didn't. Die, that is."

"Huh. Looks like silver linings do exist."

"But he's not allowed to have sex for a while," Shirley tells me, watching avidly as I approach the shared wall. I wrap a hand around the sledgehammer and give it a good tug. It comes loose easily, and when I peek through the hole, I see nothing but bright lights and hear nothing but four-letter curse words. "You know," my client adds, "because of his heart and all."

"Hey, you win some, you lose some."

Shirley laughs again, and when I turn back to her, I see her give a little shrug. "Maybe I could watch some TV while I wait?" Her eyes soften with hope. "You know I love me some *Judge Judy*."

"Remote's on the receptionist's desk." I jerk my chin toward the front. "Have at it."

"And if anyone comes by looking for you?"

Aside from potential walk-ins looking for a spur-of-the-moment tattoo, no one is coming by unannounced. Gage is working a beat, Lizzie is filming some makeup video for her

YouTube channel, and aside from the two of them, it's not like I get a lot of random visitors. I swing the sledgehammer in an arc. "Tell them you've buried my body in the courtyard and stolen all of the goods."

Giggling, Shirley practically sashays around me to pluck the TV remote off the front desk while I head for the door. Knowing her, she'll be so immersed in the world of *Judge Judy*, she'll forget that she's even waiting.

Stepping out onto Bourbon, I'm immediately assaulted by the *clip-clop* of horse hooves, the hollering for Mardi Gras beads—even though it's June—from up on the second-floor balconies, and a scent that my twin once dubbed *eau de French Quarter*.

Sewage. Booze. Vomit. Humidity.

It's a special fragrance that speaks to the soul and reminds me of my later teenage years, when Gage and I used to sneak into the strip clubs with our fake IDs and order rounds of shots like we were high rollers.

Now, Gage is a cop for the NOPD's Special Operatives Division, and I—well, the last time I got drunk down here in the Quarter—or, anywhere, really—was the day I arrived back in town from my one and only trip out to the West Coast.

Because clearly my last night in LA wasn't enough to erase the burn of Savannah's rejection.

Resting the sledgehammer's wooden handle on my shoulder, I nod to one of the street performers who always hits up this intersection, then cut left. The glass windows of the storefront next to Inked are completely blacked out.

I try the door with a jiggle of the handle, and Lady Luck must be on my side because it swings open without issue.

Option Two would have been to use the sledgehammer.

One glance is all I need to know that someone is doing some major rehab. Gone are the walls featuring Cajun spices and Voodoo dolls. The shelves of T-shirts, highlighting punny New Orleans phrases, have also disappeared, along with the alligator heads that once sat by the cash register. Instead, the floors are stripped down to the concrete slab and the walls are bare of paint and stucco to reveal the fragile, original, nineteenth-century brick-between-post foundation.

The touristy shop that routinely sent me customers every night is no more.

Damn.

How the hell did I miss this place being sold?

At the sound of activity coming from down the short hallway, my ears perk up and I follow the voices:

"Are we fucked?"

"No, dimwit. We're not *fucked*. We just have to fix the damn thing before the boss finds out, which means we're in the clear. You know they never come down here on Tuesdays."

"You know what makes Tuesdays my favorite? Tacos. Titties. Not exactly in that order but I'll take what I can—"

"For the love of God, someone please shut him up."

The end of the hall yields to a large room, and I spot a group of construction workers standing around the hole that's an even match for the one on my side of the wall.

Letting the sledgehammer's weight fall from my shoulder, I swoop it up so that it's standing vertical, the base still clutched in my palm. "Y'all lookin' for this?"

As one, they all turn in my direction.

I'm enough of a people watcher that I immediately notice a short-ish dude, who's wearing a Saints T-shirt, blanch at the sight of me. Kid doesn't even look old enough to grow facial hair, let alone work a full-time gig. Either way, he looks guilty as hell.

A fact he confirms a second later when he mutters, "*Shit*," like he's been caught red-handed by a teacher for cheating on a test.

The beefy guy behind him bops Shortie on the head, then steps around him. "Shut it," he grunts out of the corner of his mouth to the kid. He casts his attention to me, all cordial-looking. "Hey, man. You must be from next door."

Good deductive reasoning skills on this one. The sledgehammer had to have been a dead giveaway.

I dip my chin. "I own the place."

"Double shit," Shortie utters, and if I'm not mistaken, his voice sounds like a perfect match for Tacos-and-Titties Lover. He scrubs a hand through his messy hair. "Listen, it's our first day on the job and these assholes shared this video with me and I lost control. But if you'd seen it, you would've messed up too. Tits, bare tits." He makes a show of cupping a giant pair of knockers in front of him, going so far as to tweak the nonexistent nipples. "From a club up the block—"

His buddy cuffs him on the back of the head, a little harder this time. "*Kurt*, dude. What the fuck?"

Kurt lets out a frazzled breath. "Did I say too much? I probably said too much."

I don't know whether to laugh at the kid or side with his friend. Something tells me that it's not just Shortie's first day on this job site but on any job site. Kid is about to be in for a rude wakeup call, I bet.

"Accidents happen," I say evenly.

I'm sure as shit not going to touch the whole video topic with a ten-foot pole. I spent my fair share of nights at those same titty bars once upon a time. At almost thirty-seven, though, that's not the sort of entertainment I need to have a good time. Sometime in the last decade, the strip clubs lost their luster. Maybe I'm getting old or maybe it's because now I actually know the women who're working their asses off to earn a living. They're not nameless faces when you work in the Quarter and see them every night in passing.

"But I'm still gonna need to talk to y'all's boss." I set the sledgehammer down, poised against the wall. "They in?"

"*She*," the beefy one says, wincing. "The boss is a she."

"She's not in though," Kurt pipes up. "Handles everything through email. So far, at least, since she's been out of the country. I hear she's pretty though. That's what Chad said. He's done work for the family before."

"Dude," mutters another guy, this one in the back of the pack, "d'you have to say *everything* that goes through your head?"

"Honesty is the best policy." Kurt elbows his friend in the side. "Ain't that right, Chad?"

I don't know how it's possible, but these dudes might have Shirley beat when it comes to gossiping. And that's saying a lot, considering the woman only shows up to bingo so she can get the 411 on the elderly community in her neighborhood.

Give me the strength to not punch Tweedle Dum right in the mug. Exasperated, I pass a hand over my jaw. "I'll take a phone number."

Five sets of horrified gazes swing in my direction.

Chad's the first one to speak. "We can fix it, man. Tomorrow—first thing. No need to get the boss lady involved."

Kurt thrusts a hand up in the air, only to have it swatted down by the same dude who called him out earlier. Scowling, the kid clutches his hand to his chest and solemnly vows, "Screw tomorrow, I'll fix the wall right now."

When he moves to leave, two different pairs of arms pin him in place. "No," both guys mutter emphatically. Kurt frowns, and I stop just short of rolling my eyes.

Time's up.

I've got a cannolo with Shirley to eat, three more stars to ink, and that's not even factoring in the next two clients that are booked for this afternoon. The first one is getting an easy tat—a skull-and-crossbones combo that I could sketch out in my sleep—but the other scheduled appointment is gonna be a doozy. Covering up some old ink, lots of colors, intricate shading that's going to take me hours. I don't have time to be worrying about a random hole in my wall or having to listen to . . .

Christ, is that *Nickelback* playing on the radio?

I meet Chad's gaze because, out of the lot of them, he seems the one most likely to pull himself together and rise to the occasion. Though if he's the one responsible for the boob video, maybe I'm wrong.

"I'll be sure to mention it was an accident," I manage tightly, "no harm, no foul. But I need that wall fixed, and I don't have time to wait for the boss to show up whenever she damn well feels like it."

Almost as one, the group shifts their attention to something or someone coming down the hall. I hear the staccato of heels striking concrete. The sharp breath of Kurt, who honestly looks like he's about to piss himself. The scrape of my shoes as I twist around, fully prepared to take in what has everyone else looking like petrified hens.

Fuck me.

I wish I hadn't looked.

Because there, walking toward me, is the one woman who took my dead, neglected heart and dropped the damn thing right in the meat grinder. Even now it beats irregularly, like it's not sure whether it's acceptable to launch into a sprint at the sight of her or shrivel up and retreat into hibernation.

If I were anyone else but me—cool, calm, and collected, twenty-four-seven—I'd set a hand on my chest, just to ensure I haven't suffered a heart attack at a critical time, like Peggy's husband.

After all, it's not every day you come face to face with the woman who chose twenty-six other men over you.

When Savannah's sky-high heels careen to a halt, I know she's spotted me. Panic floods her gorgeous face, widening her gaze and parting her full lips and making her fingers, which are wrapped around a thick stack of manila folders, clench.

"Owen?" Her voice cracks on the second syllable of my name, and then she swallows, audibly. Shifts her weight from one foot to the other. And I'm just enough of an asshole that I don't answer, not right away, because the last time we saw each other, she looked me dead in the eye and told me that she felt nothing for me but friendship.

Pure, platonic friendship.

Savannah Rose is a lot of things—sweet, ambitious, a defender to every person around her, even to her own detriment—but I never took her for a liar.

Not until that night.

I feel the tension simmering in the air between us, and it's not just the New Orleans swampy humidity kicking into gear. It's us, this tangible chemistry that I wish didn't exist but always has, from the very first moment we met, when I was dating her younger sister.

My molars grind together. "Rose."

She sucks in a harsh breath, as though she can't believe I have the balls to use my nickname for her. Twisting away, she gives me a view of her profile and one slender shoulder. "What are you doing here? Aren't you busy with . . . aren't you busy next door?"

Ice thickens in my veins.

Did she plan on speaking to me? Or did she seriously think that she could waltz into the storefront next to mine and pretend that I don't exist? Something tells me it's the latter, and I feel emotion—anger, bitterness, and worse, embarrassment—clog my throat. Clearly, this joint is about to be converted into one of her family's many restaurants, which means she'll be in and out of here for *months* during construction. And then later, too, when the place opens and patrons flock to yet another Edgar Rose Restaurant Group establishment.

As if the city isn't already overrun by them.

I imagine Savannah sneaking in and out the restaurant, always checking to see if I'm on my way out of Inked, or always heading left, toward St. Peter Street, just so she won't risk me catching a glimpse of her out my front windows.

The embarrassment recedes, scattering like confetti on a windy day.

I step in her path.

Because I'm feeling ticked off.

Because I *am* ticked off.

Still, after all these months.

Her thick hair falls in waves down her back, nearly to her waist. Like a curtain, it shields her face from scrutiny. Much as my fingers itch to tuck back the strands—refusing to let her hide from me—I casually hook my thumbs in the belt loops of my jeans instead.

"Don't," she warns on a shaky whisper.

"Don't what? Be here?" I drop my voice to a low, unforgiving pitch. "Hate to break the news to you, but I've got an appointment with the boss."

That gets her attention.

Her eyes are almond-shaped, lashes thick and batting quickly as she stares up at me, though not at all flirtatiously. She's confused, on the verge of calling me out, I'm sure, when Kurt clears his throat behind me and ventures, "We, uh, screwed up, Miss Rose."

He points to the wall, and she follows the length of his arm with her gaze.

"*Crap.*"

Whether she's talking about the inevitable repairs or the fact that she'll now have to interact with me for the foreseeable future, I'm not quite sure. Either way, it's almost grossly satisfying to know that as much as she wants to be done with me, the universe has pulled a giant middle finger and flashed it in her direction.

Somehow, I've found myself with the upper hand and I'm not about to squander it.

I drop a hand to her stack of folders, careful not to touch her, and lower my head so we're at eye level. For a second, I let myself remember *before*. All the times she sat in Inked, watching me work. The first time she asked if I could tattoo something on her skin. The first time I *touched* her skin. Soft. So fucking soft. I'd gone home, fully prepared to do the right thing and go straight to bed, and instead found myself standing beneath my shower head, my hand wrapped around my dick. Because, Christ, everything about this woman calls to me, no matter the fact that, in theory, she's never been mine to want in the first place.

"Send me an invoice," she clips out, clearly striving for control of her emotions, "and we'll take care of the repairs."

An invoice isn't going to work for me.

"Thirty minutes," I tell her, not bothering to temper the hard note in my voice. "I'll be waiting next door."

Her brows shoot up. "We shouldn't."

I let out a short, caustic laugh. "When has that ever stopped us before?"

2

SAVANNAH

When life takes a shit on you, it does so in epic proportions.

I'm talking *epic* proportions.

In the last twenty-four hours: I've lost my luggage—according to the airline, both suitcases are currently vacationing in Tokyo; spotted my face on no less than three tabloid magazines while hustling through the New Orleans airport—"*America's Sweetheart Spotted Returning to the USA*!"; and sat down for lunch with my parents, expecting at least a hug, considering I've been traveling with Amelie all over Europe for the last four months, but instead was given the "big news."

Apparently, I'm the newly minted Vice President of the Edgar Rose Restaurant Group.

My dad beamed at me with pride from across the oak table.

My mom offered a warm smile and a toast of congratulations with her second glass of merlot.

Meanwhile, I was so caught off guard that I choked on a half-eaten boudin ball and almost needed resuscitation.

Confession: between the vice-presidency and death by boudin ball, I'd choose the latter.

And if all of that isn't enough to make my head feel like exploding, there's also Owen.

Owen.

I spent eight hours formulating a plan of action while flying over the Atlantic Ocean. Eight hours of staring out the small, oval window and picturing his reserved black gaze and his full bottom lip and, oh yeah, thinking of various ways to approach him about the new ERRG restaurant opening next door to Inked, as well as finding a way to discuss everything that went down on *Put A Ring On It . . .*

Oh, who am I kidding?

I've spent the last seven *months* thinking of ways to apologize for what I did, in front of the entire nation. I've mulled it over more times than I can count. I've pulled up Inked on Bourbon's Instagram page—because Owen has never been one for having personal social media accounts—and typed out at least three dozen apologies that have never been sent because what else is there to say?

I'm sorry. I said that when I sent him home from the show.

I hope we can still be friends. I told him that too.

Please don't hate me. I whispered those four soul-crushing words just before he stormed out of the mansion, his broad shoulders tense with fury. He'd turned back to me, then, with his normally aloof, dark eyes blazing and all that ink at the base of his throat rippling, like he was struggling for control. His mouth had parted, words clearly ready to launch and take aim, before he shook his head sharply and disappeared out into the night.

We haven't spoken since.

So, yeah.

Two hours ago, I was fully prepared to finish up my meeting with the construction crew and then stop by next door. Bury the hatchet, once and for all. Come to terms with the fact that while I won't be at the new Bourbon job site daily, I *will* be down there frequently and the chances of Owen and me running into each other are definitely greater than zero percent.

But after actually seeing him face to face for the first time in months . . .

I don't think I can do this.

Nerves pulse wildly under my skin as I stare at the antique doorknob that leads directly into the tattoo parlor.

Thirty minutes. That's how long he gave me to get my butt over here.

I'm down to twenty-nine minutes and a handful of seconds.

I'm not the sort of woman who heeds a command without a sharp retort on the tip of my tongue—unless your name is Edgar or Marie Rose, in which case, all I do is obey, earn a paycheck, and wonder how I can love and hate a job all in the same breath—but the last thing I want is Owen Harvey barging into the construction site next door and causing a scene because I failed to show up on time.

Not that I've ever known him to cause a scene.

Not until you lied to his face and told him that you thought of him as nothing more than a friend.

A friend.

Honestly, it's a miracle I wasn't struck down by hellfire on the spot.

Unexpectedly, the glass door swings open before me, narrowly missing the pointed toes of my pumps.

I don't need to glance up to know who it is. My senses are honed to everything that makes him *him*: the woodsy scent that reminds me of hiking in City Park, the way he instinctually favors his left arm, the cowlick in his hairline that causes the dark-as-night strands to lay boyishly across his forehead.

His gravelly voice resonates within me like an earthquake shuddering beneath my feet. "You stand out here any longer and the cops are gonna think you're plannin' a burglary."

I almost laugh.

Seven months ago, I *would* have laughed.

But already I can feel the awkwardness rifting between us, and I curl my toes in my heels to keep from turning tail and running away. I smile, all teeth and *please-don't-make-this-harder-than-it-needs-to-be* vibes. "With any luck, Gage would be the one to show up and I won't have to worry about being arrested."

At the mention of his twin, Owen rests a hand on the doorframe and bows down, so that we're eye to eye, the way he's always done to put us at equal height. In a soft, lethal tone, he murmurs, "Oh, you'd have to worry, all right."

I shiver. Right there on the sidewalk, in the witheringly eighty-six percent humidity, I shiver like winter is coming and my only hope for survival is burrowing in Owen's warm chest.

The way I see it, I have two options here: cower under Owen's tangible anger or push back and stand my ground.

Desperate to reassert some control over the situation, I choose the latter with probably more gumption than is necessary.

My fingers land on his solid chest and I give a sharp

push. He concedes without issue, drifting backward so I can ease my way into the air-conditioned parlor. It's exactly the way I remember: black-and-white parquet floors, nineteenth-century barge-wood walls, frames of tattooed artwork hanging tastefully throughout the space.

A half-eaten cannolo abandoned on the receptionist's desk.

The dessert I don't remember being here, but since I wouldn't mind eating my feelings right about now, I pay it no mind.

Spinning around, I plant my hands on my hips and get right down to business. "ERRG bought the souvenir shop next door three weeks ago. They went bankrupt, my dad saw an opportunity to open another restaurant in the Quarter, and the deal was done before the realtor even uploaded the listing online."

Owen stands with his feet spread apart, hips straight, bulky arms folded over his chest. He's big and brawny and I hate that even now—after everything that's happened between us—I can't help but stare at the way he's rolled up the sleeves of his blue flannel to expose his steely, tattooed forearms.

His expression remains impassive under my scrutiny.

I tap my fingers on my hips, a silent beat that does nothing to mitigate the excess energy firing through me as I wait him out.

And wait him out.

And wait him out some more.

My tapping dies a slow, slow death. "I should have sent you an email when the deal went through, just as a head's up that I'd be . . . that *we'd* be opening next door to you." Another composed email to match the dozens of others I've written to him that sound stiff and completely unlike me. This latest one is still sitting in *Draft* mode in my inbox, never to be read again. Or sent. Just like all the others. "I'm sorry for that," I add softly, "I planned to stop by after my meeting next door. Obviously"—I clear my throat awkwardly—"I wasn't expecting you to be there. That's not . . . that's not how I wanted you to find out. I know you don't like surprises."

Surprises like the way he showed up in California and shocked you right down to your core?

As if he's recalling the same night as I am, his black eyes gleam as he levels me with a swift, thorough once-over that starts at my professionally blown-out hair and ends at my chipped, end-of-vacation pedicure.

Clearly content to let me run circles around myself like a dog chasing its own tail, he doesn't say a word.

Dammit. Can't we do this civilly?

"Owen, I—"

"You're not wearin' a ring."

Words die on my tongue at his succinct pronouncement. Like my hands belong to someone else, I hold them up in front of me. Nails painted a pristine summer white. Skin the color of café au lait. Slim wrists with silver bangles tinkling noisily as they clink together.

What Owen said isn't quite true—I *am* wearing rings, just not where they count.

And not on the fourth finger of my left hand.

Has he really not seen any spoilers online? Footage leaked months ago, over the winter, that I turned down both final contestants. And there's been no shortage of talk about it everywhere else. Even while traveling in Europe, I couldn't stand in the checkout aisle of a local grocery store without seeing my face staring back.

That woman on the front pages of those magazines—she looks like me, smiles like me, but God, I feel like we might as well be two different people. Pre-*Put A Ring On It*. Post-*Put A Ring On It*. I didn't fall in love on the show—not the way that I hoped I would after that very first night—but somehow those three months traveling the world with a bunch of strangers changed me anyway.

I can't help but wonder if Owen sees those changes now. He's always read me like an open book—peeled back my layers as though my spine is only his to crack, my pages only his to flip.

Slowly, I shake my head. "No, I'm not." I pause, steeling my spine for his response. "Engaged, that is. I . . . I'm not engaged."

Owen's expression reveals nothing. He's completely aloof, and that ambivalence threatens to spark my anger in a way that dating twenty-six strangers never did. The producers lamented my level head, even when shit hit the fan—like when one of my final two contestants, Dominic DaSilva, came clean during our overnight date about how he'd been paid to come on the show. I never once screamed. I never once lost my temper. I'm sure the producers would have loved the added drama of me throwing a vase across the room or bashing Dominic in the face with my fist, but I stayed calm.

Completely unruffled.

But with Owen . . . Jeez, I already feel my cheeks burning as I stand here, completely vulnerable to whatever he might say—except that he's not saying *anything*.

And then, to my short-lived relief, he opens his mouth and grinds out, "Too bad."

My jaw goes slack.

Too bad?

Too bad?

When he turns away, heading for his office, I march right after him. "Are you kidding me?" I snap at his broad back, hot on his heels. "*That's* all you have to say? I've been gone for seven months, Owen. Seven. Months. And I tell you that I'm not engaged and all you can come up with is *too bad—*"

I don't expect his quickness.

Maybe I should have—at this point, I should always expect the unexpected when it comes to Owen Harvey—but I don't.

My shortsightedness has dire consequences.

Namely, me with my back pressed tightly against the exposed brick wall of the narrow hallway, Owen's big body looming large over mine, and one of those deliciously tatted hands planted on the wall beside my head. His eyes narrow and I feel the air *whoosh* out of my body like he's sucked it right out of me.

"What do you want me to say?" he growls, his face mere inches away from mine, his minty breath hot on my lips. "Let me hold you till you feel better, Rose." His tone, though mocking, is underlined with an intensity that scorches a path straight to my heart. "Let my shoulder be the one that you cry on." His nostrils flare, his lip curling with distaste. "Is that what you want to hear?"

Feeling the familiar pinch of guilt in my chest for hurting him, I strive for nonchalance when I quip, "That could work, except that I'm not really feeling the urge to cry right now."

He curses under his breath, and not for a single second do I think it's complimentary.

My chin lifts as I study his rugged features. A nose that's been broken a time or two in the past. A small, faint scar that's shaped like a crescent moon on the outer perimeter of his right eye. The heavy brows that act like two bookends to the seemingly permanent furrow that never, ever fades, even when he's grinning devilishly.

Any chance of him grinning, devilishly or otherwise, is about to go up in flames. No time like the present to acknowledge the massive elephant in the room.

Here goes nothing.

"I'm sorry, Owen. I'm sorry that I sent you home the way I did. It wasn't fair and it wasn't kind, and for the last two-hundred and ten days, I've regretted every moment of that night. I regret *how* it happened, but it was necessary. It *had* to be necessary. Nothing between us was ever going to work out—not for the long run." Unable to stop myself, I graze my hand over his arm. I hate the way my heart hiccups at the brief touch. Hate, even more, how my gaze seeks his out, begging him to understand. *Please, please understand.* "It would never have worked out," I repeat, this time more forcefully, maybe to remind him of that fact, maybe to remind myself too. "We both know that."

Beneath his flannel, his shoulders bunch tightly as he shifts his position. My arm falls, flattening against the wall near my hip. Coarse brick scrapes my palm. The gap between us narrows farther, all but destroyed for good when he ducks his head and rasps by my ear, "You're absolutely right."

Wait . . . *I am*?

Moving slightly to the left so I can turn my head fully, I try to get a read on him. But my Owen—the Owen I thought I knew—stares back at me like I'm nothing but a stranger. The heat, the silent need that used to warm his dark gaze, is long gone, with nothing left to remember him by but that furrow and the crescent-shaped scar and the crooked bend to his nose. "I-I don't understand. You *agree* with me?"

"Surprising, isn't it?" Nothing about the look on his face gives me the impression that we're on the same page here. A beat passes. And then, "While you've been off gallivantin' around the world, I've had those same two hundred and ten days to realize that you're not at all the person I thought you were."

My mouth is dry. So dry, not even a gallon of water could quench my thirst.

Try as I do to keep my voice level, I'm fully aware of the quiver that I can't quite hide when I whisper, "And who do you think I am?"

His gaze pierces mine, immobilizing me in place. "A coward."

Oh.

Oh.

He shoves away from the wall before I can formulate a single thought, a single comeback, a single *anything* that isn't my stupid heart letting out a keening, pained whine of despair. After everything that's happened, I deserve that verbal hit. I deserve it, but that doesn't mean I like it.

And it doesn't mean that it doesn't hurt.

My hands rise to clutch the collar of my dress. I feel my heart hammering, loud and frustratingly persistent, and it takes me a second to realize that it's not just my heart pounding wildly but that I can also hear the distinct sounds of a brass band marching down Bourbon Street.

Life in New Orleans is ongoing, but inside this building, within this narrow hallway, I'm seconds away from coming undone.

I watch, struck mute, as Owen strides for his office door, like he can't get away from me fast enough. But just before he ducks inside, he glances over his shoulder and meets my gaze. "Think I'll send that invoice over to you after all."

And then he shuts the door behind him, closing him inside and locking me out.

The way it should have been between the two of us from the start.

3

CELEBRITY TEA PRESENTS:

SAVANNAH ROSE, AMERICA'S SWEETHEART, SPOTTED IN NEW ORLEANS AFTER MONTHS LIVING ABROAD!

Dear Reader, never let it be said that you aren't hearing the breaking news here first: Savannah Rose, Put A Ring On It's *first-ever bachelorette, has returned to the Big Easy!*

America's sweetheart was spotted looking rather hassled and hurried at Louis Armstrong New Orleans International Airport yesterday morning, where one reliable source witnessed Savannah stop in front of a magazine stall, buy a stack of tabloids with her face on the front cover, and promptly drop them into the nearest trash can before she made her way outside.

"I was stunned," the source, who also provided the picture below, wrote in to me via email. "Absolutely stunned. I mean, I've been watching her on TV every week for a month now and she seems so kind. *So levelheaded. Not the sort of person at all who'd do something like that. I'll be honest, it struck me as a little . . . dramatic."*

The question remains, though: how much do we even know about Savannah Rose? She's been notoriously tight-lipped when she graces our small screens each week, and, of course, we can't forget her emotional meltdown from the season's first episode. Sending that inked god home before he even joined the cocktail party? Savage, Dear Reader, absolutely savage. (And entirely too enjoyable, so I rewound three times just because I couldn't get enough.)

Now, we all know Savannah Rose was bound to return from her travels at some point—the girl may come from New Orleans royalty, but money can't buy you an international visa.

It also can't buy Miss Savannah Rose a man.

No one has forgotten the leaked footage from this past winter, least of all me. The show may be mid-season on TV, but it's no secret that Savannah is as single as on the day she was born. (More single than I am, although that's a story for another day.)

Continue to watch this space, Dear Reader. Now that our girl Savannah is back stateside, I can only imagine that the tea will be piping hot, and it's only a matter of time before it's ready to be spilled . . .

4

SAVANNAH

Coward.

Twenty-four hours after my showdown with Owen at Inked and I've yet to scrub his accusation from my brain. It trails me as I park my car and head for ERRG's main office, an Art Deco building situated in New Orleans' Warehouse District. It dogs my heels as I step into the lobby for the first time in months, and head for the elevators.

And it'd probably follow me into our fourth-floor offices, too, if I didn't nearly pee my pants when my coworkers pop out from behind desks and computers and bookcases to shout, "Welcome back, Savannah!"

Neon-colored streamers explode in the air, and then I'm being sidelined by a pair of arms that squeeze me in a chest-compressing hug.

"Can't breathe," I wheeze out, my hands flailing where they're pinned down to my sides. "Georgie"—I knock my head gently against hers—"ease up or I'll suffocate."

ERRG's executive assistant only squeezes me tighter. "Ten more seconds."

My laugh merges with a gasp. "I don't know if I can last five."

"Serves you right for ditching us for *Europe*," she counters flippantly.

"Move aside, Harris," says a different voice, this one deeper, more arrogant. Jean Dufrene steps in my line of sight, his broad shoulders blocking the florescent lights behind him. "Your turn is up."

Georgie sniffs, her curly brown hair tickling my neck, but she lets go anyway and steps back. Her honey-colored eyes pin Dufrene with an inscrutable look. "You bitched about this entire party and *now* you want to pretend that you care?"

"Oh, I care." He taps her on the nose, like she's a good dog that he's hoping won't pee on his shoes. "But only because I knew you'd bring those delicious cupcakes that I like so much."

I barely stifle a snort when my assistant glares up at the towering Cajun chef, who's as fundamental to ERRG's success as she is. Jean may be the mastermind behind the menus at all of our thirteen restaurants here in New Orleans, but Georgie keeps the machine chugging along—even when I've been out of town with Amelie.

Coward.

Goddammit. What's it going to take to get Owen's stupid voice out of my head? Another twenty-four hours? Forty-eight?

Doesn't matter.

What *does* matter is that *I* know I'm not a coward. A coward would have turned tail yesterday instead of standing up to him in that hallway. A coward would find a way to ignore him forever, instead of—

"I didn't buy them for *you*," Georgie growls, cutting off my train of thought. She's not even five feet tall but that means nothing when you're the child of a former New Orleans Saints linebacker. Georgette Harris might not have her father's biceps or his massive build, but she's nailed his fierceness down to a T. I watch as she prods Jean in the chest with a lime-green nail, then delivers a cutting once-over. "Food for thought, Dufrene, but maybe you should leave off the cupcakes? You're looking a little . . ." She wiggles a finger at his waistband area.

Jean's mouth tightens as he stares down at my spitfire assistant. "Hot?"

Georgie's smile is all blinding white teeth. "I was going to say *round*."

Oh, boy.

I just barely manage to kick my grin off my face when ERRG's notorious chef cuts me a seething glare. There's nothing "round" about Jean Dufrene. The man might as well be a robot: he runs marathons regularly, prays to the altar of CrossFit, and walks his dogs along the Mississippi River levees twice a day like clockwork. He's nearly as active as Georgie's dad was when Mr. Harris played for the Saints, and yet I know something Jean doesn't:

Georgie goads him because she's harboring a major crush on him, and, to date, Jean has either never picked up on the clues she's been leaving behind, like red velvet cupcakes over the last number of years, *or* he's simply not interested.

My gut tells me it's the former.

"Can you fire her and put me out of my misery?" he grits out from between clenched teeth.

I grin at him. "No."

Though if you ask my parents about that, they'll say it's just business. *Family* business.

The first Edgar Rose opened a tiny corner store here in New Orleans, in 1888. He had the wherewithal to purchase the lot beside the Hotel Monteleone, which at that point—from the old newspaper clippings I've come across while researching those early days in the company's history—was nothing like the opulent hotel that stands on Royal Street today. But it was then that Edgar Rose *I* apparently got his first taste for fine cuisine, and that corner store started churning out red beans and rice every Monday. Soon enough, he graduated to fancy Parisian-styled food that he'd learned from the chefs next door.

By the time he passed away in 1923, at the age of seventy-four, the Roses had not one restaurant to their name but five. And in the last hundred or so years since, my family has expanded the business into the food empire that it is today.

Thirteen restaurants here in the city. Fourteen if you count the still-under-construction Bourbon Street site. Another one over in San Antonio because Dad liked Alamo Square and thought San Antonians deserved the chance to dine on Creole cuisine. There's been talk of expanding to Florida, maybe Miami, but I've done what I can to pump the brakes on those plans for now.

We're already stretching ourselves thin with fifteen establishments, and with my parents getting older, I'm not entirely sure I want to be tied to this ship for the rest of my life.

I love food. I love making people happy.

What I don't love is feeling as though the weight of the ERRG legacy rests entirely on my shoulders.

The pressure is . . . *stifling.*

With my knuckles to the door, I give it a little push and step inside.

Dad's face brightens at the sight of me. "Well if it isn't my new Vice President."

I try to grin, if only because I know the VP title should feel like an accomplishment. On paper, I've more than earned it. In reality, I'd prefer to just be Savannah Marie Rose, interior designer; it's what I studied in school.

Well, for a second major.

Hospitality, as was expected of me, came first.

"Heya, Pops."

He leaps up from behind his monstrosity of an oak desk and comes toward me, arms opened wide to envelop me in a big hug. He doesn't hesitate for a single second, the way he did when he dropped me off at the airport, back in the fall, for my flight to California. Then, I hadn't been willing to accept his affection, no matter how well-intentioned. All he'd needed was one look at my stiff expression to know our relationship was on thin ice, despite the fact that, even in November, the weather was hot enough to have me sweating under my shirt. He hadn't issued a single apology, not for backing me into the proverbial corner with his deals and his ultimatums, not for saying what he did to Amelie that sent her—my bold, brave sister—running with her tail tucked between her legs. No, he'd only passed over my suitcases like we were nothing more than strangers, wished me the best for the show, and somberly climbed back into his SUV without another word.

Edgar Rose *IV* is notoriously well-known for remaining silent when words would do him a whole lot of good.

And now . . . Now, I feel like that drunk balancing on a tightrope, torn between wanting to give in to how much I've missed him and continuing to stand my ground—for my sake and Amelie's, too.

Jump. Don't jump.

Indecision divides my heart, but in the end, I find myself clinging to the familiar as I wrap my arms around Dad's middle in a moment of weakness. In seven months, life has changed in so many ways, but *this*—my dad—hasn't changed one bit. He still smells like tobacco and peppermint, and he still dresses like he's prepared for an emergency and might be called to cook in one of our many kitchens at any moment. T-shirt. Jeans. Scuffed black tennis shoes that have seen better days. His shorn dark hair is a little grayer at the temples, though, and when he pulls back to smile at me, I can't help but note that the crow's feet at the corners of his eyes also seem more pronounced.

"You look tired," I tell him.

"And *you*," he counters, letting me go to sail back to his rightful place behind his desk, "look as though you've spent too much time hanging out with your sister. What kind of dress is that? It looks like a blanket."

I glance down at the "offensive" garment. I wouldn't call it a *blanket*, per se. More like . . . Bohemian. In search of some major retail therapy, Amelie and I found it at a little hole-in-the-wall shop when we stopped in Bari, Italy, before making our way via ferry to Greece. I immediately fell in love with the way the canary-yellow fabric swept over my frame, not hugging my breasts or my hips. After being stuffed like sausage meat into tight, sequined dresses and even tighter jeans during my time on *Put A Ring On It*, I'd craved the freedom of being able to walk around without Spanx or having to suck in my stomach at all times.

Taking the seat across from Dad, I cross my right leg over my left at the knee. "I like it."

His mouth settles into a small frown. "Maybe don't wear it for meetings."

"Because it's bright and looks like sunshine?"

"Because you look like a beach bum, Savannah, and ERRG doesn't employ beach bums for Vice Presidents."

Anddddd here we go.

Tempted as I am to check out the grandfather clock in the corner of the office—just to confirm that it's been less than one whole minute before Dad started harping on about something new he doesn't approve of—I instead fold my hands in my lap, squeezing them together, and force myself to exhale the frustration.

Europe was temporary. It was lovely and a total breath of fresh air, and God knows Amelie had needed me there to have her back, no matter what she might say about being just fine on her own. But *this* is my life and forgetting that will only lead to disappointment.

Coward.

I slam the proverbial lock on Owen Harvey and throw away the damn key. He has no idea what he's talking about, calling me a coward. He owes no one, not even his twin brother, an explanation for how he lives his life and why he does the things that he does.

There are no consequences.

There are no quiet conversations about destroying the family legacy by expressing a want, a *need*, to do something other than manage construction crews and hundreds of employees and whether or not the menu at five of our fourteen open restaurants needs sprucing up.

The Harveys, from what I've seen of Owen, Gage, and Gage's wife Lizzie, are a tight trio where if one teeters, the others bolster up the fallen, on their own shoulders if need be.

The Roses . . . Well, let's just say everyone wants a piece of the pie in my family. Second cousins. My aunt and uncle. Our drama has made local headlines more times than I can count, and if they ever discovered our latest scandal—actually, pump the brakes. I don't even want to think about that. Honestly, the only one who *doesn't* give a crap about the Rose legacy is my younger sister, who is currently lounging on a sandy beach in Italy, if the picture she sent to me this morning is any indication.

Amelie Rose is living the dream, even if it has come at a massive cost to her emotional well-being, and I'm just . . . living.

After one last critical side-eye of my outfit, Dad drags open his desk drawer and hauls out a folder that must be as thick as my forearm. It lands heavily on the desk. Licking one finger, he flicks it open and begins shuffling through the stack of papers.

"New project?" I ask, already preparing myself for another talk about the possible Miami expansion. When Edgar Rose *IV* gets something in his head, he can't let it go. *At any and all costs, too.* "I thought we talked about waiting until the Bourbon Street job was done?"

He leans over the files, his T-shirt stark white against the caramel of his skin. I'm nearly a spitting image of him, from my black eyes to my thick, wavy hair that usually puffs out like a triangle around my head instead of curling beautifully like my sister's. Hence, the professional blowouts. It's my one luxury. My favorite luxury.

Amelie takes after our mom: bronze skin, warm brown eyes, and a round face that is smiling more often than not. When she was a kid, she used to plant her tiny hands on my cheeks and stare at me, as though wondering how the Rose blood could run through us both, even though we barely look alike.

Both sides of my family have been in New Orleans for centuries. The Roses were free people of color, back in a time when slavery still ravaged this country. The DuPonts, my mother's ancestors, were Spanish politicians who arrived in the eighteenth century and married the local French noblewomen.

As a girl learning about pirates like Jean Lafitte and emperors like Napoleon Bonaparte, I found the history of my home all too fascinating. Instead of shelves topped off with cookbooks, mine were burdened with the past of New Orleans, stuffed with so many books about my Creole ancestry and the women who ruled this city, oftentimes better than the men, and how food tangled people together, no matter the color of their skin.

As a thirty-five-year-old woman, however, I'm fully aware that my dad is driven by his own personal need to see ERRG succeed, almost to a fault. He's determined to prove to the world that the Roses belong front and center in those same history books that I once devoured nightly—instead of being shoved aside into the margins the way Edgar Rose *I* was, as were his son and grandson. Until the last generation or so, my family's accomplishments have barely registered as a footnote.

Sometimes I can't help but wonder when my dad will think he's made it. And then I remember all the holidays and summers I spent sweating my butt off in our various restaurants, instead of doing traditional family activities like the other kids my age, and I know that "making it" doesn't belong in Edgar Rose *IV's* vocabulary. For as long as there's room to grow, we'll always be hustling for more recognition, more success, more *everything*.

Dad looks up now, his midnight eyes twinkling with the sort of anticipation I've come to dread.

"Whatever it is," I mutter, holding up my hands, "stop thinking about it. You've got that look in your eye again."

"I don't have a look."

"You absolutely do." I point at his face, twirling my finger in the air. "See, that? That smile? That means you're about to put me to work and I'll be lucky to come up for air."

The twinkle dims and the frown returns with alarming quickness. "Success is only halted by—"

"The lazy," I finish for him, having heard his life motto on repeat since birth. "I know. But when I talked to Mom last night, she mentioned that you haven't been feeling well. We both think maybe you could do with a break. What do you think—a week? Two? Some much-needed R&R and no crazy scheming."

"I want to build a hotel."

I choke on nothing but air.

Not that Dad seems all too concerned with me nearly dying. He only slaps a hand down on one of those precious pieces of paper he's got there, before spinning it around and using the flat of his palm to push it in my direction.

"A hotel," he repeats, nodding enthusiastically. "You were right about it not being the right time for a Miami expansion. They don't know us there and it would be an uphill battle from the start, but this . . ." He points to the paper sitting in front of me like a ticking time bomb. "Now *this* is an expansion that we can make happen, *cherie*."

A . . . *hotel*? Has he not heard a word that I've said about not concocting any more crazy schemes? How much clearer can I be? And, seriously, how can he even be thinking about a project of this scale when, just seven months ago, he nearly ruined *everything*?

"Pops, Mom said—"

"Your mother worries too much." He waves a hand in the air, all bah-humbug dismissiveness, then leans back in his desk chair. Like a kid, he spins it around so he can stare out the massive window that overlooks Lafayette Square and the marble Court of Appeals building beyond the green space. Hands on the chair's leather armrests, he casts me a quick, searching glance over his shoulder. "I feel fine."

"You look *tired*."

Dad stands, propping one shoulder against the glass-paned window. "And you, Savannah, are the new Vice President of ERRG."

My back snaps straight at the excited tinge in his deep voice. Something about the way he's looking at me right now . . . I don't like it and I certainly don't trust it. Though if I'm being honest, the whole trust factor with my dad has been iffy for months now. I love him—would do just about anything to make sure he's happy—but the trust? That line has totally been crossed. Stiffly, I say, "I didn't ask for the promotion."

"Not all we receive in life are things we've asked for, *cherie*. I didn't ask to be good at making food when your Uncle Bernard can't even cook eggs without scorching the pan. But I am good, and my brother isn't, and this hotel—this is how we bring more to the game here in N'Orleans. Can't you see?"

All I see is a sixty-eight-year-old man practically rubbing his hands together, he's so damn eager for world domination.

Uncomfortable with the turn of conversation, I shift in the chair, uncrossing my legs and leaning forward to plant my hands on my thighs. "I think opening a hotel falls under crazy schemes."

"Is it crazy?" Hands perched on the back of his cushioned, black chair, he drops down to his elbows and interlaces his fingers before him. "Or is it genius?"

I think of the amount of work it takes to sustain fourteen restaurants across the country. Even before the VP announcement, I've always played a fundamental role in managing each establishment as ERRG's General Manager. I put out fires and start some of my own, and it's been *years* since I've stepped away fully from the company.

Even in Europe—hell, even while filming *Put A Ring On It*—I had my laptop with me at all times and my cell phone tucked away for emergencies. Because not even the chance to fall in love meant that I could quietly reassign my responsibilities to someone else for the matter of months that I was gone.

Any other person would crumble under the weight of my daily agenda. The only reason I haven't thus far is because I know with every fiber of my being that if I were to back off, Dad would turn to Amelie to fill my shoes.

And my twenty-seven-year-old sister wouldn't last a week in them, maybe not even that.

Dad takes the seat opposite mine. "Genius," he begins, sounding both seasoned entrepreneur and impatient conqueror, "is giving you the chance to build this hotel from the ground up, Savannah. I want you to be the visionary."

My palms, now sweaty with nerves, squeeze my knees. "No."

He arches a dark brow. "No? Not even if that means turning down the opportunity to put your interior design degree to use on something that isn't rearranging tables in a restaurant?"

I'm being manipulated, I know that.

Edgar Rose *IV* is nothing if not a businessman down to

his very core, and he *knows* how to work a situation to his advantage. He knows that I'm unhappy corralling hundreds of employees like sheep for ERRG. He knows that, just before I left to meet Amelie in Europe, I emailed him a resignation letter that he refused to accept.

His response? *The Edgar Rose Restaurant Group is in your blood, cherie. Will you really abandon our family's legacy?*

I caved then.

I sucked it up and trudged through months of watching Amelie lounge in beach chairs and dance all night with handsome men and stroll through art galleries while she collected unique pieces for resale, later, back in the States. I watched it all with my laptop cracked open, and my inbox highlighting a staggering two-thousand emails, and my phone going off every few minutes because someone had a problem back here in the city and I was, apparently, the only one equipped to handle it all.

When Dad reaches out to grasp my hand, holding on tightly, I raise my gaze from my yellow Bohemian dress to look at him. "You've wanted this for years, Savannah. The design element. The piecing together of furniture and wall colors and room layouts—and I'm giving it to you. You pick the team that you'd trust to see the project through, but every decision . . . it's yours."

When something is too good to be true, it usually is.

Life as a Rose has most certainly taught me that.

"Do we really have the funds for a hotel? Investors all lined up?" I shake my hand free of Dad's to run it through my hair, then remember too late that I tied it back in a long braid today. *Crap.* Letting the strands do their own thing, I add, "And where in the world is there space in this city to build a new hotel?"

His grin is slow to rise. "We already have the property."

With an uptick of his chin, he nods to the paper he slid before me when I first sat down.

The ticking time bomb.

I reach for it, dragging it closer, and skim my gaze from the top of the contract down—only for my heart to stop. *No.* "The job site on Bourbon?" I croak, my tongue feeling swollen in my mouth. "*That*'s where the hotel is going to be?"

Looking all too pleased with himself, Dad leans back in his chair and folds his arms over his chest. "The permits have already been acquired. Same with that daiquiri shop next door. The landlord was all too willing to sell once I agreed to pay him up front."

Up. Front.

That dread that felt like it was threatening to cling to my ankles now swarms north, to my knees, to my waist, until it becomes hard to breathe. "Pops," I say slowly, swallowing past the thickening lump in my throat, "please tell me you aren't planning what I think you're planning."

He raps his knuckles on the desk. "I'm going to own the whole block, *cherie*. The *entire* block, including—"

"Inked on Bourbon."

I'm suddenly glad I didn't have time to stop for coffee or a bagel this morning—or, hell, even one of Georgie's red velvet cupcakes—because if I had, it would all be coming up right about now. Nausea swirls in my gut, and I press my hands to the edge of the desk to stem the need to find the closest toilet. Or trashcan. I'm not that particular, to be honest.

I think of Owen pouring his soul into every tattoo that he inks onto someone's skin—onto *my* skin, even—and I shake my head sharply. "You can't. It's one thing if that landlord was willing to give up his shop, and another thing entirely to force out a successful business."

"But I won't be the one forcing out a successful business."

My gaze snaps up to meet Dad's. "What? Who will, then?"

He grins. "You."

5

OWEN

Café au lait in hand, I cut around a group of tourists throwing spare change into a street musician's open guitar suitcase, as they bop their heads to the rhythm of drumsticks thwacking plastic buckets.

The sun beats down on my head. Nine in the morning and it's scorching hot already. Hot enough that I've left my customary flannel at home and opted for only a T-shirt instead. In other parts of the city, trees line the sidewalks and provide shade, but down here in the Quarter, there's nothing but narrow balconies, stucco, and the odd potted shrubbery on various front stoops. On Bourbon, you're more likely to find plastic beads and discarded Hand Grenade bottles littering the ground than you are a fancy arrangement of peonies.

In other words, I should have asked the barista for an iced coffee instead.

Grimacing, I lift my gaze to check the street for oncoming traffic, only for my stride to come staggering to a halt.

Beside the former souvenir shop, on the corner of Bourbon and St. Peter Streets, Mike's Hard Daiquiri is missing its infamous sign. Hell, it's not just missing the sign, it's missing a fucking front *door*.

What the hell?

I dart across the street, barely avoiding a collision with an oncoming horse and buggy duo hauling tourists around for a French Quarter joyride. Ducking inside the popular daiquiri joint, I call out, "Mike, you in?"

There's the unmistakable sound of drilling and then a head pops out from behind a wall. "Heya! Who're you looking for—oh, shit."

I stare at Tacos-and-Titties Kurt and he stares back at me, and yeah, my stomach right now? It's rolling uneasily like I've just boarded one of the touristy steamboats that sail the mighty Mississippi.

Careful to keep my expression blank, I ask, "Where's Mike?"

Kurt scuffs the heel of his boot against the floor. "Mike who?"

Christ. "The guy who owns this place."

"*Ohhhh*, right. Him." More shoe scuffing commences, though this time it's accompanied by a good ol' boy, *aw-shucks* whistle that instantly grates on my nerves. "Yeah, last I heard he bought himself a one-way ticket to Aruba. Don't think he's coming back anytime soon."

Hell would have to freeze over before Mike Fairfield willingly gave this place up. He's been serving daiquiris for longer than I've been tattooing over at Inked, and it'd take a huge payout for him to consider leaving, even for the sandy beaches of—

Hold on.

My gaze zeroes in on Kurt. "You're not next door."

It's not a question, and the kid must think I'm some sort of new-age bank robber because he immediately throws his hands up in the air and confesses, "ERRG bought this place too!"

Wait . . . this place *too*?

I sweep the room with a hasty once-over. The daiquiri machines are gone. The once shiny floors are covered by plastic tarps. And hell, but I don't think there's been a day in the last decade that Mike hasn't played *Two Piña Coladas* by Garth Brooks from sunup to sundown. The silence permeating the room only drills home what Kurt is saying: Mike peaced out for sand, oceanfront views, and some piña coladas of his own, all—I'm assuming—at the expense of the Edgar Rose Restaurant Group's checkbook.

Fuck. Me.

Twisting around, I toss my lukewarm coffee into the garbage can chilling by the empty doorway.

"Wait! Where are you going, man?"

To have a little talk with the daughter of Satan, that's where.

Ignoring Kurt, my feet haven't even hit the sidewalk before I'm slipping my phone from the front pocket of my jeans and scrolling through my contacts for the one name I haven't called in months.

Fact is, ERRG doesn't do coincidences. Self-proclaimed "small business" or not, the Edgar Rose Restaurant Group is a conglomerate here in New Orleans. I don't trust, not even for a second, that they ran Mike Fairfield out of his daiquiri shop under fair circumstances. Sure, he must have agreed to whatever exorbitant sum they threw at him—but beyond that?

Edgar Rose *IV* does not play fair.

I learned that during the few months that I dated Amelie. I may be quiet, more emotionally withdrawn than my twin, but I'm no idiot. Amelie liked dating me because I wasn't the sort of guy her dad wanted coming around the house. We were casual—our relationship so laid-back that it barely constituted as one in the first place—but I always wondered if Amelie understood *why* her dad hated me so much. It wasn't just the tattoos and my blue-collar upbringing.

Nah, Edgar Rose disliked me because he'd taught me a hard lesson in fairness years earlier, when I briefly worked as a busboy at one of ERRG's restaurants and he had me arrested for a theft I didn't commit. Two months spent in jail, and not even a single apology when the judge finally dismissed the charge, much to the old man's disgruntlement.

The Roses are treated like untouchable royalty here in New Orleans, and I had firsthand experience in playing the part of pawn.

So, yeah, fair? Not exactly a word that Edgar Rose knows real well, if at all.

With the phone pressed to my ear, Savannah's callback ringing, I wrench open the door to Inked and come to an abrupt stop for the second time this morning.

Standing by the receptionist's desk and talking to my second-in-command, Jordan, is none other than Savannah herself.

I'd recognize her anywhere, even though she's not facing me. The thick hair that damn near hangs down to the swell of her ass, the curvy thighs encased in a pair of tight jeans, and the slim ankles that peek out above the thin straps of her high heels. Her girlish laugh echoes in the parlor as I pocket my phone.

As though sensing my arrival, I watch her shoulders stiffen and all that lush hair swing as she whirls around, one hand clutching the desk to keep her steady. "Owen." Her fingers squeeze the lip of the counter as her mouth tips into a strained smile. "Just who I was looking to see this morning."

I cut a sharp glance to Jordan, who's doing a piss-poor job of pretending to look preoccupied with organizing the desk, and then return my focus to Savannah. Her poker face is terrible. The gentlemanly thing to do would be to let her off easy and tell her that I already know about Mike's Hard Daiquiri.

But I'm no gentleman.

Lifting a sardonic brow, I stare at her expectantly. "Is that so?"

"Yup!" She nabs her purse off the counter and hooks the strap over her arm. One step in my direction and I catch the effervescent scent of her perfume. It's light and airy and reminds me of summer days spent on the deck of my boat, the sun kissing my skin and the water spritzing my face as I hit the gas, hard. Licking her lips, like she's nervous, Savannah tilts her head to the side. "I was hoping to talk with you. It'll only take a few minutes of your time."

The last time she took a few minutes of my time, I called her a coward.

Most of me regrets the pain I saw blooming in her gaze. Part of me still stands by what I said, knowing that if she had the backbone to acknowledge that what I and Amelie shared was nothing more than casual dinner dates that never progressed further than kissing, we'd be in a completely different position right now.

And still part of me wants to punish her for denying what we have—what we *had*—in front of the entire goddamn country. I'm not the kind of person who wears his heart on his sleeve. Over the years, I've done a damn good job of caging my emotions until the past, and all my shadows, hold no leverage over who I am now.

Against my better judgment, I still took that leap of faith seven months ago.

For her.

For us.

For fucking nothing.

Like he's possessed, Jordan bangs on the computer keyboard. When he catches my eye, he holds up his hands with dramatic flair. "Sorry, that's my go-to response when I can feel the awkwardness levels in the air rising."

"You torture technology?"

"Caress it," he corrects somberly, "I caress it gently, but yeah, how about you two take this little . . ." Nose scrunching, he scratches the back of his head. "Whatever you want to call it—the beginning of the end? A heart-to-heart? Either way, take it to the office, would you? Before I feel compelled to accidentally hurl the computer against the wall, and we still don't have that hole fixed yet."

Considering that at one point in time a mother and daughter overheard Jordan having sex with a client in the parlor's storage closet, he doesn't have room to talk smack. Still, I'm not looking for an audience. What Savannah and I have to discuss isn't up for public consumption—not even for Jordan, who was the first tattoo artist I hired here at Inked.

"Man the phone," I tell him.

He palms the telephone like it's his lover. "Already being manned, boss man."

"Try not to scar any more family members by unzipping your pants."

Jordan throws up his arms. "It was *one* time, Harvey. One time!"

"And none of us have ever recovered." Let's just say that Jordan's big attitude doesn't correlate to the attitude he's packing in his pants—if you catch my drift. "You know the Yelp review from that mom still circulates at the top of our most helpful reviews, right? Two thousand likes and counting."

"It's made us famous. Come for the ink, stay for the dick."

Savannah stifles a laugh into a closed fist. "In terms of marketing campaigns, it could be worse."

Thrusting a finger in her direction, Jordan exclaims, "See what I mean? I'm a trendsetter."

"Nah," I murmur, rapping my knuckles on the counter, "trendsetting would entail that you earned yourself a solid positive review." I flash him a quick grin. "And if you read all the way to the bottom, you'd have seen that the mom complained that Yelp doesn't offer negative stars."

"Dammit, man. Who the hell actually clicks *see more* to read all the way to the end?"

Savannah raises her hand. "I did. You know, when Owen told me about it last year. That reviewer was very . . . verbose."

"It can't be *that* bad."

"It is," Savannah and I say simultaneously.

Maybe I'm caught in a weak moment—teasing Jordan with her by my side, like we used to—but I meet Savannah's gaze and hold it. One second. Two. The moment lingers, wrapping me up in memories of her visiting Inked for lunch breaks and doing paperwork in my office late at night while she brought her own to work on . . . Until it segues once more into cold, hard reality.

She dumped me.

I moved on.

Maybe Jordan is right—the awkwardness levels are practically toxic.

In silence, we trudge down the hallway until I'm elbowing open my office door and standing off to the side to let her in. I catch another whiff of that sultry perfume of hers as she slips around me, giving me a wide birth. I grit my teeth. Watch with narrowed eyes as she carefully takes the seat closest to the exit and sets her purse on my desk. Given our past, it's all too easy to imagine us the way we used to be: laughing, splitting a pizza, badly singing to whatever song came on the radio as we worked.

I don't bother with sitting down now.

Resting my ass against the corner of the desk, I link my arms over my chest. Small talk has never been my forte, so I don't start with it now. "ERRG paid off Mike."

Her brow furrows. "Do you hear yourself? You're making it sound like we're the mafia or something. We didn't *pay* him off—"

"What do you call it when a man agrees to sell off his pride and joy in exchange for sipping piña coladas on a beach in Aruba?"

"It's called giving an elderly man the chance to pay off his debts and still enjoy the rest of his life however he sees fit." Unzipping her monstrosity of a purse, she pulls out a stack of folders and drops them unceremoniously on my desk. "Mike was ready to move on. It was a mutually beneficial deal."

"What about the souvenir shop?"

"Bankrupt and about to be put on the market," she says easily, riffling through her papers.

I stare down at her, unconvinced. It took three stints in

jail—all within the same year, when I was twenty—for me to learn to trust my gut. As a kid, I was too damn gullible. Too easy to trust, too naïve to know any better. Despite the fact that I come from a long line of cops, my parents did what they could to keep Gage and me sheltered. Dad told us all the good things about his job, leaving out all of the bad. When it all got too much for her, Mom left him and covered up her heartache with smiles and hugs. Then she took us with her to Hackberry, Louisiana.

Population: under fifteen hundred.

Number of ways we could get into trouble: zero.

Maybe things would have turned out differently if I'd stayed out in southwest Louisiana. But I didn't, and life always manages to find you no matter how far you run.

And if I'm looking on the bright side, then I'd say jail has a pretty good success rate at stripping your innocence. Forces you to harden up or find yourself isolated in a place where teaming up means survival and walking the solitary beat guarantees nothing but trouble. By the time the judge dismissed my case after Edgar Rose's accusation, I wasn't the same kid my mom used to send to pick up milk from the corner store or the same teenager who shyly asked Maryanne to prom, knowing that she liked Gage more, though he didn't even know her name.

Over the years, I've learned to stay on my toes and anticipate the inconceivable. Right now, my gut is hollering at me to not trust a thing coming out of Savannah's sexy, pouty mouth.

Wanting to throw her off-kilter—to see that fake-as-shit poker face crumble—I set my hand over hers to still her anxious shuffling. "And me?" I ask, my voice low.

Her lips part on a sharp breath, but she doesn't move her hand out from under mine. "What about you?"

I lean down, slouching my shoulders so that we're at eye level. "Let's not play this game, Rose."

"I'm not—"

"Your dad bought the souvenir shop," I tell her, flattening my hand on hers so that her fingers are pinned to that precious folder she's gripping like no tomorrow. Her startled gaze leaps to mine. "It was being sold, and he picked it up before anyone else could put in an offer. Yeah, you told me that. But the daiquiri shop . . ."

When I purposely trail off, her hand flexes beneath mine. "I told you, Mike was ready to move on to his next adventure."

"Daddy dearest doesn't do anythin' out of the kindness of his heart, baby." The endearment isn't necessarily considered one here in New Orleans. It's a word bandied about by cashiers and cabbies and even sweet-tempered librarians to kids in strollers all the way to the elderly pushing their walkers. But Savannah's eyes . . . Christ, they fucking *burn* when the word slips from my tongue, and my damn cock twitches in my jeans. My head might know that we're done with her, and my heart has finally gotten the memo, but my dick is clearly not one to fall in line. *Traitor*. Releasing a tight exhalation that does nothing to relieve the ache behind my zipper, I add, "Which means it's not escapin' my notice that ERRG now owns the entire block."

"*Almost* the entire block," Savannah retorts, tugging at her hand so that I let her go. If I wasn't watching so closely, I'd have missed the way she swallows, hard, and straightens her shoulders as if she's going to war—against me. "He doesn't own Inked."

"Yet." I keep my tone soft, cool. Cross my ankles, one over the other, and settle in like I've got all the time in the world to hash this shit out with her. "Did he send you to me,

Rose? Tell you all the ways you need to convince me to roll over and play dead, just like Mike?"

"Owen—"

"Answer the question, Savannah. He wants Inked next." Our gazes clash, mine angry and resolute and hers bleak but hopeful. "Yes . . . or no?"

6

SAVANNAH

Owen Harvey is not a nice guy.

Oh, the man has the whole *I'm-such-a-gentleman* disguise down pat. There was that one time the Entrepreneurs of the Crescent City awarded him the Humanitarian of the Year award for donating a hefty percentage of his annual profits to a local foundation intended to help kids with special needs. And, okay, *fine*, he's also been known to foster puppies while they wait for their fur-ever homes. Puppies, for God's sake. Look up *Sexy Gentleman* in the dictionary, and no doubt you'll find Owen's ruggedly handsome face waiting for you as the only definition.

So maybe he is a nice guy—to some degree—but none of that matters. What *does* matter is this: Owen Harvey pulls no punches and he knows exactly how to spin this conversation so that I'll be the one sitting in the palm of his hand.

If I'm not already there, that is.

I meet his dark, pointed stare, and do my best to ignore the fluttering in my belly that has nothing (okay, *almost* nothing) to do with his close proximity and everything to do with the frustrating way he baits me to give him what he wants: my submission.

Not going to happen, buddy.

He's close, closer than he's been to me in months, and it takes every bit of willpower to keep from leaning in for a sniff of that delicious cologne he wears.

No. *No.*

I jerk back.

I'm no bumbling little girl with no idea how to hold her own. I manage hundreds of employees, millions of dollars' worth in assets, and, yes, I might not be doing what I love—not the way that Owen is with Inked on Bourbon—but there's a reason why the Vice President nameplate is now sitting front and center on my desk.

I'm good at what I do. Although I prefer compassion over strong-arming my opponents, I can be ruthless. I will *not* wither into a pile of lust just because Owen Harvey is sex on a stick and is currently looking at me like he wouldn't mind throwing me on his desk, if only to get all the answers he wants out of me.

Shifting off the chair, I rise to my full height. In my sky-high pumps, my eyes are level with all that ink at the base of his throat. Perfect. We're on equal footing now, both of us sucking up our own bubbles of power.

Confess, his thunderous expression demands.

We're getting there, I hope mine answers.

I line up my hip with the edge of the desk, my arms linked across my chest. His gaze veers south, swooping down over my loose, silky shirt to my tight skinny jeans to my hot-pink stilettos. The perusal is slow, meant to intimidate rather than seduce, but I'd be lying if I say I don't feel the flames of desire flickering at my feet. Want clenches my thighs together, but I hold my stance, unwilling to give him any ammunition to think he's bested me.

I hurt him—I know that. And I've paid the price for doing so every day for the last seven months. But this meeting has nothing to do with *Put A Ring On It* or our personal relationship or the fact that he called me a coward. It's about business, *only* business.

I clear my throat.

He plants his hands on the desk, on either side of his hips, and meets my gaze unapologetically.

My heart thuds in my chest as I force out a droll, "Like what you see?"

His smile, though barely there, is laced with a dangerous heat. "You know I do."

Breath hitching, I look away. Take a second to stitch my flustered emotions—and my stupid, flaming cheeks—back together into some semblance of control. *Throw them off their game. Catch them by surprise.* It's the first tactic Dad ever taught me when it came to business management. *Never let them see your weakness.* But what to do when your weakness isn't a thing but a person, and that person is the one your family expects you to dismantle for their own gain?

Shakespeare couldn't even make this shit up.

"You called it, you know," I say smoothly, as though I'm discussing the weather or the Saints' latest draft pick, "ERRG wants to buy you out."

Out of the corner of my eye, I see Owen's fingers flex on the desk. "Surprised you're comin' right out and telling me."

"Because I'm a coward?" I flick my gaze up to his handsome face. "Is that why you're surprised?"

His nostrils flare, and those long, artistic fingers of his drum a silent beat on the desk like he's working out his next words with careful precision. "Savannah, listen—"

"Do you regret it?" I kick my chin up, staring him down. *Do* not *let him see how much his answer means to you.* After a heartbeat of silence, I clarify, "Saying what you did earlier this week?"

He hesitates, and I can practically see him playing out all the different options laid out before him. One path keeps us tethered to this hate-infested, push-pull relationship, and the other puts us on the road to salvaging whatever we can of our friendship. I want the latter. No, I *crave* it, but I won't beg for forgiveness. I've done that, months ago, three days ago, and here we are still.

Push.

Pull.

There's only so many times I can say *I'm sorry* before I strip the words of all power they carry.

Finally, his broad shoulders sag like he's come to grips with some internal, warring struggle. "You know I fucking do, Rose."

Thank God.

Twisting around before he can glimpse the emotion—and all the grateful tears—cresting to the surface, I shakily flip open the top folder I brought from my office. The deeds to the souvenir shop and Mike's Hard Daiquiri. I set those aside and reach for the thick contract I printed out this morning. "I'm not a coward, Owen, no matter what you think about what happened that night." And what he *thinks* he knows won't even come close to the reality of it all. Still, the long-standing frustration of being misunderstood sharpens my words. "A coward would have shown up here today, willing to do whatever needed to be done to make my pops happy."

"I thought we just agreed that I regret calling you a coward," he grunts, pushing off the desk to head for the coffee maker in the corner of the office. He glances over at me. "Want one?"

"Sure."

Presenting me with his back, he grabs the glass decanter and shoves it onto the heating pad. He skipped his flannel shirt today, so there's no hiding how his black T hugs his muscular frame almost indecently. And hug his frame, the shirt most definitely does. Wide shoulders taper off to a lean waist. The cords of his back muscles play when he lifts an arm to grab two mugs from a built-in shelf. To say nothing of the way the hem of his cotton T rises, revealing a black strip of briefs—boxers?—and an even more tantalizing glimpse of inked skin.

I bite down on my bottom lip and do what is only right in the name of self-preservation: I picture Owen wearing awful, hideous tighty-whities. Not that the reprieve lasts long.

He reaches up, bicep visibly clenching beneath his short sleeve, and runs a hand down his nape.

His shirt rides up. More taut skin is exposed.

And now there's nothing I can do but stare up at the ceiling and think of all the awful things in the world.

Sex on a stick is right.

The first time I met Owen, my sister dragged me into Inked because she couldn't wait for me to meet the guy she'd been seeing recently. I'd asked her what he looked like, and she'd only flashed me a small grin and said, "Bad."

She wasn't wrong.

Owen Harvey looks like every woman's bad-boy fantasy come to life. The messy dark hair. The intricate tattoos that cover his arms and the base of his throat. One time, when I'd had too much to drink, I asked him if he had ink all over. Was his entire body a canvas of artwork? I'd wanted to know

The chance to do something with my life besides manage restaurants and be my father's lackey—gone.

Any hope of Owen and me turning over a new leaf . . . pretty much nonexistent.

His big, black *I-crush-dreams-for-a-living* boot lands on the trash pedal. The tin top smacks the side of his desk as the shredded papers drift down like plastic beads at the height of Mardi Gras season. And then he picks up my empty mug, his expression wiped clean of all emotion, and asks, "More coffee before you go?"

I don't think coffee is going to cut it.

Hell, I'm pretty sure a full bottle of wine isn't going to fix the hot puddle of *fuck-my-life* Owen has just landed me in.

"No, I'm good."

"Suit yourself." And then the jerk takes *my* mug to the Keurig and tops it off. Turns and rests his broad back against the wall, and casually drawls, "About the hole. I've got guys comin' out to fix it tomorrow, but in case they need to stop inside the old souvenir shop—that good with you?"

He casually sips from the mug I just used. Eyes me steadily over the rim that's still marked with the pink of my lipstick.

That whole *I'm so calm, the TV producers were begging me to lose my shit?* It goes sailing right out the window.

Owen Harvey is my kryptonite, my weakness—and, as of this moment, the biggest pain in my ass. And from the taunting gleam burning in his gaze, he knows it too.

Just. Friggin'. Fantastic.

7

OWEN

Savannah Rose is quickly becoming a pain in my ass.

Seventy-two hours.

That's how long it's been since she waltzed out of Inked on Bourbon with her massive purse tucked under one arm and dogged determination etched into her expression like war paint. Jordan had looked from me to her and then back again before promptly announcing, "Y'all should just fuck out your differences and call it a day."

Fucking has nothing to do with the onslaught of Rose-*everything* that has invaded my life in the last few days.

First, there were the trio of emails (and phone calls) that landed in my inbox. Each highlighted a different financial advantage to me selling the two floors above the parlor, the last of which going so far as to even pinpoint that the overall marketplace for private rentals has decreased in New Orleans since the city council voted to eliminate short-term rentals from the French Quarter.

My response was a simple but curt, *My block exists in the preapproved zoning area of Bourbon.*

No reply, which should have raised red flags but didn't—not until the construction crew next door began erecting scaffolding on the exterior of our entire block yesterday morning. *Scaffolding*, for fuck's sake, when there's nothing at all wrong with the façade, the interior, any of it, save for the goddamn hole in the wall that was just fixed.

And then there's this.

This.

Seventy-two hours after Savannah left, and I'm staring at all the roses that have infiltrated Inked on Bourbon while I stepped out for lunch. Not just one bouquet or even two.

No, there are over a *dozen* scattered around the parlor. On the receptionist's desk. The leather sofas in the waiting area. Beside the equipment. When I spot another sitting innocently atop a side table that usually holds binders with tattoo examples for clients to flip through, I curse under my breath and contemplate the legalities of storming into ERRG's headquarters, busting open the door to Savannah's office, and letting her fucking have it.

I'd enact the punishment real slow, too.

Her hands restrained above her head, my belt cinched around her wrists.

Her shirt yanked down to reveal her tits.

My hand on her thigh. High enough to have her begging for more; low enough that she'd soon be regretting every moment of sending her little "gift" to my place.

The chime of keys disturbs the fantasy as Gage slams to a stop beside me at the sight before him. He catches his car keys mid-toss. "It smells like a goddamn funeral home in here."

Appropriate, maybe, considering the fact that Savannah's days are about to be numbered.

"Looks like I had a visitor while we were eating. God

knows Jordan probably let them in—the asshole's got a sadistic sense of humor." Toeing aside a bouquet that's been left on the floor, my eyes narrow when I see a pocket-sized card resting beneath the flowers. I drop to my haunches and pick the card up, turning it over to see if anything has been written on the front.

Nothing. Totally blank.

"Someone crushing on you?" Gage asks good-naturedly, dropping down beside me. We're the same height, the same build. Save for the number of tattoos I'm rocking and the beard I haven't gone without in close to a decade, we're identical. Nearly. "Or am I gonna have to break out the cuffs and wrangle your stalker behind bars?"

The idea of Savannah being arrested for stalking is so ludicrous I almost laugh out loud. I don't, but only because if I do, there's a good chance I might choke on the cloying scent that's verging on downright nauseating.

Gage is right. It does smell like a funeral home—which would be funny, if it weren't for the fact that my temper is close to boiling. The Roses . . . nothing they do is subtle, especially not when it comes to the family business. Not their drama, nor their successes, and definitely not their inability to accept defeat.

Last I heard, Edgar Rose's younger brother Bernard was cut off from the family fortune after he placed Rosalie's—the newest ERRG restaurant here in the city—as his part of the pot in a poker tournament last year. The media ate that shit up real quick, doling out the kind of headlines that'll be branded on the memories of New Orleanians for the next century and a half.

"Not a stalker," I grunt, digging my thumb under the envelope's flap. "I can guarantee that."

My twin knocks his knee into mine. "Aw, is this what wooing looks like in the twenty-first century?"

If being wooed entails me being pushed and prodded into selling two of my rental properties, then yes—I'm being wooed with such finesse I'm shitting unicorns and goddamn rainbows by the hour. Be still, my ever-pounding heart.

"Do you seriously think I'm being wooed?" I ask, sarcasm lacing the words.

Out of the corner of my eye, I see Gage look pensively from bouquet to bouquet. He cocks his head. "Not the method I'd take—you know I'm more of a wine-and-dine-'em kinda guy—but I can't knock the hustle. This couldn't have been cheap."

For people like me and Gage, who grew up with very little besides the clothes on our backs and an ambition to make a difference in the world, a dozen bouquets is an over-the-top waste of money.

For an heiress like Savannah Rose, all of this is chump change.

Another reason why it's a good thing she ended whatever we could have had before it even began.

I may be doing well for myself now but I'm well aware of the number of years it took me to get to this point in my life. Savannah, on the other hand, has been fed by the proverbial silver spoon since birth.

Refusing to acknowledge the anxious jitter in my knees as I stand up, I peel back the envelope's flap and pull out the card. Angle it so that only I can read the words scrawled in her feminine script:

To being the best of neighbors. Yrs, Savannah Rose.

"What's it say?" Gage demands, sneaking out an arm to make a grab for the card.

The bastard is quick on his feet, but I've always been faster—even after the accident.

I spin out of his reach, shoving the card back in its envelope and then sticking it in the back pocket of my slacks. My twin lowers his gaze, and it's hard to miss the debate warring in his expression before he launches forward, hooks a hand in my shirt collar, and trips me up with his feet.

Bastard.

"We don't do secrets, remember?" he mutters. "You got a problem with something means that I have a problem with something." Before I have the chance to elbow him in the gut, he's snagged the card from my pocket and sashayed—straight up *sashayed* like a goddamn ballerina—over to the front desk. I note the stiffness in his shoulders when he shoves aside another bouquet and picks up yet another card, waving it in the air, before he's even read the first. "Fess up, bro, you're being wooed. Courted. Whatever you want to call it."

I shift forward on my feet, intent on ripping that new card right out of his grasp. God only knows what that one says. *Agree to the deal, Owen, and your twin will never have to know that you told him nothing about my proposition.* Or maybe, *Sell us the two rentals and ERRG won't make your life a living hell, the way it did for good old Bernard Rose.*

Really, the possibilities are endless.

I grimace. "You don't want to know."

"Have I met her before?"

"You could say that."

His gaze tracks the roses strewn all over the parlor, then drops to the two cards he's holding. Indecision sparks in his expression, as though he's torn between letting me have my privacy and saying to hell with it and finding out for himself. "Do I like her?"

I let out a rough laugh that rings hollow in my ears. "You did."

"Did, emphasis on the past tense?" It's not really a question, and Gage doesn't even pretend to give me time to answer. Sharp-minded and shrewd-eyed, it's no shock when my brother switches into cop mode. "Roses . . . There are roses *everywhere*, and you—" His nostrils flare with realization. "No."

"You're slow on the uptake today."

"Sue me for skipping a second cup of coffee when my lovely wife decided we should make use of our morning doing other, more exciting things."

Light on my toes, I move swiftly. "Sounds like you're makin' excuses, man."

"Sounds like you're—*hey!*"

With both cards in hand, I don't waste time in ripping open the second envelope. Same card, same handwriting, different message:

Thoughts on the roses? Too on the nose? Not enough subtlety? I'm up for feedback. Yrs, Sav.

Seven. Months.

For seven months, I've done what I can to put aside my misplaced crush on America's most eligible bachelorette. I'm not one to sleep around with random women. Never have been, never will be, and sure, we can blame it on some romantic, idealistic fantasy of me remembering my parents being truly in love—before it all went to shit—but I've always wanted to see *something* coming out of a relationship before I drop my briefs.

Doesn't mean I haven't kept myself busy in other ways since coming back to the city. I bought another real estate property, one that I'm fixing up in Barataria, a coastal town some twenty-odd miles south of New Orleans. I took on not one new apprentice at the parlor but two, because why stop at making only one kid's dreams come true? I've stepped up with the Entrepreneurs of the Crescent City, an organization I first joined because Savannah belonged to it, even going so far as to sit on the board and help young businessmen and women in the greater-New Orleans metro area reach for what they deem the unattainable.

I worked.

I hustled.

And I've done it all to keep from breeching the thin barrier that Savannah erected when she sent me home from the show because what she felt for me was friendly. *Brotherly*, even.

I honored her wishes, respected her boundaries, ignored countless interview opportunities that have sprouted up to "expose America's sweetheart" over the last month and some change that *Put A Ring On It* has started airing.

All of which I gave the proverbial middle finger.

Because you're still in too deep with her.

I inhale sharply and immediately wish I hadn't.

The scent of roses has permeated Inked.

I'm entrenched in it.

Fucking drowning in it.

Those boundaries between me and Savannah? They're about to come crumbling down.

Gripping the cards tightly, I spin on my heel. "I gotta go."

A heavy palm lands on my shoulder. "Tell me you aren't taking back up with her again, man."

I glance over at him. "Trust me, I learned my lesson the first time around."

His gaze bounces from me to the bouquets. "You sure about that? Because from where I'm standin', it looks like the two of you have learned absolutely jack squat. This is the same girl you let me assume you'd hooked up with, just once, even though you never did."

Because I was trying to save face after spending so much time with her once Amelie and I broke up. Because it was easier to let my brother think that I was pining after a woman who I'd already slept with instead of desperately wanting someone who I'd never once kissed, never once touched. Maybe that makes me an asshole, and if it does, karma delivered swiftly and efficiently. Gage had a first-row seat to watching my lie unravel before me once I returned to New Orleans, when any chance of me escaping *Put A Ring On It* emotionally unscathed went up in a flaming ball of cataclysmic fire.

"Don't worry about me. I got it." Shrugging his hand off, I step toward the door. Then, on a whim, I pivot and grab the lone bouquet seated on the front sofa. Another card is stuffed between the two cushions, provoking me with its very existence.

Read it.

Don't read it.

In the end, I cave—not because I'm willing to give Savannah another chance, the way Gage seems to think I will, but because America's favorite sweetheart is about to be taught what it feels like when you fall from grace.

Bouquet tucked under one arm, I tear open this next envelope and sweep open the card with my thumb.

Her message is simple, a taunting tease as much as it is throwing down the gauntlet for me to pick up:

I'll be at the office all day. Fourth floor. Suite 402. I'll bring my wits as long as you promise to bring an open mind. Yrs, The Woman Behind the Obnoxiously Annoying Rose Delivery.

Pressure builds at my temples, and the plastic wrap around the roses crinkles loudly under my armpit as I shove open the front door and holler at Gage to lock up behind me.

Savannah thinks she's got the upper hand in our little situation.

She may have struck the first match, but she sure as hell isn't going to win the war.

8

SAVANNAH

Moaning filters through the conference room.

Male moaning, female moaning, hell, I'm pretty sure even our office cat—Pablo—gives a beseeching *meow* as we all dig into the steaming crawfish dumplings set out before us.

"Dufrene," says Jorge, ERRG's social media manager and IT guru, "you are a god."

At the head of the twelve-person table, Jean sits like a king. One booted foot hiked up on the edge of the table, elbow propped up on his bent knee, his Saints hat askew on his head like a jaunty crown. "What was that, Jorge?" Jean prompts, tapping his ear. His chair creaks as he leans forward. "You said I'm a . . . what?"

Cheeks stuffed full, Jorge grumbles something unintelligible.

"That's right," my head chef says, snapping his fingers, "a *god*. And you doubted me for wanting to do a Cajun-style twist on steamed dumplings."

Shamelessly, I scrape my fork across the porcelain plate, then lick the aioli sauce off the tines. I swear my heart gives a little flutter of satisfaction. Thing is, when it comes to food, Jean Dufrene *is* a god. He started off as a sous-chef seven or eight years ago with Rose & Thorn, our flagship restaurant, but it didn't take long for him to catch Dad's attention. Once that happened, any hope Dufrene had of not moving up the ranks—he'd initially only planned to remain in Louisiana for another year before moving to Atlanta with his then-girlfriend—was sliced and diced. He's been with us ever since. Cocky. Confident. And clearly determined to rub it in Jorge's face that he's the best food mastermind we've ever had.

Granted, I'm pretty sure Jorge only talks smack so that Jean will feel compelled to show up to the office with bite-sized samples of all the new items going on our menus.

Truly, their bromance is legendary.

Eyeing the second dumpling set before me, it takes every bit of self-control to not eat it. Instead, I reach for my bottled water and crack the cap open. "What's the timeline for getting these moving at Rosalie?"

Dufrene shoots me one of his arrogant grins. No surprise, a few of my female coworkers squirm in their chairs. "By the weekend rush, at the latest. I'm confident that—"

The door to the conference room swings open and Georgie pokes her head through. Her gaze immediately lands on me. "You missed a call on line one."

"Ever hear of knocking, Harris?"

Georgie nudges the door wider, turning slightly so she can eyeball Jean where he sits. "Ever hear of manners, Dufrene?"

Usually, I'd let the two of them banter it out—free entertainment, ladies and gents—but not right now. Not today. Not after I special-ordered over a hundred roses to be hand-delivered to Inked on Bourbon, all in the effort of prompting

Owen from his cave. The man is the most self-contained person I've ever met, and that's saying something coming from *me*.

Licking my lips, I pretend to be sidetracked and nonplussed by scratching out *Meet About Menu Addition* from my calendar's to-do list. "Did they leave a name?"

Georgie shakes her head. "No."

Disappointment has me gripping my pen a little tighter. Probably a random caller then—someone on staff needing a day off or one of my managers wanting to gripe about the host not showing up for a shift again. Those sorts of issues are supposed to go through a chain of command, but I still end up with a handful of them every day.

Maybe Owen hasn't seen the roses yet?

Maybe. Unlikely.

The thought of him avoiding me forever churns my stomach in a way that feels like it should come with a DANGEROUS THOUGHTS label attached.

Reaching up to tug at her curls, Georgie shifts her weight, door still propped open by her hip. "He, ah, said he would be here in time for your appointment."

Our . . . appointment?

Oh.

My eyes widen and I won't deny it: my heart flutters again, this time for a reason that has nothing to do with Jean's crawfish dumplings. A year ago, I sought out Owen's company because his presence soothed me. Every minute that I spent with him felt like the antidote to the everyday chaos of being a Rose. He listened and he encouraged and, when he saw me retreating into my chain-linked shell, he pushed me to do something crazy that reminded me that I was so very much alive.

He inked my skin. He dragged me to the wine bar over

on St. Charles Avenue that I love so much. He offered his office to me like a safe haven from the constant demands of my job.

I loved that side of Owen.

But I can't help but crave this new dominant side of him too—the side he's only shown me since I walked into the old souvenir shop and saw him standing there with barely leashed fury in his gaze.

It's all kinds of wrong—and knowing our history, I'm going to be burned alive by heartbreak or regret or both—but I can't help poking the metaphorical bear to see his claws come out. Hence, the roses.

Hence, you are insane, my subconscious informs me.

Yeah, that too.

I fake a light tap to my head. "The appointment! Right, right. Will you let me know when he arrives?"

"You got it, boss." With one last glare in Dufrene's direction, Georgie flips me a thumbs-up and backs out of the room.

Tapping the next item on my task list, I turn to Jorge. *Focus, girl. Focus on the job.* Easier said than done when I can't help but listen for any new sounds coming from the main office area. "Catch me up to speed on the Rose & Thorn IGTV campaign. Where are we at?"

Jorge sits up straight. Propping his laptop open, he clicks away at the keyboard, then meets my gaze. "We're doing great. I've been tracking our numbers—for every new Behind-the-Scenes video we post on Instagram, there's a direct correlation to the number of patrons who come in to eat for about . . ." He taps some more, his dark eyes roving over the screen. "Three days or so. This week I tried posting five videos—one on each weekday—instead of our usual three but didn't see an increase in reservations."

"So it's safe to say that three videos per week is probably the max we can hit before oversaturation?" I flip to a new page in my notebook, making a note of Jorge's theory. Stop just short of doodling Owen's full name, like I'm a middle schooler with my first crush.

Savannah and Owen sitting in a tree. K-i-s-s-i-n-g. First comes love, then comes marriage. Then comes—

Embarrassed, I draw a heavy line through Owen's name.

"I've been testing for a month now," Jorge says, regathering my attention. "Maybe things will be different during Mardi Gras, but for a regular month with no major city-wide events, three seems to be right on the money."

"Perfect." I cap my pen and lean back in my chair. Try as hard as I can not to think about Owen storming in here. The reality is, I *do* need to see him. My father did not react well to Owen turning down ERRG's offer. *As if I expected anything different.* "I want you to try it out with Rosalie's account next —schedule the first video with the launch of the dumplings. See if we can get the word out that way. If it works for Rosalie, then it's safe to assume that it'll work for the rest of the restaurants."

The conference door swings open again and, once more, Georgie peeks inside. Her cheeks are flushed when she looks my way. "Sorry to interrupt. The, um"—she fidgets with her shirt sleeve—"*caller* wanted me to let you know that he's just parked his car. ETA is five minutes."

A shiver of heat works its way down my spine.

Ignoring the inquisitive glances aimed in my direction, I press my tongue to the roof of my mouth and inhale slowly. Let it out. Then calmly reply, "Message received."

As if Owen isn't giving me a countdown until all hell breaks loose.

As if I'm not watching the minute hand tick away on the clock mounted to the wall above Dufrene's head.

As if it's an everyday occurrence that the man I rejected in front of an entire nation isn't on his way to pick up the gauntlet I recklessly threw down.

Hovering in the doorway, Georgie drops her hand from her sleeve. "He wanted me to let you know that he's . . . bringing you something that you forgot at his place."

Across the table, Dufrene watches me speculatively. "You're blushing."

God, am I? Resisting the urge to press my palms to my cheeks, I reach for the water bottle. "It's a little hot in here." I look to Heather, our CFO, for backup. "Isn't it a little hot in here?"

Her expression doesn't so much as twitch. "I'm going through menopause, Savannah. I'm roasting approximately twenty-four/seven."

The men all groan, Jorge going so far as to shout out "TMI!" while Greg, ERRG's accountant, makes the sign of the cross like there's a good chance Heather's menopause will metamorphosize into, I don't know, the *plague*.

"What?" Heather throws her hands up in the air. "Women deal with menopause, men put up with using the little blue pill. Life goes on."

Sarah offers a high-five from Heather's other side. "A-frigging-men."

They slap hands as Georgie creeps back out of the door. "I'm going to go now." Before Dufrene can make another parting comment, ERRG's executive assistant escapes out of the conference room.

Act normal. You can do this! I turn back to my employees. "Where were we?"

Looking amused, Dufrene drawls, "Menopause. Rosalie. Jorge finally learning how to count."

My social media manager thrusts out an arm and punches Jean in the bicep. Only, it's Jorge who ends up wincing. "What the hell are you?" he mutters, shaking out his fist. "Iron Man? It's like punching a brick wall."

Dufrene's mouth curls in a smirk. "I work out."

I hold up my hands, palms facing out. "Children, can we please get back on track?"

For the third time in ten minutes, the conference room door cracks open, and this time I squeeze my eyes shut. "Georgie, why don't you send me a text when he gets here? That way we can wrap up this meeting before I—"

"Before you what, Rose?"

Rose.

My eyelids peel open and, sure enough, it's not my curly-haired, spitfire of an assistant standing in the doorway but Owen Harvey in the flesh. Dark, messy hair. Black slacks. A deep blue button-down that looks completely foreign on his large, brawny frame. No flannel in sight.

The fact that he's pushed the sleeves up to his elbows, though? It's the only familiar thing about the image he's presenting me with right now.

My gaze skips down to the bouquet of roses he's gripping in one hand.

Looks like he received my delivery.

Game on.

Immediately, I launch to my feet. Ten pairs of eyes from around the table swivel in my direction. I can feel them all staring openly, curiously, even as my stare stays latched on the one man who has the ability to make me question everything.

Even my decision to keep my distance from him.

I hear Georgie's jangling bracelets before I see her, but suddenly there she is, panting and heaving as she points wordlessly at Owen then at herself. "Bathroom," she manages weakly, "I left to go to the bathroom and he—he—"

Owen doesn't even have the good grace to look apologetic. "Figured I'd give myself a tour."

He would.

He *would* take it upon himself to stroll all up in here like he owns the place. Thank God my dad isn't in the office today. It's one thing for me to invite Owen to a showdown when it's just the two of us, and another thing entirely to do so when there's the very real chance that the two of them will have a potential run-in.

I don't know why Dad dislikes Owen so much, especially when Amelie and Owen's breakup was an entirely mutual decision. But the hate is real, even if seemingly unjustified, and in the off-chance that someone will recognize Owen's face from his one ill-fated episode on *Put A Ring On It*, it's probably best that I get him out of here and into my office as quickly as possible.

Grabbing the plate with the sole crawfish dumpling on it, my high heels tap against the ceramic tiled floor as I swoop in close to the man determined to throw my world upside down and keep it that way. By invitation, this time around.

On instinct, I wrap a hand around his exposed forearm and ignore the tantalizing spark of heat at the contact of skin against skin. I toss out "we'll finish up the meeting at noon!" over my shoulder, just as I yank Owen behind me and into the hallway.

"You sure you want to be alone with me right now?" he rasps softly, and if my heart wasn't pounding ruthlessly before, it definitely is now. I'm aware of his heat at my back, the tension radiating from his big body, the way he pulls out of my grasp and locks a hand around my wrist, tugging me to a stop. "Because I'm not feeling nice." His thumb slides over my stampeding pulse. "And I'm not feelin' cordial."

My gaze flicks left, quickly assessing the empty hallway. When I return my attention to Owen's rugged features, I ask, "Did you bring an open mind like I suggested?"

His lips twitch. "I brought something—can't say it's an open mind exactly."

I dip my chin toward the roses. "Tell me you appreciated the gesture, at least. A dozen bouquets of roses. Really, you'll remember this moment for the rest of your life."

The pressure of his hold on me slackens, but he doesn't let me go. "You're assuming that the gesture means enough that I'll even want to remember it."

Ouch.

Looks like I'm not the only one who brought their wits along.

Whistling low, I shake my head with dramatic slowness. "Owen, you wound me."

He jerks me close, and I nearly stumble over his feet. "*Wound* you?" he echoes in disbelief. "You've been *hounding* me. Gage thought I had a goddamn stalker and you're worried that, what? I hurt your feelings? You sent me a hundred and forty-four roses, Savannah. What the hell were you thinking?"

Cheekily, I smile up at him. "I'm thinking that your math skills are excellent. Has anyone ever told you that?"

Dark eyes narrow into slits. "You . . . you are single-handedly becoming the biggest pain in my—"

I clap my free hand over his mouth.

His trim beard tickles my palm and my heart hammers

against my rib cage and, oh God, I'm not sure which one of us I've surprised more by touching him so boldly.

I've never—not once—touched him like this.

Not when he was dating Amelie.

Not when they broke up and we spent every moment that we could together.

And certainly not when he showed up in Los Angeles and begged me to give our relationship a real chance.

I swallow thickly. Then gather all of my courage to open my mouth and say, "You ignored all my phone calls. I needed to talk to you and since you were clearly avoiding me, I took drastic action. It wasn't Plan A, I assure you."

Grasping my fingers in his, Owen lifts my hand from his mouth so he can speak. "I'm not selling."

"Hear me out."

"Nothing you can say will change my mind."

"Maybe not, but you'll never know unless you give me a chance."

Give me a chance.

It is, possibly, the worst thing I could say to him because it is *exactly* what he asked of me that night in California when he put himself on the line and I rejected him.

But perhaps this means that Owen Harvey is a better person than I am because instead of telling me to take a hike, he only studies me like he can see inside my head and read every single one of my thoughts—except I don't think he'll see my proposal coming.

I'm jumping out of the dotted lines on this one.

Taking a step that will either see me fired from ERRG or put me on the path to being heralded as a hero.

And I think . . . well, I think that if Owen listens to what I have to say, he'll see that this could be a massive opportunity for him, as well.

together or anything. Anyway. I learned French and Spanish at the same time I was taught English. Instead of sports, he encouraged us to pick up an instrument and learn to play." She gives me a small smile that doesn't quite reach her eyes. "I used to want to play lacrosse so badly."

I stare at her, unable to look away. "You'd be wiped clean off the field."

"Oh, ye of little faith." Those slouched shoulders of her go stick-straight. "I'd survive."

"Maybe. Good news: they give out participation ribbons for just about everything nowadays."

With real slick subtlety, she runs her middle finger alongside the picture frame, and I have to bite back a grin. "Please don't quit your day job. You'd make a horrible life coach."

"Your claws are showing."

"Just trying to earn myself a blue ribbon for best wit in New Orleans. You did say they hand them out for everything nowadays, didn't you?"

My only answer is a low, husky chuckle.

"*Anyway*," she says, with a pointed glare over her shoulder that doesn't even come close to putting me in my place, "Amelie and me, we were meant to be . . . well-rounded, I guess. That was the goal."

My feet move out of their volition, bringing me closer to her. "Every parent's hope for their kid."

"Yeah." She gives a soft, deprecating laugh that raises the hair on my arms. "You could say that. Only thing is, Dad was so *determined* to create these powerhouse daughters that it's like he forgot that we were human too. As soon as school wrapped for the day, he had us following him from restaurant to restaurant. By the time I was ten, I was bussing tables three nights a week. By sixteen? Dad had me helping him man the front of the house—taking reservations, seating customers. The day I graduated high school, he took the family out for dinner and brought ERRG's account ledger." Another one of those bone-chilling laughs that makes me swallow thickly. "Apparently it was time for me to look at what went into the backend of keeping a century-old business like the Edgar Rose Restaurant Group afloat."

"Why are you telling me this?"

The words emerge raspy, demanding, but Savannah turns around anyway, picture frame clasped to her chest, and meets my gaze head-on. "Because I knew then that my dad expected me to be just like *him*. The late nights and the laser focus and the ability to sever personal relationships for the greater good of the family legacy." She shakes her head, sending her wavy hair this way and that. I want to catch the strands and wrap them around my fist. Drag her ever closer until we've having this conversation the way I'd prefer: naked, in bed, with the morning light as the only veil we'd keep between us.

I drag my fingers through my hair, exhaling sharply.

"It's what he would do," she goes on, completely oblivious to the turmoil rioting in my head, "it's what he *still* does. And, you know, up until this point in life, I've willingly gone along with it all because it was either me doing Dad's bitch work or Amelie doing it, and my sister . . ." A fragile smile pulls at her lips. "Well, you know how she is."

I came here wanting to shout and rage and put this woman in her place for testing the frays of my sanity.

It's what I wanted, but standing here now, it's not at all what I do.

Because, at the end of the day, Savannah Rose softens my hard edges and brightens my shadows and, *fuck it*. I close the remaining gap between us before I even realize that I've moved. Her head tips back, gaze rising from my chest to my throat to my face. I feel that one look like she's taken a hammer to my skull.

Vulnerable. Trusting.

Christ.

I thought I was past this. I spent seven *months* getting past this, and yet it's a test of willpower that I manage to keep my hand down by my side instead of cupping her cheek and pressing my lips to her forehead.

"Rose, your sister is a great girl, but I'm not . . ." My hands ball into fists. "At the risk of sounding like a complete douchebag, I've never been interested in peeling back her layers. It wasn't like that between us."

It was never the way it's been with you.

Her throat works with an audible swallow. Just when I think she's about to finally agree to put this Amelie thing to bed, she changes gears completely: "What I was trying to say is, I've spent my entire life putting ERRG first so Amelie could put it *last*. So, I think"—she winces, fingers tapping on the frame—"that in doing so, I've become a little bit too much like my father. The cutthroat side of him, I mean. It's not who I want to be, and when I came to your office last week with that contract . . . *that's* who I was."

"You mean that you were just like your father?" I draw out slowly, trying to make sure I have this right.

Her gaze brightens. "Yes! Exactly!"

Maybe I've had one too many concussions over the years, but let's put it this way: my Thomas Edison lightbulb is not lighting up.

"Savannah?"

Her smile falters. "Yes?"

"You're nothing at all like your old man." Savannah

might think she's cutthroat but she's leagues away from pinning the blame of theft on a kid just because he *looks* like trouble. Edgar Rose did that to me. And, yeah, I'm sure my back talk didn't help matters. I'd been angry at the world, for taking my dad, for my mom taking her own life less than twenty-four hours later, for the universe taking what little naivety I had left. But I hadn't stolen a damn thing. Not then, not ever.

Voice sharp, I grind out, "You care, Savannah. Do I like you maneuvering to try and get your way? Nah, I don't. But you do it with humor and you do it with kindness, and maybe your dad worked you to the bone as a kid, as opposed to letting you live, but I wouldn't say that means you're *just like him*." I pause, letting the words sink into that pretty head of hers before tacking on, "Although I'll be honest, the roses scream of your old man. It's the exact narcissistic bullshit sort of move he'd pull just to have the last word."

Her lips part. Clamp back together. Then, "You are such a man, do you know that?"

"Why? Because I tell it like it is?"

"No, you jerk"—she rolls her eyes without heat—"because right after you make me feel good, you drop a one liner that has me seeing red. *Narcissistic?*" She scoffs dismissively. "The roses were gorgeous."

"The parlor smells like I've been receivin' mourners for a solid week. You haven't buried Inked yet, baby. Don't get ahead of yourself with an early obituary."

Rolling her bottom lip between her teeth, she pokes me in the chest. "Like I said," she mutters, "*just* like a man."

Against my better judgment, I feel a smirk tug at my lips. "If you ever had any doubt about what I'm packing in my pants, then I have a bigger problem than your dad trying to evict me from a building that he doesn't even own."

Silence.

Pure, undiluted silence.

It lasts only seconds before she manages, "*Really*? Dick jokes?"

"Savannah," I utter in complete somberness, "the subject of my dick is always important."

She stares up at me, unblinking. "Huh."

It's my turn to return her stare. Heat, the kind that has nothing to do with erections and smooth skin and crisp sheets, creeps up my spine. "Huh, what?"

"You're totally blushing."

"*What*? The hell I am."

Leaning back against the bookcase, she rakes me with a thorough once-over. "Is it the fact that I'm opening up to you that's causing all the blood to rush to your face? Or the conversation about your . . ." Here she only unhooks one finger from around the picture frame and makes a little circle with it as if that's the new sign language signal for *penis*.

My face warms.

Goddammit.

"Neither," I grit out, "definitely option C."

"*Interesting*." She hums a little under her breath, looking altogether too pleased for my comfort. "I didn't realize you were shy."

The seventeen-year-old me who shook when asking Maryanne to prom nods his stupid little head with his hands held high, shouting "Yes! That's us! Shy all the way to our core!" Thirty-six-year-old me—the me who wants nothing more than to strip Savannah naked and show her all the ways I'm bold and confident and nothing at all like my teenage self—plants a hand on the shelf beside her head.

"You're playing with fire, baby," I growl.

"No, Owen, I *am* the fire."

And then she twists the picture frame around and shoves it at my chest.

10

SAVANNAH

I see the moment that the full impact of the picture in the frame hits Owen.

His bearded jaw clenches and he falls back a step and I'm not surprised in the slightest when his dark eyes snap up to meet mine. "How long has this been on your shelf?"

This is referring to a picture of the two of us at an Entrepreneurs of the Crescent City meeting from over a year ago. His twin, Gage, had just given a speech to help raise money and awareness for a first responders charity that he'd founded. Photographers regularly attend every EOCC meeting and, on that night, one caught Owen and me unaware while we listened to Gage. If I close my eyes, I can almost remember everything about those few seconds where the ever-stoic Owen had turned to me for support.

My arms wrapped around his lean waist in solidarity. His stark, pained expression, while he listened to his brother discuss his mental state, after working on the front lines of the New Orleans Police Department, and mine . . .

God, I've stared at that photo so many times to know that my features were strained with *want*. From the very first time that we met, Owen has always reminded me of a chained wolf. His tattoos intimidate and his always reserved expression often makes me feel as though he's holding back, biding his time, before striking.

But in that moment, Owen had needed *me*. His ex-girlfriend's sister. His friend, if not his lover. And as much as I'd burned with the knowledge that he was hurting for his twin, I'd still soaked up those precious few moments where the untamed wolf allowed himself the chance to be comforted by a woman who wanted him more than she wanted her next breath.

Who *still* wants him more than she wants her next breath.

Aware that Owen is waiting for a response, I clear my throat awkwardly. "It's been about . . . oh, you know, like a year and a half or so. The photographer that night, he posted it on the EOCC website, and I thought—well, I don't really know *what* I was thinking when I printed it out. I mean, the quality isn't even all that good but when I first saw it, I realized we don't have a single picture of the two of us together and there really was no talking myself out of it once that epiphany hit me, and oh my God, please shut me up before I keep rambling."

"I like it when you ramble," Owen murmurs, his voice pitched low and smooth like the most intoxicating whiskey.

Ba-dum.

There goes my heart. It's going to beat right out of my chest and maybe that won't be such a bad thing because then I won't be responsible for swaying Owen over to the dark side and convincing him to sign his soul to the devil.

I mean, ERRG. Not the devil.

Really.

"The whole point of the story," I say, dredging up the last

bit of my courage, "is that my dad regularly maneuvers his opponents like pawns on a chessboard. I screwed you over once, Owen—I don't plan to do so again."

"My definition of screwin' would have been infinitely more enjoyable, in case that was ever in question."

Ba-dum.

It takes every ounce of self-control to hold his glittering gaze when I dredge up a pitiful retort, "I thought you were shy."

At that, he throws back his head and barks out a deep, sexy laugh. The sort of masculine laughter that spreads warmth through your limbs like liquid heat. Even now my core clenches tight, and I'm forced to avert my gaze or face the consequences of finally discovering what it might be like to kiss that grinning mouth. I'd kill to taste a little of that laughter for myself.

I clear my throat again. *Act professional!* Or as professional as I can be while simultaneously wondering what he might say if I were to unbutton that dress shirt of his and slip my arms around his waist, all so I can feel that heavy laughter deep in my bones.

"Are you done?"

Sobering, he reaches past me to set the frame back on the shelf. "Are you going to be sending me anymore rose bouquets?"

I sniff. "Not now that you called me a narcissist."

"I called your dad a narcissist."

"Same thing, really. I thought they were the perfect calling card. You'd know immediately who sent them."

"How about this"—he spreads his arms wide, like he's doing me a grand ol' favor—"I'll give you an *A* for persistence."

When he bites down on his bottom lip in clear deliberation, I wave a hand at him. "Spit it out. An *A* for persistence and a . . . *what*?"

"*C* for originality." I gasp in mock-outrage, which only prompts him to add, "Too on the nose, Rose. I'd offer you the chance for a do-over but, really . . ." He leans down so that we're at eye level. "Don't."

Don't.

Incredulous laughter climbs my throat.

My entire life has been a series of *don'ts. Don't* climb the ladder after the boys because girls don't roughhouse. *Don't* accept that boy's invitation to the school dance because his family doesn't know the right people. *Don't* complain about upholding a legacy that's existed for five generations, no matter what you *think* you want to be doing with your life.

Don't, don't, don't.

And for the first time, with Owen looking at me like he's worried I've lost my marbles, I *do*.

"I want you to be a partner in the new hotel."

Owen's jaw goes slack at the same time Pablo gets a wild hair up his ass and launches across the room to cling to Owen's slacks.

"*Christ*," he grunts—Owen does, I mean, not Pablo—before wheeling around.

The furry demon only holds on more voraciously.

"Pablo, let go!" I lunge forward to grasp the gray-haired cat, but he escapes my uncoordinated hand grab with skill.

Or maybe it's less that *he's* escaped it and more that Owen—gorgeously stoic Owen—is hopping like a can-can dancer on speed. In fascinated horror, I watch as the "inked god," as the media has dubbed him, whirls around with his right leg extended and shaking.

Pablo hisses, his little triangle ears twitching in what I can't help but feel is delight in discovering a worthy opponent, and climbs higher, from calf to knee and from knee to thigh. He sinks his talons into Owen's leg while his tail swishes in the air.

Oh. God.

"Here, kitty, kitty, kitty." I wave my arms frantically, hoping to distract him. "Come to Momma."

Owen reaches for Pablo's underbelly. "He's *yours*?" he asks, sounding appalled.

There's little point in lying. "I rescued him."

"How the hell did America's sweetheart end up with the antichrist?"

As if personally offended by the insult, Pablo hisses again and—

Oh, no.

His sharp claws inch upward, leaving Owen's thigh for a more northern region. The apex of his thighs. The firm bulge behind the soft fabric of his slacks. The reason behind women's orgasms everywhere.

I'm not sure which one of us reacts faster.

One minute I'm diving forward like a baseball player sliding onto home base, my hand outstretched to yank Pablo off before he causes major damage, and in the next, my cat is screeching as he flails through the air in a blur of somersaulting limbs.

Pablo, being Pablo, lands with all the grace of a feline who has nine lives.

I, on the other hand, do not.

I plow straight into Owen, the full weight of my forward momentum hitting him in the solar plexus. He collapses like a folded accordion, arms thrown out, legs sprawling. His pained grunt echoes in my ears as I drop like a sack of potatoes atop him, my face pressed against warm, rock-hard flesh, and my eyes squeezed closed.

Ba-dum.

The rigid muscles beneath my cheek go concave when Owen rasps, "I'll be honest, I've thought about you jumping my bones hundreds of times and this . . . this is not how I imagined the moment going down."

My mouth goes dry at the explicit visual springing to mind. I can only picture us now: Owen's big body splayed out like a Prince of Darkness Ken doll; my own tossed over his, hands planted on the floor, legs twisted up with his legs, cheek resting on his . . . on his *what*?

Seeking a distraction from the fact that it is *very* possible my mouth could be inches from his belt, I demand, weakly, "Did you just throw my cat?"

"No."

I crack one eye open.

Oh, thank God.

No leather belt in sight. Only a very inked sternum and a view of the holy grail: Owen Harvey's abdomen. There are ridges for days, cut and sharply defined, and jeez, is that a *tattoo* just above his waistband? Short of embarrassing myself by pinning him down—you know, more than I already have—so I can get a closer look, I let out a fake, *I'm-so-chill* laugh that sounds slightly more like *I-have-lost-my-damn-mind-please-forgive-me*. "Thank you. He doesn't really like men, which is sort of a problem, but he really is sweet when you get beneath all that ferocious—"

"I hurled him."

Head jerking up, my gaze climbs Owen's mountain of a chest and the thick column of his inked throat. "You *hurled* him?"

Owen tips his head to the right, clearly seeking out Pablo. "Figured he had at least one life left."

"That is . . . that is . . ."

The door swings open and Georgie pokes her head in, the way she always does when she's bored at the front desk and wanting to chat. I see the moment when she glances from the desk to the bookcase before, brows knitting, she drops her attention to the floor.

To *us*.

I scramble to my knees, only to hear Owen wheeze when my elbow accidentally makes contact with . . . with . . . Oh, boy.

Shoulders hunched, he rolls to his side, his palm going to his dick.

Just kill me now.

"It's not what it looks like." In the span of seven months, I've turned him down on national television, leveled him with an ultimatum to sell off his real estate, and now, to iron out his hatred for me, I've potentially rendered him childless.

What a grand time to be alive.

Gaping, Georgie looks from me to Owen and then back again. "Does he need ice for that?"

"Yes," I say at the same time Owen growls, "No."

"He does," I tell my assistant firmly, "and could you maybe take Pablo . . ."

"You owe me," Georgie grumbles as she snakes an arm under my cat's underside. "He hates me."

"I know the feeling," Owen mutters under his breath.

"He needs *love*," I interject lamely even though I suspect that, when I stumbled across him at the animal rescue shelter across the river in Algiers, two years ago, it was me who needed love more than my aggressively agitated pet. "He's a little prickly, that's all."

Owen drags himself up onto his knees. "He's a menace to society."

"Only to men, really." Guilt eats at me when I spot tears in Owen's perfectly nice slacks. At the rate I'm going, I'm going to owe the man a private island, equipped with a yacht, a massive house, and a constant stream of women to occupy his days. I cringe. Okay, maybe not the women. "He's not all that bad otherwise."

"Savannah?"

The door closes behind Pablo and Georgie.

Breath caught in my throat, I shift my focus to Owen's face. "Yes?"

His big, tatted hands land on his thighs. "Ask me again if I want to be a partner in your family's hotel."

Is it wrong that I've totally forgotten the reason I wanted him here in the first place? I mean, the hotel wasn't the *only* reason, of course. I wanted him to see that I'm not just my father's puppet. That I can rebel just like him and Amelie. That I'm not lost to the vision of ambition, the way Dad seems to be most days.

Ba-dum.

Anxiously, I pick at the hem of my dress, which, miracle of all miracles, has not ridden all the way up my butt to show the world my unappealing granny panties. Open my mouth and give voice to the proposal that's been nagging at me for three days, ever since I left Inked on Bourbon's office: "Keep your property, Owen. It's *yours* and no one else's, and not my father or me or anyone else deserves to strip that from you. But I think . . . I think it might be monumental for both you and ERRG if you were to come on board with this project. You've said in the past that you enjoy investing in new opportunities. If our restaurants are any indication of the hotel's profitability, it will be insanely lucrative for you—you could buy other properties; do whatever you want with the money, honestly. And, maybe, if you agree, my dad will finally see that the Edgar Rose Restaurant Group won't be . . . *tainted* if we welcome people into our midst that aren't family by blood."

And maybe then I can prove to my father that the world won't come crumbling down if we sometimes hand over the reins to someone else.

Before I *crumble from the weight of it all.*

I nearly jump out of my skin when Owen's finger touches my bare knee. Shaded black ink against unblemished caramel. A sight that balloons emotion in my chest. It feels so right and maybe just a little wrong, given our history, but I want to beg him to press his palm to my leg and let me feel the weight of him erasing the heaviness of everything else.

"Look at me, Rose."

He doesn't need to tell me twice.

In his gaze, I see nothing of that shy man I playfully accused him of being. He's all stern lines and intoxicating heat. Hard muscle and steely confidence and an unexpected compassion that I see in the set of his mouth. He looks at me now the way he *used* to look at me, back before *Put A Ring On It*, back before I ruined it all because I have never, not for long, anyway, been able to erase Dad's insistent voice from my head.

A Rose marries for the betterment of the family, Savannah.

A Rose never deviates from the plan.

A Rose—you—*will not sleep with the man who dated your sister.*

Sometimes, most days, there is nothing I despise more than being a Rose.

"No."

Disappointment, swift and fierce, pierces me at the succinct two-letter word coming from his lips.

"Right." I force out a light, unaffected laugh. *You are so, so stupid to have even thought he would say yes.* "Totally get it. I'm sorry to have even brought it up. And . . . and I'm sorry for the roses and the emails." I wave my hand. Ignore the way my fingers tremble. "It was ridiculous." *More like pathetic.* "I'll make sure to tell the crew to stick to our property. No more crossing borders."

The fingertips on my knee gather pressure as Owen slides his palm over my skin. "I'm saying no because owning a hotel is not my dream." A small pause. "I spent so many years when I was younger trying to live up to other people's expectations of me, Sav. And when I failed to deliver, it drowned me. Sent me on a downward spiral that will stay with me, always. So, no, I'm not gonna jump on the hotel bandwagon with you. I'd be doing it for you, and only you, and that's a recipe for disaster, right from the get-go." His palm skates up a half inch. "Something tells me that this hotel gig isn't your dream either."

Bull's-eye.

Dammit.

"I hate how you read me like no one else can," I whisper.

He squeezes my leg. "And I hate how you pushed me away. But it's life, Rose. Better to be hurting and hating than dead."

Before I have the chance to summon a response, the office door slams open and Georgie emerges. "The ice has arrived for the tragically wounded!"

Behind her, a droll voice mutters, "Ever hear of knocking, Harris?"

Georgie's curly head snaps back to look over her shoulder. "Ever hear of not reusing comebacks, Dufrene?"

I hang my head forward in defeat.

Owen is right.

This is not my dream. It's never been my dream. But at least my family-made prison comes with the two best friends a girl could ever ask for, even if I am the one who cuts their paychecks twice a month.

And even if I've never felt more alone.

11

CELEBRITY TEA PRESENTS:

HURRY UP AND POP THAT FIRST-KISS CHERRY: HOW SAVANNAH ROSE MANAGED TO FRIENDZONE YET ANOTHER TV SUITOR

Dear Reader, after the chaos of episode one (Do we need a recap of the man in a dinosaur onesie or Savannah Rose's epic meltdown when sending home that inked god?), I honestly prepared myself for an emotional roller coaster while watching Put A Ring On It's *first season. Maybe I set my expectations too high—can expectations truly ever be* that *high when it comes to unscripted reality TV? I think not—but I feel . . . inconsolably let down.*

Don't get me wrong: the men on this season are fine specimens of excellent trouble-making pot-stirrers. I mean, when that investment broker out of Kansas stormed into Savannah Rose's private suite because he thought ex-NFL player Dominic DaSilva was on the show for all the wrong reasons? What a delight. When Viktor (Instagram influencer, 25) instigated a fight on last night's episode by claiming that Harry (Flamenco dancer, 29) has a girlfriend back home, I stood and applauded, right there in my living room.

I'm here for the drama. We are all *here for the drama. And the men are bringing it each and every week.*

Savannah Rose, on the other hand?

I'm just going to come right out and say it: our bachelorette may have a tough-as-steel backbone, but when it comes down to her personality in every other capacity . . . Savannah is, dare I say it, a bit of a wet blanket.

America's sweetheart or not, Savannah keeps a closed lid on her emotions, rarely approaches the men with anything but a stance of friendship, and I'm tired of it. The girl is boring to watch. Gorgeous, yes, but boring as heck. I have dish towels with more personality. The paint on my wall *has more personality.*

Where is the passion? Where is the I-need-to-be-alone-with-him-so-I-can-rip-his-shirt-off *chemistry? I'm not sitting through thirty minutes of commercials each week just to watch another testimonial where Savannah claims that she believes in friendship first, desire second.*

Sweetness aside, I'm losing my patience here—and, if the dipping audience ratings this past week are any indication, so is the rest of America.

*Pick a guy—*any *guy—and lay one on him!*

At the rate we're going, my own sex life will have withered up and died by the time Savannah does more than peck a contestant on the lips. I can't let that stand. Something must be done. After last night's episode, when hot-as-Hades Lukas Hester was sent home after a tear-inducing afternoon of surfing, mind-numbing conversation about their respective pets, and a painful-to-watch smooch on the lips that left me yawning, I'm at the end of my rope.

(Never let it be said that I'm not pulling one for the team; I watch this crap, so you don't have to.)

Even so, I'm calling it here first, Dear Reader. No woman can come on a show like Put A Ring On It, *be presented with twenty-seven hot men that are sparking Twitter battles every week from obsessive fans, and somehow not make a notable connection with any of them—after she "claimed" to be looking for love.*

Savannah Rose is hiding something, and I'll be here for when the tea is ready to be spilled . . . if I don't die of sheer boredom first, that is.

12

SAVANNAH

"Good Lord, but that Dominic DaSilva has a pair of abs on him like I've never seen." One sip of champagne, a quick glance around at the crowded ballroom, and then Frannie Barron, the mayor of New Orleans, leans in conspiratorially to whisper, "Tell me, are they painted on? Photoshopped?" Her penciled-in, dark brows raise. "You never know with TV nowadays."

Dominic DaSilva, former NFL tight end, all around bad boy extraordinaire. Of all the guys vying for my heart on *Put A Ring On It*, Dom was the only one to give me butterflies. His gaze was dark, his muscles were bulging, and in those first few weeks when I had been determined to put Owen aside and get on with my life, I'd momentarily allowed myself to think of *more* with the famous ex-football player.

Unfortunately, all I needed was our first one-on-one date to realize that while my body was all too willing to give Dom a go—his abs might as well be Photoshopped they're so well-defined—my brain refused to get with the program.

Hello, my name is Savannah Rose and it seems that I'm permanently fated to pray at the altar of Owen Harvey.

It'd be funny if it weren't so pathetic.

I clink my champagne flute with Frannie's. "No Photoshop in sight, Madame Mayor. Let's just say that the man earns his ridges the old-fashioned way. Lots of sit-ups, not enough of Taco Tuesdays."

"A shame."

"I totally agree. Tacos are food for the soul."

Frannie throws her head back with a laugh, her long, Senegalese twist braids slipping over her shoulders. "I mean, it's a shame that I'm not twenty years younger."

"And not married," I tease. Frannie might be our mayor but I've known her since I was ten years old and bussing her table at Rose & Thorn every Saturday afternoon. Her husband was the first one to give me a taste for interior design—he's the mastermind behind some of the most opulent historical home restorations in the city. Between the summer of my sophomore and junior years of college, he even set me up with an internship, much to the disgruntlement of my dad.

"Bah," Frannie mutters, batting a dismissive hand in the air. "That's marriage for you. One day it's all sunshine and roses—no pun intended, of course—and then the next thing you know, conversation is somehow cemented on bathroom activities, who was the last one to put away the dishes, and God forbid you even *think* about watching a new TV show on your own—I promise that World War III will be imminent."

Trying to hold back a laugh, I sip my champagne. "It sounds wonderful."

"Marriage *is* wonderful. It's also not for everyone." She eyes me over the rim of her glass. "Don't think I didn't notice that you aren't wearing a ring."

Crap.

Not this again.

Averting my gaze, I sweep a hasty glance over the elegant ballroom. Every summer the mayor of New Orleans hosts an auction to fund his or her favorite charities. Tonight, there are Saints players hobnobbing with some of the city's oldest Creole families, like my own; venture capitalists sharing drinks with lawyers; politicians sitting beside oil tycoons. Last I checked, the minimum bid for the auction items starts at five-thousand dollars with the implied understanding that bidders ought to be raising the stakes well into the five-figures by the end of the night.

The mayor's ball is an invitation-only party for the rich, the famous, and the famously rich.

The Roses fit solidly in the latter group.

"Production asked me to keep my jewelry to a minimum once the show started airing." The lie slips smoothly from my tongue. I'm pretty sure the *Put A Ring On It* producers don't care one way or the other, since rumors ultimately fuel the show's overall audience ratings. "Am I engaged? Am I not engaged?" I wag my eyebrows playfully. "You'll just have to tune in for the finale to find out."

The mayor sips her bubbly. "Are you aware that your right eye twitches when you lie?"

"*What*? Of course it doesn't."

"I've known you since the days of hot-pink braces and acne, dear. Don't think I don't remember you lying to your old man right in front of me when he needed help at one of the restaurants and you pretended to have to study for a test."

I open my mouth, then gently snap it closed. "I did have a test."

"Sure you did," the mayor says with a sly grin, "but you

also wanted to come over to the house and talk about fabric patterns with Antoine. Your eyes always give you away."

Literally, too, I suppose.

Frannie taps my bare ring finger. "Never fear. You'll meet the love of your life someday, and then you, too, will be welcomed into the world of arguments about what shows to watch and what takeout to order, and the number of times your partner finishes the toilet paper and fails to clue you in until it's too late."

I swallow a startled laugh. "That's honestly more than I ever needed to know about Antoine."

"Twenty-five years of marriage, Savannah. If I can't make fun of him by now, who will?" She squeezes my hand, busses my cheek, then steps back. "All right, I'm off to mingle. Since you're clearly not engaged, and there are plenty of single men present, I expect to see you on the dance floor. Don't be a wallflower."

And then she's gone, disappearing into the crowd of black tuxedoes and jewel-toned ballgowns.

My feet, strapped into a pair of glittery silver stilettos, remain glued to the floor.

I've spent a lifetime attending events just like this one, where the conversations stay unapologetically shallow and the drinks are poured heavier as the evening wears on (all the better to up those bids, of course).

For years, I've played the part expected of me.

While Dad talked the ear off of some wealthy ERRG patron, and Mom hovered nearby, chatting to a woman from church, I've always held down the fort. In any other city, a family like mine would be caterers to this event and nothing more. In New Orleans, the Roses have not only provided the food for the mayor's ball, but we're also a few of the more popular guests.

Usually, I'd pack up my feelings and get on with the flirting and the chatting and the catching up.

Usually, but not tonight.

Because it's not every day that America's nastiest tabloid reporter calls you a "wet blanket" and sparks a discussion the likes of which you've never seen on social media. And I've seen a *lot* since agreeing to the role of *Put A Ring On It*'s first bachelorette.

Finally, my feet get a move on.

With my head held high, I ignore the not-so-quiet commentary that has stalked me like the worst kind of stage-five clinger since I arrived earlier tonight:

"Did you see that Celebrity Tea Presents *article? Ouch."*

"Jeez, even Entertainment Tonight *picked the story up. What's next? An appearance on* The Graham Norton Show*? I swear to God, I'm so tired of hearing about the Roses. Their duck confit is delicious though."*

"Honestly, I always thought she was *a little boring. A little too perfect, not enough substance—know what I mean?"*

A little boring.

A little too perfect.

Not enough substance.

I almost laugh out loud. Is there anything they *don't* think they know about me? These are people who have existed on the periphery of my life for years. I went to school with their daughters, their nieces. I'm not some stranger they're gossiping about. And, so yeah, maybe I do keep my relationships with them at surface level but that has more to do with them than it does with me—I can play nice with the best of them, but I don't play nice with assholes.

Guess I do have a little too much of the Rose blood in me for that.

With a sharp retort hot on my tongue, I whip around, fully prepared to give them a piece of my mind, only to be cut off by a server dressed in a sleek, black tux. "Wine?" he asks without inflection, his gaze resting somewhere above my head, a black tray balanced on one hand.

"You know what? I think I will." I pluck a glass off the tray, then go back for a second. His bushy brows don't even twitch as he nods curtly before drifting off to another partygoer.

How boring can a girl be when she's double-fisting wine, dressed to the nines in a sapphire gown, and planning to do major damage to her checkbook, all in the name of charity?

Boring, schmoring.

I won't apologize to Mr. *Celebrity Tea Presents,* whoever the hell he really is, just because he thinks I should have spread my legs more, during filming, for his and America's entertainment. That isn't me. It will *never* be me. I'd rather be labeled as a total snooze-fest than screw twenty-six men just to prove a point. At least my self-respect is still intact.

Blood piping hot, I toss back some wine from glass number one, then turn my back on jerk central over there. They aren't worth even a second of my night.

For what has to be the hundredth time since I've returned to New Orleans, I find myself wishing Amelie was by my side. I know Europe is doing her good right now and I know she has no immediate plans to come back to the States, but still. My younger sister knows how to turn these dull parties on their head, even if it comes at the cost of making other people uncomfortable.

Pretty sure no one has ever accused Amelie Rose of being boring *or* too perfect.

As I sidle up to the auction table, I drink from glass

number two because I'm not cruel. Don't want it feeling left out or neglected, of course.

I peer down at the items that have been staged for viewing.

There's an autographed Drew Brees football. Next to it are a pair of intricate diamond earrings from a popular jeweler on Magazine Street. I step to the right, my gaze roaming the table and taking note of the various pieces: a delicate sculpture with copper-painted flowers, a pair of tickets to Machu Picchu with an all-inclusive stay near the world heritage site, an abstract-style painting that looks like it's been done by a kindergartner who devoured way too much sugar.

Beside each item is a placard listing its value, the person who donated it, as well as its specific auction number so that bids can be placed on the corresponding app created for tonight's event.

I finish off glass number one, set it down on a nearby, empty, high-top table, and grab my phone from my clutch. There are approximately a gazillion text messages winking back at me, all from acquaintances and family members asking me what I think of *Celebrity Tea Presents'* "wet blanket" remark.

"I think he's a total tool," I mutter under my breath, before downloading the auction app and waiting for it to load.

After a quick "miss you and wish you were here" text to Amelie and another sip of wine, I take in the party that's in full swing.

Couples are making their way onto the dance floor, including Frannie and Antoine and even my own parents. The two couples look so damn different, it almost seems blasphemous to compare them. Whereas the mayor and her husband are clearly whispering to each other, heads bent close, their arms locked tight around the other's frame, Dad and Mom dance at an arms' width apart. Over Mom's head, Dad scans the room like he's searching out his next business acquisition. Around Dad's shoulder, Mom mouths something to a friend of hers, as if she's counting down the seconds until she can go back to doing her own thing. It wasn't always this way with them, but in the last few months, there's been an obvious chasm rifting between them. And, if I'm being honest, that chasm has divided our entire family. Three of us here in Louisiana, one in Europe.

Familiar bitterness squeezes my lungs, only to be matched by the dampening of my palms as I clutch the wineglass tighter.

Don't go there—not tonight.

Easier said than done.

Turning my back on the dance floor, I drink more chardonnay and sigh a breath of relief when my phone pings, letting me know the app finally downloaded.

One swipe of my finger against the screen shows that Frannie went all out for this year's bidding process. There are multiple photos listed for every item, some with wordy descriptions, others without.

Resting the base of my glass against my collarbone, I study my options. The painting would be a safe bet, even though it isn't to my taste at all. I swipe left. The earrings? No, I don't think so. They're beautiful but also a little too safe, and who needs more of that when you're already being labeled as boring by all of America? Hard pass.

"Come on, Machu Picchu. I'm ready."

I've never been to Peru. Scratch that, I've never been farther south than Mexico. Tilting my phone like it's a foreign object, I stare at the picture of a couples' massage that's being offered with the all-inclusive package. Both parties are grinning from ear to ear like they're keeping a massive secret. I bet it was staged. Every family vacation that I can remember as a child ended with Mom and Dad staying in different rooms.

I scroll down to find the current bid, then blanch at the bold red number staring back at me.

"Twenty-thousand *dollars*?" For that much money, that all-inclusive trip better come with a helicopter ride all the way up to the top of Machu Picchu, my own personal masseuse, and an oxygen tank for when the realization hits that I've spent a college tuition's worth of money on a romantic trip meant for two.

Absolutely not.

I swipe again, then once more—

Wait, was that . . .

I backtrack, my thumb freezing when Inked on Bourbon's logo flashes across my screen. Heart pounding, I toss back the rest of the wine and get rid of the glass. Then quickly skim the offer. Unlike the Machu Picchu listing, Owen's is classically simple. There are no pictures, save for the business logo, and only a short description listing off a custom tattoo, to be designed by Owen himself, along with a sketchbook. That's it.

Except that it can't be *that's it* because if he's donating something, he must be somewhere in this ballroom right now.

That's how the mayor's auction works. How it's *always* worked.

My gaze snaps up, phone still clutched tight in my grip. I search the faces in the ballroom, looking for familiar inky-colored eyes and dark, messy hair.

Owen has never been invited to one of these parties—I

would know—but Frannie does things her own way. It's why the city adores her, and why New Orleans' richest have come out tonight to write their checks while hoping to sneak in a quick chat with the woman who's leaving her stamp on the Crescent City each and every day.

A crazy idea smacks me right across the face.

Did Frannie invite Owen on purpose? Clearly, she's been following *Put A Ring On It* all season, enough to know what Dominic DaSilva's abs look like, at least. Did she catch the first episode when I sent Owen home? Did she—God, the thought alone makes me want to crawl into a hole—decide to take matters into her own hands and ask him to donate something for the auction, all so she could lure him to the party and watch me lose my cool?

It's an insane theory.

Totally improbable.

Against my better judgment, I find myself moving along, searching for Owen's donation. My gaze sweeps over the table.

Another all-inclusive trip, this one to Croatia.

A trio of Roman daggers that look like they've only just been excavated from Italian soil.

An impressively sized bayonet dating back to the Revolutionary War.

And then I see Owen's contribution to tonight's event: a simple certificate with the promise of a custom tattoo positioned beside a leather-bound notebook that's been cracked open like a rare book in a museum.

Don't touch it, Rose.

Another *don't* to live by.

So, I do.

Instinct leads my fingers to the spine. The leather is soft, worn. The pages crinkle as I pick it up, staring down at the image sketched on the open page.

I'm not sure what I expect to find. Maybe a drawing of something that is very clearly the beginnings of someone's tattoo—but it isn't that at all.

Instead, I find myself absorbing the harsh lines of an unfamiliar masculine face. The man's hair stands on end; his eyes, shaded to be almost eerily translucent, stare out from the page, hard and emotionless; gray discoloration paints his cheek, like maybe he's taken a punch to the face. It takes me a moment to realize that the man is actually positioned behind bars, the tips of his fingers curling around the metal. And as soulless as his gaze reads, there is nothing subtle about his grip on those bars. Knuckles straining, veins popping, he looks ready to leap from the page.

My hands grow clammy.

I flip the page, turning past a selection of French Quarter sights: the spire of St. Louis Cathedral caught in a rainstorm, the dilapidated, curved shape of a balcony caving under the weight of people drinking to their heart's content.

Another turned page, and this time my heart thuds a little faster when I see the hourglass figure of a woman dancing on a stage. She's dressed in nothing but tiny panties and even tinier nipple pasties. From the bottom of the page, hands reach toward her, dollar bills thrust in the air. I can almost hear the boisterous catcalls and the heavy music pounding, but it's not until I look at the woman's face that my breathing grows labored.

Her features are drawn, her mouth tipped up in a smile that screams misery and isolation. A single tear carves its way down her cheek, a direct contrast to the eager hands grasping and groping and demanding all of her.

And even though I've never once removed my clothes for money, I feel my eyes water and my chest's sharp rise and fall, because this woman—the emotion that she feels that no one else sees—is *me*. How many times have I put on the so-called "airs" required of me, even when I've wanted to flash the world the middle finger instead? How many times did Matilda or Joe on *Put A Ring On It* demand that I give one of the guys a little more attention, because they knew he'd make for good ratings, even though he made my skin crawl?

How many times have I stripped myself down to build someone else up?

My stomach churns uneasily.

Unable to look at that woman's tear for one more second, I flip to another page, and then yet again to another.

I'm so entranced by the sketches of New Orleans life that Owen has created that I fail to miss the solid presence at my back . . . that is, until a familiar husky voice rasps, "Trying to buy a piece of me, Rose?" and everything in me goes still.

13

OWEN

I catch Savannah just before her elbow collides with my gut.

"Angling for further mutilation?" I grunt, cupping her arm and steering her wide before she gets any more dangerous ideas.

"You caught me by surprise."

"I was makin' enough noise to sound off an alarm."

"Well now you're just lying." She spins around to face me. "If I wanted to hurt you, I would have aimed south."

"Already going back for round two?"

Her expression clears and feminine laughter closes in around me. A little husky. A whole lotta sweet. "Pablo sends his apologies," she tells me.

"Pablo needs to send a lot more than an *I'm sorry*." My gaze drops to my sketchbook, which she's clasped tightly to her chest, the same way my mom used to clutch the fake pearls my dad bought her every year for her birthday. She'd finger each of the beads, rolling them back and forth as though the action alone might soothe her. It's damn near impossible to think of anything else when Savannah rubs her thumb up the spine of the leather-bound book. Seeing her with it is fucking with my head. "My legs look like a scratching post," I add.

"It could be worse." She releases the notebook with one hand, turning over her wrist so I can see the inside of her forearm. Old, faded scratches cut through her skin. "I sort of lied the other day."

My gaze collides with hers. "Yeah?"

"Yeah." She returns to gripping my sketchbook. "Pablo kind of hates everyone equally. He doesn't discriminate."

"Like I said, you adopted the antichrist."

"Like I said," she says pointedly, her chin tipping up, "he just needs some love and affection."

I cock a brow, folding my arms over my chest. "You totally sleep with your bedroom door closed, don't you?"

The second she starts shifting her weight and cutting eye contact, I know that I hit the nail on the head. "He surprised me a few times when I first brought him home, that's all." More shifting. Her gaze bounces from my face to her feet and then back up again. "I woke up at three in the morning—"

"The witching hour," I murmur, just a little sarcastically. "Want me to say it a little louder for the folks in the back? Your cat is possessed."

"He is *not* possessed. I think I would know."

"Could be trying out for the role of Binx in a *Hocus Pocus* remake."

She rolls her eyes, but there's no hiding the telltale curve of her lips. "Has anyone ever told you how dramatic you are? *Anyway*, he just . . . he liked to pounce on my face while I slept. I think he wanted to play."

"Or suffocate you."

"If that's the case, he clearly didn't succeed. Here I am."

Yeah, here she is.

Her makeup is heavier tonight—longer and fuller lashes, lips painted a darker hue. Shiny earrings dangle from her ears, matching the pendant that rests above her breastbone. Her dress is modest compared to so many of the other gowns I've spotted around the ballroom: thin straps snake over her shoulders; a neckline that teases more than it reveals.

She looks every inch the sweetheart that the media has dubbed her, and I feel every inch the alleged bad boy for wanting to muss up her perfect bun and yank that too-mature neckline down, down, down, until she's dirty and messy and fucking *living*.

"You never answered my question," I say, aware that my voice sounds too damn husky but unable to do anything about it. "Looking to make a purchase?"

Not for the first time tonight, I fight the urge to snatch back the sketchbook and hide it away. My first mayor's auction and instead of taking part in the drinking and the dancing and the general debauchery of the upper echelons of New Orleans society, I've found myself watching this table.

When I haven't been stealing glances at Savannah, that is.

"Why would you give this up?" she asks, cleanly side-stepping my question. "You could have stuck with doing the tattoo. *Only* the tattoo."

Again, her thumb grazes the spine. Again, my head feels like it might explode—vulnerability and confidence war with each other, each fighting for the upper hand.

I tear my gaze away from the sketchbook and zero in on her face.

"Nobody's gonna pay five grand for a tattoo," I tell her. "I'm good, Sav, but not that good."

"You *are* that good. Celebrities come to Inked all the time."

"They don't pay five-thousand dollars a pop."

Her lips pull tight, the bottom one catching my eye when she bites down in clear frustration. "This journal is way too personal. You can't auction it off."

Up until a few weeks ago, I would have said the same thing. Hell, I *did* say the same thing. But then Mayor Frannie Barron stopped by Inked so we could discuss the Entrepreneurs of the Crescent City—in particular, my vision for the organization and how we can increase numbers among New Orleanians who don't think they have anything to offer, due to their circumstances—and she'd spotted the sketchbook on my desk. I'd drawn in it the night before. Forgot to put it away. And while I'm a confident bastard, I'm not stupid; you don't tell a public figure like the mayor to stop what she's doing. So, I kept my mouth shut. Watched uncomfortably as she cracked the spine and pored over the drawings that I've created over the last fifteen years.

I never would have opted to sell my art. Not until Frannie Barron personally asked me to show the world what I've drawn. She wanted to stir up awareness for the slices of New Orleans life that so many people ignore when they come solely for the partying and the drinking and the chaos.

"Donate it to the auction," she'd encouraged, "give people something to talk about that really matters."

And then she'd intended to outbid all of her competitors.

Savage, really. Part of me even approved.

I pluck the notebook out of Savannah's grasp. "I'm ready to let it go."

"I call bullshit."

These pages have been with me since the time of my parents' deaths. I have other sketchbooks—countless others—but I always come back to this one in particular when I have something I need to expel from my brain. Sometimes that leads to a series of sketches, all tied together by a common theme; sometimes I end up with only a single image.

Either way, letting it go into someone else's hands tonight is going to steal a piece of my soul. I'm choosing to look at it as a cathartic experience that might leave an impact on someone else, even if that someone else is the mayor of New Orleans.

Plus, memories are meant to carry you forward, but certain ones . . . all they do is shackle you in place.

And I've already had enough shackles in my life.

"Not bullshit." I set the book down on the table, letting the weight fall as it will. When the pages flutter open to a penciled sketch of Savannah standing in front of the *Put A Ring On It* mansion, her expression weighted with dread, I immediately flip to another. She sure as hell doesn't need to see that and I sure as hell don't need to relive that night anytime soon. I glance at her over my shoulder. "How'd your dad take to me sayin' no to the hotel?"

The tension in her shoulders go slack. "Not great."

"Y'all still going forward with it, then?"

"As if my dad would have it any other way." Demurely, she clasps one hand around her opposite wrist. Then, as if realizing how bitter she sounds, she forces a tight grin that I see right through. "We have a projected opening date, so long as everything goes according to plan from here on out. It'll be an exciting venture—a break from the restaurants, that's for sure."

I step away from the auction table. "An exciting venture?" I repeat, huffing out a sarcastic laugh beneath my breath. "Who are you trying to convince of that? Me? You? Or your old man?"

"*Owen.*"

"You ever going to tell him that you're miserable?"

Her eyes pop open wide, head jerking right then left as she catalogs the people standing near us. No one is paying any attention, but that doesn't stop her from hissing, "Not here."

"Everyone's drunk, Rose. You could start doing jumping jacks in that dress of yours and no one would bat an eye."

"I highly doubt that."

"Which part? The fact that they're plastered or the fact that you could do something completely bizarre and no one would stop drinking to even applaud you?"

"Have you seen me exercise? No one would applaud me, even if they were stone cold sober." Her brows furrow. "Plus, hypothetically speaking, I'm pretty sure that if I were to even *attempt* a jumping jack in this thing, I'd risk flashing the mayor, my parents, and—"

"Me," I interject with a slow grin, "you'd also risk flashing me."

Her gaze leaps to my face. "Reason number one right there as to why I should refrain from working out for the rest of my life."

I don't rise to the bait.

It doesn't take a rocket scientist (which I'm definitely not) to see that Savannah is feeling out of her depths here. The nice-guy thing to do would be to step back and let her carry on with her night without inserting myself into her business, but I'm not always a nice guy.

Maybe it makes me a masochist, but I've spent the last

14

SAVANNAH

Is it possible for a man to deliver an orgasm when he hasn't even stripped me naked yet?

Because that's what we're working with here, ladies and gents. Owen Harvey feels like perfection. Rock-hard chest. Big hands drifting down my back. Thick, muscular thighs that slip between mine as he spins me around the floor. Like I said, pure perfection, even if he's not particularly adept at—

"*Ow*."

Panic dashes across his features. "Shit. *Shit*."

Toe smarting from the weight of his massive foot—seriously, I think he crushed a bone or two—I fight off a wince.

When Owen wrapped an arm around my waist and led me to the dance floor, I'd expected greatness. A smooth, seductive sway that made my heart pound fast and my core ache. Owen Harvey *looks* like the sort of guy who'd be a dancing prodigy. He moves with a panther-like confidence, like a man who knows *exactly* what to do with a woman in his arms.

And maybe he does—between the sheets—but when it

comes the more *vertical* type of dancing, Owen is . . . Well, I'm pretty sure the potted plant in my office has more rhythm than the man currently trotting on my feet.

I scoot my heel back at the last second, effectively tipping our combined balance to the right. "In case you were wondering, dancing is not like riding a bike. How long has it been?"

Looking flustered, Owen grunts, "Does it really matter?"

Probably not. Practice may make perfect, but it can't fix the unfixable.

And Owen's sense of rhythm? It is *long* gone, if it ever existed. I give a moment of silence for women's feet all over the world, my own included.

Wanting to brighten that dour look on his face, I poke him in the side. "Just trying to see if you're out of practice."

"You're trying to lead." His mouth flattens in disgruntlement. "That's the problem."

I grin. "Actually, I think the problem is that you have two left feet. We're supposed to be swaying."

He frowns, as though the sounds of the John Legend cover playing personally offends him. "I only know how to dance zydeco."

Do not laugh, do not laugh, do not—

I suck in a sharp breath when his foot lands on mine again. "Owen," I gasp, both from the way he enthusiastically spins me around and also, because, *dear God, the pain*, "don't take this the wrong way, but you're about to do permanent damage."

"I'm not that bad, Rose."

As if the universe is all too pleased to prove him wrong, there's a small shriek off to my right when Owen turns us a little too sharply. My dress catches under my high heels, and I teeter, hovering between that moment of safety and oblivion. Right before I go down, I spot a woman limping away on the arm of her partner, and then my vision is swallowed by all things Owen Harvey.

His arm securing me to him like a band across my back, my nose grazing the lapel of his tuxedo, my flailing hand accidentally brushing his cummerbund.

My heart skips a beat.

There's no doubt about it: if we keep up with this, we're going to leave a trail of injured partygoers behind us.

I smooth a hand up Owen's chest. The thick strands of his hair tickle the back of my fingers as I cup the nape of his neck. "Let me lead."

Dark eyes flit down to my lips. "I'm nearly twice your size."

"So you'll look like a giraffe being led by a mouse for the rest of the song. What'd you say earlier about my jumping jacks, that everyone is too plastered to even think about applauding?" When I catch his eye, I add, "Humor me, Harvey." *Trust me.* "I won't let you wipe out. Better yet, if I do, at least you know we'll go down together."

Almost reluctantly, he does.

The tension still strains his shoulders but, second by second, I feel the rest of him cede control. My left hand stays looped around the back of his neck while my right slips down his side to the waistband of his black pants. With gentle encouragement, I slow our pace until we're matching the rhythm of the song. It's a sexy blues number now, a little too fast for a traditional slow dance but way too slow for the Cajun zydeco jig that Owen was determined to set us upon.

"I was a debutante," I murmur after a moment, once Owen has matched me for two eight counts in a row and I'm ninety-percent sure that we won't pull a domino effect and send the rest of the crowd tipping over. "I'm not sure if I ever told you that."

The pressure of his hand at my back slips up my spine. Lingers there, between my bare shoulder blades, before lazily coasting down all over again. Goose bumps flare to life on my skin, just as Owen murmurs, "Nah, you never did. But I can see it."

Because I'm boring? A little too perfect? Filled with no substance?

I bite back the words. I'm not going to go there, not with him. It's one thing to read comments from strangers online and another thing entirely to hear someone I respect—someone who means so much to me—agree with the tabloids. Not that I think Owen would agree, necessarily, but best to avoid that conversation altogether.

Just in case.

My thighs brush his as we turn. "I was given private dance lessons when I hit the ninth grade—nothing ever fun, though. No jazz, no hip-hop. It was like taking a page out of *Pride & Prejudice* and realizing no one else ever received the script." I let out a little laugh. "You should have seen me at my first high school dance with our brother school. Everyone was bumping and grinding along to Next's *Too Close* and there I stood, off in the corner, wondering how I could possibly be so clueless."

"No one asked you to dance?" Owen's voice is pure grit, pure sex. My fingers dig into his side a little deeper. "I find that hard to believe."

"I'm pretty sure I looked horrified. Only one of the chaperones approached me—my English teacher. She wanted me to know that she really enjoyed the meal she'd had at Rose & Thorn." I scrunch my nose, tipping my head back. "Come to think of it, I'm pretty sure she asked me for a friends-and-family discount for the next time she went back."

Owen shakes his head, sending the dark strands of his hair flopping forward boyishly. It nearly destroys that whole *I-eat-children-for-breakfast* bad boy appeal that he rocks on the regular. Nearly. Like the ink on his skin, Owen's brash outlook on life isn't the sort to ever be tamed. "Your teacher doesn't count."

"Then, no, no one asked me to dance."

Back then, I'd felt embarrassed and confused. Going to an all girls' school meant that my interactions with guys my age had been severely limited. Flirting, talking with the opposite sex—all of those skills had skipped right over me in the genetic pool. Embarrassment aside, I hadn't minded much. While everyone sweated through their clothing and worked out their quads while they touched their toes, I ate my heart out at the buffet table. Who the hell needs pimply-faced boys when there are cupcakes? Priorities.

"It was probably for everyone's benefit," I tell Owen, letting the memories of high school fade with a boot to the mental file. "I'm pretty sure no one cared to see my pirouettes."

The right corner of Owen's mouth curls. "Oh yeah? They as good as your jumping jacks?"

"Now let's not get ahead of ourselves here." I pretend to hike my nose up in the air like the pampered heiress I've been accused of being my whole life. "It's not my fault that I missed Broadway's call."

"Is that what happened?" Owen asks, sounding all too amused. "Just one phone call and your dancing career was over before it even began?"

In an exaggerated, New Orleans drawl, I murmur,

"That's right, sir. Sometimes, I still shed a tear or two over a lost opportunity. Breaks my heart, you know?"

"Must be the case, especially since Broadway is the home of actors and not necessarily dancers."

I blink. "Well, then."

"If it makes you feel any better, high school dances spark fear into even the bravest souls."

"So you're telling me you were clueless too?"

This time, his mouth tugs up into a full-fledge grin. "Rose, you think anyone was really tryin' to dance with me when I have all the rhythm of an elephant on ice?"

Laughter bursts out of me, unapologetically loud. "Now *there's* a visual I won't forget."

"Not just a visual, apparently."

"My feet have never felt better."

Owen's gaze flicks between mine, studiously assessing. "Your right eye is twitching."

Dammit! "Not you too," I groan, momentarily dropping my head back and forgetting all about the fact that I'm supposed to be the one leading the cause. But what Owen is missing in rhythm, he triumphs in persistence. He doesn't let us miss a beat, even when I say, "You're the second person to tell me that tonight."

"Who was the first?"

"The mayor."

"Frannie Barron is a smart woman."

"She's a bloodhound," I gripe good-naturedly, seeking her out in the crowd. "A lovable, nosy bloodhound." My gaze finally lands on her tall frame—only, she's not alone. Dad stands beside her, his head bowed to listen to whatever it is that she's saying, even as I realize that his gaze is locked on me.

On *Owen*.

I open my mouth, fully prepared to ask the question that has nagged me for years—*why* is it that my father despises Owen so much—but the words are swallowed by a gasp when I'm tipped backward over a muscular arm.

My gaze flies to his face in shock. "You dipped me."

"Thought you wouldn't mind being my first," he says, his voice pitched low, his breath hot on my lips. His dark hair falls in front of his eyes, and just like that, my control snaps.

With eager fingers, I brush the strands back. Meet those midnight eyes of his like my soul depends on it. Give him my full weight because I know he can take it, and just *once*, I want to feel as though I belong to him and him alone.

My heart is pounding so fast, so loud, that I swear I can't hear a damn thing over it. *You can do this. Ask him to kiss you.* Screw that. I can be bold and brave, too. A coward would ask for a kiss. America's goddamn sweetheart would ask for a kiss. I'll kiss *him*. "Owen, I—"

"Mind if I cut in?"

Dad.

Crap, crap, *crap*.

At the sound of my father's voice, Owen's hold tightens around me. His hand veers south, toward the curve of my butt, as though he's unwilling to let me go. *Or unwilling to dance to my father's fiddle.* I feel that one touch like a brand on my soul.

Slowly, Owen lifts me back to standing on my own two feet. I feel the loss of his embrace immediately.

The magic, as my grandmother used to say when things went sideways, *is broken.*

"Harvey," Dad says through a thin smile, "good to see you joining the mayor's ranks."

A step up from the tattoos, isn't it?

My father doesn't say it, but I know that's what he really

means. And, God, but it *infuriates* me. Yes, Owen dated Amelie. Yes, they broke up. So *what*? Amelie has had a string of ex-boyfriends in her twenty-seven years—a lot more than I have, that's for sure—and yet I can't remember my dad reacting to any of them the way that he reacts so viscerally to Owen, as though Owen has personally wronged him.

It drives me insane, and though I'll probably regret it come tomorrow, I loop my arm through Dad's before Owen can even get a word in. "I think we need to have a chat." I look to Owen, giving him a small nod that I hope he'll correctly interpret as *I've-got-your-back*, before gently steering my dad toward the bar.

No one ever said we can't have this conversation with booze.

Once I've shoved a flute of champagne at him, I cock my hip and cross my arms over my chest. "You were rude."

Visibly unconcerned, he sips from the crystal glass. "All I did was greet him, *cherie*."

Looks like I'll be needing champagne for this conversation too, then. I swipe a glass, take a healthy drink, and then jump into the proverbial fray. "It was what you insinuated. Like he can't be here because he's not worthy enough."

Black eyes, so very similar to my own, stare back at me as though I've lost my damn mind. "We aren't having this conversation again, Savannah. Once was enough."

When he moves to leave, I step in his way. Out of the corner of my eye, I notice heads begin to turn in our direction. I ignore them all, focusing instead on the man who has had a firm hand in directing every avenue of my life.

Softly, I hiss, "I agreed to your ultimatum, didn't I? I went on that stupid show and I *stayed*. ERRG got its notoriety. I'm the new VP, just like you've always wanted. Profits are bursting through the roof ever since I came home." Fearing the wineglass stem might snap, I loosen my grip. "Tell me, Pops, is there really anything left for me to do? Because from the way I see it, I've fulfilled my side of the bargain and you *haven't*."

His expression stiffens. "We are not doing this right now."

"Why not? Because you're scared someone might overhear that your picture-perfect family isn't so very perfect after all?"

"*Savannah*."

I don't heed the rigid warning in his voice. Couldn't, even if I wanted to, because the champagne has loosened my tongue and the crisp memory of Owen teasing me about my lack of athletic prowess has strangely emboldened me—if you can't accept your failures, then how in the world can you even begin to succeed?

"Have you called her like you promised you would?" I demand.

A small pause. "No."

Of course not. Because why would the all-powerful Edgar Rose *IV* bother to fix his own mistakes? Mistakes that include lying to his youngest daughter for *years* about who she really is. Amelie doesn't look like me—doesn't look like him—because she doesn't have a single trace of Rose blood in her. Something neither of us discovered until two weeks before *Put A Ring On It* was due to start filming.

She'd told the world that a business opportunity led her to Europe. Good timing, I suppose, because that wasn't a lie. But the reason she's stayed gone for so long—why I chased after her as soon as my contractual obligations ended with the network—has everything to do with having my sister's back.

Loyalty, it seems, is not something my dad has figured out real well, despite the millions he's worth.

A harsh laugh leaves my throat. "Only you would have the nerve to drop a bomb like that on your daughter and then expect her to fall dutifully in line."

"She's a Rose," he says, almost stubbornly. "She'll come home when she's ready."

"She's *human*," I reply sharply, "and she's reeling from the fact that you aren't her father. At least Mom tried to apologize and explain, whereas you've just . . ." Anger tangles my words and I inhale sharply. One deep breath. Then another, for good measure. I step toward him. "For her entire life, you've made it out to seem like she's the odd duck out, the one who disappoints you even though you should be *proud* of her for all that she's accomplished. And then she actually learns that she *isn't* a Rose, not by blood, because you flung that fact in her face. Suddenly everything you've ever said to her takes on a new meaning. You killed her, Pops. Maybe not physically, but emotionally, you slaughtered her and then had the gall to tell her to stop being childish and do the family proud by going on *Put A Ring On It*."

For the first time, Dad's expression fractures. His hand comes up to rub his chest in small circles. I want to believe that he feels bad. My father is not a horrible man. He's fair to his employees. He believes in helping those less fortunate reach for their dreams. He is *good*, the sort of father who never shied away from playing with dolls or wrapping me up in a tight hug the first time a boy broke my heart.

Unfortunately, he's also blinded by his own ambitions.

America may believe that I'm too sweet, too passive, but I know better: I've spent the last decade with the weight of ERRG on my back. I did so because it was expected of me.

"Even ones named Gage?"

She salutes me with her can. "*Especially* ones named Gage. I'm miserable." Dramatically, she wiggles her toes again, as though to prove her point.

"You look great."

"I'm not sure that I'm meant for motherhood."

"We'll hook Gage up to one of those labor simulators, so he'll know the exact pain you're gonna experience. Turn the voltage way on up. Do it right and he'll be lookin' at this pregnancy situation as a one-and-done type deal."

Lizzie's mouth curls in a grin. "You're evil, you know that?"

"I'm the older brother, baby girl. I created evil."

At that, she throws back her head with a bubbly laugh. It's the same warm, infectious laughter that's earned her over ten million subscribers on her makeup YouTube channel. On paper, she and Gage shouldn't have even lasted more than a date or two. Former playboy. All around spunky good girl. A total recipe for disaster—if not for the fact that Lizzie brings out the best in Gage and my twin, in turn, pushes his wife to reach for every damn dream that enters her head.

Marrying Lizzie is the best decision Gage has ever made. It brought her into our life, made our duo into a solid trio. After so many years of being a family of only two, it's been nice to welcome someone new into our midst.

She's also the only one who knows just how much Savannah's rejection rocked me to my core.

As though she's got a radio tap on my brain, Lizzie casts me a sly look. "I heard through the grapevine that you and Miss Rose were dancing it up at the mayor's auction last weekend."

More like I was tromping all over her toes, but yeah, we

can call it dancing. What could have ended disastrously was saved by Miss Rose herself. The woman moves with complete fluidity, better than any fantasy I've ever drummed up. Letting her lead ought to have been embarrassing but, hell, it had been all kinds of sexy instead. Her soft hand at my waist. The other tangling with the short locks of hair at the base of my neck. The way she looked up at me, her eyes twinkling with delight.

Facts of life I don't recommend, though? Dancing with a hard-on.

There's nothing quite like admitting to a girl that you don't have rhythm while also rocking an erection that could double as a coat rack, especially when her dad appears out of nowhere to break up the party. Young, troubled Owen would have snapped back after Edgar Rose's not-so-sly comment about me being at the mayor's ball; thirty-six-year-old me doesn't give a damn. If Rose hadn't felt threatened by my presence, he wouldn't have said a word. That, in itself, holds more power than worrying about the man not liking me. Doesn't mean I didn't notice his and Savannah's uncomfortable exchange after I'd walked away, though. And it doesn't mean I easily forgot the embarrassed expression on her face once I'd left for the night, long before the final call for bidding.

"You're not denying that you danced with her," Lizzie drawls, eyeing me speculatively. "*Interesting*."

I take a long pull of the soda. "You didn't swing by today to tell me your butterfly tat achievement, did you?"

She doesn't look even the least bit guilty. "I needed a subtle opening. Thought I'd bring it back to where it all began, when Gage inked a butterfly on my butt."

"Lizzie," I say slowly, "you're about as subtle as that pregnant belly of yours. Do you even know how to be discreet?"

each other, I promised myself that I wouldn't ever use *I love you* until I meant it. The forever kind of mean it.

And while Savannah makes me wonder *what if?* that doesn't mean that I love her.

It's just lust. Just like.

"Fine," Lizzie says, fishing her car keys out of her pocket, her gaze still locked on my face. "You don't love her. But answer me this: if you had the chance to have sex with her . . . would you?"

My face heats at the question.

Immediate, gut response? Hell yes.

Given the chance, I'd fuck her six ways from Sunday. On her back. On her stomach. On her knees, the rug scraping her skin as I hold her in place and work my hard-on inside her wet pussy.

Lizzie and I are close but this . . . I'm not going there with her. My relationship with Savannah, whatever is left of it, is too damn personal. Maybe she wants me back, maybe she doesn't, but I'm not going to violate her trust by discussing our nonexistent sex life with my sister-in-law—no matter how well-intending Lizzie is.

"No," I finally say, diving recklessly into the lie, "I don't want to fuck Savannah Rose."

"*Oh.*"

My head jerks to the right, only to find the woman in question hovering in the doorway. One glance at her expression is all I need to know that she heard what I said. And instead of that singular look of desire that the reporter from *The New Orleans Daily* caught, Savannah stares back at me wearing the same impassive mask I've grown to loathe.

The heiress mask.

The holier-than-thou mask.

The you-can't-hurt-me mask.

"Sorry for"—she visibly inhales, her nostrils flaring —"not calling in advance. I had something of yours. Figured you might want it back."

I tear my gaze away from her face to the small bundle she's gripping to her chest. With slow, measured movements, she slips the scarf out from around the bundle until my heart is in my throat and I'm standing here like an idiot.

She brought me my sketchbook. *The* sketchbook.

Which means that she spent at least five-thousand dollars on purchasing something she always intended to return to me . . . Meanwhile, she walked into Inked, just in time to hear that I have absolutely zero plans to strip her naked and make her come.

God-fucking-*dammit*.

16

SAVANNAH

So, this is how Owen felt when I sent him packing.

Raw.

Embarrassed.

Hurt.

My head is a jumbled mess of barely cohesive thoughts that do absolutely nothing to propel me into motion. I can't turn away. I can't *run* away. As though I'm reliving a nightmare, I stand immobile, playing Owen on repeat:

No, I don't want to fuck Savannah Rose. No, I don't want to fuck Savannah Rose. No, I don't want to—

Dammit!

His words burn. Like the worst kind of toxin, they seep into the crevices of my insecurities, dredging poison through my veins, pouring sludge into my heart. I open my mouth. Snap it shut a second later. In my arms, his sketchbook feels like a beacon of my own vulnerability. He didn't ask for this—to be fair, he didn't ask for much aside from that one dance—and here I am, showing up unannounced yet again when he's made it all too clear that we've hit the end of our road.

Honestly, I'm surprised there's no DEAD-END sign waiting to greet me with booze, chocolate, and at least a dozen sappy romantic comedies. *10 Things I Hate About You* has always been my go-to breakup movie.

Pull yourself together.

Do not *fall apart.*

I've spent a lifetime living up to the Rose name. When the other girls in grade school teased me about my wild hair and my awkward demeanor and my penchant for being the teacher's pet, I turned up my nose and walked away before they could see my tears. When guys in college chose my more outgoing, bubbly girlfriends, I pasted a smile on my face and wished them the best of luck. And when my dad demanded that I fulfill my contract with *Put A Ring On It,* I did so with my head held high.

A Rose with her unshakable pride.

It's too bad my thorns are currently nowhere to be found.

As though I'm not feeling like I've been punched in the gut, I meet Owen's gaze boldly. Do my best to scrape together every inch of my father's arrogance when I carefully unwind the scarf from around his sketchbook. "Sorry for not calling in advance." *Perfect.* That's perfect. I sound calm, totally collected. Running my tongue over the back of my teeth, I hiss out a short breath, then add, "I had something of yours. Figured you might want it back."

Owen's impassive black gaze drops to the leather-bound notebook I'm holding to my chest. Brows knitting together, he drags his thumb across his bottom lip before sinking his hand into all that thick, midnight hair. The strands stick up when he lets his arm fall back to his side. "Jesus," he mutters, so low I nearly miss it, "Savannah, I didn't hear you—"

Beside him, a very pregnant Lizzie Harvey awkwardly coughs into a balled fist, cutting him off. "*Soooo*, I think that's my cue to go." She looks from me to Owen and then sharply nods her head. "Oh yeah, I'm pretty sure I'd rather be anywhere else right now—even the DMV, which, I'm just going to say it, is hell personified." She shoots me a half-grin. "No offense, of course."

I slip a glance over to Owen, who still looks like he's composed of marble. God, the man could *seriously* beat out my dad when it comes to expressionless faces, and that's saying something. "None taken."

Under different circumstances, I'd give Lizzie a hug and ask her how she's been. We aren't best friends, but she's always been extremely kind to me in the past. Of all the people I've met, she's always given me the feeling that she enjoys talking to me for *me,* instead of determining her next move so she can get something out of me. Under *these* circumstances, however, I only watch with sinking dread as she busses Owen's cheek with sisterly affection.

When she turns to me, it's with a knowing look in her sharp, blue eyes. "Good to see you back in N'Orleans, Savannah," she says, moving in for a swift, one-armed hug before heading for the front door. And then, with a parting "don't kill each other, please" vote of confidence, she escapes out onto Bourbon Street.

Leaving me and Owen alone.

Oh, how fun this will be.

I drag in a heavy, chest-filling breath. Tap my fingers against the leather-bound notebook and sketch out a quick plan: drop off the book, play pleasantries for no more than three minutes max, and then get the hell out of Dodge.

Easy peasy.

And then I can make a pitstop at the closest bar for a

pick-me-up in the form of a cocktail or five. Maybe even make it a fish bowl so when I start to cry, everyone will think I'm just regretting my life decisions.

Not completely untrue.

Doing my best to ignore the awkwardness permeating the parlor, I sidestep Owen and head for the receptionist's desk. "I'm just going to leave this here for you, then I'll be out of your hair."

Strong fingers circle my wrist, stalling my flight. "You bid on it."

Only, I hear what he doesn't say in that rough New Orleans drawl of his: *You bid on* me.

So we're going there.

Sinking my teeth into my bottom lip, I glance down to where he holds me. Ink crawls down his forearms, his wrists, to the tips of his fingers, in intricate geometric shapes that look only that much more complex the longer I stare. I once heard that tattoos, much like pets, are a reflection of their owner.

I'm not sure what that says about me, since I have a homicidal cat who runs my life like a power-hungry dictator, but if we're rolling with that theory, then Owen is the most complex person I've ever met.

He hides his vulnerabilities well—behind all that intimidating ink, behind the trim beard that half conceals his smile when he openly grins, behind those aloof eyes of his that see so much and reveal so little.

So, yes, I did. I bid on the sketchbook.

I bid on *him*.

Because, charity or not, I saw something besides fury and impatience glinting in his eye on the night of the auction. I saw fear and sadness, and yes, even a sliver of vulnerability. The man who shows the world nothing suddenly verged on showing it all.

I couldn't let that sketchbook go.

The thought of it landing in an art gallery or being sold alongside tickets to Machu Picchu churned my stomach in such a way that I felt physically sick.

And, yeah, I spent a good deal of money to outrun Mayor Frannie Barron, who, I would just like to add, did *not* go down without a fight.

Pretty sure that in her eyes, I went from being the acne-prone little girl who used to bus her tables, to enemy number one in less than two hours flat.

No regrets.

In a clear, sharp voice, I clip out, "I did."

I watch as Owen's thumb finds my skittering pulse on the inside of my wrist. The heat of him, the slight pressure . . . I close my eyes just as he demands, "Why?"

Swallowing past the sudden lump in my throat, I set the sketchbook down. "We both know why."

I sense his solid presence behind me a second before I feel his touch all over. And I'm talking *all over.* His chest collides with my shoulder blades and his thighs brush the backs of my legs and then he takes it one step further by arrogantly pinning my captured hand to the desk. Does the same with the other, locking me in place.

Caging me between the desk and his muscular frame.

Oh, my God.

My nails scrape the desk as he rasps, "Tell me anyway, Rose." The words are whispered against the shell of my ear, his breath rustling my hair. An intoxicating shiver works its way down my spine. "*Why.*"

Shoulders shuddering at his close proximity, my head lolls forward.

We're crossing so many boundaries here, tromping over

them like they've never even existed. Maybe for him, they've always been a negligible issue, but for me . . .

How many times have I imagined a scenario just like this one? With him taking me exactly as he wants, heedless of the consequences? Too damn many to confess.

It was wrong of me. I knew that then, even as I know it now. Amelie is my sister, my best friend, the one person I'll protect above all else. But that didn't stop the fantasies of Owen from storming my head, almost right from the start.

I imagined his mouth crashing down on mine, his fingers tracing the line of my underwear before pushing aside the fabric to touch me *just there*, his cock bobbing against his firm stomach when he pushed me to my knees.

Crushing on Owen Harvey when he was dating my sister was the worst kind of hell.

But wishing that he'd choose me over her felt like the worst kind of sin.

And when they broke up—the honest-to-God most civil, most *unemotional* break up in the history of breakups—Dad swooped in to remind me that getting together with my sister's ex-boyfriend was *not* in the plans.

Firm, masculine lips land on my sensitive skin, ripping me from my thoughts, and boldly kiss the hollow curve where my neck and shoulder meet. A second kiss follows, a few inches north. Another shudder of want tears through me, the chasm between *do* and *do not* growing ever further apart.

"Answer the question," comes his guttural demand.

God help me, but I do.

"You would have let it go," I whisper, tilting my head to the side in a wordless command for *Give me more*. "Just like that, you would have let it go. Because that's who you are, Owen. You're tough and stoic and you can pretend all you

Oh, God.

"Because I'm done watching other guys flirt with you." His palms skim up to the tops of my thighs, his fingers finding the crease of my hips. "So, I'm going to put this real simple." Thumbs digging in, he snaps my ass forward so that the bulge behind his zipper aligns perfectly with the apex of my thighs. I moan. Right there, out loud. The bridge of his nose finds my jaw, nudging upward so I'm giving him all the room to play with my neck. His tongue flits out when he finds my fluttering pulse. "I'm gonna fuck you, Rose. And it's not going to be elegant and pretty, like you're accustomed to." Another flick of his tongue, another shameless moan torn from my lips. "You're going to beg. Beg me to make you come, beg me to give you more, and if you're real good, maybe I'll do it all over again before you have to beg for that too."

I can't breathe.

My chest heaves, my mouth sucks in air, but it all feels completely pointless when faced with this new reality:

Owen wants me to beg. He wants me to submit.

What he doesn't realize is that I've wanted this for so long that my desire for him feels like it's been sewn into my very being. I breathe in, and I catch his scent. I breathe out, and my fingers are already prepared to latch onto his frame and tug him close.

No one else will do. I've tried. God, have I tried. I went on blind dates while he went out with Amelie. I ended up on a TV show that set me up as the sole girlfriend to twenty-six men for *months*, only to leave exactly the way I showed up: alone. I stayed away out of respect for Amelie, for my dad's stupid ultimatum, and yes, for me, too.

A man like Owen Harvey will destroy me. He'll take my life that fits perfectly within the Rose plans and he'll dismantle it piece by piece, not out of maliciousness but because he believes I can do better. Because he believes that I shouldn't ever settle for the status quo.

Call me crazy but I'm ready to be ruined.

I *want* to be ruined.

One big hand slicks up my spine until it's cradling the base of my head. "You have three seconds to tell me you don't want this to happen."

Crooked nose. Furrowed brows. Crescent-shaped scar. *Gorgeous.* He'd scoff if I said it out loud, but Owen . . . he's the most gorgeous man I've ever met. Inside and out.

"Three."

I kick off my other high heel. Hear it fall to the floor.

"Two."

I don't wait for him to move first.

Throwing caution to the wind, I cup Owen's face with both hands. His beard tickles my palms and his hot gaze homes in on my mouth, like I'm the sole patch of light in a night of complete darkness.

"One," I whisper with finality, and then I take fate into my own hands and press my mouth to Owen Harvey's.

He tastes like self-destruction.

And I've never had better.

No, she tastes like she's mine.

Warning bells sound off in my head, clanging loudly, but I shut the door on thoughts of the future and focus on the now.

After almost two years, I have Savannah Rose in my arms. Finally, we're on the same page.

Half expecting baby cherubs to burst into the hallway, shooting confetti into the air in congratulations, I flex my hands under her ass, clutching her tighter, thrusting my hips upward. The web of her slim-fitting skirt stops me from making direct contact, and I tear my mouth away from hers to growl, "Drag your skirt up around your hips."

Hastily, she maneuvers the fabric up between us, leaving her in nothing but her unbuttoned shirt, that lacy bra, and a pair of boy shorts that shouldn't be as sexy as they are.

She's beautiful. Almost too beautiful for me to ruin.

Almost, but not quite.

My eyes slide shut, and my mouth finds hers on instinct alone.

We collide in an inelegant meetup of lips and teeth. For all my talk, I know that we should take it slow. Work our way up to whatever comes next. She must sense my momentary hesitation because she pulls back long enough to demand, "Don't you dare stop now," before diving back in.

She doesn't need to tell me twice.

With my left hand, I circle her wrists and drag them up above her head. Pin them to the wall and crash my mouth down over hers again. My kiss is bruising, my touch demanding, but Savannah . . . *Christ.* Her hips roll seductively into mine, telling me exactly what she wants me to do, despite the fact that I've got her mouth otherwise preoccupied with my tongue.

I thrust upward, needing more, needing *this.*

Almost eight months ago, she sent me home. Sent me spiraling, more than I'll ever admit to another soul. And yet, having her in my arms now is unlike anything I ever believed possible. It feels like an elusive dream. Like at any point I'll wake up and the morning sun will be a total bastard, shining bright in my face, and I'll turn, hand outstretched to see if the bed is still warm from her body, only to find it cold and empty.

The thought adds an aggressive bite to my kiss, a possessive urgency to the way I hold her.

"Owen," she gasps, breaking away to let her forehead fall to my shoulder. "It shouldn't—it shouldn't feel this good. It's *never* felt this good . . . not for me."

Another forward thrust, and I drag my jean-clad erection over the spot she needs me most, earning myself another one of those breathy moans of hers that has my vision blurring. One glance downward seals the deal: her breasts are threatening to spill from her bra; her unbuttoned shirt looks sultry and inviting, as opposed to the equivalent of a modern-day chastity belt; and her underwear and skirt are inching down with every drive of my hips like they're willing to give up the good fight and bare all.

America's sweetheart is no more.

I need inside her, *now*.

"It was always going to feel this good." Slowly, I release my hold on her ass so she can slide down the length of my body, her wrists still pinned by my left hand. "With you and me, it was always going to feel like you're coming out of your skin, chasing a high like you've never known. I knew it, even when I shouldn't have. I wanted you. Craved you like nothing else in my life."

Chin tipped up, her pouty lips seek mine. A swirl of her tongue before she whispers, "Careful, or I'll get addicted."

memory of Owen's mouth ravaging mine to set the guilt into motion.

At the sound of an attention-seeking *meow,* I turn my head just in time to see Pablo leap onto my office desk in a blur of gray and white. Spine arched, he slinks along my open laptop, his thin tail curling around the corner of the screen.

"This is all your fault," I mutter, reaching out to run a hand over his sleek back.

He spares me a haughty look, his blue eyes narrowed, as though to retort, *Really, wench? Mine?*

"All your fault," I repeat, petting him again. Pablo may be homicidal, but I like to think that we understand each other. I feed him the good stuff that costs me an arm and a leg, and I regularly bring him into the office so he can terrorize my employees. In exchange, he listens when I have a problem. We're a perfect match. "You just had to go for the goods, huh? None of this would have happened if you hadn't tried to castrate him. You broke mine and Owen's ten-foot-tall boundary wall. Smashed it to smithereens."

In response, Pablo merely flicks his tail, pounces on my keyboard like it's a trampoline, and promptly closes me out of the video chat app.

Rolling my eyes, I concede the point. "Fine, the blame isn't all on you."

It's on me too. I kissed Owen. I begged for his dominant touch and his possessive mouth. And, so long as this conversation with Amelie goes well, I plan to do it all over again. As many times as Owen will have me.

Because what I want from the inked tattoo artist has no business being shown on Hallmark.

Looks like I'm going for a revised version of option one, then.

Peeling Pablo off the laptop before he can do any further damage, I set him on the floor. Promptly, he reclines on his side, hikes up his front right paw, and starts to go to town cleaning his genitals.

If that's not the cat form of flashing me the middle finger, then I don't know what is.

I nudge his furry butt with my foot. "Live your best life, Pabs. One of us has to."

Logging back into the app, I move the mouse over Amelie's contact name and find myself hesitating. For as long as I can remember, I've treated my sister with kid gloves, acting more like an aunt or a motherly figure than an older sibling. With eight years between us, we've always been in two different phases of our lives.

When she hit kindergarten, I was already watching my peers grind their little hearts out to Next's *Too Close.*

When she got her driver's license, I was already logging fifty-plus hours per week for ERRG.

This conversation has the possibility to tear the fabric of our current relationship in two, if we let it. *Which I won't.* I'm fully prepared for it to be uncomfortable. Sure, she and Owen may not have had some blown out, dramatic breakup, but she stilled cared about him. And I care too much about her to even consider keeping Owen a secret.

Honesty. Loyalty. Love.

That's the Rose way—or, at least, it's *my* way.

With a click of the mouse, the little green telephone bobs up and down on the screen. When the call *pings* to signal that it's been accepted, I paste a big smile on my face and ignore the anxious butterflies fluttering in my gut like tiny missiles. "Amelie! I—oh, my *God.*"

I don't know which one of us says it.

Me, my younger sister, or the person whose hairy ass is

dancing on the fifteen-inch laptop screen like a Magic Mike audition gone wrong.

"Close your eyes!" shouts Amelie. There's a loud thud, an equally loud masculine grunt when a flash of movement darts across the screen, and *way* too much bare skin. "It's not what it looks like!"

Correction: it's exactly what it looks like.

Male butt cheeks the color of a White Alaskan Malamute. Hair the color of charcoal. A neon-pink G-string that leaves absolutely nothing to the imagination. And I mean *nothing*. I don't know whether to laugh hysterically or buzz Georgie in so I can ask for some bleach, ASAP.

In the end, I lower my computer screen and stare up at the ceiling. I blink, and see the G-string crawling all up in there like dental floss. I blink again, and see nothing but a very distinct banana-shaped imprint as he tried to scurry away from the scene of the crime.

What has been seen cannot be unseen.

"Sav, we're good now," Amelie says over the sounds of distinct rustling.

With my gaze still trained on the ceiling, I demand, "What color pants is he wearing?"

"Well, technically they're nude since he's not wearing any . . ."

"*Amelie*."

"Blue shorts," a very non-Italian accent tells me hastily. *Spanish? Greek?* Doesn't matter. All I know is that I'll never be able to look him in the eye again. A second later he adds, "I am wearing blue shorts."

Blue shorts are better than no shorts.

Tentatively, like I'm prepping for the worst, I lift the screen. My sister's familiar face is grinning back at me, and, next to her sits a good-looking, olive-skinned guy wearing a black Polo shirt and a blinding white smile.

"Sav," Amelie says, jiggling the phone as she points to Mr. G-string, "this is Pablo."

Pablo, owner of the incredibly hairy buttocks.

At hearing his name over the laptop speaker, my own Pablo looks up from his place on the floor, his head cocked. His glance screams *what now, peasants?* while I'm sure mine begs *save me*.

Clearly, we're all just living in a Pablo-dominated world.

I push a weak smile to my lips. "It's nice to meet you."

Amelie's friend grins. "Your sister, she is fabulous! She has been—how do you call it?" He makes a ripping motion with his hands, his bushy, black brows arching high like we're playing a game of charades and I'm failing us both by not figuring it out quickly enough.

"Waxing," my sister chirps. "We're going to a nude beach! Pablo wants to wear a Speedo."

Unceremoniously, my mouth falls open.

That is . . . that is honestly more information than I've ever needed to know about a stranger.

I clear my throat and try to summon words that aren't *please, stop now before I'm scarred forever.* In the end, Amelie saves me from myself by patting Pablo on the shoulder. "Give us a few minutes, would you? I forgot it's Thursday."

Pablo pops a kiss on my sister's cheek, then—oh, God, please no—stands, showing off a pair of as-promised blue shorts. "Talk soon, Savannah!"

Silence reigns for a solid ten seconds before Amelie breaks it. Leaning forward, she rearranges herself wherever she's sitting before propping her phone on the top of her knee. "So, what do you think?" she prompts, her warm brown eyes shining happily.

"I think . . . I think"—*that I will never be able to look at my cat again without seeing that G-string*—"he seems nice."

"*So* nice. And he's from Spain! Did you hear that accent?"

"Spain? Is that where you are right now?"

Amelie shakes her head. "No, I actually got into Dubrovnik the other day. I needed a change of scenery. And let me tell you, Sav, it is *gorgeous*. Otherworldly. I wouldn't leave if you paid me. Here! Let me show you the view out back."

The video freezes on my sister's face before cutting to a modestly sized living room. The rental is cute, if not simply designed, and is mostly decorated in beachy whites. Big French doors open directly to a balcony that overlooks the glistening sapphire water of what I'm assuming is the Adriatic Sea.

"Isn't it stunning?" she asks, panning the video from side to side, giving me views of a rocky beach down below and, in the far distance, the façade of limestone buildings sprouting up from the sea. "Ditch N'Orleans and come hang out with me. Croatia and I would love to have you!"

My smile wanes.

Eight, I try to remind myself, *that's how many years separate the two of us.* Looking out at that water through my laptop screen, I feel just a little old, just a little weighted down by life. Eight years ago, I was doing something just as thrilling as living in Europe, wasn't I? I want to believe that's the case, but as I wrack my brain, sifting through the memories, I come up blank.

Pretty sure that eight years ago, I was doing exactly what I am right now: sitting in this same office, overlooking the same bookcase that I inherited from ERRG's former general manager.

My life could seriously use an overhaul.

Picking up a pen, I click it open, then shut, just to occupy my hands. "I really wish that I could."

I hear her massive sigh as she flips the camera back around. "You need a vacation."

"Pretty sure I just came off a seven-month vacation." Kind of. Sort of. Not really.

"Pops is going to work you to the bone, and when you can't deliver anymore, he's going to step right over your limp body and move on to one of our cousins."

It's not supposed to be funny, but I can't stop the snort of laughter that escapes me. Dad is ambitious, but not so ambitious as that. My cousins, Uncle Bernard's children, escaped the chains of the family business at the tender age of eighteen. Daniel works in tech, in Silicon Valley, and Gerard does something with stocks up in New York City. The last time I saw either of them, we were celebrating Daniel's wedding a few years back.

A wry smile tips the corner of Amelie's mouth. "All right, fine. He's not going to go to them. Wouldn't that be something, though?"

Before I boarded the flight from Athens to New Orleans, Amelie sat me down and asked that I not bring up Dad. I understand why—she's spent *months* thinking of nothing else but the matter of her birth—but since she mentioned him first . . .

Gently, I ask, "Has he called?"

One bronze shoulder, gleaming with a golden sheen from one of her favorite beauty oils, hikes up in a half-hearted shrug. "He texted me earlier this week."

Not nearly the same thing as letting your daughter hear your voice when you apologize for outright lying for twenty-seven years. Frustration boiling deep, I drag a hand over the top of my head. "What did it say?"

"It was screenshot of a plane ticket."

My jaw goes slack. "*What*?"

"Actually, that's not quite right. It was a *one-way* plane ticket from Rome to N'Orleans."

It's official: Edgar Rose *IV* is the most clueless man to ever breathe life into his lungs.

"So," Amelie goes on, a satisfied gleam brightening her eyes, "I decided to head north. Can't use a plane ticket out of Rome when I'm in Croatia, am I right?"

Eight months ago, if someone had claimed that my sister wasn't actually related to Edgar Rose, I would have laughed in their face. They're two peas in a pod, brandishing identical stubbornness and too much pride for their own good. Honestly, it's enough to make my head hurt. Amelie might not be Dad's by birth, but she's more his daughter than I am in every other way.

"You know I support you, Am. You want to live in Croatia, I'll ask for a cot when I visit. You want to come back to N'Orleans and open that art gallery you've always wanted, and I'll be right there with you, helping to build it from the ground up."

"I know," she says quietly.

"I have your back, always, but I can't—" I shake my head, not even knowing where exactly I'm going with this. All I know is that striking back against Dad doesn't do anything to repair the fracture in our family. Hasn't there been enough hurt already? "I gave Pops shit for him not reaching out to you, and he deserved that," I tell her, my voice thick with emotion, "but you picking up and traveling to Dubrovnik, of all places, just because you want to stick it back to the old man that you can't use the ticket he bought for you, is just as immature as his silence for all these months. Y'all are playing some weird chess match and I'm not sure I want to stay on the board anymore."

"Savannah."

"I don't mean to sound harsh." Guilt threads through me as I watch my sister sit down, her back to the balcony and all that pristine water. "I know you're processing everything. You have the right to go at your own pace."

"That's not what I was going to say," Amelie murmurs, shaking her shaved head. The day she cut off all her beautiful, natural curls, my mother cried big, fat tears. I've never seen her so worked up, at least not until Dad spilled her secret. My sister's shoulders inch upward, like she's steeling herself. "I was *going* to say that I didn't ask you to step on the board at all."

Shock has my head snapping back. "I'm your—"

"Sister. That's exactly it, you're my *sister*. Pick me up when I'm down, laugh with me five years from now because you're still scarred over Pablo's hairy ass, but you don't need to be in the trenches with me every second of the day. I'm twenty-seven, Sav, not seventeen."

Letting my palm land on the desk, I stare at Amelie's familiar face like I've never seen her before. Part of me feels that way. From the day she was born, I've felt like her protector—but the woman staring back at me, with her brown eyes drawn and a little disappointed, is not the newborn Mom placed in my eight-year-old arms so many years ago. My sister is gorgeous in a way that most people will never be. High cheekbones like a goddess, full lips that the boys in college all wanted to kiss, a sharp jawline that belongs in a fashion magazine. Had she actually shown up on *Put A Ring On It*, she would have knocked America dead on their feet.

My back collides with my chair as I slouch down. Feeling antsy, I balance the chair on its hind legs. "I feel like you just kicked me off the island."

"Never. We're just going to get you a new island right next door."

"Does it have a pool boy?" I ask wryly, trying to roll with the punches. Prospective neighboring island notwithstanding, I feel like I've had the wind knocked out of my sails.

"Only if the pool boy gets to be Owen Harvey."

I nearly go down.

The chair squeals as I do, too, and it's only by some miracle that I manage to right myself before toppling over. Pablo—the cat, not Mr. G-string over there—eyes me like I'm a public embarrassment. He's not out of line in assuming so.

Gripping the lip of the desk, I croak, "Did you just say Owen Harvey?"

The look Amelie levels me with is all droll, sisterly affection. "I'm in Dubrovnik, Savannah, not the middle of the ocean without access to the internet. I saw the two of you in *The New Orleans Daily*. Great dress, by the way. You looked beautiful."

I swallow, hard.

I didn't even realize there had been an article of us in the local newspaper. Has Owen seen it already? My heart pounds so forcefully that it seems unsustainable for long. *Heart attack, here I come.* Wetting my lips, I graze my thumb along the edge of the computer keyboard. "I wanted to tell you myself. That's why I called."

"I thought you called because you love me."

My eyes widen. "Yes! That, too. Obviously."

Amelie laughs, her head thrown back. "I'm messing with

you. I know you love me."

Oh, thank God.

"I also know you want to bang Owen's brains out."

Someone, somewhere, just dig me a grave and let me crawl my embarrassed butt right into it.

I press my palms to my heated cheeks. They're on fire—or maybe it's that I'm seconds away from hyperventilation. Could go either way, really. Wouldn't the *Put A Ring On It* producers get a kick out of seeing me now?

"This is not how I envisioned this conversation going," I finally manage.

"Can't catch all these curveballs I'm throwing your way?"

Just because I know it'll make her laugh, I grumble, "Hey, not all of us are natural-born athletes."

"Must have been my birth dad's DNA," Amelie quips with a kiss to her Pilates-toned bicep, shocking me into startled silence. "What? You think it's been all sexy boys and nude beaches since you went back to the States? I've been working on things, too. Wrapping my head around it all, including the fact that Mom won't tell me who he is until I agree to come home. She wants to sit down face to face. *Anyway*, back to Owen. Spill."

This is way too weird.

"Why aren't you mad at me?" I zero in on her face, unable to look away. "You should be calling me out—"

"For a duel?" She cocks her head to the side. "I mean, I'm down for that if you are. Toy Nerf guns. Real booze. I'll be a total gem and shoot you in the butt."

Concerned for the well-being of my ass, I raise a brow. "Why the butt?"

"Yours is better," she says, like that answers everything. "So, Owen. Have you kissed him yet?" She brings the phone closer, so I get a zoomed-in view of her freckled face, diamond nose piercing, and supermodel cheekbones. "Aw, are you *blushing*?"

Clearly, this is karma for saying nearly the same thing to Owen just yesterday.

"Can we not"—I wave a hand in the air, grasping for words—"go into the specifics of it all? Please?"

Looking put out, Amelie frowns. "*Fine*." Then, beneath her breath, "Fun killer."

Her comment hits a little too close to home, considering all the "wet blanket" commentary of late. Back snapping straight, I jab a finger into the screen, even though it's not like she can feel it. "You've kissed him too! You aren't weirded out by this—or angry, for that matter—and it's honestly weirding *me* out. I don't know what to say and I don't know how *much* to say, and all I know is that I need to see where this goes with him, and if you have a problem with that, you need to tell me right now."

A pause, in which the screen goes momentarily black and I hear Amelie tapping away on her side of the call.

"Savannah?"

I drag in a sharp breath. "Yes?"

"Check your phone."

Reaching for it, from where it sits beside a bottle of water, I drag it close and see a message from my sister. Curiosity makes my fingers twitchy as I tap in my passcode and swipe to open the text. I feel my brows pull together in confusion. She sent a series of screenshots.

Amelie's voice echoes from my computer. "Owen was fun, Sav, but I never had any illusions that what we had was the real deal. Mr. Right Now, not Mr. Right For Forever. We joked more than we kissed. We hung out with friends more than we were ever together alone. And when he met you, it was game over for him."

Heart lodged in my throat, I slowly lift my gaze to look at her on the screen.

"He watched you in a way that Pops has never once looked at Mom," she says, speaking softly, like she's worried I might freak out in the face of her raw honesty, "the way I've never seen a man look at a woman before . . . and you watched him, too, Sav. Like you were too scared to approach but unable to stay away. That sort of chemistry can't be duplicated. He knew it. I knew it."

"But y'all . . ." I sink my teeth into my bottom lip. "Y'all still went out for a few months after that."

Her warm brown eyes hold no apology in them when she admits, "I asked him to. Point-blank. Pops kept forcing me to attend all those BS events, and I wanted a tagalong who wasn't trying to get in my pants."

"I don't understand. I can see why you might have asked him, but if he liked me, then why would he—"

"Agree?" Amelie smiles slow, smug. "Savannah, let me ask you this: why did you drop everything and fly to Europe after filming wrapped?"

My answer is instant: "Because you needed me."

"Looks like you and Owen have something in common, except that I didn't ask you to fly to Europe and you did so anyway." After a small pause, she adds, "I hadn't planned to show you this because you'd clearly made a decision by sending him home, but . . . Look at that screenshot, big sis, and then let me know if you think I should be mad about a man who will do anything to be with the most important person in my life. 'Cuz, from the way I'm looking at it, the both of you should be kissing my feet for even bringing him into our lives. Name y'all's first kid after me, will you?"

And then, before I can say anything else, the video chat screen goes blank as she logs off.

Down by my feet, Pablo meows plaintively, pawing me in the shin.

His five minutes of cuddle time per day.

After patting my lap, he jumps up and curls in a ball. When he lays his little head on my knee, I nearly coo out loud. He's cute as heck. Not even close to being Satan incarnate.

No one ever sees him the way I do.

Stroking a hand over his gray-spotted fur, I tap my phone, bringing it back to life. Immediately, my gaze stops on the name at the top of the screenshot: *The Harv Man.*

Leave it to my sister to give Owen a weird name in her phone. I'm listed as *Savannah Banana,* and that was only after I begged her to change it from *Sav The Van.*

Heart stampeding in my chest, I read the back-and-forth between them:

Amelie: Did the casting director call you?

The Harv Man: Martin Quell? Yeah, just got off the phone with him. Tell me I'm not making the biggest mistake of my life.

Amelie: My sister is not a mistake, Harvey.

The Harv Man: Never said she was.

The Harv Man: Now going on a reality TV show to win over a girl? Different story. This isn't me, Amelie. I don't do this sort of shit.

Amelie: It's called being romantic. Did I or did I not tell you that the grand gesture is the way to go?

The Harv Man: You did.

Amelie: You're panicking. I can tell you're panicking.

The Harv Man: I'm double-fisting whiskey and considering a cigar when I don't even smoke. The time for panicking is already in my rearview mirror.

Amelie: And texting me at the same time? You're a modern-day superhero! Now, stop.

Amelie: I practically got you on the show. All you had to do was not sound like a complete idiot when Quell called. I'm sorry you chose the stubborn Rose sister, who won't back out of a contract, but you ARE going to go show up in LA, and you ARE going to make your big ol' grand gesture and it is going to be MAGICAL.

The Harv Man: Likelihood of her shooting me down? Ballpark percentage.

Amelie: I know she's hard to read, Owen. I know she puts up a front. She was raised that way (the parentals failed with me, in case you were wondering), but I promise you . . . you are going to walk away with the girl.

The Harv Man: I owe you one. Seriously.

Amelie: Don't break her heart, Harvey, and we'll call it even.

Except that he didn't break my heart.

I did that all on my own. And then I stomped all over his in the process, too.

All these months, I always wondered how he got on the show in the first place. How, in the thousands of submitted applications, he managed to show up that night and steal my breath away simply by stepping out of that limo. And now I know the answer:

The one person I've always protected, the one person who I've always supported, no matter where her dreams led . . . my little sister.

her eyes move to the brass, circular mirror positioned above it.

In it, her steady gaze collides with mine.

I'd be lying if I say that one look doesn't make my damn heart pitch forward in my chest.

I want her eyes on me. Always. It's been that way since the day we met.

Slipping my thumbs through the front belt loops of my jeans, I dip my chin. "Want a beer? Tap water?" I don't keep much stocked in the fridge here, since I only come by when it's time to work on the house—or, alternatively, when I need to escape the city by jumping in my boat and feeling the waves crest beneath the hull. Probably why it's taken me longer than usual to finish this house and get it posted on short-term rental sites online. Nothing beats the tranquility of living on the water. "Wish I had some of that chardonnay you like so much, but I wasn't expecting company."

It's a pointed comment, but Savannah only slips the purse off her shoulder and drops it on the sideboard. "I wasn't expecting for my sister to drop a bomb on me the way she did today, either, so it looks like we're rocking the same boat."

It's a sexual innuendo if I've ever heard one, but nothing in her expression reveals that she's thinking about naked bodies, desperate kisses, or coming so hard she'll see stars for days.

Damn shame, that.

My fingers sink into the pockets of my jeans. Tone neutral, I ask, "Everything okay with Amelie?"

"She's fine. I mean, I'm pretty sure she was waxing this guy's pubes when I called, but otherwise she seemed okay."

"Waxing?" It takes every bit of self-control not to cup my dick in sympathy pain. It's one thing to manscape on your own, another thing entirely to have someone—potentially a woman you're interested in—rip all those suckers out. "Sounds"—I grimace, envisioning the worst and wishing I hadn't—"enlightening."

"It wasn't. Enlightening, that is."

With one hand gripping the sideboard, she toes off her right stiletto, then her left. She drops by a solid four inches, and fuck me, but the way she flexes her feet, like a ballerina at the bar or whatever it is that they use, does something to me—like I'm finally getting an intimate glimpse beyond the powerhouse woman who sits behind her desk like a queen.

Then again, she's either about to kick my ass or strip naked.

Not sure what it says about me that I'll gladly take either, so long as she's in my arms.

Pathetic.

"Did you drive all the way down here to tell me that Amelie probably made a man cry today?"

"Not exactly."

I drag my gaze up from her bare feet to those slacks that cling to her slender thighs, and then farther up, until I'm searching her face for answers. "I'm not a patient man, Sav. And I'm pretty sure we agreed to cut the bullshit yesterday. Tell me what you want."

She pushes away from the sideboard, her hips swaying seductively, though I'm not at all sure she even realizes the power she wields. That walk of hers is hypnotic. Naked, she'd have the power to make men lose all rational thought. After yesterday's spontaneous hookup session, I'm more than already halfway there.

As she nears me, her fingers work the first button of her shirt open, then follow through with the next. *And the next.*

Like I've been abandoned in the Sahara for days on end, my mouth goes dry.

Seeking reprieve, I press my tongue to the roof of my mouth.

No dice.

Savannah's shirt falls to the floor in a whisper of cotton hitting slate. She's wearing nothing but a plain bra. No lace. No frills.

She's the sexiest damn thing I've ever seen.

"Rose," I rasp, somehow managing to find my voice, ragged though it is, "what're you doing?"

Her hands land on my chest. "I'm taking what I want," she says, pushing me backward. I dwarf her slender frame, easily, but it's like she's looped a collar around my neck, then cinched the bastard tight, because I follow her lead without objection.

Sidestepping the coffee table.

My ass landing on the brand-new couch.

The cushions sinking beneath the sudden onslaught of my weight, even while my focus is singularly centered on the woman in front of me. Gracefully, she takes a seat on the glass table. Legs spread, long, thick hair draping in front of her bra-covered breasts. Her bare toes dig into the plush rug, and yeah, mine are doing the same.

I don't know where she's going with this but I'm in.

All in.

"Thirty-five years of doing what people want of me," she says now, her voice husky, her gaze locked on my face. "Go to Tulane, they told me. I went to Tulane. Work in restaurants, they said. I slaved away more hours bussing tables than I ever cared to." She reaches behind her, and that plain bra of hers comes loose. The straps slip down her arms, until she's holding the bra up by one finger. "Date the good boy," she murmurs, her thumb idly gliding up the strap, "marry the good boy. No one ever said anything about loving the good boy. No one ever said anything about the good boy loving *me.* Not once."

I swallow, tightly, my fingers digging into the sofa on either side of my hips. "Move your hair, sweetheart." *Give me a peek of those perfect tits of yours.*

The bra lands on the floor. "Not yet."

A frustrated groan barrels its way up my throat.

She's going to kill me. Fucking destroy me.

Probably karma for the way I tested her limits yesterday. I deserve it—maybe—but that doesn't mean I have to play fair. Tit for tat, and all that jazz.

Leaning forward, I grasp the fabric of my T-shirt by the nape, then hike it up and over my head. Toss it on the floor, on top of her discarded bra.

Savannah's mouth falls open. "What are you doing?" she demands, a little breathless. That haughty heiress expression of hers is good, but not that good. Her gaze hungrily soaks me up, tracking the tattoos on my chest, my arms, the base of my throat, before dipping down to the waistband of my jeans. "*Oh.*"

I feel my mouth tug up into a smirk. "You're oglin'."

"You—you have a tattoo—"

Sinking back into the cushions, I splay a hand over the angel wings inked just above my belt buckle. They span from hip to hip, but instead of heavenly feathers, the wings are composed of bones. Skeletons. For every bit of beauty in the world, there's always the darkness that follows. You either cave to it, or you crush it to the ground. I've spent a lifetime struggling to come out on top.

"You can lick it," I drawl, feeling not the least bit

remorseful about throwing her rebuttal back in her face, "but not yet."

Her teeth sink into her bottom lip, her gaze slipping shut. Closing me out like she can't bear to look at me without wanting to fall to her knees. Oh, yeah. I'm all in for this.

I grin.

Spread my arms wide across the back of the sofa.

Drop my voice to a gravel-pitched whisper, when I push, "Keep takin' it, sweetheart. What you want. What you crave. I promise that I can handle it all."

She audibly swallows. Peels open her beautiful eyes a second before she reaches for the button of her slacks with trembling fingers. Hesitates there, like she's not sure whether to take the next step. *Please, please do.*

"All my life," she murmurs, "I've done what's expected of me. It was my own doing, too, of course. I could have pushed back; I could have flashed the world the bird and gone on my merry way . . . but I didn't."

"There's no time limit on dreaming," I say. "You don't suddenly hit a certain age and find yourself imprisoned by your past mistakes."

I should know. If that were the case, then I'd still be in and out of jail for stupid, immature decisions, instead of sitting on a multi-million-dollar nest egg—created by my own sweat, blood, and tears. Literally.

She pops the button free.

Lifts her ass off the coffee table that I only just put together and wriggles the material down over her hips, her thighs, her slender calves.

My cock, impatient asshole that he is, grows impossibly hard in my jeans.

And this time—*this time*—she must take pity on me

because instead of knitting her knees together, she spreads them wide, feet firmly planted on the rug. With her hair covering her breasts, and a pair of tiny underwear covering the triangle between her legs, Savannah looks like a wet dream come to life just to screw with my sanity.

I drag in a heavy breath.

Curl my fingers into the top of the sofa, so I won't be tempted to reach for her.

Somehow find it in myself to not bark at her to ditch the coy act and climb her pretty ass on my lap.

You are patient, I tell myself firmly. *You are a gentleman. You are a saint.*

Pretty sure God, or whoever the hell is up there, is laughing mightily at my expense right now.

And then Savannah moves, except that it's not toward me. No, she hikes up a foot and balances her heel on the lip of the table. Like an addict cut from his drug of choice, my gaze zeroes in on her underwear-covered pussy.

Fuck, I can't.

I am not this strong.

No one in the history of earth has ever been this strong.

You will not move from this couch. You will let her dictate the pace. You will not—

Her hand lands on her stomach, fingers inching south toward paradise.

I bolt up off the couch, prepared to haul her into my arms, only to be halted by a hand to my shoulders. "Let me," she whispers, leaving me no choice but to fall back against the couch and prove to her that I can take it all, just like I promised.

But I can't.

I can't take it all because this woman . . .

"You're gonna kill me," I mutter raggedly, returning my

arms to the back of the sofa with all the enthusiasm of a man being told to walk the plank. "Make my heart stop. Put together a funeral. Send a gazillion roses that I'll smell, even down in hell."

"Pretty sure they don't have roses in hell." Her fingers brush the waistband of her panties with teasing strokes obviously executed to make me lose my mind. "But even if they did"—a flirty, naughty smile tugs at her lips—"this is all your fault."

I'm not one to ever feel truly caught off guard, but there's no stopping my jaw from popping open at that. "Hold on. *My* fault?"

"You walked into my life, Owen. You walked into my life when you shouldn't have, but you did, and you threw all of my carefully orchestrated plans right in the garbage. I was fine doing what was expected of me. Would have probably been content to suck it up and do the same thing for the rest of my life, not causing waves, not pushing buttons, but then I strolled into Inked on Bourbon and learned what it means to *thrive*."

All comebacks die on the tip of my tongue when she slips those questing fingers down, down, down. Beneath the fabric of her underwear, her knuckles move in a small circle. Once. Her head tips back, full mouth parting on a silent moan, hair slipping to the side to reveal heaven itself. Her breasts are gorgeous: hard-tipped nipples; that imperfect mole on her left breast; just enough weight to make for a perfect handful.

Her name is ripped from my throat, needy and fucking desperate.

"I'd never seen anyone so enthralled by their work before," she says, that damn finger of hers still circling, still rubbing her clit beneath the shield of cotton, even as her breathing grows labored. "Did you know that you bite down on your bottom lip when you're concentrating hard? Or that you make this sound—this little growl of approval—when you stand back and let your client see their tattoo for the first time? Your pride is contagious, your ambition a drug that I wanted for myself . . . and then the fantasies started."

I growl now, but not out of approval and definitely not out of pride. Precious control slips through my fingers as I shamelessly cup the bulge straining behind my zipper, squeezing my erection just enough to alleviate the mounting pressure.

Savannah arches her back, loops her other hand under her bent knee, and knuckles her underwear to the side, leaving her pussy completely exposed to my hot gaze. Holy *fuck*. I die, right then and there, my muscles tight with tension, blood pounding furiously in my head—both of them—my teeth gritted to the point of pain.

Without a hint of embarrassment, her finger teases her clit, swoops down to her wet folds, then retreats up again. Her breathing hitches, like she's working against her own desire, and then she meets my gaze, hers glassy with lust, mine no doubt reflecting the same desperate hunger.

"You aren't the only one who tangled the sheets around your waist, your hand wedged between your thighs." As if to prove her point, she sinks a finger into her pussy, pumping slowly, in and out, and I all but come like a schoolboy with absolutely zero stamina. "I thought of you stripping down to nothing, and me slipping to my knees. Your hand going to the back of my head, and mine going to your thigh. Your mouth telling me to open wide, and mine sucking the crown of your cock."

"*Fuck*."

She curls her fingers, dragging them up again to press

Midnight-hued eyes flicker to my face, and in them I finally see so much. The former hurt, the current lust. The hard planes of his naked, inked chest heave with a jagged breath. "You didn't, then."

"I was scared," I admit softly. "Scared of how easily I'd cave if I let you."

The rasp of his leather belt sliding past the denim loops of his jeans echoes like a foghorn in my ears. "I was gonna kiss your hand," he says, his voice so low that I nearly miss the words, "sweet. The quintessential gentleman."

My heart trips over itself. "Oh."

"I'm not going to kiss your hand now, Rose. You hold them out to me and I'm gonna cinch this belt nice and tight around your wrists, and then I'm going to spread your knees and worship you the way only a sinner can." A small pause. "Scared now?"

I drag in a breath that seems to rattle its way past my lips. I am *shaken*, right down to my core. Shaken, but not scared. Although I've never once pictured Owen tying me up, I can't say that the thought disgusts me. If anything, my toes are digging into the rug with budding anticipation. I want it. I want *him*. However he'll give it to me, leather belt looped around my wrists and all.

Like I'm some sort of bold temptress, I hold out my hands. "I don't scare easily." And then, to slam it home, I wink at him. "Sorry to disappoint. I feel like I'm crushing your illusions of me, one sexual act at a time."

He throws back his head with a bark of rich, masculine laughter that I feel like a caress down my spine. The belt finds my wrists even as his mouth comes down, hard, over mine. He tastes like fresh mint and slightly bitter, like beer, and then all rational thought hits a dead end when my wrists kiss behind my back and the belt tightens and Owen

—my big, tatted, stoic Owen—lets out the sexiest groan I've ever heard.

"Gorgeous," he mutters, maybe to me, maybe to the universe, "and all mine."

That one, I think, is to me.

His hands spread my thighs. Then, just like he did yesterday at Inked, he drags my ass forward, so I'm poised off the edge of the table. He holds my weight like I'm his most treasured possession, his grip cupping my butt cheeks, his nose trailing up my inner thigh, breathing me in.

Owen is a vision between my legs.

A dark-haired, bearded, inked god of a vision. *The Prince of Darkness*. It fits—perfectly.

I make a move to reach for him, to sink my hand into all that luscious hair, but the belt is a firm reminder that I'm meant to beg—for now, at least. He's taking what he wants, putting his will into action, while acknowledging that I'll demand the same of him later.

And that's okay.

It's a compromise, a back and forth, and then—

"*Owen*."

His tongue flicks out against my clit, so softly, such a teasing caress that my back arches in want of more. Immediately I struggle against the restraints. But the smug bastard only lifts his unholy gaze, holds mine for *one* . . . *two* . . . *three*, and then swirls his tongue in a slow, torturous circle.

"I hate you," I manage on a tight, breathless moan. "I take it back. No belt. I need . . . I need—"

His beard scrapes the inside of my thighs as he offers me a rare, devilish grin. "All you need is me, sweetheart. And I got you."

Like he's prepared to feast, his hands tighten their grip on my ass, and then everything in me positively deeper into my mouth, and then I'm being abruptly yanked off the table.

"I need in you. I can't—" He looks at me, this little helpless question in his gaze that tells me he's just as deep in this moment as I am. There's no going back. No rewinding the clock. It's both thrilling and terrifying, all at once.

"I'm on the pill," I tell him.

"You're gonna ruin me, sweetheart," he mutters, his hands linking around my back to fiddle with the belt. It grows tight, then loose, and then it's off and falling to the floor with a clink of metal. He nuzzles my neck. Presses a soft kiss to my pulse. "And I can't find it in myself to care."

My wrists are sore, a little tingly, but it doesn't stop me from circling my hand around his cock and squeezing up, up, up the hard length of him. "Make me beg, Owen."

"Today," he says, turning us around so that I'm being backed up to the couch, "tomorrow, five fucking years from now."

It's as much a declaration as either of us have ever given but as I fall onto my back on the couch, cushioned by Owen's muscular arm looping around my waist as he lowers me gently, it feels like a promise. A vow. His mouth crashes down on mine, taking me savagely but with the sweetest desperation that inflames my soul.

My arms are stretched out above my head—his doing, not mine—so that my back arches. I have my right leg down on the floor, the left hooked around his lean waist. So long. We've wanted this for so long, and call me emotional, but my chest constricts with need, and I feel the bite of tears threatening to spill.

I return Owen's kiss just as fiercely, expressing everything that I shouldn't say so soon in a relationship—or whatever this is between us. *I need you. I crave you. I'm falling.*

I've been *falling*. I feel him line up his erection with my entrance, and then he pushes forward, just far enough that I know he's going to be big and I know it's going to hurt so good. Goose bumps erupt over my skin at the thought of that metal barbell dragging back and forth inside me.

Complex. Untamed.

Owen Harvey takes no prisoners when it comes to sweeping a girl off her feet.

He drags his mouth from my neck to my jawline. "This is never gonna be a one-time thing," he rasps, sinking in another inch. "You know that?"

I roll my hips, needing more of that fullness. "I know," I whimper. "*Please*, Owen."

"Say it again."

"Please," I beg, not even caring that I'm caving because, God, it feels so good already, "give me more."

"Nah, Rose, I'm not gonna give you more." He rears back, the head of his cock once again positioned to make my naughtiest dreams come true. Then he growls, "I'm gonna give you *everything*," and thrusts forward, sinking in to the hilt, and it's true.

He gives me everything.

And it feels *wonderful*.

I cry out, ignoring his silent edict to leave my arms above my head, and drag my nails down his back. His thrusts are steady, perfectly composed of rhythm—just like he promised—and it seems impossible that I already feel my body tightening. I push down against every one of his thrusts, trying to give as good as I'm getting. And Owen is nothing less than raw, masculine perfection.

I feel the graze of his piercing stoking the fires within me. I feel his hot breath on my neck, as well as the corded power in his frame as he plants one hand down by my side, having sex with Savannah Rose would not have ended up on my agenda for the day.

Looks like I'm in debt to Amelie—again.

With my wrists resting on my bent knees, I lean my head back against the house. "When did she tell you?"

Savannah shifts beside me, rearranging her legs so that she's sitting cross-legged, her beer clasped between her hands. "Today. Earlier. She, ah, sent me a few screenshots of your texts . . . from when she got you on the show."

Even with as far as Savannah and I have come since then, I hear the bitter laugh that dredges its way up to the surface. "Turned out to be the wake-up call of the century. I climbed out of that limo so confident and then—well, we both know what happened."

Out of the corner of my eye, I see her grip tighten on the bottle. "Owen, I—"

I cut her off with a shake of my head, raising my beer to my lips for a cool drag. "We don't need to rehash it. We've done that. Multiple times."

"Owen, just let me—"

"I *can't*," I grunt, wrenching my gaze away from her slender legs to the wooden balcony railing. "Maybe that makes me a pussy but talkin' about it, relivin' it"—I drag a hand through my hair, pulling on the strands—"it leaves a bad taste in my mouth, Rose. Let's just leave that shit in the past. Move on. Move forward, me and you."

She's silent for a moment. Long enough that I find myself looking over at her, wanting to make sure I haven't completely pissed her off. But instead of looking ticked, she has this sort of resigned expression that flatlines her mouth and turns her gaze steely. My heart, riding on the high from having Savannah naked beneath me, slows to a crawl. Nothing about the look on her face screams good news.

Shit.

Propping herself up, she scoots forward and turns to face me completely. Setting down the beer by her knee, she clasps her hands together in front of her, and instead of the gorgeous, tempting woman who just fucked me like her life depended on it, I feel like I'm being given a glimpse of a much younger Savannah. More innocent. More vulnerable. She worries her bottom lip, and then blurts out, "I'm going to ask you a question, and I need you to give it to me straight. No bullshit."

I drape an arm over my left knee, leaning in. "I don't make a habit of dabbling in BS, sweetheart. You got a question, just ask it."

She meets my stare without trepidation. "Why does my father hate you?"

Fuck.

Instinctively, I take another draw of the beer. Cast my gaze over to the railing. Briefly wonder if throwing myself to the gators—not that they're usually out at this time of day—would make for a more appealing option than diving into this conversation.

"Owen?" Her fingers brush my jean-clad knee.

Guess we're doing this, then.

Wanting to be anywhere else but here, I close my eyes. Do my best to sift through the memories with an objective eye that won't leave me feeling like the scum on the bottom of my shoe. It doesn't matter how many years have passed since, I still feel the ache of grief, of utter self-loathing.

Softly, as though she's worried that I might make a run for it, Savannah's hand drifts up to mine. Intertwining our fingers, she offers silent encouragement with a telling squeeze of her hand.

Jesus, this girl. The weight of the world always seems to

around. She was dead that night, and Gage found her the next morning."

"Oh, my God." Voice soaked in anguish, Savannah jerks forward, heedless to the fact that she's in only her underwear, and slips her hands over my jean-clad thighs. Drops a kiss to my bare bicep, then lets her forehead rest there on my arm for a long, silent moment. I breathe in her scent, fingers flexing down by my sides. When she finally peers up at me, it's with her beautiful eyes drowned in sorrow. "We don't have to do this. If it's too much—if it hurts—we can lay it to bed. Right now."

This topic is always going to burn a hole in my chest. But I've had nearly sixteen years separating today from then to reconcile that my tumultuous emotions, while threatening to crest the surface, can be shoved back down. I've had good practice. Become something of a professional at it.

"Not that Gage was particularly bad before the accident, but I was . . . I was the good kid. I was the kid who never caused trouble in class. Real shy, too." I brush my lips over Savannah's forehead, needing the contact. "Gage and me, we grew up with this plan to enter the police academy together. Live up to the Harvey legacy for another generation. Do what our dad and our grandpa and his dad had done. But burying my parents—it changed something in me, like a switch going off. I spiraled. Dropped out of the academy within days."

As though hearing everything that I'm not saying, Savannah sweeps a hand over my inked arm. "I once overheard you say that you got into tattoos in jail."

I let out a humorless laugh. "Yeah, you could say that. I went from being the ultimate nice guy to every parent's worst nightmare. I got wasted at biker bars. I got *pummeled* at biker bars. Landed myself in jail twice for that—too much drunken brawling. Ten out of ten, wouldn't recommend it."

"I'll take your word for it."

Letting her go, I drag my knees up and drop my wrists on top. For this, I need space. "I met your dad around then."

Her shoulders jerk. "Oh."

"I needed a job. Turns out booze and drugs don't pay for themselves." When her expression falters at my admission, I almost bark out a laugh. *Yeah, meet the real Owen Harvey, sweetheart.* A real class act. Just another case of a kid having a decent upbringing only to go off on a bender. Scrubbing a hand over my face, I mutter, "Rose's was hiring. Bus boy. Nothing spectacular, but I went in and somehow nailed the job interview, considering that I was tanked."

Savannah's questioning gaze lands on my face. "This was how long ago? Did I—did I ever see you there?"

I shake my head. "Don't think so. You were probably in college."

"*When*?" she demands, this time a little more sharply.

"Shit, I don't know. Summer of '06? Something like that."

"The internship," she whispers, mostly beneath her breath. Louder, she says, "I begged Frannie Barron's husband for an interior design internship. Summer between sophomore and junior years. It's one of the few times in my life where I haven't been full-on in with ERRG. It literally took me months to convince Pops to let me off the hook for an entire summer break."

I guess there are small graces. I would have hated for her to have seen me then . . . the way I used to be.

"Two times in jail that year already." Reaching for the beer, I drain it dry. "Even Gage sat me down—the irony used to kill me. Gage, the former troublemaker, telling me, the kid who'd done everything *right* for so long, to pull my shit together. So, I did. Quit drinking. Dropped the coke. Was doing everything in my power to block out this goddamn need to drown the world out by drowning myself in the process, and then . . . then over a hundred bottles of wine went missing."

"Oh, God." Savannah's hand goes to her throat, and she looks positively sick. "I remember this. My dad, he never once said your name, but I remember him talking about it at dinner. It was *all* he could talk about for weeks. Some of those bottles were worth thousands of dollars."

My lips tug upward sardonically. "He pulled the entire staff in for questioning. One by one they all walked back out, and I remember sitting there, waiting, and knowing it was about to be a shit storm. I hadn't done anything, but I was the new guy on the block, and I was the druggie the manager kept an eye on at all times. The look on your dad's face when I walked in—I was guilty before my ass even hit the seat."

Savannah's brows furrow, her knees tucking in so she's hugging them. "I feel sick," she whispers.

Yeah, we both know where I'm going with this.

"Innocent till proven guilty—something I knew well. My dad was a cop. My brother was in the academy. Great in theory," I say, my voice pitched low, "shit in practice. I was arrested within the hour. Told I'd be given the chance to make bond, but that moment never came."

"Owen, I don't even know what to say." Her hands knot together, anxiously twisting as a flurry of emotions cross her face. "Did you hire a lawyer? How long were you in jail? *Shit, shit shit.*"

"There are a lot of things I love about N'Orleans. The food. The culture. Hell, even the drunken tourists. What I don't love are the back-end deals. The greasing of palms.

The turning a blind eye. The pretending you didn't just wrong someone because they fit the stereotype—yeah, I had a rap sheet. Yeah, I was reckless and stupid. But I wasn't a thief." My molars grind together. "Two months later, the real culprit came in and confessed. Turned out he was one of the dishwashers. Apparently his conscience couldn't handle me sitting behind bars for a crime that he'd committed." I pause, briefly. "I was released twenty-four hours later."

A panicked, high-pitched laugh escapes Savannah. "So, what? My dad hates you for something you didn't do?"

"Nah, sweetheart. Pretty sure he hates me because I'm a very obvious example of where he went wrong. I'm a living, breathing mistake that could have turned around and sued his ass to kingdom come."

"But you didn't."

"No," I murmur, shaking my head, "I didn't. Because despite everything, your dad taught me a good life lesson: success isn't winning when you're stepping on the backs of others to achieve it. At any point, he could have stopped and really done a thorough investigation of the staff. Done his due diligence as a business owner. It's not the route he took."

Her hand finds mine, our palms kissing. "How are you not bitter? How can you even look at me and not want to screw my dad over? Strike up revenge. Whatever you want to call it."

"All you can do is play the cards you're dealt." At the end of the day, landing in jail isn't the hardest card I've ever been dealt. Not even close. But that—that one will stay a secret. *Always*. "Because playing to the *what-ifs* only gets you so far in life. Ending up behind bars gave me a different perspective." With my free hand, I tap her forehead gently. "The world may tell you to sit down, or to get back into place, but the only person who gives them that power is *you*."

A slow, understanding smile spreads across her face. "Take what you want."

"Take what you want," I confirm, running my fingers through her hair. I cup the nape of her neck because touching her is quickly becoming my new addiction. "Plus, revenge is useless. Unless we're talking punishment of the sexual variety, then I'm all in."

"You would be."

"A man has to have his prerogatives."

"You're ridiculous," she teases.

I tip her head to the left, pull back her hair, and eye the tiny, delicate bird that I tattooed behind her ear months and months ago. Next time I get her naked, I'll find each and every tattoo I've marked on her skin. Kiss them, touch them. For now, I only brush my thumb over the black bird caught in mid-flight, relishing the shiver that wracks her shoulders. "Chasing shadows only steals the light, Rose."

Startled, her wide gaze slips up to my face. "Who told you that?"

"My cellmate. First time I was in. Big, hulking bastard that was in for armed burglary. Nice enough guy if you didn't bring up poker." His is a motto I've lived by ever since. "That's when the ink comes in for me. I feel the emotion. Allow it to submerge me and capture the downward spiral. And then I purge the fuck out of it by putting it on my skin. A memory. A piece of me etched in deep. Then I let it go."

I don't miss the way she scours me with her gaze. She studies my bare chest, my arms, the base of my throat, with more concentration than she ever has before. "Did you ever ink something about me? After California?"

Take the leap of faith.

Trust her.

I circle her wrist with my fingers, then bring her hand to my chest. In a low, guttural voice, I confess: "Hope is a funny thing. You beat it down. You starve it from within an inch of its life. But the shit goes nowhere. You may have sent me home, and you may have stayed on with twenty-six other dudes, and you may have told me we were nothing more than friends, but hope—stubborn as it is—didn't take a hike."

She draws in a sharp inhalation, looking at me like she can't quite believe everything she's hearing. "*Owen.*"

"So, no, I never did." I offer a half-smile. "I take what I want, sweetheart. And one day, I knew I was gonna have you. I didn't know how, and I didn't know when, but you and me? There was always going to be a tomorrow. Always."

Without giving me time to protest, she climbs onto my lap and drops her hands onto my shoulders. "Kiss me."

So, I do.

Thoroughly.

22

CELEBRITY TEA PRESENTS:

AMERICA'S SWEETHEART SPOTTED IN THE ARMS OF THE INKED GOD!

Dear Reader, I wouldn't have believed it if I hadn't seen the evidence for myself, but Savannah Rose was spotted in the arms of Owen Harvey earlier this week. Yes, that *Owen Harvey. The inked god from* Put A Ring On It. *(Have the drama gods finally answered my prayers? Yes, yes, I think they have.)*

The New Orleans Daily *reported multiple sources spotting the couple dancing at what seems to be an infamous mayor's ball in the Big Easy, and boy, did they look positively* smitten.

For the sake of full transparency, I will admit that this is absolutely unprecedented. Eight weeks ago, we witnessed Savannah's only emotional meltdown while on the show. The crew captured it all—the tears (Savannah's), the stoic expression (Harvey's), and the total pandemonium it caused within the Put A Ring On It *mansion once the other contestants realized that someone had been sent home before the cocktail party had even gotten under way. #FeelTheScandalBrewing*

Now, I'm not one to gossip (HA!) but I will gladly partake in a little shameless speculation for the sake of you, my readers: I think Savannah has been seeing Harvey on the slick for months now, possibly even as soon as the show wrapped up filming back in February. Obviously, more evidence is needed before I can really solidify this theory, but, Dear Reader, you don't do this for as long as I have without being able to read the clues well enough.

Savannah Rose and Owen Harvey clearly have a history, and it's only a matter of time before it unravels before the entire world. The tea, as they say, is piping hot, and I'll be waiting with bated breath to catch every moment of the impending Dram-aggedon.

Because I know *you are dying to learn more about Owen Harvey, I've done a little research on Savannah's current love interest—don't say that I don't have your back. Keep reading to discover the tea on our inked god, who may or may not be officially dating* Put A Ring On It's *very first bachelorette.*

Owen Harvey: The Details

Born: August 5, 1983 / New Orleans, Louisiana

Occupation: Tattoo Artist / Inked on Bourbon, Owner

Siblings: Gage Harvey, twin / New Orleans Police Officer

Social Media: Nothing (who is *this man??) save for Inked on Bourbon's online presence.*

Interesting Factoids: Harvey seems to be a bit of a wild card. I did some digging (you're welcome), and, when he was twenty, my research shows that he spent a total of three months in jail, on three separate occasions. One article linked to the Orleans Parish Prison even mentions him having been involved in a prison-yard brawl, which resulted in Harvey earning himself a fractured collarbone, a broken tibia, and a shattered arm. (Anyone else picturing a scene right out of Prison Break? *No? Just me? Perfect.)*

My Humble Opinion: It figures that a girl like Savannah Rose would go for the ultimate bad boy instead of the various contes-

tants from the show who went above and beyond to romantically woo her. My only question is this . . . will she even be able to keep up with a man like Owen Harvey? Or, better yet, will she manage to snag his attention for longer than a lay or two? Doubtful, Dear Reader. Very, very doubtful.

23

SAVANNAH

The minute I walk into ERRG's office on Friday morning, it's mayhem.

I'm talking *utter* insanity.

Phones are ringing off the hook, Georgie looks like she's on the verge of hurling her computer across the room, and even Jorge grimaces when I catch his eye as he scurries past me, cell phone clasped to his ear and his voice sharp enough to cut glass when he growls, "No, we are *not* available for comment on the matter. Now please, lose this goddamn number before I—"

The rest of his sentence is swallowed by the door swinging shut.

What the hell is going on?

Bending, I unlink the leash from Pablo's cat harness. Immediately he slinks off, probably to cause mischief in someone's office. Balancing the coffee tray in my other hand, I set it down on Georgie's desk. My gut twists when I hear curses exploding from down the length of the hall—Heather, if I'm not mistaken.

A seed of panic floods my veins as I turn back to

24

OWEN

We've been swarmed by twenty-something-year-olds.

It started five minutes after I opened Inked's doors at nine. The first chick walked in, looking nervous but excited, and asked for a trio of turquoise stars on her ankle. I hadn't even finished the set when the door swung open again and another girl strutted in, this one decked out in a miniskirt that threatened to reveal all, and a crop top that stopped right under her breasts. She wanted a pink gradient butterfly on her shoulder blade. No big deal. I had her sit in the waiting area for Jordan to show up—he was due in at nine-thirty.

But then the door popped open again, and this time it wasn't just one girl waltzing in but *five*. Twenty minutes after that, another ten strolled in, all giggly and doe-eyed and looking at me like I was a meal they wouldn't mind snacking on.

I called Gage in. I called Lizzie.

I called both Kyle and Sammy, our two apprentices, and even with the six of us trying to manage the growing crowd of giggling women in my parlor, there's no denying the truth: it's a fucking shit show of epic proportions.

"Oh. My. *God!*" shouts a chick from the waiting area. "Owen! Owen, can you be the one to do my tattoo? *Please*?"

I offer her a placating grin and turn to the girl lying flat on my table. Her denim shorts are dragged down just far enough so that I can work on the crescent moon she wants inked on her hip bone. Incessant feminine laughter drowns out the heavy metal sounds of Five Finger Death Punch on the surround system.

"Ooo, that tickles!" the girl coos, brushing her fingers over my arm. "Is it supposed to tickle, Owen?"

Careful to not screw up her tat, I roll my stool to the left by a margin, giving her the subtle hint to *do not touch*. Maybe I need Gage to make me a sign. Better yet: put it on a T-shirt and sell it as merchandise. *Don't touch your tattoo artist.* I bet I would sell millions. Fastest get-rich scheme there ever was.

I don't know what the hell is in the air today, but something must be going down. We're the number one tattoo parlor in the city—maybe even in Louisiana—but I've never seen Inked as packed as it is this morning. There has to be at least thirty or forty women waiting out front, not a single one of them willing to make an appointment and come back on another day. Like I said, epic shit show.

"Sometimes," I grunt, in answer to the chick's ridiculous ticklish question. "Depends on the person."

"Are you ticklish?"

"Uh . . ."

"Sorry, what I meant to ask is, are you single?"

Christ.

I lift the iron, then grab a damp paper towel to wipe her skin clean. "Yellow, right?" I ask, picking up the color chart I use on the regular, to help customers go with the perfect fit. "How deep do you want the shading to get?" I point at the column of various yellows on the laminated trifold. "G5? Lighter than that?"

Propping herself up on her elbow, the girl takes the chart and studies it. "Canary yellow, I think. G3."

"Great."

She lays back down, and I pick up G3's bottle and add some to one of the ink caps in my color tray.

I haven't even started shading the first half of the moon when she asks, "Sooo, are you single? I mean, I saw that you and Savannah Rose might be . . . *together*." I cut my gaze north, to her face, just in time to see her frown. "But, really," she continues, a touch petulantly, "she doesn't deserve you, Owen. I mean, she sent you home."

She sent you home.

Wonderful. I've got my hands on a *Put A Ring On It* fanatic.

Wait. Are the *rest* of the folks waiting for ink also *Put A Ring On It* fanatics?

Leaning back on my stool, I make a show of fiddling with the coordinating colors that match G3, all while eyeing the group of women gathered at the front of the parlor. Unlike Lizzie, I'm not someone who keeps up to date on social media. If it weren't for maintaining Inked on Bourbon's Instagram and Facebook pages, I wouldn't have an online presence at all. I like it that way. Keeps a certain divide that lets me live my life the way I want to, without running the risk of someone jumping in with an opinion I sure as hell didn't ask for.

Except that clearly *something* happened this morning.

Casting a quick glance at the chick on the table, I casually ask, "Y'all all friends?"

The girl's head tilts toward the other women. "With them?" She scoffs. "No way."

"Just felt like comin' to get a tat on the fly, then?"

I'm shit at small talk, but it must get the job done because she flashes me a predatory smile that's more than a little terrifying. Pretty sure my nuts just shriveled up and called mercy. "Oh, no," she says, still grinning like a piranha on the hunt, "pretty sure we're all here because we saw that article from *Celebrity Tea Presents* this morning."

Celebrity Tea Who?

I wheel back over to her, tattoo machine returning to her hip to finish off the job. "And he talked about Inked?"

"He talked about *you*." Her fingers brazenly touch my wrist, stroking my pulse. "Don't worry, I don't really care that you've been to jail." Giggle, giggle, giggle. "It's actually kinda . . . hot."

Everything in me goes still.

Over the years, I've done what I can to bury my past. I've volunteered on the board for the Entrepreneurs of the Crescent City. I've taken on countless apprentices like Kyle and Sammy, because in an industry like mine, opportunities to climb the ladder are slim to none. I've given my time and money to supporting charities and nonprofits all around New Orleans.

I've done anything and everything to erase a period in my life when drugs and alcohol quieted the roar in my head and the pain in my heart. I hate that Owen. I hate his recklessness and his selfishness and his desperation to play up this tough-guy-asshole persona that has *never* been me.

I may be broody. I may be shy—though I hate this word. I may take a while to open up to new people. But I'm not an asshole, and I'm definitely not a user.

You were, though. You were the worst one of them all.

Swallowing past the hard lump in my throat, I return my attention to the crescent moon. The colors swirl before me, like a kaleidoscope shoved under a magnifying glass. *Focus, man. Just finish this off and get her the hell out of here. You. Can. Do. This.*

The girl's fingers dance up to my left elbow. "Is this the arm you shattered?" she asks, a sly gleam in her stare. "That's what the article said, that you were in a prison fight. But I think you look good, Owen. Sexy. I like the beard. Did I mention that I'm single?"

Everything is too much. The endless chatter. The rough vocals of Five Finger Death Punch, a band that I usually love. The chick's relentless flirtations. The damn colors that won't stop swirling.

Focus, focus, focus.

I breathe in. Let it out.

Manage only three more seconds of shading before screaming erupts from up front. It's only down to years of experience and perpetually steady hands that keeps me from fucking up this moon beyond all recognition.

"Uh, Owen," Gage drawls from the workstation to my left. "We've got company."

Chest squeezing tight with dread, I snap my gaze to the waiting area. I see Pablo, the homicidal cat, before I spot her. He's prancing along the receptionist's desk, sending papers flying left and right, and Savannah—

"Oh, my God!" someone shouts. "Savannah Rose, will you sign this for me?"

"You are so, so pretty," exclaims someone else. "Here, let's take a selfie for Instagram!"

"Are you hooking up with Owen Harvey? Is that why you're here?"

Mass. Chaos.

I'll deal with it if I have to, but I'll be dead before I allow customers to maul Savannah right in front me.

Leaving the chick on the table, I push to my feet and cup my gloved hands around my mouth. "*Quiet!*"

Silence descends over the parlor, dozens of eyes zipping in my direction.

Savannah's included.

I look to her first, trying to get a read on her expression —her features are completely neutral, and if it weren't for the fact that the hair at her hairline has begun to curl, I would have missed the fact that she's sweating and clearly uncomfortable with the spotlight.

I got you, sweetheart.

I drop my hands to my hips. "Listen up, folks! We're game to stay here all day if that means we get everyone the ink y'all are wanting. But I'm calling it quits right now on the personal questions or anything to do with *Put A Ring On It*. You stay, you know the score. That goes for me, my staff, and Savannah Rose over there. It's your call."

A few girls exchange annoyed looks, then slip through the crowd to head for the door.

The rest shift their weights, rocking back on their heels, but don't move.

"I'll take a few pictures," offers Savannah, picking up Pablo from the desk and snuggling the crazy beast to her chest. She drops a kiss to the top of his head, and I'll be damned—the cat doesn't whip around, claws bared and prepared to shred Savannah alive. "I don't mind."

"Rose."

At my gruff tone, she spares me a quick glance. "I'm good, Owen." A small, fake smile widens her mouth. I doubt anyone else even realizes how much she wants to run. But I see, and I know the only reason she's here is for me. *To have my back*. She returns her attention to the group of twenty-something women milling around her. "If y'all can promise not to ask about *Put A Ring On It*, we can even do a few videos? For Instagram, I mean."

Cheers explode like she's pulled an Oprah Winfrey and given everyone a set of keys to their own Lamborghini.

Gage's client slips off the table, a square-shaped bandage on her upper arm, and swings past me with an open expression. "I told my friend there was something going on between you and Savannah Rose," she tells me blithely. "I called it on that first night when she sent you packing. No woman reacts that strongly unless feelings are involved."

She leaves me standing there, speechless.

Words have officially deserted me.

I watch as Gage hits the front, calling out the next name on the list. Jordan is right behind him. I don't know who this *Celebrity Tea Presents* asshole is, but they've brought pandemonium to my front door. Literally.

Hitching my jeans at the knees, I sit on the stool and get back to work finishing the crescent moon. I shade G3 into G4, careful to blend the two yellows perfectly. And then I do it all over again, when the next customer sits at my table wanting a yellow butterfly.

Butterflies for all.

I really should make sure that's the first line in my eulogy.

WE CLOSE EARLY.

By the time 5 p.m. rolls around, and the line has finally dissipated, we're all exhausted. Kyle and Sammy head out first, muttering something about hitting up the first bar they come across on Bourbon. Considering you can't go two feet without stepping in front of an establishment peddling booze, I figure they'll be toasted within the hour.

"I wish I wasn't pregnant," Lizzie moans as she flops onto the sofa. "I need wine. Actually, I probably need more than wine, but I'll settle for pretending I'm classy for at least the next thirty minutes."

Savannah collapses next to her. Her long hair is pulled up into a ponytail, and her high heels are long gone. "I think I've lost the ability to smile. Here's to a lifetime of having resting bitch face."

My sister-in-law tips her head to the side, her face flattening the sofa cushion, and gives Savannah a lackluster poke in the cheek. "You could never have RBF. You just *look* friendly."

"It's a curse," Savannah mutters wryly.

"I bet it brings all the boys to the yard."

That makes Savannah laugh out loud. "I'm really only concerned about one boy."

"Real subtle, there." Lizzie pins me with a haughty look. "I bet she knows how to spell discreet too."

Rolling my eyes, I watch as Gage heads straight for his wife. Bending at the knee, he slips one hand behind her back and the other beneath her knees. "Hold tight, princess," he says warmly, just before he lifts Lizzie clear off the couch.

She doesn't even shriek. Instead, my sister-in-law tucks her head against Gage's chest and lets her eyes fall shut. "Okay, you win. You can be my favorite Harvey twin again."

Gage looks my way, his brows raised.

I shake my head. "I didn't want the title, man. Your wife is tenacious."

"I heard that," Lizzie protests with a little laugh. "And

I'm not tenacious. I'm pregnant. Seven months pregnant. And this is after you fired me, Owen."

"You *fired* her?" Savannah asks, drawing her feet up under her to sit cross-legged on the sofa.

Here we go again.

Rubbing the back of my neck, I mutter, "It's just until she gives birth. More for her sake than mine."

Jordan comes down the hall, his backpack slung over one shoulder. He looks from me to the rest of the group. "Lizzie, don't you dare take his shit. Did you hear about what happened earlier this—"

"*Jordan,*" I growl. "I will fire you. Don't think I won't."

The asshole only puckers up and blows me a kiss. "You love me."

"I really, really don't."

"Eight years with me at your side, man. You think you could actually run this ship without Jordan Knight?"

He moves toward me, arms outstretched. I try to duck out of the way but there's no escaping his grasping fingers. He fake-boxes my ears, drags me close, and blows a wet-sounding raspberry on my forehead. *Fucker.* I push him back with an arm to the shoulder, wiping the spittle off my face with the back of my hand.

He turns to the rest of the group, a mischievous grin lighting up his face. "For the record, I am now not the only one to have christened Inked on Bourbon with the appearance of a dick. Owen. Savannah. Why don't you tell the class how I caught y'all dry humping in the hallway?"

The man clearly has a death wish.

For her part, Savannah only holds her arms open for Pablo to leap onto her lap, then tilts her head to the side. Her gaze skims over Jordan with a speculative gleam. "I don't know what you're talking about. Who was dry humping who again?"

Jordan's eyes narrow. "From the looks of it, it was a case of mutual humping."

"Huh. Sounds exciting." Looking unperturbed, she strokes Pablo's fur. "Can't say I remember that at all, though. Are you sure that you aren't just having flashbacks?"

My second whips around to face me. "Seriously?" he demands. "Y'all are *not* just gonna pretend it didn't happen."

I hold my hands up. "What the lady said."

When Gage barks out a sharp laugh, I sneak a wink in Savannah's direction.

Lizzie pats her husband's chest. "Just fess up, Jords, you're still upset about that one-star. I know, it can have a real lingering effect on your psyche, but you can't let it define who you are."

"I am *not* mad about the one-star!"

My sister-in-law swaps a look with Savannah, who murmurs, "I don't know, Jordan, you sound upset to me."

Jordan rolls his eyes. "Y'all suck, you know that? I'm going to get laid."

"Stay away from closets, buddy!" Gage hollers at Jordan's back. "We don't need any repeats."

Brandishing his middle fingers like guns being drawn from his belt, I catch Jordan's face in profile when he blows fake smoke from one finger, then the other. "See ya later, jerks," he mutters seconds before escaping out onto Bourbon.

Lizzie glances my way. "Were y'all actually dry humping? Because if yes, I approve."

I slip my hands into the front pockets of my jeans. Rock back on my heels like I'm nothing but fifty shades of innocent. "A lady never kisses and tells, Liz."

My ridiculous comment has the desired effect—both my brother and sister-in-law laugh hard. Then, with a wave from Lizzie and a short nod from Gage, they follow Jordan's lead and head out.

Leaving Savannah and me alone.

And Pablo.

I eye the cat suspiciously. "Is he wearing a harness?"

Shrugging, Savannah rubs the spot behind his little ear. "What can I say? He likes to go on walks."

Laughter climbs my throat. "You really are the definition of a cat lady, aren't you?"

Her mouth tugs upward in a tired smile. "I'm an equal opportunist, Owen. I willingly give affection to anyone I think needs it. Cats. Dogs."

"People, too?" I ask, closing the distance between us. After the day we've had, all I want is to hold her—and I don't give a damn if that makes me a sap. "Or just animals?"

"Depends."

"On what?"

"How they make me feel," she murmurs when I slow to a stop in front of her. She's completely relaxed against the sofa. Shoes gone, legs crossed beneath her, shirt collar parted and slipping down her shoulder. It's been a long eight hours, but I feel my cock stirring even now. This woman . . . Christ, she ramps me up like no one else ever has.

"Rose," I say, huskily, "get rid of the cat."

"Or what?"

"Or you're going to be responsible for when he draws blood because I'm kissing the hell out of you."

That tired smile of hers widens. "Well, when you put it that way, say no more. I'm all for protecting your oh-so-sensitive skin."

The sentiment heats my blood even as I laugh heartily at her wise-cracking humor.

With a little scratch to his twitching ears, Savannah releases Pablo. He jumps to the floor, skirts around me like I'm enemy number one, and slinks off. Needing Savannah close, I drop to my knees on the cushions, straddling her thighs. Prop my hands on the back of the sofa and lower my head to press a kiss to her temple. "Thank you," I whisper.

Her hands land on my back, on either side of my spine. Softly, she digs in her fingertips, like she's trying to relieve my tense muscles. "For what?"

"You came." I shake my head, my eyes squeezing shut. "I'm not even sure what went down today." *Aside from all my dirty laundry being aired for the entire world, that is.* "But when you walked in that door . . . I didn't even realize how much I needed you until that moment. You handled the crowd like a pro."

"You did the heavy lifting. I only smiled and posed."

"Yeah, for how many times, though? Fifty? A hundred?"

"I honestly lost count."

Yeah, me too. One butterfly. Fifteen butterflies. Thirty butterflies. At one point, they all melded together. If I never have to ink another butterfly again, it'll be too soon.

Finger to her chin, I inch her head back so I can brush my lips over hers. The last few times we've kissed, it's been raw, an all-consuming desperation. This kiss is gentle in comparison. I keep it light. Easy. A promise for what's to come more than any sort of delivery right now. Pulling away, I push off the sofa and onto my feet. Hold out my hand for her to take. "Let me walk you back to your car so you can head home and get some sleep."

Ignoring my hand, she clambers off the sofa with a groan. Looking like her worst nightmare has come to life, she toes over her stilettos and slowly begins to put them on. "I'll stay. Tell me what you need me to do."

"Savannah."

"Don't Savannah me. Do you need me to sweep?" She glides past me. Okay, more like she hobbles. The woman is too stubborn for her own good. "Maybe take out the trash after all those towels y'all used?" She faces me, her hands planted on her hips. "I promise I'm not so much of a princess that I don't know how to work a dumpster. I even have moderately toned arms capable of heavy lifting."

Fuck, this girl.

I step toward her, then. Without preamble, I cup her face with both hands and crush my lips down over hers. She tastes sweet. Tempting. *Affectionate*. Her fingers circle my wrists, holding on, holding *tight*, while I ravage her mouth. Kissing Savannah—wanting Savannah—is what got me on *Celebrity Tea* in the first place, but I can't find it in myself care.

Only . . .

My lungs squeeze at the memory of *exactly* what the tabloid reported. Jail. The fight. Shattered bones and hospital beds. With tense shoulders, I tear myself away from Savannah and fall back a step.

"I'll sweep," I grunt, unable to meet her stare while long-ago embarrassment floods my system, "if you don't mind picking up, up front here."

When I turn on my heel, it's only to have her fingers wrap around my elbow. My *left* elbow. It never healed correctly. On bad days, I can't get my arm to extend fully. On good days, there's only a twinge of pain.

My feet remain locked in place.

"What's wrong?" Savannah's fingers trail up, up, up until they're cupping my shoulder as she steps around me, blocking my escape. "You were with me and now you're where?"

No bullshit.

I established that aspect of our relationship weeks ago. Easier said than done when we're talking about her and not me. *Hypocrite.* Yeah, I'm no saint. Never have been, especially during my early twenties.

"Owen," she pushes gently, "talk to me."

I open my mouth, tongue feeling thick and swollen. "You read the article, didn't you." Not a question. "It's why you showed up here."

Her chin dips in a shallow nod. "*Celebrity Tea Presents* picked up an article from *The New Orleans Daily*. They . . . Well, they threw a lot of accusations around. About us seeing each other after filming wrapped up on the show, and even before then." Lips firming, she hastily adds, "Everyone's calling, wanting to know about our relationship. *People. Entertainment Weekly.* Jimmy Fallon. I was worried that you might have been stampeded."

"One of the girls earlier"—shit, this is hard—"she left the impression that everyone knows now . . . about me. Jail." I grit my teeth, then rip off the proverbial bandage. "About the fact I was an idiot and got myself hospitalized."

Savannah swallows, her fingers coiling tightly in my shirt. "Were you jumping into the fight? Trying to help someone who was in trouble?"

A caustic laugh rattles in my chest. That would have been preferable. *Good guy Owen Harvey rushes in to save the day.* For a second, I let myself imagine those headlines hitting the news outlets. Fiction is always better than cold, hard reality. "Nah," I mutter, staring down at the way her hand is gripping my shirt, like she's desperate to reconcile who I was then and who I am now. *I've been trying to do the*

considering her position. "For what it's worth—I don't mind his shadows. They make him human, and I've spent too much of my life being told to search for perfection."

Fuck.

I drop my head to stare at my feet. Pressure builds in my chest. As much as I'd like to blame it on exhaustion, I know the root cause is the woman staring at me, waiting patiently for my response. She's tearing me inside out, forcing me to look myself in the mirror and accept all my faults, all my successes. It makes me want to spill it all. Bare every bit of my soul. Tell her what no one else has ever known, aside from my parents.

The always present spark of fear at the thought of going *there* clamps my mouth shut, though. There's no going back if I open up fully, and with the media in a frenzy as it is now . . . I could lose it all if my secret got out. All of it, gone in a blink of an eye. It's a risk I can't take, not even for her.

"Black ink, right?" she asks, nerves coating each word.

I glance over at the workstation, tracking the placement of the bottles. "Yeah, black."

Straightening my shoulders, I press my fingers against her back to hold her steady, then slowly, gently, begin to trace the words she chose for herself. Words that I've spent years doing my best to live by, no matter the cost.

She hisses, this soft sound that has me pausing when I finish off the *B*. Wiping the needle against the Vaseline to keep the ink good for another round, I murmur, "Breathe, sweetheart. Don't keep the air in your chest."

"I always forget how much it hurts."

"Hurts so good," I correct, checking her gaze to make sure she's okay before returning to the next letter. "It's an addiction for me, just like any other."

"Have you ever counted how many you've had done?"

"Nah." Shaking my head, I pull back, reach for a paper towel, then glide it across her skin to collect the ink and spots of blood. Go back in for more, my focus glued to tracing the lines of the letters. "The way I see it, you don't need to count the memories. They belong to you, shape who you become. And most of my tats I don't care to revisit once they're done."

Another small hiss. Then, "Not to sound like I'm trying to go all Shakespearean on you, but it's like you've cloaked yourself in all your shadows."

I've never thought about it in those terms before, but yeah. "Guess I'm poetic like that."

After a small pause, she says, "All of mine are about chasing life. Some form of it, at least."

I think of the delicate tattoos I've inked on her skin. The tiny bird in flight behind her ear. The dandelion caught in the wind, bursting apart, on her right shoulder blade, where the band of her bra sits. The words "be as you are" scrawled in typewriter font just above the waistband of her pants, to the right of her spine. All the others that I've tucked away in corners of her body that no one sees.

No one but her and me.

If I'm all shadow, then Savannah is all light.

We fall into silence as I work on the rest of the tattoo. Once the spiral hit, sketching became as necessary to me as breathing. And even though I never had the chance for pencil and paper while I was locked up, those memories stayed with me. Tattooing is an extension of that. The chance for me to bring a vision to life and let the artwork speak for itself.

Grasping the paper towel again, I dab the settling ink. "You're done. Just let me clean you up and then you can take a peek before I put a bandage on it."

"I bet it's beautiful."

My gaze flicks up, finding hers. "For eleven thousand dollars, it better be."

The corner of her full mouth tugs north. "I have faith in you."

Once I'm done getting her sorted, I step to the side and make room so she can slip off the table and onto her bare feet. The ink looks good there, following the line of her bra. Seamless with her skin but still visible to the eye when she gets ready in the morning or glances in the mirror. A constant reminder of where she is now and where she's trying to go.

When her fingers absently trace her stomach, I growl in my throat and she shoots me a smug grin. "Told you, didn't I? You're vocal when you approve."

She steps up to the mirror in nothing but her slacks and that bra of hers. But instead of smiling with happiness when her gaze lands on her reflection, I watch as her brows knit together with obvious consternation.

My feet move toward her of their own accord. "What?" Unease curdles in my stomach, like I've eaten something rotten. Her ink is an exact replica of the stenciled outline that I marked on her skin before using the iron, but still . . . something in her expression isn't right. "Do you hate it? Savannah—"

"What color did you use? For the tattoo?"

Oh, *fuck*.

Bile rising in my throat, I twist on my heel, immediately heading for the workstation. *Gage's* workstation. Not mine. Panic tangles with dread as I snatch the bottle of ink off the counter, exactly where I always, *always*, place the black ink over at my spot. Ripping the plastic baggie off, I turn the bottle over, hoping, praying, but there's no label.

No label because Gage is Gage and I'm me, and *I'm going to be sick.*

I don't want to turn around, but I force myself to. Slowly. With the bottle still gripped in my hand that I thought for sure was black ink.

Savannah is still standing in front of the mirror, one hand pressed to her belly as an indecipherable emotion work its way across her face.

I can't bring myself to move any closer to her. Couldn't, even if I wanted to.

"Savannah," I utter, my voice cracking on the last syllable of her name, like I'm some prepubescent boy instead of a thirty-six-year-old man who has been to hell and back. Right now, I feel like that same shy, fumbling teenager who asked Maryanne to prom, knowing she didn't want me at all. "I'm so sorry. So fucking sorry."

"The ink is dark blue." Her eyes lift to meet mine in the mirror. "Not black."

And that pretty much says it all.

The famous tattoo artist, the supposed inked god, is colorblind.

25

SAVANNAH

A thousand thoughts tumble chaotically through my head.

I hear Owen's broken apology.

I see that his face has gone ashen, like he's caught in the midst of a nightmare.

But none of it is clicking together, not even when I look down at the sensitive, reddened skin around the words *Be Fearlessly Unapologetic*. The script is exactly what I wanted—feminine and dainty and slanted just so—but instead of the words being done in black ink, they're a deep navy blue.

Close, but not quite.

Something is not adding up.

"It's okay," I hear myself say, as though I've been submerged in water and can't catch a single sound. My hand drops to my side, and I deliberately unfurl my fingers so that Owen doesn't mistake my confusion for anger. "I shouldn't have pushed for this. You're clearly exhausted, and, really, I don't mind the blue. It's beautiful."

But instead of responding, Owen twists his big, brawny body and plants his hands on the table I was just sprawled out on. His head falls forward, that thick, black hair of his hanging boyishly over his face as he visibly draws breath into his lungs in such quick succession that concern pierces my heart.

He's the very picture of desolation.

Is he worried about what I might think of him—about the drugs and the fight? Yes, it hurts my heart to know that he felt so alone in his grief. And, yes, it's hard to align the man I know with the vision he painted for me of his twenty-year-old self. Thing is, he was *twenty*. Still practically a child. No matter what *Celebrity Tea Presents* or any other tabloid might say about his past, *I* know that the Owen Harvey standing before me now is the man he was always meant to be.

Kind. Gracious. Humble.

You can't fake those sorts of qualities, not for the long haul.

Moving on silent feet, I reach out and kiss my palm to the broad planes of his back. "It's no big deal," I tell him, my voice hushed since I'm pressed up against his side, though I'm careful not to mess with my still exposed tattoo. "Accidents happen." In an effort to tease him, I slip my hand down his arm, then whisper my fingers over his wrist. "Never fear, Harvey, I'm not going to demand that Frannie give me back my eleven thousand. You're in the clear."

"I'm colorblind, Rose."

I blink. "I'm sorry, I think my ears still might be malfunctioning after undergoing six hours of screaming *Put A Ring On It* fans, because I could have sworn that you just said—"

"I don't see color."

Oh.

Oh, God.

Shoulders slouched, he flexes his hand beneath mine on

the table before stepping out of reach. "I mean," he says, his voice gravel-deep, "I *do* see color. All of it. I just . . . don't see it the way that you do."

I've always been the sort of person to react to crises with very little fanfare—thanks, Dad—but this . . . this . . .

My fingers dart to the very first tattoo Owen gave me—a little bird caught in mid-flight that he placed behind my right ear. As I sat backward on a chair, my hair scraped up into a bun so the strands wouldn't get in the way, I never once thought anything about the man wielding the tattoo machine in his hand, like it was an extension of himself.

I mean, I *thought* about him.

The deepness of his voice. The broad shoulders that I wanted to run my hands over. The aloofness in his black eyes that always sparked in challenge when I engaged him in witty banter.

But I never . . . I never once suspected *this.*

Colorblind.

Owen.

Slowly, with my hand scraping my lower belly as I snag my shirt off the ground, I turn in a small semicircle. I keep my eyes locked on the framed photos of tattoos strung up around the parlor—some of the tats were done by Gage and Jordan and Lizzie, but almost all are by Owen's own hand. While a few are diluted black and white, more than half are color in full bloom.

Reds.

Blues.

Greens.

A single word is torn from my throat: "*How?*"

With stiffness radiating from every inch of his frame, Owen moves toward the portable workstation. Ink bottle clutched in hand, he stares down at it like it's personally betrayed him, tense silence cloaking us both, and then releases a gritty chuckle that doesn't sound at all humorous.

A shiver works its way down my spine.

"Practice," he grinds out, roughly shoving the bottle of ink onto the workstation, between a mauve and emerald green. "Years and years of practice."

"I don't understand. You and Gage are—"

"Fraternal twins."

My chin snaps back in shock. "But y'all look identical. I mean, maybe not *identical.*" Unlike his twin brother, everything about Owen is more potent to me. The sheen of his hair. The structure of his face. The body that is so powerful that standing in his proximity has always made me feel slightly breathless.

"Not identical," Owen tells me, crossing his arms over his burly chest when he plants his ass against the side of the table. His pose is casual, but his expression is nothing less than restless. Black eyes sweep past me, like he can't bear the thought of looking too closely, only to return to my frame intermittently. A tick pulses to life just below his jawline, and then keeps on ticking. "We're the same height, almost the same weight—but none of that is truly indicative of anything. We're not a match. Well, not an exact one, anyway." His mouth curls sardonically. "Which means that, DNA-wise, I can be colorblind while he isn't. Doesn't defy the laws of twinness."

On wobbly legs, I inch closer to him. I want to catch his gaze and make him look at me. Owen and I, we might not be *together* by definition of boyfriend/girlfriend, but that doesn't mean I don't know him well enough to push past his carefully crafted walls. Walls that, if I'm being honest, are taller and thicker than I ever anticipated.

Questions fire at me from every which way, but I stick

It's pure genius. Absolutely innovative. And still, Owen looks like he's on the verge of turning tail and running.

He nods, slowly. Sets the ink bottle back in its place and reaches for the trifold, taking it back from me with an almost embarrassed sense of urgency that cranks up my compassion tenfold.

"Owen," I whisper, "I'm not judging you. Please know that."

His gaze flicks down to my new ink, regret etched in his features. "I fucked it up. I was tired and not thinking straight, and it didn't even occur to me that Gage wouldn't put his black where I set mine." Beneath his breath, he grunts, "Rookie move."

"Rookie move or not, why hide this?" I throw out an arm, pointing at all the examples of his craftsmanship framed on the walls. "You've built up this entire business. Celebrities come here. Locals come here. You're amazing at what you do, Owen. Better than amazing—your work is an experience unto itself. You should be sharing it with the world."

"I *am* sharing it with the world!" Nostrils flaring, he flattens the trifold on the counter with a rough slap of his palm. "I've spent almost ten years sharing it with anyone who walks in those doors."

I stare up at him, noting the tense lines creasing his forehead. He's unraveling, coming undone. Still, I push: "Who knows the truth?"

And just like that, his harsh expression crumples. "Savannah, don't."

I cup his hip, my thumb skirting under his shirt to brush his skin. For our entire relationship, this man has forced me to take a good look in the mirror and accept pieces of myself that I'd rather not. He's called me out on not living up to my dreams and my potential, for staying at ERRG when we both know I'd rather be anywhere else. He does so because he wants to see me happy, and something tells me that keeping this part of himself a secret has more to do with survival and a fear of the inevitable consequences than it does with bringing him any amount of joy.

"Who, Owen."

His hand comes down on mine, gripping my fingers hard. I feel the slight tremble in each digit. Feel, even more, the anxious rush of his breath against the crown of my head. And then, in the lowest, most devastating tone I've ever heard, he answers: "You."

Tears well in the backs of my eyes. I want to hurl myself into his arms. I want to strip his pain or, at the least, take it within myself because my Owen—the cocky, broody man—is nowhere to be found. Vulnerability radiates from every inch of him, and this time, he doesn't release my hand. Not even for a second.

"It started out harmless enough," he says, so softly I have to strain to hear every word coming from his mouth. "I was a quiet kid. Painfully shy. Gage was the boisterous one and I took his lead. It was . . . it was my kindergarten teacher who noticed something, but by then, some of the other kids had started to push me around out in the playground. Typical kid shit. She had my parents come in for a meeting, and they all agreed it would be best if the other students didn't know. Why give them more ammunition to fuck with me than they already had?"

A protest leaps to my tongue. The *right* thing to do would have been to tell the other kids to cut the crap and respect their fellow peer. In the end, I swallow it down. Whether or not I would have taken that route doesn't matter. This was thirty-something years ago and what's done is, unfortunately, well done at this point.

Even so, that doesn't explain why Gage wouldn't be told. They're *twins*, for God's sake. When I vocalize this, Owen only squeezes my hand. "Gage at five is not the Gage of today. Dude couldn't keep his mouth shut for anything. I think my parents knew that—they were trying to protect me, just in case he let it spill to someone else at school."

Incredulity floods my body. "They made you lie about who you are, like—like you should be *ashamed* of yourself!"

Owen's mouth flattens. "I'm not ashamed."

"Then why doesn't Gage know?" I demand.

"Because it got weird, all right? Awkward as fuck. What am I supposed to say? Hey, bro, we're almost thirty-seven and you think that you know everything about me but surprise! I can't tell if your shirt is red or purple or fucking maroon. Good talk, let's grab a beer."

I growl—actually, *growl*—deep in my throat. "Yes. And while you're at it, maybe you can tell the world too. Let them see the real you."

"Not happening, sweetheart." He brushes past me, hands locked on his hips as he starts to pace. "I'm not about to sign myself up to be the next freak show. Either business is gonna dry the hell up because no one will trust me, *or* everyone is going to want to make money off the colorblind tattoo artist."

"You are *not* a freak show."

For the first time since he confessed, his expression softens imperceptibly. "You have no idea how much it means to me for you to say that."

"Well, it's the truth. If anything, I'm in awe of you. Take what you want." I huff a soft laugh under my breath. "It gives that motto an entirely new meaning now that I know this about you. You are the most . . . the most—"

"Stubborn?"

I shake my head, searching for the right words. "I was going to say complex, but I think I'm going to go with something else." Sneaking a glance at the artwork hanging on the walls, and the trifold tucked away on his workstation, it's hard not to feel inspired by the greatness of the man before me. People always advise making lemonade out of lemons, but it's as though Owen has dominated the market and forced everyone else out of the lemonade-making business. Conceding defeat has clearly never been an option for him.

"I don't agree with you keeping your color-blindness a secret and I really think you should reconsider, at least with Gage, but that doesn't mean you aren't the most driven person I've ever met. Learning how to tattoo couldn't have been easy, and yet you've done it anyway. You took what you wanted, you made it yours, and you're living out your dream every day, despite probably feeling like the world is waiting for you to fail." I shake my head. "Is there anything you can't do once you put your mind to it?"

Rocking back on his heels, Owen rubs the nape of his neck. Then, gruffly, he admits, "I'm shit at interior design. It's painful in a way that tattooing never is, even at its worst. But when I bought Inked, I decided, what the hell. Who's gonna really complain about mismatched furniture when the drunkest street on earth is down a flight of stairs? Bourbon cures all."

My heart kicks into overdrive as a realization sets in. "The rental units upstairs," I manage to get out, "that's why you wouldn't sell to us for the hotel."

Black eyes zero in on my face. "I didn't lie, Rose. They make me a fuck ton of money as they are, but . . . yeah. I guess, if we're digging a little deeper, then they hold sentimental value, too. They're the first units I ever overhauled on my own. All my life, I've tried to push back and find ways the computer so he can get a good look at the email. His mouth is straight up gaping open by the time he finishes reading. "She dumped me."

He says it like the thought alone is completely unfathomable, and I swallow a laugh. "Probably serves you right—you gave her our email, you douchebag. What? Your number wasn't good enough?"

"It wasn't like that."

"Sure it wasn't."

"I was hoping it would make me look like I'm a catch. You know, *Hey, here's my email. Oh, look! I'm employed even though I have the humor of a teenager and just moved out of my parents' house!*"

I blink, then find myself asking, "You just moved out of your parents'? Seriously?"

Jordan hooks a finger under the collar of his T-shirt, his expression strained. "It's perfectly normal for my generation. Studies show that millennials are often living at home longer than previous generations. Student loans are a bitch."

"You didn't go to college."

"Dammit, man, why am I gonna live in a shoebox when I can live in a mansion?"

"But you don't live in a mansion. I've seen your place—your *parents'* place—which now makes so much sense. What almost thirty-year-old man regularly sets his porcelain China out in the dining room like he's prepared for a dinner party at all times? I didn't want to say anything but you had me worried."

"Bite me, Harvey."

I hold my hands up. "Do I need to put on my Dr. Phil hat again? Like last time, when you were trying to decide between buying a motorcycle or a car and it took you six months to figure out your life?"

"No comment," Jordan clips out.

"I'd do it for free, but I'm worried I'd just be enabling you even more. Poor Jane." I cluck my tongue, not even feeling the least bit bad about giving my buddy hell. Turnaround is fair play, and all that. "Is that what happened? Did she wake up one morning, only to find Mama Knight collecting her underthings off your bedroom floor?"

"I seriously hate you."

I cock a brow. "Are you quitting? Am I finally free?"

Jordan's fist collides halfheartedly with my shoulder, and I throw back my head with a bark of laughter. Moving the mouse, I delete Jane's email. "No more handing out Inked's info so you can feel better about your life."

"Yes, Mom."

I flash him the bird, then return to sorting through Inked on Bourbon's inbox. Most days, it's a mixture of junk and clients seeking appointments, but ever since *Celebrity Tea Presents* put Savannah and me on blast last week—along with all of my dirty laundry—we've been slammed with media requests too.

There's not a chance in hell that I'm putting myself out there like that.

In rapid succession, I delete interview requests from *Life & Style, In Touch,* and *The National Enquirer*. Every day is more of the same, and not for the first time, I catch myself wondering how much longer this can possibly go on for.

Unlike what a lot of these reporters seem to think, I'm not interested in capitalizing on my newfound "fame" by revamping my lifestyle into that of a social media influencer. I've made it a personal ambition to always look for new ways to prove to myself that having Deuteranopia—or being

"America's Sweetheart Can Do No Wrong Except When It Comes to Picking a Man."

"Boring or Self-Absorbed: We're Diving Deep to Understand Why Choosing Savannah Rose as Put A Ring On It's *First Bachelorette Was the Wrong Move for the Show."*

"Will Savannah Rose Ever Find Love? Or Will She Sabotage Her Own Chances By Friend-Zoning Every Man She's Met? New Source Reveals Insight into A Younger Savannah . . . And How Not Much Has Changed Since High School."

And then one uploaded from *Celebrity Tea Presents* just this morning: *"Recapping Last Night's* Put A Ring On It *episode: How One Date With Savannah Rose Led to This Contestant Walking off the Set."*

I don't click on any of it.

Can't, not without losing my temper.

Savannah doesn't deserve this. No one does, but hell, Savannah deserves it the least among everyone that I know. She is so damn good—down to her core—and to see her being ripped apart online because of her love life seriously makes me see red.

Or not red.

A brownish hue.

Doesn't matter.

What matters is that not a single one of these news sources have bothered to comment on how much of a badass she is. Whether she likes her job or not, she manages ERRG like a boss. She's the first female vice president the company has ever seen—something *The New Orleans Daily* reported on last month—and she's done it all so competently, so seamlessly, that watching her in her element is like watching an Olympian perform.

She kills it, each and every time, and yet none of those accomplishments have ever hit the tabloids.

Instead, she's been stripped down to the basics: her looks, her TV persona, and whether or not she's successful in bagging a man.

Hands balling into a fist, I force myself to take a deep breath before I pick up my phone and pull up her contact. I fire off a single text:

How do you feel about doing something crazy? Just you and me?

27

SAVANNAH

Seated on my front-porch swing, I watch the street for Owen's truck.

When I said yes (rather enthusiastically, I might add) to doing something crazy with him, he didn't give me anything more than the basics: wear a bathing suit, bring sunscreen, don't bring the harbinger of death.

Pretty sure he meant Pablo by the last one.

Currently, the little furry demon is sitting in my bay window, pawing the glass like we've been separated for decades instead of a whopping five minutes. Trying not to draw attention to the fact that I'm seeking him out, I slide a surreptitious glance his way, and yup, there he is.

One paw pressed to the windowpane, his little mouth popping open wide in a soundless *meow*.

I shake my head. "You can't come with me, Pabs."

When his paw slides down the glass in the most pitiful, slow-motion glide that there ever was, regret pierces me right in the gut. Considering that I take the little guy almost everywhere, I know he's ticked at being cooped up while I have fun without him.

Owen was right: I am the very definition of a cat lady.

I steel my spine against Pablo's begging blue eyes. "We're going swimming," I tell him, even though he can't 1) hear me, and 2) understand a lick of what I'm saying. "And you don't do water."

He tilts his little cat head to the side, whiskers flicking, as though to say, *I do whatever I want, and get me out of this house.*

Dammit.

Owen is going to kill me for this.

Hooking my purse strap over my shoulder, I fumble for my keys and then insert them in the lock. All it takes is the creak of the door opening for Pablo to fly off the cushioned window seat like he's Superman in training. Ignoring the chance to escape into the wide-open world, he hightails it after me.

I give him a firm side-eye as I head down the length of my traditionally shotgun-styled house for the master bedroom. "If you scratch him, your feather toys will be thrown in the trash."

Pablo meows and slinks between my legs.

"In fact, be prepared to say *sayonara* to the mouse squeaker too."

My cat's only response is to pounce on one of the stray plastic bottle caps that I keep around the house because he adores them so much.

Figures.

My Carrollton neighborhood shotgun dates back to the 1870s. It's modestly sized, artfully decorated—thanks to me—and has approximately *zero* closet space. Old houses, you have to love them. Opening the only closet door in my home, I stand on my toes and grasp the cat backpack from the top shelf.

The pet carrier. Pablo. The fact that I agreed to this outing in the first place.

I stare at the selection of paddleboards propped up against the shed that belongs to City Park's Watersports. There are blue paddleboards and red paddleboards and even a pink one, but really, the only thing to say is: "Of all the crazy things to do in N'Orleans, *this* is what you decided on?"

Beside me, Owen links his bulky, tattooed arms over his hard chest. *Damn the man for being so good-looking.* It's incredibly unfair, honestly.

Looking a little too smug for my liking, he bumps his hip with mine. "Just lookin' to get you out of your comfort zone, sweetheart."

"Do you not remember our conversation about me lacking all athletic abilities?"

"Oh, I remember."

"You're evil, you know that?" I toe one of the paddleboards with my shoe and it slips out of sync with the rest. "I'm going to wipe out, which means that there's a good chance Pablo and I are both going to drown before the day is over." I pause, feeling my cat resettling himself in the backpack. "Wait, is this all part of your grand plan for vengeance? Pablo tries to steal one of your nuts and you decide that—"

"*Anddd*, I'm gonna stop you right there." Stepping behind me, Owen slips his thumbs under the padded straps. His beard tickles my cheek as he leans in close, his presence solid and warm at my back. "You know, maybe this cat thing isn't so bad. Look how close I can get to you without him trying to—how'd you put it?—steal one of my *nuts*."

"Are you making fun of me?" I ask, just barely resisting

the urge to relax into his chest. "Because if so, I take exception."

"You really, really should. This pet carrier is a goddamn eyesore."

The backpack stirs, like Pablo has taken exception to Owen's close proximity. "It's fashionable," I protest weakly.

"Rose, you look like you've got the planetarium on speed dial. Tell me, is your idea of a fun Friday night cuddling with the antichrist while watching *Ancient Aliens*?"

I snort under my breath. "Nothing wrong with outer space, Harvey. A dream of mine has always been to see the Northern Lights."

"My eyes might make it a bit difficult to see all that," he murmurs, one hand falling to my hip and squeezing, "but I'm down to make the trip with you . . . if that's ever up for consideration."

Giddiness slips through me at the prospect of us vacationing together someday. I think of us strolling through the airport, luggage rolling beside us, as we grin at each other. I think of him curled behind me in some hotel bed, his arm looped around my waist, my body cradled by his. And then I let myself visualize the moment when we're standing beneath a foreign sky, our fingers intertwined, our heads tipped back as we wait for the aurora borealis.

My eyes might make it a bit difficult to see all that.

Instant regret slams into me. Dammit, dammit, *dammit.*

Feeling my stomach lurch, I turn my head, just far enough so I can glance up at his face. His features are relaxed, as though he's unbothered by my obvious faux paus, but still . . . Guilt sits heavy, like curdled milk, in my stomach. "The Northern Lights are green and purple. Oh, God, Owen, I'm so sorry. I didn't even think—"

He cut me off with a kiss to the top of my head. "It's an

experience I wouldn't want to miss. I'd get to see your face when you look up at the sky—it's enough for me."

My lips feel parched. Seeking reprieve, I run my tongue along the roof of my mouth. It doesn't help. Probably cosmic karma for speaking without consideration first. "You . . . you are a good man, Owen Harvey."

"That good, huh?"

"Don't let the compliment go to your head."

"Definitely too late for that." I feel his hot breath on the back of my neck, just as the pressure of the backpack straps eases off my shoulders. Whirling around, I watch in surprise as he gently slings the pet carrier across his back. When he catches me openly staring, slack-jawed, he rolls his eyes. "Don't make this out to be more than it is. Chances are, you're gonna wipe out. We can't have Pablo going down with you."

"You're bonding," I whisper dramatically, going so far as to press my palm to my heart. "I can't believe this is really happening."

Owen's mouth twists in a frown. "We are *not* bonding."

"It warms my heart. It really, really does."

"Rose," he mutters, in warning.

"Wait!" I throw up a hand. "I need a picture. Don't move!"

"Savannah, if you take your phone out, I can't be held responsible for what I—"

Hands looped around the backpack straps, a scowl tugging at his lips, that baseball cap on his head—Owen looks flustered and irritated, and with Pablo glaring at me from his little space-capsule window, I snap a picture of them both. What a pair. For real, a total match made in heaven.

"—do," Owen finishes, biting out the words.

I check the image, then nod to myself in satisfaction as I pocket my phone in my purse. "One step at a time. You'll grow to love each other at some point. Preferably in this lifetime."

A moment of silence, and then, "Savannah?"

I glance back at Owen over my shoulder. "Yes?"

"You better ditch those shorts before I do it for you."

Stifling a laugh, I bite my bottom lip, solely to tease him. "Is that a promise?"

He growls deep in his throat, and, knowing not to push his restraint any further, I do as he commands and push my shorts down the length of my legs. I stuff them into my over-the-shoulder purse but choose to leave my tank top on. Turning, I hold out the bag to Owen, kicking my chin toward it. "Want to add anything before I put it in the locker?"

"Yeah, hold on." Setting Pablo down, Owen grasps the nape of his T-shirt in that sexy way that men seem to know will incite a woman into losing her clothes, along with all of her sensible decision-making skills. Seriously, do they learn that move as children? Is it taught in Sex-Ed classes, with the tagline: *How To Make Women Hot And Bothered?* Whatever the case is, my heart positively flutters as every inch of Owen's naked chest makes an appearance, inch by excruciating inch.

First the angel-wing tattoo, then all those ridged abs, and, finally, his tatted, hard-as-stone chest.

It is a certifiable *crime* that he's expecting me to put myself on a paddleboard instead of dropping to my knees and putting my tongue to work.

The white T is shoved into the depths of my bag, just as Owen releases a deep, masculine chuckle. "You keep eye-fuckin' me like that, and it'll be a miracle if you last ten seconds on that board."

"I still think you're playing dirty by bringing me here."

Big hands grasp the hem of my tank top and reel me in with slow, seductive intent. Dropping his head, his mouth finds mine for a hot kiss that has me straining on my toes to get even closer. He pulls back, just enough to graze his lips over mine again, before murmuring, "With any luck, you'll be wet all day and won't mind at all."

My mouth falls open at the blatant sexual innuendo.

"You did *not* just make a joke about—"

"Pick a paddleboard, Rose," he says, all sunshine and happy rainbows as he winks at me, "any paddleboard. And give me one, too. Time to get the antichrist into position."

Because I have all the revenge tactics of an eleven-year-old girl, I select the pink one for him and fake a neutral expression when he takes it from me. But, beyond an arched brow on his part, Owen doesn't comment on my choice for him. Instead, he drops to his haunches, clearly being careful not to disturb Pablo, and then wraps a black strap around his ankle that's also attached to the board. From there, he drops the paddleboard into the bayou, a scant foot over from us, and somehow slips his massive frame onto the pink surface without wobbling all over the place.

His balance is perfect, his instinct for how to position himself right on par, and it's pretty obvious that this is not his first rodeo.

From his back, Pablo watches me with a gleam in his sharp, blue eyes that would worry me if he actually had access to Owen's junk for round two.

Time to make the magic happen.

After grabbing my own board from the lineup of rentals, I try to follow Owen's experienced lead. Black strap around my ankle. Paddleboard in the murky water. I don't bother asking if there are gators in here because I already know the answer is yes.

All the better to not end up face-first in the shallow water.

Still on my knees, my stomach muscles clench as the gentle waves push the board up, and I try to hold on tight to the sides. I can do this. I can absolutely do this.

One foot up, right? Then the other?

All or nothing.

"Savannah," Owen says as I struggle to plant one foot down and gain enough traction to do the same with the other, "take it easy. You don't need to—oh, shit."

It's the last thing I hear before my weight teeters to the side and my knee, already wet from the water seeping onto the board, slips left, and then I'm going down, down, down. Down in a flurry of wet legs, a waterlogged shout that gets caught in my throat, and with the sudden realization that my bikini and tank top are all white, white, and you guessed it, white.

It's a damn good day to be me.

28

OWEN

Here's the thing: the waters where we're paddleboarding don't even reach my waist.

Which means that when Savannah topples off the side of her board with all the grace of a gazelle caught in an ice storm, I do the ungentlemanly thing—I laugh.

I laugh so hard that, when she bobs to the surface with moss stuck to her hair and her face dripping wet with a look of abject misery, it's all I can do to keep me and Pablo from meeting the same fate.

The fact that I have a cat strapped to my back in an astronaut-themed pet carrier has made this day unique all on its own, but watching Savannah Rose—Miss Heiress, Miss America's Sweetheart, Miss Prim and Proper Debutante—find herself submerged in the shallow bayou, has tipped the scales of my good mood to OVERLOAD.

"Please stop laughing," she growls as she grasps her paddle from where it's floating away. "Forget about me owing you after this—sir, you will owe *me* for life."

I'm counting on it.

Paddle gripped in hand, I rearrange my weight on the

board so I can head in her direction. "Would you look at that," I drawl, a real fake Southern accent kicking in, "she's wet already."

Her usually warm eyes narrow to slits as she hurls herself onto the board like a beached whale. "Wearing all white," she mutters glumly, "was a mistake."

Damn.

Sometimes, white is a tricky color for me. In certain light, I see it clearly—or, at least, as everyone else sees it, I'd assume. And, hell, it's definitely the easiest to pinpoint when I'm looking at my trifold color chart, if I even need it then. But once in a while, depending on the exact hue and the surrounding environment, white can be a deceiving bastard too. Like right now, with a slight gray cast to her tank top and bikini, the subtext beneath Savannah's words doesn't carry the same weight for me as it would for the next guy.

That's fine.

I'll just strip them both off her later. Naked is better than clothed any day of the week, in my book.

Finally close to her, I tap my paddle against the side of her board. "Climb on up, sweetheart. You can do it."

"I like when you call me that."

Mouth curling in a small grin, I ask, "Sweetheart?"

"Yes." She curls her legs beneath her, so that she's on all fours. Her tank top is plastered to her upper body, clinging to her shoulders and trim waist and leaving her bikini bottoms exposed to my gaze. "Honestly, I should hate it, since every tabloid under the sun has taken to calling me that. It's sweetheart this and sweetheart that, and it feels patronizing coming from them, but you . . ." The board leans to the left as she plants a shaky foot down and *slowwwwly* stands up. "You make it sound intimate, like anytime it slips her arms a little faster, driving the board forward with more momentum. I match her pace easily, drifting along beside her. "When we hit the tarmac, I knew there was no going back to the way things were before *Put A Ring On It*. I guess I just didn't realize how much of me would be caught in the upheaval. Before the show, I knew who I was—maybe there were things I'd like to change or improve, but I was still *me* and I felt confident in all that."

I drag my gaze over her damp hair and her drying tank top and the curve of her ass. "And now?" I ask, huskily.

"Now?" She pulls the paddle out of the bayou, holding it parallel with her hips. Water drips onto the board, but instead of worrying about it, she simply coasts along. "Now I feel like I don't know who I am at all. Am I the VP of ERRG, the woman who handles everything and doesn't take crap from anyone? Am I the bachelorette, the girl who flirted and simpered accordingly, whenever the producers gave me the signal to amp up my game—even when it made my skin crawl? Or am I the woman whose character is being smeared across the internet, and all because the world can't align the real me with the version that *they* want to be true?" Her mouth tugs downward, as though she's thinking hard on something, and then, softly, she says, "I made the mistake of going online last night and searching my name. Wrong move."

My throat tightens. From what I briefly saw earlier, during my own internet search, I can't imagine she found anything worth seeing. Nothing that wouldn't break her spirit, anyway. "Sav, whatever they're saying, it's not a reflection of *you*. The authentic you, the you that everyone who knows you personally adores."

Just like I adore you.

Adore. The word seems paltry in the face of the

emotions squeezing my lungs. Emotions that are honestly making it hard for me to remember that I have her goddamn cat strapped to my back, and that I can't just dive into the water and swim over to her. I hate seeing the frustration harden her features, hate hearing the disappointment in her voice over other people's lackluster opinion of her, and I don't know . . .

Hell, I don't know if it's really just adoration that I'm feeling or something else entirely.

Maybe even love.

I know that I love Gage. I know that I loved my parents.

But the love for a woman is something entirely different. It wrecked my parents to the literal point of no return, but even knowing the possibility of a destructive outcome doesn't stop me from thinking that if love is the jagged emotion clawing at my chest, wanting to knock the lights out of every person who's made Savannah feel less than, then I'm too fucking late to turn my ass back around and head in the other direction anyway.

Savannah and I have been at opposite ends of a string for so long, that, now that we're all tangled up, it's impossible to even consider winding my way back out.

I wasn't lying when I said this thing between us could never be just a one-night-stand.

I want tomorrow too, and the tomorrow after that, and all the hundreds of tomorrows that trail in their wake.

Voice hushed, Savannah says, "Someone created a fake Instagram profile of me. The pictures are mostly stills from the show, but the captions are disgusting, the comments even more so. Obviously, I reported the page as soon as I saw it, but I spent the entire night thinking about how not a single soul stood up to defend me in the hundreds of comments." Her gaze lands on my face. "It made me realize and that it's not only my hand jerking him off, but now his too.

His breathing comes in harsh, shallow pants that have me squirming with desire in my seat.

It's broad daylight and though the windows are tinted, they aren't *that* dark. Not dark enough to hide the fact that Owen's head is thrown back against the headrest or that his chest is rising with each ragged inhalation or—and especially this—that this feels absolutely crazy but so right all at once.

I'm a thirty-five-year-old woman giving a man a hand job in the front seat of his truck—I didn't even pull these sorts of wild stunts back in college . . . or ever.

Owen's calloused palm tightens around my hand, silently urging me to pick up speed. My gaze darts to his face, taking him in, and *oh, God*. He is, hands down, the sexiest thing I've ever seen. Veins popping in his throat, white teeth digging into his bottom lip, black eyes hooded and trained on me—on my mouth.

I whisper his name, plaintive and needy, and match his pace, moving our fists faster as his pupils dilate, and a sweep of color warms his cheeks.

He groans, deep in his throat. "Fuck, sweetheart, I'm gonna come."

I don't allow myself time to think. Hastily, I rearrange my body, aware of the gear shift digging into my side, and swipe my tongue over the crown of his cock. His free hand flies to the back of my head, and words are tripping off his tongue—endearments, too—but they're lost to the roar of blood rushing through my head and the sudden realization this might be the single most erotic, spontaneous hookup session of my entire life.

I swirl my tongue over his pierced head, all the while

wholly aware that Owen is fucking my mouth just as we are, together, fucking his cock with our hands. It's a heady thought, completely lewd and brazen, and I'm so turned on that all my concerns and worries from the last week take a hike as though I've flipped a switch.

"Shit," he whispers harshly, "Rose, if you don't want—"

I tighten my grip, sucking him in a little deeper, and he comes with his hips flexing off the seat and that hand in my hair twisting through the strands to keep me close. I squeeze my eyes shut, swallowing every drop of him, and only slow the pumps of my hand when I hear him breathe out, "Sav . . . your cat is watching us."

My head jerks up, and sure enough, Pablo is staring back at me like I've just done him dirty.

"Oh, my God, we've scarred him," I whisper.

Owen combs his fingers through my hair, his thumb grazing the tattooed bird behind my ear. "He had to learn about the birds and the bees at some point."

"He's three!"

"What is that? Twenty-one in cat years?" Owen's entire body shakes with deep laughter. "After what he just saw, Pablo might have to see a cat therapist. You think he'd go to Satan for a session?"

The fact that Owen is having the time of his life with this shows me all that I need to know: life with Owen Harvey would always be an adventure, and it would always be fun, even if "fun" entails discussing much-needed therapy for my cat after he just watched me give Owen a hand job.

Some things, you just can't make up.

Pulling back, I grab my bag off the floor, pop a kiss on Owen's cheek, and throw open the passenger-side door—but not before nabbing the keys from the ignition. "Catch me if you can, Harvey, and we'll finish off somewhere that Pablo can't play voyeur."

I'm out of the truck and hitting the steps up to the second-floor entrance, all in the span of a heartbeat. I hear Owen's muttered curse and Pablo's annoyed *meow*, probably as Owen tries to grab him, and then the telltale *thwack-thwack-thwack* of my flip-flops hitting the wooden rungs. Fumbling with the keys, I try one, then another, in the lock.

Third time is a charm.

As soon as I'm in the house, I kick my sandals to the side. Fling my bikini top onto the floor. It lands on the slate tile with a wet slapping sound. My bottoms are halfway down my thighs when the sound of my phone going off snaps my attention toward the direction of my discarded purse.

Dammit.

I don't want to answer but it might be Amelie or, potentially, another emergency. I answer without looking at the Caller ID.

"Hello?" I ask breathlessly as I wriggle my damp bottoms down my calves.

"Savannah, hey."

My back snaps straight at the familiar voice—a voice I haven't heard in months. *Dominic DaSilva.* He'd reached out to me over email around the time that I returned to New Orleans, wanting my input for an article he planned to write about how the paparazzi were hounding him and his new girlfriend, Aspen, and her son. I gave him my blessing, then. If he'd asked me in the last two weeks, I would have given it to him ten times over. "Oh! Dom. I didn't expect you to call."

Behind me, the front door slams shut, and I turn, my past in my ear with my present and future closing the distance between us. Pablo scurries off to do whatever cat things it is that he does, but my sole focus is concentrated on the Prince of Darkness. He strips off his T-shirt. Throws it to the side with a confident flick of his wrist. Inked fingers descend to the waistband of his board shorts, but instead of pushing them down over his hips, he flashes me a predatory grin that has me clutching my phone tighter.

I'm wet.

Truly, truly wet.

In my ear, Dominic keeps talking: "I know. Sorry, this is probably bad timing. You might be busy."

Black eyes flit to my phone, and oh boy, I do *not* like the look on his face right now.

Strutting toward me with all the grace of a panther on the hunt, Owen doesn't stop until he's all up in my space and his hands are on my ass and his mouth is—*Oh. My. God*—closing around one of my nipples.

The man knows it won't be possible for me to carry on a conversation when he's doing *that*, but he squeezes my butt anyway, like he's challenging me to go ahead and give it a try.

I'm going to kill him—but not before he makes me come.

Priorities.

"No!" I exclaim to Dominic. "No, of course not. Not busy at all."

Owen's teeth scrape my nipple, tugging the bud sharply into his warm mouth. My knees threaten to give out, and it's a complete miracle that I manage to pull myself together at all to listen to my sort-of ex-boyfriend on the phone.

"Are you sure?" he asks. "You sound like . . ."

Think, Rose, think! Inspiration strikes with a classic, age-old excuse. "I'm on the treadmill!" The words fly out of me just as Owen sinks down to his knees, putting him at eye me come while your cat played Peeping Tom."

"I didn't know!" Biting down on my lip, I swivel my hips, begging for more pressure, for more of that sharp-edged dominance that he loves to dole out the minute we get naked. "He's peculiar."

Owen's finger glides down, dragging through my wetness. "He's yours," he says simply, before using the tip of his finger to pump ever-so-gently into my heat. It's a tease, not nearly close to satisfying, but I play the game willingly.

Between us, there's no such thing as losing.

Owen's finger plunges deep, just as his thumb grazes my clit. It's an overload of sensation all at once, and I bite back a cry as I sink my hips down. The muscles in his arm tighten around my leg, keeping me still as he fucks me with his finger. It feels good, it feels *wonderful*, and when he takes it one step further by replacing his thumb with his tongue, I'm all but done for.

Yes, yes, yes.

I stare down at him, this big, brawny man dropped to his knees before me, and it's enough to turn my desire for him into an inferno. The last time I was in this house, I didn't know all there was to know about him, but I do now.

The two of us, we're stripped down to the studs.

Raw.

Vulnerable.

And it's for that reason alone that I feel no hint of shame when I beg, "I want to feel you, too. *Please*."

His swirling tongue stops, just for a second, as he looks up at me with an emotion in his gaze that I can't quite read. "I got the place a bed."

It's all he says but I nod, eagerly. "Lead the way."

Trust Owen to do things his own way, though. He stands tall, all powerful lines and rippling ink, just as he hooks an arm behind my legs and another around my waist. He cradles me to his chest like I'm a bride, his most prized possession—but his face is all harsh lines and masculine hunger.

He turns us sideways as we enter the hall, careful not to bang my head on the walls, then takes the second door on the right. Light from the bare windows trickles in, startling in its brightness, and it takes me a moment to fully grasp what I'm seeing.

A king-sized bed backed up against the far wall.

A pale green rug rests beneath it, soft and inviting.

A white dresser sits opposite them both, sleek and glossy with brass hardware.

Twin nightstands bracket the bed, their color a more rustic off-white that's not an exact match for the other pieces of furniture.

Tears burn behind my eyes. The design isn't harmonious, and it certainly doesn't go with the furniture in the living room, but when I glance up and cup Owen's bearded jaw, I find that I don't care in the least. For once, my HGTV-loving soul is quiet of all critiques. "You decorated the room," I whisper.

He nods curtly, his eyes a little hesitant when they meet mine. "Expedited it all last week after you left. I hope . . . I hope you like it." He visibly swallows, then cuts his gaze from mine. "If you don't, it's easy enough to fix. Doesn't matter one way or the other. It's all replaceable."

Oh, Owen.

My heart beats a little faster as I grasp the back of his neck and shift myself up in his arms to kiss his neck then the underside of his chin. "I love it."

His mouth parts with a hitched breath. "Don't lie, Rose. I can take the truth."

Another moan reverberates in my chest as I coil the sheet in my hand.

If having him take me on all fours was heaven, then this is somehow better. I'm stretched open, splayed wide to his ministrations. His hand grips my waist, tight and possessive. I lean my head back into the cradle of his left arm, which is propping my head up, turning just so in a silent request for a kiss.

He gives it to me without question, driving his tongue into my mouth. The kiss is messy and desperate and when his hand slips down my stomach to find my clit, it's his mouth that captures my cry, his cock that captures the spasm of my core.

"Please," I whisper, pulling back long enough to let the word slip past my lips. "*Please.*"

Owen's thrusts turn hard, his hips pistoning into mine, two of his fingers circling my clit, and it's too much all at once. Too much pleasure. Too much sensation. Too much *Owen*. My orgasm splinters through me, dividing and conquering, and the man surrounding me only chuckles, low and raspy, before angling his hips to hit me deeper.

He comes with a groan, his hips still slamming into me, the sounds of sex percolating in the room.

It's only when our heart rates have slowed that Owen lifts his head, takes a look around, and announces, "Good news: we've fulfilled your wish. The comforter is on the floor."

I whisper my fingers over his forearm, which is still wrapped around my waist. "Is there bad news?"

I feel him kiss the soft skin behind my ear, right over my bird tattoo. "Just that I don't think I was bad enough for you—you got me a little sentimental—which means we're gonna have to redo everything, unfortunately. Comforter is going back into place. My shorts gotta come back on. We'll start from the top. Count this round as a dress rehearsal."

I giggle—actually, *giggle*—at the smugness in his voice. "Is that so?"

"Yeah," he rasps, "it is so."

"Well, then."

He licks the shell of my ear, the *one* place he knows where I'm ticklish, and then tucks his feet around mine before I can thrash against him. "For the record, I'm pretty sure my neighbor caught you jacking me off in the truck, which means the next neighborhood crawfish boil is bound to be interesting."

Laughter bubbles up out of me. "Good thing you'll be going on your own, then."

Owen rolls over on top of me, pressing my back into the mattress. His nose grazes mine as he pins me to the bed with his hands and feet. "Correction, sweetheart, it's a good thing you'll be goin' as my date so you can take full responsibility for your actions."

I raise my brows. "What a taskmaster, you are."

He grins, a wide, happy smile that fills my heart with joy. "I know," he murmurs, brushing his mouth over mine in an indulgent kiss, "I let the entire city of N'Orleans down by dropping out of the police academy. Just think about what I would have looked like in my uniform."

"You could borrow Gage's."

"Good plan. How about I get some practice in now?" Mischief gleams in Owen's gaze as he stares down at me. "You've been a naughty, naughty girl, Miss Rose . . ."

I don't hear the rest of what he says—I'm laughing too hard, holding onto him a little too tightly, and loving life in a way that I never have before.

menu. But, honestly, you can't go wrong. The Rockefeller oysters? Delicious. The crawfish-stuffed fried shrimp? Mouth-wateringly good. And don't even get me started on the boudin balls—they come with this jalapeño-cheddar stuffing that I would eat every single day if I could."

With the lights turned down to set the atmosphere, it's tough for me to make out everything. The color of Savannah's dress melds with the hue of her hair, and my brother's suit and tie combo appear to be a wash of a singular shade, giving his head a bit of a floating appearance. The Headless Horseman effect in the middle of July.

Good times.

Clearing my throat, I grab the leather-bound menu and slide it open with my thumb. Savannah wasn't wrong—everything sounds great. And, honestly, it makes me wonder if the new ERRG hotel opening next door to Inked will end up having a restaurant like this one. Best to hope not, since I'd probably find myself heading over there for lunch and dinner, maybe both.

When the server comes around to take our drink and appetizer order, we settle on a bottle of red wine for the table and a virgin margarita for Lizzie. The wine comes a few minutes later, and no surprise there, it looks brown.

My version of red.

I drain half from my glass and try to rule with my head and not my heart. I'm nervous as fuck, yeah, but Savannah is right: Gage is my brother, my only family, and he's not going to judge me for something that I can't change.

And even if I could miraculously fix my vision now, at the age of thirty-six, I'm not sure that I would. A decade ago, my answer probably would have been different, I'm sure, with a resounding *hell yes* loud enough so all the folks in the back of the room could hear me. If I weren't colorblind, I wouldn't have had to teach myself everything I know about tattooing; I could have trusted people to have my back instead of looking at me as a lawsuit in the making if they took me on.

Then again, would I have been so determined to succeed—to be better than everyone else—had I been just *like* everyone else? I'm not so sure that would have been the case, and I'm not willing to rewrite history and give it a go.

Like I told Savannah, there is never a sliding scale when it comes to memories or life experiences. And with things as are they are now, I would never risk all that I've gained for the chance at *what if*.

The appetizers come, and the four of us pounce on them like it's the last supper. The boudin balls *are* orgasmic, and I go for a fried, green tomato with so much vigor, I nearly scald my tongue.

"It's delicious," I tell Savannah, once they've taken away our empty appetizer plates. "Seriously, I've never tasted anything better."

She reaches out across the table, breaking Debutante Protocol, I'm sure, to grip my hand in hers. A satisfied smile curls her lips. "Thank you. This is the menu that Dufrene—he's the chef who made the crawfish dumplings that you tried—and I have worked on the hardest. When a restaurant is 131 years old, it's hard to keep it modern while still maintaining a sense of heritage and tradition."

I stare at her, aware that Gage and Lizzie are listening in, but unable to stop myself from murmuring, "You love it."

She lifts one bare shoulder, and there's just enough light for me to tell that she's wearing some sort of lotion. It glows with a subtle sheen, making her skin look dewy. "I do." For a moment, she drops her gaze to the table before looking at me again. "I used to love being in the restaurants, especially this one. Rose & Thorn has always been my favorite. You can *feel* the history when you walk in. Upstairs, in one of the old offices, we have menus going as far back as 1922. *1922!*" Her eyes brighten with unrestrained excitement. "Back in high school, I spent a single month organizing all of them. I wanted to put them on display, somewhere that patrons could stop by and see them too. I-I felt so much pride, so much happiness, at knowing I was making someone's day a little better by stopping by and telling them our story. The Rose story, I mean."

"And you stopped telling that story?" I prod, digging for more information.

"The pitfalls of climbing the corporate ladder, I guess. I spend more time behind my desk than mingling with guests nowadays."

I squeeze her hand. "Then maybe you need to get back to what makes *you* happy. Watching you, listening to you just now—this place has your passion. It might not be your only passion, but it clearly has it still in spades."

A contemplative look sweeps over her face before the servers come back around with our entrees. We feast like kings, and my waistband protests every step of the way. By the time we're done, and Lizzie is commenting on how she can't afford to outgrow her current maternity clothes so close to the birth, we look like stuffed turkeys ready for Thanksgiving dinner.

"Chloe told me you were here, but I didn't believe her."

I start at the heavy masculine voice booming from behind me, then watch as a guy wearing a chef's coat dips low to kiss Savannah's cheek. I mostly remember his face from when I burst into ERRG's conference room, and when he turns my way, it's clear he's recalling the same moment.

He sticks out a hand. "Harvey, right? The one who made Savannah blush."

The woman in question darts out an arm to punch the chef in the side. "Dufrene, don't embarrass me."

"Can't have that," he says, grinning, "or you'd fire me and this whole enterprise would come crumbling down. ERRG wouldn't survive without me." His gaze sweeps over the rest of the table, stopping on Gage. "Jesus, there are two of you."

Gage throws his head back at that, sticking out a hand for the chef to shake. "Gage. I'm the better-looking one."

Dufrene's expression doesn't even budge. "I'd dispute that but y'all don't have the necessary downstairs equipment for me to be making those sorts of judgment calls." He turns to Lizzie. "I'm assuming you belong to the alleged better-looking twin?"

Lizzie's smile is all female satisfaction. "I think it's safe to say that he belongs to me."

Gage reaches for her hand. "Damn right I do."

Standing up, Savannah pushes her chair back. She cuts a sharp glance my way, and my heart—lulled by the good wine and the even better tasting food—trips over itself. Guess that means it's show time. "Dufrene, care to give Lizzie and me a tour of the Hummingbird Room?" To Lizzie, she adds, "You'll love it. Rose & Thorn has twelve dining rooms in total, not including this one, but the Hummingbird Room is my absolute favorite. When news of D-Day hit N'Orleans, my grandfather decided to close its doors in commemoration of the fallen soldiers. We haven't used it since, so it's a bit of a walk back in time. Everything is exactly the same as it was then, from the utensils set on the table to the crystal ware."

I note Gage's brows shooting up with interest. "I'd love to see that. I'm a huge military history buff."

easy enough to come out with the words: I. Am. Colorblind. Specifically, I've got a rather severe case of Deuteranopia. It fucks with my sight. Makes me see things differently.

That's what I *should* say.

But it isn't what exits my mouth: "When we were kids, we used to play with toy fire trucks. Remember them?"

Gage locks one forearm down on the table, the other planted on his knee. "Dad hated that we didn't want to use the police car ones he bought us, which made Mom laugh so hard that I used to think she might pee herself."

"Yeah." My smile is small, unsure. "Whenever you'd take them to a friend's house, I used to tell Mom that I wanted the brown truck." I was six, then, and my art teacher had already figured it all out. My head knew they were red—were *meant* to be red—but my eyes . . . well, they told a different story. They still do. "I asked for it every time, and every time I knew that meant Mom would be having a sit down with me."

I see confusion in the twist of my twin's mouth, but to his credit, he lets me navigate the story without interruption. I run my damp hands over my slacks. Swallow past the growing lump in my throat. "*You know fire trucks are red*, she'd tell me. Then she'd grab one of the toy cop cruisers and point at the lights, saying, *Red, white, blue*. Over and over again, she'd repeat it to me. *Red. White. Blue.* But I didn't see it—not that I didn't try."

I steel my shoulders. "She told me to follow your lead. Hang back and watch what you did. That was her way of helping me, I guess, accept the fact that I would never see color the way you do, the way most people do."

My twin's Adam's apple dodges down the length of his neck. "Owen . . ."

"Mom and Dad wanted me to keep it a secret, so I did.

They wanted me to learn from you, to take mental notes on how you handled certain situations, so I did that too. And all the while, I did my best to never let it slip that I learned to read traffic lights based on what I *knew* was the correct order, even though I sure as hell couldn't tell the difference between red and green, and, sometimes even the yellow. When we went to prom, and Maryanne told me to buy some red flower for the boutonnière, I stood at the florist's for nearly an hour before I worked up the courage to admit that I was a fraud who needed help because I was so fucking lost."

Gage scrubs a hand over his mouth, then threads his fingers through his hair. "You're an artist. Deep down at your core, that's who you are. How the hell—"

I cut him off with a dip of my chin. "I'm quiet, bro, but I'm not dumb. I look for clues. I focus on order so that there's no chance of me slipping up. And, sometimes, when no one is looking, I say *fuck it all* and draw the world as I see it. No judgment. No fear. No waiting for someone to lean over my shoulder and tell me that the colors don't match or that I've screwed the whole thing up."

At my house, I have an entire closet worth of oil paintings that might as well be strung up next to a sign that reads, *Owen Harvey Doesn't Care About Your Opinions*. I do what I want. I paint how I want. I see the world how I want, without trying to fit into the stereotypical boxes that society hands out like candy corn on Halloween.

My twin falls back in his seat, shoulders slouched. "Why are you tellin' me this now? If you've kept it a secret for all these years, why bother coming clean?"

Instinctively, my gaze flicks to where Savannah took off with Lizzie and Dufrene. Inhaling deeply, I confess, "I told Savannah, once, that chasing shadows doesn't leave much room to find the light. So when she found out about . . . about me, it was by accident." I meet my twin's eyes, a color that I know to be identical to my own. Black, one of the few colors that doesn't try to play tricks on me, no matter the shade—unless, of course, another color is masquerading as it, just for shits and giggles. *Lucky me.* "She called me out for being a hypocrite, then told me I was doing a disservice to our relationship by not being open with you." I breathe in, holding the air in my lungs, then let it all out. "She was right. I can't rewrite Mom and Dad's decision—they did it to protect me, I know that—but me and you, we've got a whole life in front of us still. No secrets."

Gage is quiet for a moment. Then, "I'm pissed I was left out of the loop and hurt that y'all all felt like I couldn't be trusted. That said, I'll get over it."

"That's . . ." I swallow, thickly. "That's good."

"But I'm telling you right now, this has opened the field to me roasting you for life. When you buy a pillow for one of your rentals, I'm gonna swap it with a different one, just to see if you notice. When you ask me to go shopping with you the next time—which now makes *so* much sense—because you claim you have awful taste, I'm going to lead you to the most horrendous shit you will ever find and smile with glee when you pay for all of it and Savannah looks at you like you've lost your mind."

Laughing roughly, I grumble, "Fucking bastard."

"You owe me," Gage says, shrugging, "for thirty-seven years. When we're seventy-four, I'll reconsider and possibly leave you alone."

"Take a year off—our birthday isn't until next month."

"Speaking of, joint red birthday cakes."

I roll my eyes. "You're enjoying the shit out of this, aren't you?"

Gage drains his wine. “I combat hurt feelings with misplaced humor, what can I say?”

“How the hell does Lizzie put up with you?”

“By shutting me up in other, more exciting ways that you will never, ever hear about.” My twin perks up, his gaze sweeping the dining room. “Speaking of, is that why Savannah took Lizzie off to that Hummingbird Room?”

“She wanted to give us time to talk.”

“That’s just a little evil.” Looking impressed, he points a finger at me. “Get me a tour of that room and we’ll call it even. Seventy-three, and I’m not budging on that.”

I know there’ll be more conversations to come, more questions from my twin once the information really sinks in —the guy is a cop through and through, and leaves no stone unturned—but I soak up the brotherly camaraderie, knowing that we’ll be okay. “Love you, bro,” I tell him.

He raises his empty wineglass in a toast. “Love you back. Now, tell me, what color shirt am I wearing?”

I throw my head back with a laugh.

He’s an asshole, but he’s my asshole, and while we wait for Savannah and Lizzie to make their way back to us, I ham it up and give him hell.

“Pink,” I lie, “the same color as your puke that time we hit up Bourbon when we were nineteen and you swore you could handle drinking Pepto-Bismol before we hit up the bars. Turns out you couldn’t. Turns out, we’re still banned from that bar for life.”

I wouldn’t want to be banned with anyone else.

mirror or Owen. "No, I mean, I'm stepping *down*. No more being the VP."

"*Oh*."

I'm not sure if that's an approving *Oh* or if Georgie thinks that I've lost my mind, but I paste a big smile on my face anyway. Fake it till you make it, and all that. "I should have more time to grab cocktails now, which should be fun. I haven't had a girl's night in, well, it's been awhile."

Georgie's lips part—any wider, and she'll be catching flies. "Wait, you're serious?"

I pluck my café au lait from the tray, flicking open the tab so the steam can escape. "Deadly."

"You're actually quitting?"

"Not quitting, just . . . moving departments. Or, rather, creating a department that doesn't exist yet." I blow the steam away, watching my executive assistant over the plastic rim. "I have a plan, and without causing a revolution up in here, I'd like for you to make the move with me."

Now, Georgie's mouth is flapping open. Flies? She could catch a small bird in there. "Y-you"—she runs a hand over her curly hair—"you want me to *move* with you."

"Yes." I nod, tilting my chin toward the long hallway. "Bernard's office has been empty for months and it's large enough for two desks. Didn't you go to college to be an archivist—and then ended up here when you couldn't find a job in your field? I swear I'm not making this up and remember it from your interview."

Georgie's coffee cup collides with the desk. "I—I mean, yeah. *Yes*." Her gaze turns panicked. "I mean, *not* that I don't appreciate what ERRG has done for me, which is a lot, like making sure I don't eat Ramen for the next decade while having five roommates that all smell like cheese."

When I raise a brow, she plods on: "Will this—will this new position have something to do with history?"

"History all day, every day. Also, food and tours and if I haven't said this officially yet, you're hired." I sip from my coffee, then step back. "Can you send my dad to my office when he comes in? I have to break the big news."

And pray that he doesn't want to kill me in the process.

Once Georgie gives me the affirmative, and I'm sure that she's not going to faint from excitement, I head for my office. Or what will be my *ex*-office sometime soon. I'll miss the large windows that overlook Lafayette Square—a view that Uncle Bernard's old office doesn't have—but atmosphere is what you make of it.

I kick my shoes off before I take my seat, then boot up my laptop. As it whirrs to life, I grab my phone from my purse, only to find a series of notifications filling my home screen. In the last week and a half since *Celebrity Tea Presents* shared that picture of Owen and me dancing, I've been bombarded with requests for interviews—all of which I've ignored.

But this isn't one or two emails; there are *hundreds* of messages.

Notifications from social media.

Texts from friends and acquaintances, and even one from the mayor.

I tap on Frannie's, my breath clamped tight behind my teeth while it loads:

Mayor Barron: Here is my publicist's contact info. She already knows you'll be calling. And, Savannah—do not be stubborn with this. Please let me know if you would like me to pass along my lawyer's information, as well. I am here for you, dear girl. Always.

"What in the world," I mutter under my breath, sitting

up tall in my seat. My heart races at a fast clip. Frannie Barron has been in my life since I turned eleven, but she rarely texts me. She calls, often, but she's always been of the opinion that texting is the killer of modern-day relationships. Then again, she once said the same thing about Buzzfeed, and I swear to God, she takes those little quizzes they publish more than anyone else I know.

I scroll through my notifications, only to find that I have missed four calls from her. She's left two voicemails, and I play them both:

"Savannah, you're probably on your way to work. I can't believe this happened—I'm calling your father right now. When you get to the office, stay there. Don't leave. I'm here for you."

"Savannah, just got off the phone with your father. He's on his way now. Do not panic. Everything will be okay. I've handled worse scandals than this, I promise you."

What scandal?

My fingers tremble as my computer finally kicks into gear and I open the internet browser. *Just do it. Type in your name.* For the last eight months, my life has been turned upside down more times than I can count—and I'm terrified, downright *terrified*, to search myself and discover what someone else is saying about me now.

Boring.

Perfect.

Self-absorbed.

Whoever came up with the saying that *sticks and stones may break my bones, but words will never hurt me*, was a filthy liar and clearly never grew up in the age of the world wide web.

"Do it, Rose," I order myself.

As though hitting the ENTER button may cause the end of the world, I type in my name like I'm ninety-five years old and have never touched modern technology. Draw in a sharp breath and wait for the page to load.

The first headline hits me like a freight train: *"Emails Leaked: America's 'Sweetheart' Has Been Hacked!"*

"No," I whisper, and there's no one to hear me in my office, but I say it again and again, my chest squeezing, my heart palpitating. "No, no, *no*."

My gaze slides to the next article: *"Good Girl Savannah Rose Isn't So Good After All: Forbidden Love, Betrayed Sister, and Messy Love Triangle Breakup!"*

And the next: *"Is Amelie Rose a Thorn in the Rose Legacy? Leaked Emails Reveal the Mysterious Secrets Surrounding Her Birth."*

I can't breathe.

I can't—Oh, my God, I can't *breathe*.

With shaking fingers, I reach up to the high-neck collar of my shirt to undo the top button. I drag in air, in through my nose, out through my mouth. Do it all over again, in the hopes that it will dissipate the oppressive cloud sweeping over me. It doesn't work. It doesn't do *anything*. Panic seeps into my veins, tuning my body like a live wire that might implode at any moment.

Those emails . . .

I wrote dozens of them to Owen over the course of my time on *Put A Ring On It* and while I was in Europe. I wrote them riddled with apologies for hurting him the way that I did. I wrote them drunk, with raw honesty as my only weapon as I bared my soul. I wrote them cold-stone sober, my every punctuation, my every paragraph, littered with intent to make him *see* . . .

How much I loved him.

How much I worried about Amelie, who deserved none

of Dad's disappointment for something that would never, ever be her fault.

I spilled every dirty little secret—including some of my fantasies. I detailed them with precision. I imagined him devouring every word, his hand sneaking beneath the sheets. Some of the emails were bold. Some were tame. But the nature of them all were the same, always. They started with a greeting and ended with a simple: *Yours, forever.*

And I wrote them often. Every day, every night, every time he crossed my mind and I wanted someone to confide in, someone to hold me up after hours of pretending I was all too happy to be dating anyone *but* him.

I never hit send.

And now . . . and now—

"This can't be happening."

Feeling my stomach churn, I grab the trash can from under my desk and drop to my knees. I make it just in time. My eyes water and my hair hangs in front of my face and my brain seems to have ditched me because the only thoughts flitting through my head are:

How—

—Owen.

Why—

—Amelie.

My stomach heaves again, but miracle of all miracles, nothing comes up.

I need to get off this floor. I need to be proactive. Those are all things I know, but God, everything *hurts*. Haven't the tabloids taken enough? Haven't they dragged me through the mud *enough*? Fear and dread mingle like the most debilitating cocktail, swirling in my system until I'm barely aware of my office door crashing open.

"Savannah—*Savannah*."

Dad.

A sob wracks my body. He'll never forgive me. *Amelie* will never forgive me. And my mom, who's waited all this time to tell my sister face to face, to answer all of her questions . . .

Self-loathing slithers inside me, and I can't stem the cry that rips from my mouth just as familiar black tennis shoes round the corner of my desk and stop inches away from the trash can.

"*Cherie,*" he utters, and I hear it in his voice—the brokenness, the pain.

"I'm so sorry." I whisper the words, or maybe I bawl them out, but I lick my dry lips and try again, determined to make things right. *If that will ever be possible.* "I didn't mean for any of this to happen. I don't even know *how* it h-happened."

I hear the crack in my father's knees as he drops to his haunches. The trash can is moved to the side, and then I feel his lean arm come around my shoulders as he drops his head on top of mine. "Listen to me," he says, the shallowness of his breathing undercutting his tough tone, "this is not your fault. Do you hear me? This is *not your fault.*"

I feel five, not thirty-five, when my hands coil in his white T-shirt. "Pops, everyone knows. About what you said to Amelie, about Mom's affair. Everyone. *Knows.*"

"Get up, *cherie.*"

"Pops, did you hear anything of what I just said?"

His hands clasp my head, forcing me to look at him. His eyes are red-rimmed. It's obvious he didn't have time to shave before Frannie's call woke him up because his stubble is thick and uneven. He looks fragile and exhausted, and it hits me again that my father is not so very young anymore. When he sees that he's caught my attention, he demands, "What did I tell you and your sister as kids?"

I swallow, roughly. "Success is only halted by the lazy."

"No." His voice cuts like a whip through the room, like he's determined to reach past my tears and my panic and my fears. "Are you dead?" He says it, just like he always did when we were young—when we scraped our knees or when we failed a test or when we tried our hardest to make something happen, only to be met with failure. "Are you dead, *cherie*?" he repeats, his jaw tight.

I shake my head, my answer nothing more than a whisper: "No."

"Then get back up."

Then get back up.

The Rose way.

Our way.

He stands, leaving me to do so on my own because that's how my father raised us. Tears cloud my vision for an entirely different reason. I've spent so many years looking at my dad as though he's ruled our lives with an iron fist—instead of considering all the ways he's worked to see us as independent, strong-willed individuals. He made us *fighters*, and never once did I stop to appreciate it.

My legs are weak, and my face feels tight, but I push myself off all fours and climb to my bare feet. "I love you, Pops."

"Love you, too, Sav." He grabs my phone from my desk, shoving it inside my purse. "We have twenty minutes to get to the airport."

I eye my laptop like it's the gateway to hell, then jab the power button. "We're leaving?"

He shoves my things toward me. "We're not going anywhere. Amelie called last night—she used the ticket.

The ticket that I"—he rubs the back of his neck, looking sheepish—"I bought for her. She asked me to pick her up, so we could talk. But now . . ." My father's shoulders hunch, before he's standing upright again with a look that tells me he means business. "Twenty minutes, then we get home to your mom."

"Is Mom—is she okay?"

Dad's fingers brush mine. "She's a Rose, *cherie*, and she isn't dead. She'll get back up too."

32

CELEBRITY TEA PRESENTS:

BREAKING NEWS! OWEN HARVEY'S SECRET IS EXPOSED!

My, my, Dear Reader, what a day it has been! It's the sort of day that I've been waiting for my entire life—and now that it's here, there is simply not enough time to put fingers to keyboard to collect all of my thoughts.

And, trust me, I have a lot.

If you've been living under a rock (or are still hungover from your weekend debauchery), then you may have missed the SAVANNAH ROSE SCANDAL OF THE YEAR. Her personal email account was hacked, and all her dirty laundry was aired just this morning, including hundreds of emails penned (but never sent) to Owen Harvey—more on him in a second. With the Put A Ring On It *series finale coming this Wednesday, and the live reunion special to be aired next week, there is no doubt in my mind that many of the booted-off contestants will be spending the next twelve days deliberating on what exactly they'll tell America's (Disgraced) Sweetheart when they see her next. Bloodshed will be spilled, I'm sure of it.*

Back to Owen Harvey, Savannah's not-so-secret beau.

Things started innocently enough on Friday night when Harvey and Rose went out for a double date at one of Savannah's family's restaurants in New Orleans. Accompanied by Harvey's twin brother, Gage, and his wife, Lizzie Harvey (YouTube Mega Beauty Influencer ThatMakeupGirl), the foursome seemed to be having a fabulous time.

That is, until Rose and Lizzie Harvey stepped away from the table.

An anonymous source—who has my undying gratitude for life—happened to be sitting next to the Harvey brothers when he overheard information that shocked him to his core:

New Orleans' most famous tattoo artist is colorblind.

Yes, Dear Reader, the tea has been spilled here first!

Now, much speculation could go into why Harvey decided to keep this secret to himself for all of these years, but I think we all know the answer to that question: would you truly trust someone with your skin when there's a very *large possibility that they will screw it up? I'm not trying to be ugly, but don't tell me you aren't thinking it too. Harvey clearly knew how customers would react and, instead of seeking transparency with his clients, he opted to keep that integral information to himself.*

If you ask me, it reeks of duplicity—but, hey, what do I know? I'm nothing but a journalist seeking the truth. #DoOrDieTrying

It remains to be seen what the fallout of this sort of news will entail for Harvey's popular tattoo parlor, Inked on Bourbon. Will business continue to flourish? Will customers show up, but demand an artist that isn't *our inked god from* Put A Ring On It? *The ramifications for this sort of reveal are endless, but never fear: I'll be here, ready to spill the tea as soon as it's ready, and until then . . .*

Please enjoy a special video clip submitted by our anonymous source. I hope Harvey is ready for all the speculation that will be coming his way.

33

SAVANNAH

I watch from the backseat of Dad's car as he and Amelie step out of the rotating doors at the airport. If there are any paparazzi waiting in the flanks, they're really good at what they do because I don't see the flash of lights or a swarm of folks holding cameras to their faces. Still, Dad has his arm wrapped around my sister's shoulders, as though if he does so, he can protect her from the world.

Eight months ago, he couldn't even protect her from himself.

Suitcase clasped in one hand, Dad guides Amelie across the junction where the cabbies wait, and then, finally, they're here. Instead of hitting up the front seat, my sister yanks open the door I'm leaning against and motions with her bracelet-laden wrist for me to move over.

I scoot down the bench, reaching for my seat belt—and don't even have the chance to buckle up.

My sister's arms wrap around my neck, her breath warm on my shoulder as a shudder wracks her slender frame.

"I'm so sorry." I hug her back, tightly, and fight a fresh

wave of tears. *Then get back up*. Crying won't solve this mess. It won't rewind the clock and allow me to rewrite history. I press my tongue to the roof of my mouth and count to three full seconds. Only then, once I'm sure I'm not on the verge of another breakdown, do I say the words again: "I'm so, so sorry, Am."

Her answer is a mumbled whisper in my hair. "Not your fault, Sav. This isn't on you."

Except that it kind of is.

At any point, I could have deleted all those emails sitting in *Draft*. There was no reason to keep them—except that I did. I kept them all, like they were a secret diary that allowed me to voice my deepest fears and my biggest regrets and my most desperate fantasies.

Nothing says *Here's a Monday for you; have all the fun*, like having your email hacked and all your innermost feelings exposed for the world to see.

I smooth a hand over my thigh and realize that I've yet to stop trembling.

The driver's side door squeals open and then Dad slides in, already pumping the gas before he's even slammed the door closed. In the rearview mirror, he meets my gaze, then searches for Amelie. He clears his throat. "Did you—did you have a good flight, *cherie*?"

Amelie lets me go but stays on the middle seat like she used to when we were kids. "It was great. Just, you know, absolutely fantastic until about an hour ago when a notification popped up on my phone." She throws her hands up in the air. "Remember way back when, when we all used to bitch about not having WiFi on airplanes? Well, let me tell you, *this* is the reason we should go back to the Dark Ages."

Leave it to my sister to infuse a little humor into the situation. Smiling weakly, I nudge her in the side. "Is it really the Dark Ages when we're talking about just a few years ago?"

She turns her head to stare me down. "Absolutely, one-hundred percent yes."

In the front seat, Dad fiddles with the temperature. "Your mother will be happy to see you."

"Are *you* happy to see me?"

Another thing I've ruined this morning. This moment was supposed to be for them only and here I am sitting like an interloper. Amelie specifically told me to find myself a new island, and so I avert my gaze to the window and watch the I-10 highway speed past us. Nothing to see here.

"I am," Dad says softly, and if I could see his face, I know it'd be etched with remorse. "A Rose has his thorns and I . . . I have my pride. I wanted to include you, Amelie. All these years, I wanted you to feel as though you were my daughter, my baby girl—and when you told me that you would rather do anything else over working for ERRG, I . . ." He swallows, audibly. "It felt as though you were rejecting *me*. I lost my temper. Years of feeling inadequate—"

When he cuts off roughly, Amelie leaves my side to climb into the passenger's seat. "Why would you feel inadequate, Pops? You have the world, don't you? Money? Success? Anything you want is yours."

"Your father . . . I mean, your biological father"—here, my dad's voice turns bitter—"No, we should wait for your mom. We can't have this conversation without her."

But Amelie will not be dissuaded. "Have it with me now, and then let me have it with her later. There are always two sides to every story—you told me that when I used to lie about doing the chores around the house. So, give me your side, Pops. Mom will give me hers when we get home."

Try as I do to make myself as small as possible, it's

utterly futile. I find myself staring at Amelie with my own pride ballooning in my chest. The woman sitting up there, staring at our father and begging him to talk, will never again be the little girl who used to pull on my untamed hair or beg for sister nights when I was a freshman in college.

I loved that Amelie with every corner of my soul.

But I respect this one sitting diagonal from me now—and then her hand flattens on the center console, her fingers drumming a silent beat, and I know she'll always need me, even just a little bit.

I drag my butt over to the uncomfortable middle seat, scoot forward to the edge, and slip my hand under hers.

The Rose sisters against the world.

Dad pulls off at the Esplanade Avenue exit, curving the SUV along the off-ramp. Finally, he confesses, "Your mother left me."

My hand tightens around Amelie's. "I don't remember that."

He looks right, checking for oncoming traffic—but, also, I think, to sneak a peek at the two of us. "It wasn't for very long. I had . . . I had loved your mom for a long time, though she didn't much notice me. I was lanky and a bit of a nerd. Dropped out of high school. Why finish when I would end up at ERRG in the end? No one convinced me otherwise, but the one thing I missed about school was Marie. She was beautiful and smart and the sweetest soul I'd ever met, and so I convinced her to tutor me. It was a way to see her, in between working in the kitchens."

"You've never told us this story," Amelie says, giving voice to the confusion I'm experiencing in my heart.

"It was a long time ago." Dad slows the car for a red light, his fingers tapping on the steering wheel. "So, the tutoring went on. I pined after her. She fell for some boy at school. It was messy. They dated and we ended up going our separate ways." The light turns green, and he accelerates. "I saw her again when I was in my late twenties. She was just as beautiful—turns out she'd been traveling the world. She'd lived in Prague and Paris and, for a time, in London. And, this time, it seemed she liked me too."

Wetting my lips, I clutch the back of Dad's headrest. "I don't understand how it goes from y'all liking each other to her leaving you."

"He came back, *cherie*. That boy from high school that swept her off her feet—and I was still that lanky nerd who spent too much time in the kitchen, except this time, that meant I spent too much time away from your mom. I . . ." He blows out a sharp breath, shaking his head. "She was looking after you, Savannah, and the house, and I was always doing something else. Always working on the business. Always focused *elsewhere*. Her leaving is on me."

Amelie's hand leaves mine to land on Dad's forearm. "Pops, it's *not* on you."

He nods sharply. "It is. The night she packed her bags, she begged me to reprioritize. The work had to stay at work, but the family was for always—and instead of falling to my knees and asking her to forgive me, I told her that being a Rose would always come first."

My throat thickens. "Pops," I whisper, my voice strained. "Please tell me you didn't."

In profile, I watch his face grimace. "I did. So, she left to stay with your aunt, just for a few days."

Amelie's mouth twists. "I hear a *but* coming."

Another grimace, this one deeper, more severely drawn. "But she was ripe for the pickings, emotionally distraught, so angry at me that I swear she could have lit up an entire power plant with all her fuming. Aunt Bea took her to a bar and guess who happened to be there?"

"My dad," Amelie says, which she hastily amends to "my biological dad" when *our* dad coughs awkwardly.

"Yes, he was there. They . . . they slept together, only once, but I guess the once was all it took. She was home within a week. I-I begged her to come back, and she was always upfront. She never hid what happened that night at the bar. We just never expected—"

"Me."

My sister's tone is forlorn, and one look at her face reveals so much heartache that I nearly launch myself into the front seat so I can hold her to my side and protect her the way that I always have.

"You were *mine*, Amelie," Dad grinds out fiercely, his gaze tracking from the road to her face and then back again, lightning quick. "From the day your mother told me, I have never felt any differently. I'd loved her for almost half of my life, and I would be damned if I stopped then. You were a Rose. You *are* a Rose. I will always have one regret in my life, and that was eight months ago when I allowed my own insecurities to boil over onto you."

"You don't regret the day you didn't beg Mom to stay?" I ask.

He shakes his head. "I can't. If I had asked, then I wouldn't have Amelie." He takes one hand off the wheel to grasp my sister's, bringing their intertwined fingers to his mouth so he can kiss the back of her hand. "You are the best of your mom, *cherie*. Her zest for life. Her inquisitive nature. Her need to push the boundaries of what is acceptable and what isn't. But I'm sorry to say that your worst traits—those are all that belong to me."

Amelie hiccups a watery laugh that pulls at my heart. "I'm more of a thorn than I am a Rose."

Dad sends her a quick, hopeful smile. "Only the best Roses have a thorny nature, Am. Lucky enough for our branch of the family, we're all rather untamed."

Dad pulls up to our family home, a nineteenth-century Greek Revival that we moved into when I was twelve. It's a bright teal with white and magenta trimmings and in possession of so much character that it's always been the talk of our neighbors.

There, sitting on the front steps, is Mom.

Her long hair, tied in braids, hangs down the length of her back. A shocked gasp nearly leaves my mouth when I realize that she's still in her PJ's, fuzzy slippers and all. I try to look at her as Dad sees her, as this woman who is just like Amelie—rebellious and revolutionary and real.

And then her head jerks up at the sound of Dad parking the SUV along the curb, and I see it: not a single tear graces her face. She's composed and queen-like, a fighter at heart, but then the façade slips, threatening to crack and unfold, and reveals her true colors.

She launches up from the porch steps, her slippered feet walking fast, then running, until she's at the passenger's side door. It's yanked open and then my mom, the one woman who always told me to be brave and to keep my head held high when the girls made fun of me in school, leaps into the car as though the passenger's seat is meant for two.

Her arms come around Amelie's shoulders, and her husky voice whispers, "You're home," and then my sister breaks.

Her sobs fill the SUV as she's huddled on both sides from our parents, after being unceremoniously shoved up onto the center console like she's five years-old all over again and can actually fit there without her knees bopping her in the chin.

Then get back up.

I stare at my family, feeling particularly waterlogged myself, and think of Owen telling me that memories can't ever exist on a sliding scale. If we axed the brutal one of Dad lashing out in hurt, then we wouldn't have this one now—and, possibly, we never would.

I kick my chin up. "Is there room up there for one more?"

In unison, Dad and Mom throw their arms open wide. And at thirty-five, I somehow find myself in a family huddle in the front seat of my parent's SUV. I'm practically chewing on Amelie's knee, and sure enough, my mom's jaw is a little pink from when I tried to get comfortable but only managed to clock her in the face with my elbow instead.

It's perfect.

No, it's *imperfect*.

And that makes it all that much better.

34

OWEN

3:37 p.m.

I don't know the precise number of seconds, and if you asked me, I'd probably tell you to fuck off because the difference between one second and five seconds and thirty seconds wouldn't change a thing in the end.

At 3:37 p.m., the world found out.

All it took was a click of a button, some asshole named *Celebrity Tea Presents*—a fact that I'd discover way later, when I finally tuned into the news—and an even bigger asshole listening in to my conversation at Rose & Thorn last Friday night, and life, as I knew it, was obliterated.

It started with a phone call—some jerk-off named Mark White who wanted his appointment canceled.

No big deal. Cancellations happen at every business. I didn't give it another thought.

But then the phone rang again, and this time it wasn't an existing client, it was someone new, someone who breathed heavily into that goddamn headset, wherever they were, and had the balls to say, "You should be ashamed of yourself for lying for all these years. Nobody wants a fuckin' colorblind tattoo artist."

My heart twisted and my stomach plunged, and when the phone rang next, I had to force myself to pick it up. Someone from *US Tonight* was calling, wanting a tell-all exclusive where they'd pay me just shy of a hundred grand to tell the world how I managed to live under the radar for so many years.

Like I was some sort of criminal stowaway—still—and not someone born with a different genetic trait than the Average Joe on the street.

Like I was nothing but a goddamn story for them to hem and haw over, then plaster in every grocery store all over the country before forgetting I exist two weeks later.

Meanwhile leaving me to deal with the fallout.

I hung up so fast I hope she got whiplash.

The next time the phone went off, I ripped the fucking cord out of the outlet and threw it clear across the parlor.

I don't need to look online to know what I'll already find: I've been outed, and there's nothing I can do to wind back the clock.

Rapid banging on the glass door snares my attention. *Lizzie*. *Gage*. Thank fucking Christ.

I practically hurdle over one of our tattoo tables in my haste to get to the front door, and when I rip it open, I halfway worry that I might pull the damn thing off the hinges. My sister-in-law scoots in past me, my twin hot on her heels.

Once they're in, I bolt the door.

"It's fucking bad," I blurt, hands moving up to my head.

Hands on her pregnant belly, Lizzie lowers herself to the sofa. "I got dumped on Instagram, Owen, in front of at least a million people. It wasn't the end of the world. It's all in how you manage this."

"Manage it?" I pace the reception area, sidestepping her massive bag that's on the floor. "Liz, my entire livelihood comes with people trusting me with color, with ink. How the hell do you think they're gonna react when they find out I use a fucking *color chart* to determine what they want and what I can deliver?"

Gage drops a hand on my shoulder, stilling my agitation. "You have a system. It works for you."

Until it didn't. Until I was so wound up and so consumed by Savannah that I messed up—bad. *I need her*. I've needed her for hours, ever since that first phone call. I don't give a damn if that makes me sound like a pussy. She puts things into perspective; she forces me to see that if I'm true to myself, my gut can't lead me astray. She's smart and savvy and she'd handle this problem fast.

I look at Gage and Lizzie, who keep exchanging glances like they're part of their own secret language that no one will ever understand but them. They're wearing identical expressions of sympathy, of worry, but it isn't enough.

No.

I need Savannah for *me*. I need her here to hold my hand and whisper that it'll be all right. I need to feel her weight at my back, her arms looped around my waist, and know, deep in my soul, that she's going to keep me standing.

That she's going to keep me *moving*, even when anger is crashing through me like a tornado left to wander the open plains.

All afternoon, I've kept my emotions tethered by a string, mostly by staying far away from the internet. One snip, one wrong headline that I read, and I'll spiral. I close my eyes now and it's like I've fallen into a time warp. Bleakness radiates from the darkest depths of my soul. I hear my heavy breathing. I hear my brother and Lizzie discussing our game plan.

But my vision continues to swim, those goddamn colors moving and swirling until I'm hightailing it to the bathroom, my arm already outstretched because I'm going to be sick. One hand lands on the porcelain sink and the other flips up the toilet lid, and nothing, *nothing*, comes out.

I dry-heave and fight back the memories. *Not a sliding scale*, I try to remind myself. I can't change a thing of the past, not without altering who I am now. But the memories assault me, anyway, and for the first time in years, I find myself descending into the blackness—into all the shadows that I've purged out on my skin in an effort to find the light. It grips my soul with its gnarled fingers and mocks me with its wicked, sinister grin.

Spiraling never hurt during, only ever after.

I hear my brother shouting, but I slam the bathroom door shut before he can see me like this. Falling. Splintering. *Crashing*. I see it all. My parents in their matching coffins, just before we slid them into the family tomb in Metairie Cemetery. The bottle of Jim Beam that I swore I wouldn't drink completely, until I woke up the next morning, still wasted, and covered in my own vomit. The line of coke that an old friend laid out on a table before leaning down, one finger to his nostril, and snorted it all. The line that he then laid out for me.

Savannah's nervous face, just before I brushed back her hair and traced the fragile skin behind her ear before her first tattoo.

I fumble for my phone in my pocket, my back hitting the wooden door, my knees giving out as I slide down, down, down, until my ass is on the floor and my eyes are squeezed shut and the panic is crowding in and I'm struggling to find air.

Everyone knows.

Everyone *knows*.

They want a tell-all. They want me to say that I'm guilty for lying to customers for years. They want to tell me I shouldn't strive to make my dream a reality—a dream that pulled me out of the depths of hell—because I'm not like *them*.

But I only want *her*.

"Hey! This is Savannah Rose, I can't come to the phone right now, but you know the drill. Leave your name and number and I'll get back to you real soon." *Beep!*

The back of my skull collides with the door. "Hey, it's me." My voice is rusty, raw, and I try to clear it but it's a hopeless case that took a turn for the worse at 3:37 p.m. on a fucking Monday. "Some shit happened—no, *it* happened." *Freakshow. Guilty. Liar.* "Someone listened to my conversation with Gage at the restaurant, I think. Had to be, there's no other way. I'm heading to the house . . . Barataria. I need to get out. No, I need—I need you, Rose. I don't know what I'm supposed to do, I don't know what I'm supposed to say, but all I know is that I need you here. With me. *Please*."

I hang up, the phone going to my thigh.

And then I try to remember to breathe . . . and try even harder to keep my shadows at bay.

35

SAVANNAH

South of the New Orleans metro area, the roads are nothing but winding two-lane highways. During the day, it's a ten-and-two-hands-on-the-wheel sort of drive. Eyes on the road, foot always ready to pump the brakes for when the sharp turns come along—or for when a gator decides to stalk its way across in search of prey. At night, there's nothing but a car's high beams illuminating the Spanish moss hanging from Cypress trees and the flashes of reflective traffic signs instructing drivers to slow the hell down.

When it's raining, like it is now, the world feels like it's closing in.

Or maybe it's that *my* world feels like it's caving in.

Rain pelts my windshield, giving my window wipers a run for their money.

"C'mon," I mutter, sitting forward in my seat as I squint to see through the torrential downpour, "give me a friggin' break already!"

When it rains, it pours. Literally.

I spent the entire day with my family, huddled together

in the home I grew up in. Nothing is perfect—and I doubt it will be for a long time to come—but for the first time in months, I felt the fissured cracks begin to heal, just enough to give me hope. As promised, Mom gave us her side of the story, and then gave Amelie her biological father's email address. He lives in Miami. Never married. Never had any other kids. "We've kept in touch just enough so I could tell him about you," Mom told my sister, "but he wasn't prepared to step into your life when you were young and we —we were, admittedly, selfish in wanting to keep you to ourselves."

Amelie didn't say she would reach out, but she didn't discard the idea either.

For once, I'm choosing to step back and move to my own neighboring island.

An island that needs Owen more than it does the sandy beaches or the towering palm trees or the taste of salt on the breeze. I'd claim an island in the Arctic if it meant we could be together.

The tires slice through the rising water on the road, and I give up all attempt to follow traffic laws and drift between the two lanes. One wrong move and I'll end up stuck in the two-feet deep ditch that sections off the back-road highway from the tangled wetlands of the bayou.

My car makes a chugging noise, the wheels spinning fast when I just manage to avoid hydroplaning off the side of the road.

"Come on, come on, *come on*." I smack the dashboard. Almost there. Maybe another two minutes. Three at the most. I may have missed Owen's call and heart-wrenching voicemail while I was with my family, but I will *not* let him down.

A year and a half ago, I stood by his side at that EOCC

meeting, holding him up with quiet support while he listened to his brother—but my hands were still tied. My fingers couldn't dip beneath his shirt to soothe his tense muscles. My lips were forbidden to touch his cheek, his arm. And my heart . . . Well, I did what I could to lock it in its cage before it gave me away completely.

Tonight will be different.

The rest of our lives will be different.

So long as he doesn't blame you for putting him in the spotlight in the first place.

Ruthlessly, I shove the thought away and exhale a sigh of relief when his street sign comes into view. Blinker on, I make the turn, moving slower than I did on my very first day behind the wheel when I was fifteen. When I pull into his short driveway, alongside his black truck, I honk the horn to let him know I've arrived.

Ignition, off. Umbrella, ready to be popped open. Heart, beating uncontrollably fast. The wind whips at my tiny Miata, the gust all the more powerful since the house sits beside open water.

Swinging the car door open, I bow my head, already lifting the umbrella above me to shield my body from the rain, and promptly run into a brick wall.

Owen.

Big hands find my shoulders, drift down to my elbows. "You're getting wet!" I angle the umbrella, so it won't bop him in the face. Rain pelts the cement like tiny rubber balls, pinging back to splash my sandaled feet, my bare calves. A chill sweeps down my spine when thunder cracks overhead, and then it's all being replaced by heat, by rain, by *Owen* as he slicks his hands down to my butt and lifts me clear off my feet.

The umbrella falls from my hand, clattering against my car.

Owen's mouth finds mine in the darkness, his lips wet, his beard damp against my skin. The kiss isn't polite, and it isn't a hello—it's a blending of hearts, of unspoken hope and a promise of safety. I fall into it eagerly, chasing his tongue, wrapping my legs around his hips and linking my ankles so that I won't go slipping down his soaked frame.

On swift, agile feet, Owen turns us for the stairs that lead up to his front door, never once breaking the kiss. My clothes cling to my skin as he climbs each rung, an urgency to his step that I have a feeling has nothing to do with the summer storm and everything to do with what happened today.

I need you here.

I don't think I'll ever purge that voicemail from my head—a confident, successful man brought to his knees by the prospect of losing it all. The bleakness in Owen's voice ruined me, yanking a whimper from my mouth that my parents heard clear across the living room. And when Dad asked me what was wrong, I gave it to him straight: "Owen needs me, and if you have a problem with that, I don't want to hear it. You can hate yourself for what you did to him, but you can't hate him for your mistake. You're better than that, Pops. *Be* better than that."

Amelie gave a slow round of applause and Mom lifted her glass of wine in support, and Dad . . . he nodded and drove me to the office so I could grab my car.

It was a truce that I willingly accepted.

The kiss turns heavier, deepening, as though Owen can read the tumultuous thoughts flitting through my head and seeks to vaporize them. My fingers rake through his soaked hair, just as he swings the front door open and whisks us inside. The door slams shut with an echoing *thud* that comes in conjunction with another boom of thunder outside.

Droplets of water slick down my skin. Owen moves his mouth over mine, working us backward through the living room with me still cradled in his arms. My purse slips off my shoulder and falls to the floor, followed shortly by the cheap, one-dollar flip-flops that I always keep in my glove compartment for an unexpected occasion when sky-high heels won't do.

Breaking from the kiss, I gasp, "You don't . . . Sex isn't what you need from me right now."

Owen's black eyes never leave my face, not even dipping down to my beyond-wet shirt that I bet reveals all. "No," he says with a vulnerable edge to his voice, "I need you to breathe."

Oh.

My heart quickens at a fast clip. Hands moving to cup his face, I pause only when I hear the sound of my name from the TV:

"*—Savannah Rose experienced major backlash on social media after her personal email account was hacked this morning. Several sources are reporting that it might be Savannah Rose's very own family who have, allegedly, exposed her—all in the name of bringing more attention to their restaurants down in the Big Easy. This is Jeff Noonan; more on these unfolding events after this break.*"

I press a firm hand to Owen's chest. "Let me down."

His grip tightens on my ass, bolstering me farther up in his arms. "You don't need to hear that shit, sweetheart."

Pulling back so I can see his face, I trace the lines of his firmly set mouth with the tip of my damp finger, then note the hollow look in his dark-as-night gaze. "There's no hiding from it, Owen. There's no standing back, clicking your heels together, and hoping Dorothy will sweep you away to twenty-four hours ago."

Jaw clenched tightly, he cuts his attention to the ceiling. Surrounded by his arms as I am, I feel the heavy breath that inflates his chest. The hem of his drenched T-shirt sits on the tops of my thighs, lending a chill to the air that seeps into my bones.

"Owen, please—"

"I bought this place to flip it," he edges out, his voice smooth like whiskey poured over ice, "no secret, there. Buy it, rent it, sell it. Same as I've done with all my other properties. But then you showed up here and we had sex on the brand new couch I bought because I figured guests would like it. And then I found myself ordering a bed big enough for two—with enough space that your crazy cat could be isolated in one corner—and I didn't stop there. I bought nightstands and a dresser, and then I started imagining what it would be like to have us fighting over who got stuck with the bottom drawers."

My stomach dips, every one of my limbs stringing tight like they might snap at any second. "I'm shorter," I whisper, "so I'd be willing to take one for the team." Owen doesn't smile and his eyes don't gleam the way they always do when we banter, and my heart breaks a little more for him . . . and maybe even for us too. Nerves ricochet through my body when I push the dreaded question past my lips: "Are you—are you breaking up with me?"

"Not in this lifetime, Rose." Tension seeps into his body as he wheels me around to plant my wet butt on the sideboard table. His chin juts forward defiantly. "No, in this lifetime, we barter for drawers and we have only this one TV in our house because if we're in our bedroom, that means I'm too busy makin' you come."

Core aching, I try to bring my knees together, but Owen's big body keeps them spread wide. "*Our* bedroom, huh? You have this all planned out."

"I thought I did."

"What changed?"

"Everything," he grinds out, his hands locked on my hips like he's desperate for the tangible connection. "Nothing about what happened today feels like a coincidence, Sav." Then, without warning, he wheels around to head for the TV stand—the brand new, teal TV stand, the one he bought for us. It doesn't match the coffee table, but my eyes don't care when my heart is practically singing for having been on his mind. Snatching up the remote control, he jabs a button and the video on the screen leaps backward until Owen freezes it on the newscaster, my name blocked out in red along the bottom of the clip. Controller pointed at the TV, Owen's gaze snaps to mine. "News of your email account being hacked hit around nine this morning. Six hours later, that fucker *Celebrity Tea Presents* uploaded an article about me."

My stare flits between him and the frozen image on the TV. "*Celebrity Tea* didn't even report on me—at least he hadn't yet when I left my parents' house an hour ago." I think of the article I found, directly after I listened to Owen's voicemail. "I was pretty much a footnote in the piece he wrote about you, nothing more." I want to ask if Owen's read them yet, any of the hundreds of emails I'd drafted to him, but I bite back the question before I can make a fool out of myself. Sliding off the sideboard, I move to his side. "For eight months, *Celebrity Tea* has always been the first to report on anything relating to me or *Put A Ring On It*. Always."

Slinging the remote control onto the couch, Owen falls back with his hands linked behind his head. "I'm the son of a cop, Sav. Brother to a cop, too. All that information being leaked on the same day fucking *reeks* of something rotten."

I've never been slow on the uptake, but a part of me doesn't want to believe in Owen's theory. It's one thing to have your life upended by secrets leaking, another thing entirely to believe that it was all schemed and conducted for the sake of some grand master plan. If my life were a movie, I'd want it to be a romantic comedy—I've never been into thrillers where my heart rate ticks and my most harrowing fears become reality.

"When I was with my family earlier, we called Frannie. She offered her lawyer to us—I guess he has a lot of connections with the FBI—and he's already started moving on trying to figure out who's behind this."

"We know who's behind this." Before I can edge a word in, Owen turns on his heel, striding into the kitchen. Shocked at his abrupt departure, I find myself rooted in place. Heavy footsteps return moments later, and I watch as Owen sets a laptop on the coffee table. Without fanfare, he reaches for the hem of his shirt and draws the nearly translucent fabric up and over his head. He throws it off to the side, avoiding the new rug, where it lands on the slate floor with a wet smack.

The chill returns with a vengeance as I sit next to him on the couch, our knees bumping, his clad in sopping wet jeans, mine sheathed in equally wet cotton khakis. When I shiver, Owen jumps up, wordlessly heading for the hallway. Two minutes later, he comes back with an oversized T-shirt and a pair of mesh shorts.

"I tried to pick out your size," he says gruffly, handing

them over with a dip of his chin. "But when I saw the shirt, I couldn't resist—grabbed the smallest size they had."

Unfolding the black T, my eyes take in the cat illustrated in white. It's flashing a middle finger that looks a little too human-like to be remotely feline. Surrounding the cat are the words inscribed in white font: *They call me a cat lady like it's a bad thing*.

A watery laugh catches in my throat.

Owen shifts his weight. "Not too on the nose?" he asks, his voice low. "I'm always up for feedback."

This time, the laughter escapes in a rush. It's exactly what I wrote to him in one of the cards that went along with the 144 roses. And leave it to him to hold onto that memory until it served his purpose to repay the favor.

Owen is not like any other man I've ever met. He's brash and he's confident; he's shy at all the strangest times; and when I somehow manage to make him blush, all I can think is *I love you.* I love that his spontaneity is under-laced with steel grit and determination. I love that his gruffness and intimidating looks are dredged in kindness, a certain compassion that feels so rare in the elitist world where I grew up. I love that even though he grumbled the entire time, he wore my stupid astronaut pet carrier so Pablo could hang out with us, and that in my hands I'm holding a T-shirt announcing me as the cat lady I've always been destined to be.

And I love him because he pushes me to be as I am, to take what I want, to live and thrive and be the Savannah Rose that *I* see, no matter how anyone else feels. I've loved him for so long that the words are pressing at my rib cage, demanding to be released, and it's only a testament of strength that I shove them back down.

Not yet. Not until he knows everything.

"Savannah?"

Feeling my cheeks warm under his stare, I nod quickly. "I love it." There's a part of me that never wants to take it off. "It's perfect . . . but maybe a little too on the nose."

His mouth curls in the first true smile I've seen from him tonight.

While he sits, I hastily strip out of my wet clothes and pull on the shorts and cat T. When I slide in next to him on the couch, he's already pulled up multiple internet tabs. "As soon as I got back here, I started researching."

I set a hand on his thigh, gently squeezing. "You worried me, on the phone."

His shoulders hike up, then release on an exhalation. "I worried myself. Feeling like—no, *knowing* that I'm possibly hours away from everything I've worked toward for a decade going to shit is absolutely gutting. Within minutes of the article going live earlier, the phone started ringing. I hadn't even *seen* the article yet, but it's like Inked had found its way onto everyone's speed-dial list. Appointment cancellation. Some asshole calling to tell me that I was a fraud who lied to customers. A magazine wantin' an interview." He rolls his bottom lip under his top, sitting forward as he drops his elbows to his knees. "It was an instant throwback."

I try to hide my wince. "To before?"

"Yeah." One whispered word, and immediately my hand goes to his tattooed back, rubbing in small circles. "To before. Back then, I chased the shadows away by turning to ink. Teaching myself, because how could I trust another artist to take me on when I was such a liability? I worked myself to the bone at multiple jobs while I built up a portfolio tattooing friends and family for free. Then I struck out on my own. No one could say *don't* if I'm my own boss."

Don't.

Ironic how that word always seems to percolate when we want it least.

Even more ironic that Owen and I came from different backgrounds, and yet somehow found each other. Two people who were always told *don't* finally leaping into a permanent desire to *do*.

"So, today . . ."

He presses his balled fist into the opposite palm, cracking his inked knuckles. "I came here and worked myself to the bone . . . and watched that door like a hawk, praying you would come through it to hold my hand."

God, this man.

I lift my gaze to the ceiling and blink back the sting of tears. I will *not* cry. I've done enough of that already today. If my cat hasn't turned Owen off, then it's possible my mascara-streaked face might seal the deal.

Clearing my throat, I drop my fingers from his back and meet his gaze, the same one that's always seemed to anticipate my every move. On a ragged murmur, I say, "Give me your hand, Owen."

His Adam's apple bobs down his throat, but he doesn't hesitate. When he sees me rest my hand on his thigh, palm up, he tangles our fingers together. Lifts them to kiss the back of my hand, then each one of my knuckles, before setting our clasped hands on his leg once again.

Over the next twenty minutes, he points to page after page on his laptop screen. When he said he spent the entire day researching, he wasn't exaggerating.

"Every major spoiler that's come out of the *Put A Ring On It* franchise," he's telling me now, our hands still clasped together, "*Celebrity Tea* has reported it first. Stamos and Mina's engagement? *Celebrity Tea*. All that leaked footage with you rejecting DaSilva and Stamos, within minutes of each other? *Celebrity Tea*."

"Maybe he has a source from within the show?"

Owen tilts his head, and I can't pretend I don't notice the way the ink on his chest seems to move over the finely corded muscles. The man is seriously hot, in a way that makes me flustered, even now when we're discussing possible fraud. "Nah," he mutters, "I'm thinking he's *in* the show."

My eyes widen. "You mean like a contestant?"

"No." A firm shake of his head. "I'm talking crew. Cameraman, casting director, producer."

"Why in the world would someone on the crew be sidelining as *Celebrity Tea*? Wouldn't that defeat the entire purpose of the show—to spill all its secrets before it's even aired?"

"Look at any reality TV show, Sav. When the drama is hot, the ratings are even hotter. Spoilers don't matter when people tune in just to see how it all plays out."

"Jeez," I breathe. "Small miracles, I guess. Originally, the show was supposed to be done in real time. Film one day, release the next. Could you imagine the chaos?"

"Still plenty of time left for that," Owen says roughly, raking the fingers of his free hand through his almost dry hair. "Amidst all the chaos of today, I got a reminder email for the live taping of the reunion show next week."

My stomach freefalls. I can only imagine the backlash I'm going to receive from the contestants on the show. They're going to be absolutely furious. And while I'm sure that I at least partly deserve the kickback from the guys who went on the show to find true love, I know it's not going to be easy.

And it's definitely not going to go perfectly.

I force myself to breathe in through my nose and out through my mouth, then repeat the process two more times.

Independent.

Strong-willed.

A fighter.

A Rose and her thorn—I'll take the heat, but I won't accept being bashed. I've done that for months now. I've accepted the scrutiny and kept my head down when the rumors spread. Not anymore.

Mouth dry, I ask, "What do we do next?"

Owen squeezes my hand. "I work myself to the bone at Inked and go back to the basics—show the world why I got on the map in the first place, no matter what I can and can't see. You draw up a list of every person who seemed sketchy while you were on the show so we can give it to the lawyer, and then you tell your dad about your plan for ERRG. No more VP."

"No more VP." I smile, then, and it's big and wide and genuine. "And after we've done all that?"

Owen takes our linked hands and loops them around his shoulders, leaving mine there as he pushes me back onto the couch. His jeans are wet on my thighs and his cool chest leaves the most delicious-feeling pressure in my soul. His nose grazes mine, and then his lips trail down to kiss the corner of my mouth. "After that, you come with me to the store and pick out whatever you want for this house."

"Sounds like you're hoping there might be more to this than just sharing a bedroom."

Vulnerability and hope spark to life in his black gaze. "I'm bettin' on it, sweetheart, I'm betting on it."

36

CELEBRITY TEA PRESENTS:

OWEN HARVEY AND SAVANNAH ROSE GO SILENT WITH THE PRESS, FOLLOWING WEEK OF UTTER SCANDAL!

Dear Reader, it's been one whole week since the Scandal of the Year rocked the internet to its core.

In case you've been living under a rock, here's the 411:

Formerly known as America's Sweetheart, Savannah Rose's emails were hacked last Monday in what US Tonight *dubbed, "An unprecedented invasion of privacy."*

While nothing so illustrious as nude photos were released—Savannah would never—the repercussions following the massive leak are damaging enough. One of the contestants on the show, Richard Thompson (he who wore the most godawful dinosaur onesie from night one), tweeted just yesterday, "The fact that I laid it all out on the line for Savannah Rose while she was cheating on all of us—yeah, I'm talking emotional—just goes to show she's no one's sweetheart. #PutARingOnIt #BrokenHearted #EffYourCastingChoice."

Another contestant, Viktor Macky, uploaded an Instagram picture of himself with his arms around Rose. It was clearly taken during filming—only, juxtaposed on top of Rose's face was a cartoonlike crawfish, in a clear jab to her home state of Louisiana.

His caption reads: "How are you gonna come on a dating show when you're clearly in love with someone else? I quit my job for this! #PutARingOnIt #OverItOverHer #HappyAndSingle #YouHiring?"

It should be noted that Macky is an alleged Instagram influencer, so I'm not entirely convinced that one can lose a job in which you report to no one but yourself. Just my humble opinion, of course.

Strangely, all attempts to reach out to the final two contestants, Nick Stamos and Dominic DaSilva, were met with variations of the same response: "Leave the girl alone and get a life."

Ahem. This is *my life!*

Moving on.

While all of the internet is in a frenzy over Rose's deception, things seem to be looking up for her beau, Owen Harvey. Although he has not spoken out to any media sources, that has not stopped the media from talking about him. (Hey there, Owen, check your email would you?)

If there is any clapback from the revelation of him being colorblind (and a tattoo artist!) it's not happening online. Praise for Harvey is being slung from all over like shit in a barn. Other folks who are colorblind—to you, Dear Reader, is there a better way to phrase this?—drop me a line because I expect this to be a hot topic in the coming months. I'm not trying to offend all the lovely fans who are coming out of the woodwork to express how much they find Harvey a true inspiration in helping them follow their dreams.

~ Cue us all singing Kumbaya together like one big, happy family ~

While one crumbles, the other soars.

Oh, how I love humanity.

With the Put A Ring On It *reunion show due to air this*

coming Wednesday, I'll be back with a recap and all the tea. I have your best interests at heart, Dear Reader, never fear.

Till next time,

Celebrity Tea.

37

SAVANNAH

LOS ANGELES, CALIFORNIA

If looks could kill, then I'd be dead.

The Hollywood studio, where the reunion show is being aired live, is bustling with men. Men in suits. Men in bow ties. Men all wearing identical *I-hate-you-so-much-my-nostril-hairs-also-feel-the-burn* expressions. All of whom, if you want to get technical about it, are my ex-boyfriends.

Twenty-six in total.

Twenty-seven if you count Owen, which I don't.

I have never dreaded something so much in my life.

"Drink this," he tells me now, standing at my side and looking just as powerful, just as savage, as he did on the first night of filming. Black suit. Black tie. Black dress shirt. It's possible he chose it because going with all black is an easy decision for him to make, but secretly I think he enjoys the way I look like I might start drooling at any moment.

Our fingers brush as I take the proffered wine. As though we've stripped naked and started having wild sex on top of the bar, at least five pairs of eyes swing in our direction and don't move on to something bigger and better.

Honestly, it's starting to creep me out.

"It's not like you weren't on the show to begin with," I mutter to Owen after a sip of my wine. "You were a contestant. If we're looking at technicalities here, I did end up with one of the guys who came on the show."

"You knew me beforehand, sweetheart. These guys aren't gonna be looking at technicalities once we hit that stage."

Not one to be put off by nosy, beady eyes, Owen lowers a hand to the small of my back. Out of the corner of my eye, I watch as he levels a look on the group of guys that might as well come with a *Fuck Off* label. Viktor, an Instagrammer out of San Francisco, stiffens before strutting away. The rest follow him, one by one, until it's only me and Owen left in the green room.

I haven't seen Nick or Dom once since we arrived, but I have a gut feeling production is holding them captive—well, until we're all on stage, anyway. Then, I'm sure, they'll be hoping for some major drama to unfold. Jokes on them, though. Nick and Dom may not be my soulmates, either of them, but I like to think we're friends. If there's any drama at all tonight, it won't be coming from those two.

I take another sip from my glass.

Fifteen minutes until showtime.

"They're going to rip me to pieces out there."

Owen's hand moves north, to the center of my back. "Be *you*, out there. For the first time since you started this, there won't be any editing and splicing in post-production. No extra takes because you said something they didn't like; no pretending you give a shit about something that you don't."

I tilt my chin so I skate my gaze up from his broad chest to his face. Dark, messy hair. Dark, heated eyes that see so much and, now, reveal it all too. I raise my wineglass in a subtle toast. "If I hadn't booted you off, you would have put all these men to shame."

He grasps the stem of my wineglass, fingers curling over mine, and raises the glass to his lips for a deep drink. Then, over the rim, his mouth curls in a smirk. "If you hadn't booted me off, I would have had you quitting within the week. Resisting me is your one weakness."

"Is that so?"

"Yes, ma'am, it sure is."

I bite my lip, playing coy. "Then how'd you feel if I told you I decided to go without underwear with this dress?" Withdrawing the wineglass from his grip, I match him, pose for pose, smirking at him over the rim. "I just couldn't afford hundreds of thousands of people catching sight of my panty lines."

"*Fuck*," he growls, raking me over with his gaze, "you play dirty."

"I think the phrase you're actually looking for is, *I play even*."

"Is that you, Harvey?" a female's voice demands from behind me. I don't even need to turn around to know who it belongs to: Matilda-friggin'-Houghton. After listening to her bitch at me for three long months about everything that I was doing wrong, I'll probably be haunted by the sound of her shouting, *Savannah, no! Absolutely not*, until the day I die.

And then probably after that, too.

In typical Owen fashion, he doesn't start at the sound of her footsteps barreling toward us. Two sets of footsteps, if I'm not mistaken. Aaron, her always present cameraman, probably.

Voice eerily calm, Owen asks, "There a problem?"

"Yes! How many times have I had to say this? You're in

waiting room B, not A." I turn, just in time to see Matilda careen to a stop, her ever-present clipboard in her arms. She doesn't spare me a single glance, even though we haven't spoken since the end of the show. "The whole point of a real-time episode is so we can get your *real*-time reactions when you see Savannah."

"We're dating," Owen says in that no-bullshit tone of his. "The only real-time reaction you're going to get out of me is if someone acts out of line and gangs up on her."

"And *that* right there—that is why I told Joe you weren't allowed to come on the stage until the end of the episode."

What?

Setting the wineglass down on the bar, I step in front of Owen and face-off against the woman who told me on night one that I wasn't just cast to "sit and look pretty." Just because I was a debutante doesn't mean I'll roll over and cry wolf. "What do you mean Owen isn't allowed to come on the stage?"

"Exactly what I said, Savannah." Matilda eyes me up and down. From the way her lip curls, it's not a far reach to assume she hates the black cocktail-length dress I chose from wardrobe. It glimmers under the light, cuts off at my knees, and hugs my body in a flattering style. For shoes, I chose my own kick-ass teal pumps. If she has a problem with the outfit, she can take it up with my back when I strut away. "You," she says, pointing at Owen, "go in B. And *you*"—this time, she clamps a hand on my shoulder—"it's time to get the show on the road. This season has been an absolute shit show. I've gained ten pounds. I have more gray hair than I did six months ago. And when this crap is done tonight, I'm going to pour myself a bubble bath, watch *The Bachelor*, and call it a fucking day."

I raise my brow. "*The Bachelor*, really?"

Matilda's mouth pinches. "At least they have their shit together."

That they sure do. This season, *Put A Ring On It* has paid a contestant to come on the show, brought someone else on who had a girlfriend, allowed a fight to break out that sent one guy to the hospital for a rhinoplasty job—and, oh yeah, possibly has a rat to *Celebrity Tea Presents* or *is* the rat.

Tough call on that score.

A familiar hand grazes my wrist, tugging me into his arms. I go willingly, cheek against the planes of his hard chest, my hand slipping under his suit jacket so I can find his hip. "I don't like this," he says, voice hushed. The minute we walked in the doors an hour ago, we were sidelined by the entranceway and hooked up with wireless microphones. Mine sits just below my bra line, on my back. Owen's is on his hip. I clasp my hand over it now, so that if anything is picked up, hopefully it's only static.

Feeling his hand falling flat on my bra clasp, where the mic is, I brush my mouth on the underside of his chin and feel the bristles of his beard against my lips. "Let me be fearless."

The tension in his frame doesn't ease.

In the nine days that have passed since the so-called Scandal of the Year, the lawyers we hired have found out absolutely nothing. Thanks to Frannie pulling some strings, our case has been given to one of her FBI friends, but other than that . . . crickets. On the flight over to LA, Owen and I discussed a hundred different ways that we could approach the reunion show with a critical eye.

Five hours later, we came to only one conclusion: *Celebrity Tea Presents* has to be here, somewhere. Listening.

Watching. *Reporting*. And with absolutely no leads to work off, all we have is my list.

I mentally scratch Matilda off it. Not even a true fraud could fake the irritation she's wielding like a blade right now.

As if she's got a read on my mind, she tsks. "Save the kissy faces for after, would you, love birds? I've got places to be."

Over my head, Owen grinds out, "Your bubble bath isn't goin' anywhere."

Oh, my God.

Another kiss to his chin, and then I pull out of his embrace. His jacket falls back into place, leaving him to look way too dangerous and sexy for his own good. His bearded jaw strings tight and he gives me a subtle nod that I interpret as, *I got you*.

I know that he does—always.

Matilda's hand clasps my wrist and she gives me a small tug, leaving me no choice but to follow. With each crew member that we pass, I find myself scrutinizing their features. Most blink back at me, not even bothering to wave or say hello. Looks like they're all pretty much ready for the season to come to an end.

We pause by a door decorated with elaborate black curtains. "This is us," Matilda says, reaching for her radio on her hip. She points the rubber antenna at me. "Get in there, smile—"

"Pretty," I cut in, irritation peppering my tone. "You've given me this speech before."

She leans in, jabbing the antenna into my bicep. "And you've screwed it up before and nearly lost me my job in the process. Answer Joe's questions, pretend you actually give a shit that you deceived us all, and for the love of God, do *not* say anything about regretting the decision to come on the show."

And with that, she shoves me through the door and I stumble out onto the stage.

38

OWEN

As instructed, the cameraman drops me off in waiting room B. Unlike the producer, however, who looked ready to bite off the head of anyone who crossed her, this guy only shrugs his shoulders loosely on his way out the door. “Try not to get into any trouble, yeah?”

He says it like he expects me to do just that.

I don’t bother to correct him. With a sarcastic two-finger salute, I reply, “Yeah, man. I’m all good here.”

And then I’m left alone.

Considering that I’ve spent a lifetime being surrounded by cops, I’ve never been all that good at following orders. I wait a solid five minutes before making my move.

On silent feet, I hit up the narrow corridor that leads from Room B down to the rest of the prep rooms. With all the crew and contestants on stage filming the show, the hallway is blessedly empty.

My gut is telling me to take advantage of being the one left behind. One rather big problem is: I don’t know who the hell I’m looking for.

Whoever *Celebrity Tea* is, he's done a real good job of covering his tracks.

In nine days, we've discovered a whole lot of nothing. No new breaks, no new leads, nothing but the very obvious realization that we may be chasing our own tails forever with this case.

But I've never been the sort of person who sits back and lets shit fly. I take what I want, no matter the obstacles standing in the way. Which means I'm going to snag this opportunity for what it is: a chance to do a little digging of my own.

From my pocket, I pull out the list Savannah scraped together on our flight over from New Orleans. Mentally, I take off the producer's name—Matilda Houghton. The only vibes I was getting from her were *fuck-off-and-let-me-live* ones.

It takes me two different tries to find the hallway that houses all of the main crew's personal dressing rooms. With Savannah's list clutched in hand and my gaze trained on the doors, I note the paper taped to each one, indicating who the room belongs to.

Matilda Houghton, Producer.

Greg Wilson, Assistant Producer.

Allie Jenkins, Set Designer.

Joe Devonsson, Director, Creator, and Host.

Martin Quell, Casting director and Producer.

The sole of my shoe squeals against the laminate tile as I stop abruptly. Martin Quell. Wasn't he the one Amelie put me in touch with, the one who got me on *Put A Ring On It* in the first place? I try to recall the conversation, only to come up mostly blank.

I'd been nervous as fuck during that call, nearly as shy and uncomfortable as back in high school when it came to

Maryanne. I'd stammered, at least once, but Quell had laughed my concerns off. *"Talk about big, romantic gestures,"* I remember him telling me, *"she's gonna eat this shit up, man."*

We hadn't stayed on the phone for much longer after that, but hadn't he emailed me the next day? Immediately, my hand goes to the pocket of my slacks. *Shit.* No phone. We'd exchanged cell phones for microphones when we first entered the studio, as was protocol.

Glancing down the length of the hall, I check to make sure that no one is coming before putting a hand to Quell's doorknob and giving it a shimmy. No go. "Dammit," I mutter under my breath, "think, *think.*"

The casting director never made it onto Savannah's list, but my gut is telling me something is way off here. That email . . . part of the application process had been to submit all kinds of information. While Quell had let me skip the audition tapes, since he personally was inviting me on the show, I hadn't been able to avoid the other prerequisites demanded from every contestant.

Health records, criminal records.

Wait.

Fuck.

In that original article—the one where *Celebrity Tea* first put my jail time on blast—hadn't the asshole claimed he'd discovered the information based on an old article from the Orleans Parish Prison? Which would be impossible because New Orleans' main lockup doesn't have a blog, of all things, and it sure as hell isn't going to spend the time and money hiring someone to detail every digression that goes on behind bars. The list would never end, which means . . .

Hell, *Celebrity Tea* must have had the information leaked from another source while using the supposed blog as a coverup, hoping that no one would notice. Except, the *only* people who knew about that instance are Gage, the other inmates who joined the fight, and . . . Quell. He promised the information would remain confidential.

I feel like an absolute idiot for not connecting the dots sooner.

Hand moving from the doorknob to the door itself, I plant my shoulder on it and shove, pathetically hoping that it might jar loose off the hinges.

I've done a lot of bad shit in my life but accomplishing the art of picking locks has never been one of them.

The door doesn't budge.

Frustration coils deep in my gut as I bang my fist on the door, once, twice. Twisting around, I plant my back against it. Sink the heels of my palms into my eye sockets, running through possible scenarios in my head. While stalking down Quell and forcing him to confess is a real enticing thought, who knows if he's even here today. Not to mention that I've never seen him in person, making the chance of me recognizing his face while walking down the hall slim to none.

Either I get my ass back to Room B before someone notices that I'm missing, or I say screw it and do my own thing anyway.

Because I'm me, I opt for the second.

Hands shoved deep into the pockets of my slacks, like I'm going for a casual stroll, I retrace my steps and then keep moving. When I hit the stage area, I hang a right, looking for one of the entrances that lead to the platform area where the fans are seated.

There we are.

I slip through a curtained doorway. Glance right, then left, checking for anyone who might recognize me, then take an empty seat at the end of a row. The overhead lights are turned down low, centering the entire room's attention on Savannah and the *Put A Ring On It*'s host, Joe Devonsson. With their backs facing the far wall, all twenty-six contestants are seated in three rows. I drag my gaze down to the first, looking for the two guys who got down on one knee and proposed to Savannah.

Nick Stamos.

Dominic DaSilva.

Neither man looks all too happy to be sitting there. Both dark-haired and dressed in equally dark suits, they watch the stage with identical expressions of displeasure. I wonder if Mina Pappas, Nick's fiancée, is in the audience, then recall reading about Dominic's girlfriend online, and wonder if she's joined, as well.

Both men came on the show and ended up with different women.

I got kicked off and ended up with the bachelorette.

I seek her out now, catching the tail end of her response to whatever question she was asked: "—wasn't my intention to hurt anyone. That's not the sort of person I am."

Opposite her, Devonsson sits with one ankle propped up on his other knee, a stack of notecards gripped in his hand. Looking like a king posturing before his court, he idly drums the stack of cards on his thigh, then waves a hand at the contestants. "The fact of the matter is, whether that was your intention or not, many of our guys feel utterly destroyed by your betrayal."

My fingers grip the armrest. *Destroyed?* Christ, could the guy be any more dramatic? No one in those seats is shedding a tear, not that I can see.

Savannah opens her mouth, only to be soundly cut off by Devonsson. "Before we give you the chance to defend yourself, Savannah, I'd like to take it to the floor and give some of these guys some much needed closure. Viktor," he says, pointing the notecard stack toward the group, "you've been rather vocal on Instagram regarding your feelings on the matter."

A guy in the second row pops up, and I immediately recognize him as one of the assholes who was hounding Savannah earlier in the waiting room. With slicked-back hair and a suit with lapels the size of Texas, Viktor fixes his bow tie and then sticks his head out like a chicken pecking at feed. "Savannah, I just want to say that I quit my job because of this experience and for you to—"

"I want it to be clear for those watching on," Devonsson interjects, looking over to the audience, "Viktor is an Instagram influencer."

Off to the side, a projector on the wall flashes a word that reads ACT DISGUSTED.

As one, the crowd promptly draws in a heavy breath, amplified by the fact that there are at least a hundred women seated around me.

I roll my eyes. What a load of shit.

Up on the stage, Savannah uncrosses her legs. "There's absolutely nothing wrong with being a social media guru," she says thinly, snapping the room into silence. "My family's business wouldn't be nearly as successful as it is without the critical eye of my staff member, Jorge. We owe him everything." Turning to Viktor, she sets a hand on the sofa, beside her hip, and leans forward. "And I'm sorry you feel that way. Truly, I do. I wish you nothing but the best, and I hope your pages really take off for you."

There you go, sweetheart.

Looking shell-shocked, Viktor sits down to the chorus of clapping from the audience. I keep my hands on my thighs, not wanting to draw attention to myself from the women sitting nearby. Subtly, I shoot a glance around the room. Is Quell in here? It makes me uneasy that he could be, and I wouldn't even know it.

Meanwhile, Savannah doesn't even realize that anything's wrong. Maybe that's a good thing—let her handle the contestant mess before I clue her in to the fact that we've found our *Celebrity Tea*.

Another contestant launches up, this time without being called on. He straightens his thin tie, then waves a hand toward Savannah. "My problem is that *I* was accused of having a girlfriend and you sent me home. I sat at home watching every week, while seeing spoilers hit the internet, and the hypocrisy kills me. You're just as much of a liar as I am."

I watch as Savannah closes her hand in a fist. "Harry, listen—"

"The difference is, man, you went on a show *with* a girlfriend. An official one."

One of the overhead lights drops to Dominic DaSilva's head, highlighting Stamos's right arm at the same time.

In the row behind them, Harry visibly bristles. "Weren't you *paid* to come on the show?"

DaSilva only stretches out his legs and crosses one ankle over the other. "Sounds about right."

"So, what? You're trying to make me feel guilty right now? Dude, none of us received a paycheck. You did."

"And I paid the price for it," the ex-footballer says smoothly. "She found out, she turned me down, and that's that. I'm not out here whining like a little bitch about someone following their heart. Savannah came on here to find the person who works for *her*. You signed up, knowing she could send your ass packing on night one."

Damn.

An unexpected grin curves my mouth.

One of the producers off to the side starts waving her hands like she's directing a plane touching down on the tarmac, and suddenly the black projector screen swaps over to LAUGH LOUD. On cue, the audience starts tittering awkwardly. One of the ladies in front of me gets so into it, she nails the chick beside her with an elbow to the kidney.

"Uh, thank you, Dom," Savannah says, clearly trying to hold back a grin. Sobering, she folds her hands in her lap. "And, Harry, I really did try. Yes, I had feelings for Owen that started before the show began filming, but I still had . . . hope. It's why I stayed all the way to the end."

Devonsson clears his throat. "Although that's not the only reason you stayed, right?"

Savannah's expression turns wary. "I'm not sure what you mean by that, Joe."

He flips to the next notecard, snapping the old one down on the coffee table that's situated between the two sofas. As though the table's been wired with a mic, too, the *thwack* of the card hitting glass echoes loudly in the studio. "Of all the emails that were released last week, one of them *really* caught my eye."

Unprompted, immediate silence falls over the room.

My heart kicks into gear, thumping faster.

That heiress mask that I hate so much neutralizes Savannah's expression. She sits, hands clasped, her head tilted to the side, like they're discussing what wine to pour next. "There were a lot of emails, Joe. I can't even begin to imagine which one you're talking about."

"I think we've talked enough about the emails, haven't we? How about we discuss the fact that DaSilva over here won the wet abs contest and put the rest of us to shame?" *Stamos,* thank Christ.

I'd kiss the guy if I were standing anywhere nearby.

"What can I say?" DaSilva drawls. "My abs are memorable. Once you touch them, you never forget 'em."

Devonsson doesn't even spare them so much as a glance. The projector screen's instruction to the audience remains on LAUGH LOUD but there's not even a peep from the crowd. Total quiet reigns, and all I hear is the rush of blood pounding furiously in my head. My fingers curl tightly around the armrest, as though that alone can keep my ass seated instead of bum-rushing the stage for Savannah.

"I'd like to read the one that really got to me." Clearing his throat, Devonsson draws the card up so it's at eye level. "Owen," he says, in a tone that tells me he's trying to impersonate Savannah's soft, New Orleans drawl, "I can't believe I'm still writing these, but my heart feels so torn in two. I'm lost. So goddamn lost. What do I choose? A chance for my dad to repair his relationship with my sister . . . or you? The deal of the century, hand-delivered by Daddy dearest to keep me in check. I chose Amelie, not because I don't want you—not because I don't *love* you—but because she's spiraling, and I can't see my family break more than it already has. The thought of you hating me for this is—"

"*Stop.*"

The whispered word flies off Savannah's tongue and I feel it like an arrow aimed right at my heart. Her pain is palpable, but my brain is rooted on that email.

A deal.

A choice.

In the last week, I chose not to read any of the leaked emails, opting instead to trust in what Savannah and I have built, what we've reached together after everything that's happened. But I can't deny the hurt that ricochets through me, like splintered glass slicing through every one of my organs.

I smash the emotion to smithereens.

Eight months ago, if the choice had come down between Savannah and Gage, I would have felt the same impossible chasm between choosing my sibling and choosing the love of my life.

Because *that* is who Savannah is to me.

She took a man who hid from the world behind his ink and his attitude, and she stripped him down until nothing remained but vulnerability and hope. And every step of the way, she's shown me how much the feeling is reciprocated. I think of the sketchbook that I left on the coffee table in Barataria before catching our flight to California, the one she didn't need to buy back for me but did, with no expectations of receiving anything in return. She wanted me to keep every piece of my soul, never bartering a section off.

Last night, before I picked her up so we could head to the airport, I slung open my closet door and pulled out all of the oil paintings I've locked away over the years, in fear that someone might see them and pass judgment. I drove to Barataria at three in the morning, those paintings propped up on the back bench of my truck, and proceeded to hang them up in the living room once I arrived.

Because I want Savannah to see all of me.

I want her to know that when she steps into our house next, that every move I make to strip another plank from my shield, is because of her trust in me.

If I've bartered off anything at all, it's my heart.

I've given it to her, and I don't want it back.

Low murmurings pick up behind me, but I never tear my gaze away from the woman on the stage. Ignoring all protocol, she slips off the couch and snatches the notecard from Devonsson.

"Savannah, give that back."

Producers fly into motion all around the studio, but I'm already on my feet and moving toward the back wall so I can get closer without anyone noticing me. If Devonsson touches her, he's a dead man walking.

Savannah evades his grasp by ducking under his arm. Her high heels puncture the stage floor with a quick staccato as she stumbles back. "Where did you get this?" she demands, her voice clear, sharp. Her hand, I note, is trembling as she waves that card in the air.

Hold on, sweetheart. I'm coming for you.

From my periphery, I see DaSilva and Stamos launch to their feet.

"Savannah, I think it's safe to say that you're overreacting." Devonsson throws a panicked glance at the cameras, which are angled toward the stage from all areas of the room. He makes a slashing motion across his neck, but I don't see a single person move to stop the cameras from recording. "That email was leaked with all the others."

"No, it wasn't." She takes another step backward, the toes of her shoe feeling around for the edge of the stage. "I read every single email that was leaked. Every. Single. One. But this one wasn't, Joe. Want to know why? Because I wrote it on *Monday*. This past Monday, and I hoped that whoever the hacker was, would be so desperate for more gossip that I didn't even change my account password. Just left the door wide open for him to screw himself over." A satisfied grin curves her bottom lip. "I only have one question for you . . . are we still live?"

39

SAVANNAH

Chaos explodes in the studio.

There are producers yelling to "shut the fucking cameras down!" and the audience is talking a mile a minute in a confused uproar, and me—I'm being driven backward by a pair of toned arms that smell like coconut lotion and feel like anger.

Joe—*Celebrity Tea Presents* in the flesh—shoves me out of the way like I'm nothing but a rag doll. I trip, trying to catch my weight on something stable, and go crashing down instead. My back smashes against the corner of the stage, turning my vision blurry when pain supersedes the shock.

Don't black out, don't black out, don't black out.

"Get everyone *out*!" someone screams. Matilda, I think. Maybe another crew member who didn't anticipate the blow of their boss—the guy who friggin' *created* the show after working on *The Bachelor* franchise for years—stooping so low as this.

To be honest, I didn't suspect Joe either.

The scent of coconut infiltrates my senses a second

before fingers grasp the back of my dress. "You fucking bitch," he snaps, hauling me up to my knees, "you think you're just going to, *what*? Rat me out on national television?"

It's on the tip of my tongue to tell him that hadn't been the plan at all. Timestamping an email back to November had required me promising Jorge at least two dozen of Dufrene's crawfish dumplings, an extra week of vacation time, and a pay bonus, since he viewed the whole thing as a little illegal. I'd expected the culprit to out themselves behind-the-scenes or at least to leave a trail that the FBI could hook their teeth into while Owen and I traveled to California.

Having that email read out loud by *Put A Ring On It*'s director, host, and creator, on the other hand, in front of the entire world? Now *that* is the scandal of the century.

Breathing sharply through my nose, I focus on not crying out.

Instinct would have me begging him to let me go.

I won't give him the satisfaction.

He's dragged me through the mud for *months*. He's made me question my own self-worth. He's made me the butt of every sly joke and every derogatory comment online. And then, he put the cherry right on top by dealing out my innermost feelings to the world like they were nothing but cheap tickets to a rock show.

Are you dead? I hear my dad's voice in my head, that stern but affectionate look in his eyes, *then get back up*.

"You're making a scene, Joe." I jab an elbow back, hoping to hit soft flesh. Disappointment slams into me when I collide with nothing but air. I squirm in his grip, trying to find leverage. "The whole world already knows what you did. Why make it worse when you're already looking at an orange jumpsuit in your near future?"

For the merest second, that hand lets go. I take the opportunity for what it is: an opening. In a move that my dad taught me when I was thirteen, I snap my head back and make a little prayer. *Crack!* Stars explode in front of me. My teeth crash together, sending a shockwave of agony through my body. I feel the tingle in my toes, in my fingertips.

But then that hand releases me completely, followed by the distinct sound of a pained grunt, and I don't hesitate to take advantage.

Up, up, GET. UP!

I haul myself off the ground, my vision swimming, swimming, swimming as my head continues to throb. One step forward and I nearly collapse on wobbly legs. *Dammit.* My beautiful teal pumps do absolutely nothing in the way of making a hasty retreat. Kicking them off would be too time-consuming. Short of stripping one off and using the spiked heel as a weapon—and landing myself in prison, no doubt—I scrap the idea and whip around, already winding my arm back to pummel Joe in the face.

Only, one second he's there, clutching his nose, and, in the next, a blur of black is coming out of nowhere and tackling Joe to the ground.

Owen.

Familiar inked knuckles jab once into Joe's gut, and then another time into his jaw. If it were possible for a person's head to actually twirl like a spinning top, Joe's would be flying off his body and rolling into the stands of horrified fans. As it is, there's a solid *crunch* of cartilage snapping and then a squealed, "You broke my nose, you bastard!"

Owen's answer to that is another one-two punch to the

gut that has Joe's limbs flexing in the air like they've been attached to a puppet string.

Is it wrong that I'm feeling the need to pump my fists in the air and shout, "That's my man right there!"

Then again, probably not the time or the place. Or maybe it is, considering this is a reunion show and Owen and I didn't have the chance to go public with our relationship.

Unexpectedly, strong arms circle my waist, dragging me backward from the fray. "If you get hurt," says a deep voice in my ear, immediately settling my impulse to go for another headbutt, "Mina will rip my nuts out and force me to eat them for breakfast."

Nick.

Despite the fact that I trust him wholly, I dig my heels in, anyway. "If Owen gets hurt, I'll rip them out myself and hand them to her on a silver platter."

Joe squeals again, and I return my attention to the fight just in time to see him crawling along the floor as Owen links a hand around his shin to halt his escape.

Behind me, Nick lets out a throaty laugh. "Yeah, I'm pretty sure that's never going to happen."

Coming up on the other side of Nick, Dom says, "That fucker is the one who hacked your emails?" The former NFL player flicks his dark eyes over me, as though to make sure I'm all in one piece.

Another squeal.

"It's *Celebrity Tea*," I tell them both.

Dom's mouth drops open. "Hold on, *Joe* is *Celebrity Tea*?" When I nod, his eyes turn flinty and zip over to Nick. "You got her?"

What in the world?

Nick pats my shoulder like I'm a good dog. "Take a swing

for me, would you? Just trying to live up to the old Saint Nick reputation, you know."

"Never would have expected anything less from a mama's boy like you, Stamos." With a grin and a shoulder pat of his own, Dom strides over to the all-out brawl, shoves Owen to the side like he's nothing heavier than a bag of feathers, and announces, "Nice to officially meet you, Mr. *Celebrity Tea*. It's been a long time coming."

His fist connects with Joe's jaw, and I cringe.

"Should we stop them?" I ask Nick. "You know, before they do permanent damage?"

The Greek Adonis only grins. "Oh, I don't know. I think good ol' Joe can take one more round for the team."

And then he stands back, arms crossed over his chest, and waits for security to arrive.

JOE DEVONSSON CONFESSES TO HIS SIDE HUSTLE OF BEING THE anonymous owner of *Celebrity Tea Presents* through a new gap in his teeth, a gift from the inked god himself.

From my seat on the hospital bed, I stare at the tiny TV as Joe lisps, "There's no crime in being a reporter. You can't send me to jail for that." He slaps at the hands of the police officer who tries to bind him in shackles. "Where are my rights as a US citizen? I didn't hack her fucking emails!"

The news station bleeps out his cursing while he's escorted into the back of a police cruiser, then swaps over to a reporter standing in front of the camera, a microphone in her hand. "John, this is going to be one for the books. Never, in the history of reality TV, has there ever been a scandal quite like this one. All fingers point to Devonsson as being the email hacker—maybe with a helping hand or two along the way—but that'll be left to investigators to figure out. For now, let's go to a clip of the moment when everything exploded on the air."

I hit the POWER button on the remote controller.

Within minutes of security appearing, chaos erupted all over again. Along with Dom, Owen was pulled off Joe before being escorted to talk to the cops. Nick stood vigilantly by my side, especially when paramedics arrived. Of all people, Matilda was the one to bring them over to me, and before I knew it, I was being shuffled into the back of an ambulance.

If I have to guess, I'm thinking that the show will do anything to ensure I don't turn around and sue their asses to the moon and back. This hospital visit, to check if I have a concussion, is apparently "on them."

And for the last forty-five minutes, I've been stuck in this room with nothing but Joe's scuffed-up face on the TV for company.

I fall back against the pillows, then wince when the base of my skull connects with the metal headboard. "*Ow*."

Hand to my head, I rub the sore spot, then cringe all over again when the bedside phone starts ringing. I throw out a hand, palm smacking the surface until my fingers grasp the receiver and I answer it, croaking out a weak, "Hello?"

"Savannah!" my mom shrieks in my ear. "Oh, God, we saw on the TV! We've been calling every hospital in the LA area for over an hour after we couldn't reach your cell. Are you okay? Of course you're not okay. I can*not* believe that man—"

There's a shuffling of hands, I think, and then Dad's voice is coming through the line: "*Cherie*, I love you but are you *crazy*? Taking on that man like you're some sort of superhero?"

A weak smile pulls at my mouth. "You told me to get back up, Pops."

Silence greets me for a second before he exclaims, "That is *not* what I meant."

"Pops, what other situations call for a headbutt like that?" I hear Amelie ask in the background. "She did good."

"Well, now she probably has a concussion, and whose fault is that, Edgar? You never told me you taught them to headbutt people."

Dad groans. "Marie, it was self-defense. I didn't want to worry you."

"Too late for that! My baby is on the other side of the country with a probable concussion. I am worrying. I am past worrying. I *am* worry."

Right, then.

As it turns out, I do have a minor concussion, but it's probably best if I keep that diagnosis to myself. For now, at least. "Pops, Mom, Amelie, I love you all so much, but maybe we could hold off on the arguing until a point when my head doesn't feel like it's going to explode?"

It's the wrong thing to say.

My family promptly launches into a discussion of flights that they can hop on and Mom telling me to get a second opinion of everything the doctor tells me, and I can't help it —I smile, so wide, so big, it hurts. The Roses are not perfect, not in the slightest, but in this moment, I feel *loved*.

Dad's voice jogs me back into the conversation when he says, "And you tell Harvey thank you, *cherie*. I don't . . . I'll tell him for myself when y'all get back, but please let him know how much I appreciate him defending you. He's—he's a good man. I would have seen it sooner if not for my pride."

I know how much it takes for him to admit that. Throat tight, mouth dry, I whisper, "I'll tell him, Pops. Thank you."

When a knock sounds on the door a second later, I issue a quick good-bye that's met with protests all the way around, and then sit up tall in the bed. *Please let it be Owen*. I haven't heard a word from him after I was carted away in the ambulance, and my patience is wearing thin.

I need to have him here with me.

And I need to know that he won't hate me forever for not telling him the truth.

"Come in!"

The door cracks open. Only, it's not Owen's familiar face that I see but Nick and Dom's, followed by a tall blonde that I immediately recognize as Aspen Levi—from *Celebrity Tea Presents*, of course. I fight the urge to roll my eyes. Joe Devonsson really did have his fingers dipped in all of the pots.

Doing my best to ignore the throbbing in my head, I smile at the trio. "Hey, guys. Long time no see." I look to Aspen, and for her, I try to smile a little harder. God knows I look a hot mess. "It's so nice to meet you. Is Topher here?"

Her blue eyes go wide at my mention of her son, like she's surprised I remembered his name. "No, he's at home. In Maine, I mean. We were going to bring him, but Dominic thought we could use a small adults-only weekend before the school year starts up."

Dom stands at the foot of the bed, his hands resting on the metal footboard. "She's lying. Topher ditched us last minute for his friends. Apparently, a week of nothing but playing video games trumps three days in California."

Aspen laughs, hooking one finger into the back of Dom's jeans in a way that speaks volumes to the familiarity between them. My heart warms. Dom may have come on *Put A Ring On It* for all the wrong reasons, but so did I. I'm happy he found his person, and by the way he glances over at her, his black eyes practically glittering with affection, I know without a doubt that he has.

I turn to Nick. "Where's Mina?"

It's Aspen who answers with a wry grin. "Probably slapping herself silly for going to a beauty convention instead. Do you know what she texted me when the fight broke out?"

Nick glances over at her, his brows furrowed. "She texted you?"

"Oh, yeah. She wanted me to pass a message along to Savannah."

"She did?" I ask. Over the last number of months, Mina and I have exchanged a few messages here and there. It started as a question on her end, wanting to know what hotels she and Nick should stay at for their honeymoon because they planned to go to Greece, and I'd just been there. Somehow, we fell into a habit of chatting every few weeks about something random. "What did she say?"

From her purse, Aspen pulls out her phone. "Ahem, this is a direct quote: Tell Savannah that she is the badass bachelorette that all of America deserves."

I laugh at that, my head tipped back. It pings off the metal again and I end up biting back a curse.

Nick steps forward, an arm already reaching for the bell on the bedside table that's meant to ring for nurse assistance. I swat him away. "I'm okay, really. Just a little bruise, that's all."

"I'm pretty sure that's not all," he says with a frown. "I can get someone if you need it. Just say the word."

I shake my head. "No, no! Totally fine. I just . . ." Taking a deep breath, I stare up at the three people who wouldn't be in my life, or in this hospital room at all, if it weren't for a crazy reality TV dating show. The irony kills me, but at the same time, I wouldn't have it any other way. *Sliding scales.*

Truth be told, I'm rather content to harbor all these memories close to my chest, especially the one of me headbutting *Celebrity Tea Presents* himself, right into the grave. "Have y'all seen Owen at all? I need—"

"I know exactly what you need, sweetheart."

Owen.

Against my will, I gasp like a besotted idiot at the sound of his voice. And when Dom steps aside to give me a view of the doorway, I all but break down in tears. His hair is all mussed and somewhere, along the way, he lost his suit jacket. The tie, too, is gone.

I hear Dom, Nick, and Aspen shuffle around and promise to give me a call when I'm discharged. With a look of kindness in her blue eyes, Aspen offers an invite for Owen and me to grab dinner with them before they leave on Friday, if we want.

I want.

But I want to be alone with Owen more.

The door closes behind Nick, and then Owen is walking in, his shoulders hunched, his face set in that familiar brooding scowl of his. My heart gives an unsteady thump of anticipation. I ache to feel his muscled arms around my frame, his sturdy weight pressing into the mattress beside mine.

"I wasn't sure if the cops had arrested you," I say, coiling the blanket on the bed between my fingers. "You sort of treated Joe's face like a trampoline."

Black eyes dart to my face, to the bruise on my elbow. "Were you lying?" His gaze lifts again, meeting mine with such startling intensity that my entire chest heaves. "When you said that you wrote the email this past Monday?"

Guilt, the fickle, fickle thing, slams into me with riotous force. "I should have told you."

He sits down on the seat that's positioned next to the bed, close enough but not close enough to touch. *Dammit.* "You didn't, though. Why?"

I swallow, hard. "I didn't know if it would work, but also . . . I wanted, no, I *needed* you to be surprised if it came out. I didn't expect Joe to be *Celebrity Tea*, not at all. That—that was a major shock."

"That's not an answer, Savannah."

Savannah, not Rose.

My skin grows tight as I sit there on the bed. Every part of me feels primed to launch myself at his solid frame and beg for forgiveness. Except right now, as it is, I'm not sure if he would be on board with that. There's a stillness to his expression, a stiff resolve, that I haven't seen since I brought him his sketchbook and he kissed me so hard I nearly cracked.

I flatten my palms on the bed, then curl my fingers tight into a fist. "I was scared," I finally whisper.

His deep baritone answers roughly, "To trust me?"

"That you would leave me, if you knew the truth." There's no stopping the tears. I feel them rush forward and I blink, again and again, to try to quell them before they make an appearance. "I-I knew that I needed something monumental for *Celebrity Tea* to find. I had Jorge move the time-stamped email into another folder, with the hope that Joe would simply think that he had missed it on the first go-round. But another email talking about me missing you wasn't going to cut it." My lungs squeeze at the memory of sitting at my computer and typing up the words that I knew would devastate Owen. Even worse, they could tear us apart.

I stare at the way his knuckles are clenched around the armrests of his chair.

It's tearing us apart right now.

Air seems harder to find when I continue, "Every word he said is true. My dad did put me in that position, and I felt so torn that"—I swallow down a sob, burying it deep so it won't completely betray me—"it had come down to that. You told me you don't want to relive that night again but, Owen, I hung on those moments of you climbing out of that limo for *months*. You looked at me like I was someone worth keeping. You asked for my hand, and my stupid brain replayed those seconds where instead I did as you asked, and you got down on one knee."

My chin quivers and I whip my head to the side because I will *not* let the tears come.

Be fearlessly unapologetic.

He asked me to be fearless. He asked me to be unapologetic in all that I want. And maybe this wasn't what he had in mind, but I ignore the little voice in my head telling me to be composed and pulled together.

For the first time in so many years, I give myself permission to be perfectly imperfect.

A splash of wetness hits my cheekbone. I don't wipe the tear away and I don't hurry to make an excuse for it either. Instead, I give voice to the words that have lived inside my soul for so long that, to let them fly free, feels nearly cathartic.

"Every time I wrote another email, I promised myself that *this* one, this was the one I would finally send to you. But I never did, not for any of them. I did that for seven months, wanting you so badly while I tortured myself with every possible *what-if*. What if I hit send? What if you want me back still? All the while I kept that secret locked within me, like a ticking bomb strapped to my back that I couldn't escape. And when I saw you in the souvenir shop, I finally remembered what it was like to *breathe*."

I shake my head, the sight of him blurring among all my tears. "Because that's what you've done for me since the moment we met, Owen. You showed me how to find the light and you showed me that it was okay to dream the impossible. And every time you looked my way, I fell a little harder—for you, for the life we could have together." I swipe my eyes with the back of my hand, but only because I'm crying too hard to see. "My dad always says that success is only halted by the lazy, but I think he's had it wrong all along. Success is only halted by the fearful . . . and I was terrified of losing you."

Silence crackles its fiery wings of death between us, and my stomach churns with dread. *Fight for him!* "Owen, please, I—"

His big body lifts from the seat and then drops on the empty spot to the right of me on the bed. Hands balled into fists, he drops them to the mattress on either side of my body, caging me in. "I watched you today," he says roughly, "from the audience."

A lump sticks in my throat. "You were supposed to be in Room B."

His black eyes pin me in place. "I've never been all that good at doing what I'm told, Rose."

Everything in me goes still at my surname on his lips.

Do not hope. Do not hope. Do not hope.

But still my heart strains in want, and my fingers grip the bedsheets even tighter to keep myself from reaching for him.

"I sat in that audience and I watched you navigate those questions and I thought to myself, the world does not deserve her."

A nervous laugh leaps to my lips. "I don't know about all that."

"That Instagram asshole berated you, and you wished him the best. Those men took aim and *fired* at you and not once did you take any cheap potshots back, even though I'm sure you could have." Owen's elbows bend a notch, his face inching closer to mine. "The whole time you sat on that stage, I thought only one thing: *I'm yours*."

"But the email—"

"I forgave you in that moment, sweetheart."

"*Oh*." Here come the waterworks all over again. I squeeze my eyes shut, but calloused fingertips tracing my cheeks have them popping back open.

"Life throws many choices at us," he says, his voice pitched low, "and all you can do is hop on the one that feels right in your gut—even if your gut is telling you two different things." Owen moves his hand to the nape of my neck, the pressure in his touch light, so as not to hurt me. "Six months ago, I never would have considered opening up to you about being colorblind—and I thought that same thing, even, that night when we were in the parlor. It would have been easy to pretend I hadn't noticed the switch in colors. It would have been easy to let the fear of rejection or judgment keep my lips sewn shut when you'd given me the perfect excuse to walk away, my secret safe and sound."

"Then why did you tell me?" I whisper, leaning back into his comforting touch.

His gaze flicks between mine, searching. "Because you can't take a leap of faith with the woman you love if you aren't ready to strip yourself down to the studs."

My breath hitches. "*Owen*."

"Because there is no other woman I'd ever wear an astronaut cat backpack for," he goes on, destroying me with the absolute sincerity in his voice and the warmth in his gaze, "because there is no other woman in this world who slips her hand into mine when I'm spiraling, and it's all I need to feel righted again." He takes my hand, the one balled up in the sheets, and lays it over his left pectoral. Beneath my palm, I feel the quick tattoo of his heart beating fast. Nearly as fast as mine. "And because if there was any chance of me even thinkin' it might not be love, you killed that thought in an instant when you headbutted Joe like a total badass."

"Just like a man," I say, strangled laughter fighting to escape, "to say all the sweet things and give me the flowery words, and then give me a virtual high-five for breaking a guy's nose."

Owen's brows arch high. "Now let's not get carried away now. Pretty sure I'm the one who broke his nose."

"Like I said, just like a man."

Eyes sparkling, Owen sits back. "Is it just like a man to ask to keep his fiancée locked up in the hospital room until he could get there?"

My heart stops. "Did you just say *fiancée*? And what do you mean that you kept me *locked up* here?"

He ignores me completely, merely grasps my legs by the thighs and gently turns me, so that the back of my knees rest on the lip of the mattress. With a shove of his thigh, he pushes the chair out of the way. Then leans over to turn on the bedside lamp that looks like it belongs in the 80s.

"Owen," I breathe, "what are you doing?"

He drops to his knee, his *one* knee. "Eight months ago, I took a risk and showed up here in California, hoping to win your heart." He flashes me a wry smile, one corner lifted higher than the other with boyish charm. "It didn't go so well. The girl of my dreams crushed my heart."

My tongue flies to the roof of my mouth, biting back a grimace. "Too soon. Way too soon."

That grin widens, like he's enjoying making me squirm.

"I spent the next few months living in misery. Hoping she would show up and beg me to give her a second chance. Alternatively praying that she would never show her face again."

"You are *not* warming me up with this speech."

A deep, satisfied chuckle reverberates in his chest. "But then the girl came back, and no matter how much I tried to shake her loose, it didn't work. She waltzed into my parlor and made me crave. She went to bat with me, a total test of the wills, and I'll admit that though I beat her solidly on that score, she got me back by siccing her cat on me like a privately hired assassin."

"Oh, my God, *Owen*." Dammit, I don't want to laugh but I can't stop the flow. Pressing my palms to my cheeks, I manage out between fits, "But y'all have bonded! Give me a little credit here."

"Speaking of binding—"

"I said *bonding*, Owen, not binding." Heat rushes to my face.

"—she loves it when I tie her up."

My eyes squeeze shut. "I hate you."

"No," Owen says, humor in his voice, "you love me."

I peer down at him, my heart in my throat. "Yes," I whisper, the laughter dissipating when I notice the slight tremble in the hand that he has planted on one knee. Owen Harvey will always have a bit of the shy boy he used to be, and I adore him all the more for it. "I love you so much that it hurts."

"Hurts so good," he returns, and I jerk my head in a shaky nod. One of his inked hands dives into the front pocket of his slacks and comes out with a black velvet box that, on sight, has me trembling too. "I had a whole plan for this, you know," he husks out, "I was gonna put Pablo in a cat tux and bring you both down to Barataria. I wanted to do it on the balcony with the sunset behind you and a piece of art I'd painted for you resting on our bed. I wanted you to see me, all of me, and know that you're marrying a man who may see the world a little differently, but when he looks at you, there aren't any colors that are lost to him because you bring them to life, sweetheart. For him—for *me*—you bring them to life."

My lungs squeeze and I press my fist to my mouth, joy ripping through me like beams from a thousand splintered rainbows.

"So," Owen murmurs, "it's unfortunate for you that you got yourself a concussion because it occurred to me, while you were being shuttled into that ambulance, that this was my chance to propose when you weren't in your right mind to say no. I went to every jeweler I could find in the last hour."

A startled laugh shoots out of me. I hate him and I adore him and I love him too much to say anything other than, "Don't be shy, Owen. Take what you want."

"Oh, I am, sweetheart, I definitely am." And then he reaches for my hand, skipping over asking for it, and slides a gold ring to the base of my fourth finger. A gold ring with a marquise-styled ruby gem—the deep red stone winks back at me. I raise a startled glance to his rugged face, only for him to offer a shy smile. His black eyes shine with raw vulnerability. "So when people ask me why I can't see certain colors," he says, "I can say that you're keeping them captive right there on your finger. Turns out you made a promise to me on our wedding day that if I kiss you enough times, you'll give them all back."

I reach out to grip his hand, holding on tightly. "What if

I never give them back because I love my husband just the way he is, shadows and all?"

His smile turns lopsided and he rises, his inked fingers cupping my face as he presses his forehead to mine. "I'd love you just the same. Today, tomorrow, and for all the tomorrows that follow."

40

THREE MONTHS LATER

US Tonight:

Breaking News! Joe "Celebrity Tea Presents" *Devonsson Sentenced to Three Years in Prison*

Much speculation has occurred over the last few months on whether or not Joe Devonsson, formerly the head creator, director, and host of the reality show Put A Ring On It, *would face time behind bars. While Devonsson's legal team continued to try to save face by claiming that Devonsson was not the culprit behind the email hacking, yesterday he ultimately pled guilty.*

In court he reportedly exclaimed, "No show has ever had higher ratings than Put A Ring On It *in the history of television," when the judge passed his verdict.*

Already news is circulating that Devonsson is looking for television networks interested in creating a documentary on his rise from anonymous celebrity tabloid reporter to the director of the hottest reality TV show ever aired.

Commentary from the victim, Savannah Rose, has been slim. From all appearances, the former reality TV star seems to have picked up right where she left off before the show began filming a year ago. No one can find fault with that, considering the trauma she experienced at having her entire life upended.

With that said, there has been only one instance where her name has circulated online in recent months, and that has been with the creation of a new Instagram page, shared between her and her fiancé, Owen Harvey.

Harvey, who also suffered at the hands of Devonsson, was forced to come into the limelight about his color-blindness—and his lifelong work as a tattoo artist. The Instagram page, titled "Be Unapologetically You," documents the new weekly workshops held at Harvey's tattoo parlor, Inked on Bourbon (New Orleans, LA) that are designed to help those with disabilities learn how to tattoo. Although Harvey has never spoken to any magazines about his color-blindness, critics have reportedly been hammering on his door, hoping that he might give them a glance into the inner workings of a man who approaches life with such inspiring gusto. To date, it does not seem that he'll ever answer to their knocking but that doesn't mean his impact and drive hasn't been heard or felt.

All over the world, people have taken to using the trending hashtag #BeUnapologetic when cataloging experiences that they once believed unattainable or not accessible to them, for whatever the reason.

While Put A Ring On *It has reached its tumultuous end, and will not be renewed for another season, it's lovely to note that those who live authentically, dream big, and lead with kindness, will always get ahead.*

Signing out as today's guest columnist,
Matilda Houghton

EPILOGUE

OWEN

Two Years Later

Marrying Savannah Rose Harvey came with its ups and downs:

The ups: waking up to her beautiful face every morning; seeing the joy spark in her eyes the very first time she held our baby boy, who we named after my dad, in her arms; and knowing without a shadow of a doubt that when she reaches for my hand, it's still because she loves me with every ounce of her being.

The downs: if she's asking me, there are none because I'm a smart enough guy to know when self-preservation is necessary. If she's not, then here they are in all of their miraculous, shortlisted glory: she has an obsession with cats, and since we got hitched a little over a year and a half ago, we've somehow ended up with five.

Five.

She's single-handedly made me into a cat man, through no assistance of my own, and the only one who feels my pain is poor Pablo. The antichrist sticks to my side nowadays like glue on paper, as though I'm his only saving grace in a world of rambunctious *other cats* who are not nearly on his level.

Which is probably why I'm hiding from my wife in our hotel bathroom, for the honeymoon we never found time to take, and video-chatting with Pablo. And Gage, too, but mostly the cat.

My adopted, firstborn son paws the screen and, goddammit, the little fucker is cute, I'll admit it. "You're feeding him the good stuff, right?" I ask Gage, careful to keep my voice down so I won't wake Savannah while she's sleeping in the room. I stick out a foot and crack the door open some, so I can make sure she's still snoring peacefully.

Another down: the woman can wake the entire house with all that racket, but I haven't smothered her in her sleep yet. Ironically, Savannah's snoring was the first step to me bonding with her dad, after he apologized to me personally when we returned to New Orleans post-reunion show. An apology I readily accepted for the sake of Savannah and our relationship and for my own sake, too. Edgar and I may never be best friends, but we're working on it and I know, with every bit of me, that he loves seeing Savannah and I together.

As it turns out, though, chronic snoring is a DuPont trait, and is single-handedly the reason why Edgar often ends up sleeping in another room halfway through the night. "Just wait until she's pregnant," the old man told me one night when we tentatively agreed to hang out by watching the Saints and drinking beer, "it gets worse. I promise you, Harvey, it gets so much worse."

I probably should have prepared myself for the inevitable—me investing in a good set of ear plugs—but I didn't, and when Savannah got pregnant, she refused to believe me when I called her out for snoring, which she should have realized I would take as a challenge.

One more up: unveiling her thorny side is still my favorite pastime, particularly when it's Ben's naptime and therefore I can seduce his mother the way she likes it best. Her begging, me on my knees, and my face buried between her legs.

I grin, which I hope Gage doesn't notice.

On my tiny phone screen, my twin glares down at Pablo. "You know you've spoiled him rotten, right? The little asshole stole my tuna right off the sandwich I put down on the coffee table today, and you know what your son did?"

My chest puffs up with pride at the mention of seven-month-old Ben. God, even now my heart aches with being away from my little guy. This is the first time Savannah and I have taken a trip alone since he was born. Neither of us wanted to step away, but it felt like a now or never sort of deal. We want another baby—more than I want another cat, that's for damn sure—and then our already tight schedules will string even tighter. "I don't know, man," I tell my brother, "what'd he do?"

"He laughed so hard that he pissed himself."

"That's not so bad," I say, "it's not like you haven't been there yourself with Ari. How many times did she wet herself before y'all potty-trained her?"

Gage's eyes narrow visibly, over the top of Pablo's furry head. "Owen, somehow the kid managed to whip off his diaper and throw it clear across the room. It hit one of the cats."

"Not Pablo, though, right?"

My twin stares at me, unblinking. "You're ridiculous, you know that?"

I shrug. "We have a special bond, what can I say?" I shift

my ass on the closed toilet lid. "Plus, the way I look at it, Ben's clearly just prepping for a throwing arm. Little League, I'm already seeing it. You gonna bedazzle some signs for him the way you did for Ari's dance recital this year?"

"That's *your* job as Ben's dad."

"But you're so good at them. Everyone in the family knows it. Keep it up, and one of them might end up in Amelie's new art gallery. Can you imagine the sort of press you'd get?"

"I hate you, man, just so you're aware."

I grin widely. "That's fine. Hey, can you pan back over to Ben again? I know he's conked out but—"

The bathroom door swings open and while I don't do anything so unmanly as shriek, I definitely shoot an inch off the toilet lid and slam the phone down on the sink counter. "Hey."

Wearing nothing but a pair of my mesh shorts that she stole after we had sex this evening, and a T-shirt, Savannah looks from me to the phone to the toilet. Her hair is a wild, tangled mess, just the way I like it. "Were you video-calling Pablo again?"

"Me?" I point to myself, as though insulted she'd suggest such a thing. "I was scrolling through Sports 24/7 highlights."

She raises a brow. "One call to Lizzie and I'll know the truth."

Heaving a sigh, I plant an elbow on the counter. Is this what love in marriage is like while you're on your belated honeymoon in Iceland? Bantering while sitting on a toilet that you're not even using? Because if so, I want it for the rest of my life with the woman staring down at me like she doesn't know whether to laugh or hop in my lap. "I missed them," I finally confess.

Folding her arms over her chest, she cocks her hip out. “You’re not talking about anyone but Ben and Pablo, are you?”

I shrug. “The rest of them, we’re still feelin’ it out. Testing the waters.”

“You’re ridiculous.”

“Ridiculous enough to fuck?” I wag my brows playfully, and then I’m off my feet in a heartbeat. Arms looped around her upper thighs, I storm into the bedroom to the sounds of her shrieking “Oh, my God, Owen!” as I drop her on the soft mattress and crawl on top of her.

I pin one of her hands beside her head, then grab the other to move to the back of my neck. Her eyes flash good-humor and so much damn love that I feel downright blessed to be here, with her, after everything that it took to get us to this moment. *Sliding scales.* I wouldn’t replace a single memory because what we have, what we’ll *always* have, is so damn strong that I feel its impact every morning when I roll over in bed to link my arm around her waist.

Savannah stares up at me, her full lips curving in a beautiful smile that makes my heart pound fast. “A quickie,” she says, “or we’ll miss the show.”

My heart strings tight because of what’s to come tonight.

Two years ago, she told me that she wanted to see the Northern Lights one day. And for two years, she’s told me repeatedly how it isn’t necessary, how she’ll go anywhere else in the world that I want for our honeymoon. I know she says it because she doesn’t want me to feel as though I’m missing out on something monumental when we look up at the sky blanketed in strips of colors that never quite look the same to me as they do for everyone else.

I took her here anyway because love—at least the love

that I share with Savannah—has me putting her first. Always.

Gently, I grab her left hand. Nowadays, a simple gold band is nestled next to the engagement ring I found in LA, after the reunion show, but it's the ruby stone that steals my attention. Not because I can see it like she can, but because it's my heart trapped on her finger and I never want her to forget how much I love her.

I kiss her knuckle, right over the stone, then set her hand back on the blankets. Leaning down, I press my mouth to hers. Our kisses have evolved over the years, some soft and relaxed when we wind down after a long day, others hurried and messy, our need for each other edging out all the pleasantries of trying to play it cool.

This one is somewhere in between: I kiss her like it's our first time all over again. Unyielding but desperate, my tongue sweeping between her lips so I can taste her fully. She still tastes like the good girl, the debutante who wasn't asked to dance in the ninth grade, but underlying all of that is the woman my wife is at heart: a sweetheart who enjoys being a little bad.

She moans under me, her bound hand fighting the restraint of my weight.

I grin into her mouth, then pull back to husk out, "You gonna beg for me, sweetheart? You gonna show me what you want?"

Her hips buck beneath mine. "Always so arrogant."

I thrust upward, my cock gliding right over the heart of her. "You like it."

"No," she whispers, "I love it."

Drawing back, I inch down her body. My hands skim the T-shirt up her slender frame, past the scars from her C-section that I pause to kiss once, twice. The fabric skirts up another few inches to reveal her breasts, larger now after giving birth but still gorgeous, still perfect handfuls. I drop my head to swirl my tongue around her nipple, chasing the shiver that wracks her body with a nip to the sensitive bud.

Her fingers dance over the back of my neck, then sink into my hair. "*Yes*, more."

I give it to her. My fingers tweaking her other nipple, my tongue gliding over that imperfect mole that always steals my attention. I release her captive wrist, but only so I can kiss my way down her diaphragm and her belly button and then to her hip. I glance up at her face, which is partly concealed in the shadowy room. "Lift your butt, sweetheart."

She does so eagerly, and I strip my shorts off her and toss them to the side. Spreading her knees wide, I drop back on my heels and breathe out. Fucking gorgeous. I knew she would be, from that first day I met her. Gorgeous all over.

Her fingers graze my knee, drawing my attention back up to her face. "When you look at me like that, I feel like it's our first time all over again."

My heart beats faster as I sink down into the sheets. "I told you it would be, that day in the hall. We'd always feel like we're coming out of our skin, chasing a high we'll never find with anyone else. I feel the same as I did then, but only . . . more. Loving you. Wanting you. Devouring you."

I flick my tongue out against her clit, and a sexy moan filters through the room. I keep my palms on the inside of her thighs, forcing her to take everything that I'm giving her. I circle the sensitive flesh, teasing it with fast strokes that taper off whenever I feel her frame tense with the beginnings of a release. She's gonna come with me inside her, not a second before.

Her frustration leaks when I pull back yet again, and

with a chuckle, I climb up her body, only to still when she whispers, "All the way up, Harvey."

If possible, my cock stiffens even more at that. In a guttural voice, I manage, "Thought you said this was a quickie?"

"You always manage to change my mind. Get up here, baby."

I hear the wry note in her voice, and fuck it, but if she's wanting the pressure, the edge to the sex, I'll give it to her. I push her up, so she's sitting on the edge of the bed, and then I follow, trailing my hands over her full hips and the narrow dip at her waist, cupping the breasts that I just laved with attention until she was panting with need.

Standing before her, I take hold of my cock with one hand. Cup her jawline with the other and brush my thumb over her pouty lips. "I love you," I rasp.

She sighs, this warm, happy sound that fills my chest. "I love you today, tomorrow, and for all the tomorrows that follow."

It's what I told her the day I proposed, and somehow it's become our thing. A thing I whisper into her hair when she's sleeping, a thing I say when Edgar is driving her batty at the office because he wants to help out with ERRG's food tours now that he's "officially" retired, a thing I vow when she cradling Ben and I'm holding her and everything feels so damn *right* in the world.

The head of my pierced cock taps her lips, and then I'm palming her jaw, the way I once promised I would, and she's sucking me in. Pleasure zips down my spine and, *hell*, that feels good. She grips the base of me, pumping my length while she circles the crown with her tongue. My hands find her shoulders and I try—I *try*—to hold still but that's never been our style.

I take what I want.

She takes what she wants.

And we always find ourselves tangled in the middle, never wanting to let go.

I thrust forward, just a little, and she moans in the back of her throat. My head falls forward, sensation rippling through me. "God, *yes*, sweetheart. Just like that."

She bobs her head, sucking me deeper, one hand coming around to grasp the back of my thigh. Chest heaving, I feel lightning pierce my skin, a warning that I'm going to come *now*, and I yank back before the orgasm takes hold.

"Need in you," I growl, planting a kiss on her swollen lips as I push her back onto the bed. I work my way down her body and, once I have her legs looped over my forearms, I drive inside her on a single thrust. She cries out and I groan, both of us so loud that I fear we're going to wake our floormates. But there's not a chance in hell of me stopping now.

I rock into her, settling into a pace that I know drives her wild. My cock glides in, creating friction on her clit with each thrust, and soon her nails are digging into my shoulders and her back is arched and my gaze is roaming every inch of her skin that's memorized like a prayer in my head.

"Owen, *please*. More, right there, right—"

Her pussy squeezes down on me as she orgasms and then I'm right there with her, coming so hard I swear that I see stars as I spill inside her. I drop my head to her neck, my mouth finding her collarbone as I try to regulate my breathing. "Think we'll still make it tonight?"

Fingers trail down my spine before swatting my ass playfully. "With the way you drive like you're trying to take Gage's job? Oh, yeah, we'll be fine."

She's not wrong.

Our hotel is in the Snæfellsnes Peninsula, away from the hustle and bustle of the bigger Icelandic cities, and I get us to the designated meeting spot for the tour just as everyone is lining up to see the Northern Lights. I set my hand on Savannah's back, tucking her close to my chest while I brush my kiss over the top of her head. "I'm glad we're finally getting to do this."

She leans back, giving me her full weight, and tilts her head so she can see me. "You're going to love it, Owen."

Frowning at the subtle undertone of her words, I only smile and wait for the tour to get a move on. Soon, the guide is leading us through the national park. The sky is pitch black. Around us, there's nothing to see—not at this time of night, anyway. I chose this area of Iceland when booking our tickets because I figured if we were going to do this, we were going to do it right. With no night pollution, Snæfellsnes is a feast for the eyes.

During the day, at least. Right now, as things are, I can't make out much of anything.

Slowly, we make our ascent to the top of the hill where the guide, a Scottish guy named Kieran Sinclair, tells us to find a spot and get comfortable. I unravel the blanket I stuffed into my backpack, then set it out for us to sit on.

"Excited?" I ask Savannah, my voice hushed. As quiet as it is out here, it feels like we're in a church.

Savannah rummages around in her purse. "I've been waiting for this day for a while."

Another up: making my wife happy. God, I love being married.

Contentedness fills my chest as I drop to the blanket and motion for her to come over. The ground is cold, but we're so bundled up, I can't feel a damn thing. "Lay on me," I tell her, offering my lap.

Weirdly, she drags her purse with her, even though all the other tour-goers are doing their own thing and definitely aren't concerned with us—or with stealing her bag. She settles down, the back of her skull cradled by my thighs, and I brush my fingers through the ends of her hair, careful not to move the beanie she's pulled down over her ears to keep them warm.

"Look!" someone shouts with excitement. "It's happening!"

All around us people jump to attention, and I tip my head back to look up at the sky. While I can tell that there's some sort of rippling effect occurring, as though the black sky is on the move, the colors that everyone else sees are completely lost to me. My stomach twists with the long-ago emotions of a little boy who couldn't see the red fire truck like everyone else, before I shove the disappointment down deep.

I love my life.

I love my wife, my baby boy, and, yes, I even love Pablo.

Mouth a touch dry, I ask, "Is it beautiful?"

"See for yourself, baby."

My gaze drops to Savannah, who is holding out a set of glasses. A frown tugs at my lips, even as my lungs pump a little harder. Over the last few years, since the world learned about my color-blindness, thousands of people have hounded Inked on Bourbon's social media pages, along with my shared page with Savannah, Be Unapologetically You, to ask why I haven't given colorblind correction glasses a chance. The truth is: I'm no longer ashamed of the way I see the world, and when those with a similar genetic trait walk through Inked's doors to learn how to tattoo, I don't want them ever thinking that they're not good enough. Or that they are somehow *less than* because of nothing more than our vision. Strangely, and maybe ridiculously, it almost feels like their self-acceptance begins with *me*.

Staring at what Savannah is holding, I don't know whether to reel back or grab for the glasses without thought. In the end, I only say what's in my heart, what's kicking my gaze back up to the sky again and again, as though if I look hard enough, for once my eyes will do as they should. "What if they don't work?"

"Then you've lost nothing." Savannah's voice softens. "Why don't you see color, baby?"

My throat grows tight as I find her left hand in the darkness, my palm skating over her engagement ring. "My beautiful wife stole them all."

She grasps my hand and turns it over so she can press her chilled lips to the back of my wrist. "Take what you want, Owen. Be fearless. Be unapologetic."

With admittedly shaky fingers, I take the rather bulky glasses from her hand and, with my eyes closed, I put them on. Their weight feels foreign on my face. Foreign and potentially capable of emotional devastation. Fear guts me, because what if they don't work? *What if they do?* Will I suddenly find myself wishing this could be a permanent solution? Will I feel differently when I stand in front of my apprentices, most of whom are colorblind themselves, and tell them that I was wrong all along? That saying that we look at the world more uniquely is all just a lie we tell ourselves to feel better?

It's my wife's softly murmured encouragement that finally steels my spine. I tip my head back and peel my eyes open and *see*.

Light streaks across the sky in a color that I can only imagine is green, though I know I only think that because it's what Sinclair told us on the way here. But still it glows, so bright and so effervescently that I find myself grabbing Savannah's hand and holding on, tight. It's striking. Stunning. And even if I never put these glasses back on, I will always treasure this moment.

"Is it beautiful?" Savannah asks quietly, still gripping my hand.

Angling my face to look down at my wife, I note the tear that slips over her smooth cheek. Silently, I take the glasses off, setting them beside me on the blanket. There are some things I'm willing to view how the world does, but there are others—those that are the most precious to me—that I refuse to look at in any other way but how my eyes naturally see.

Things like my wife.

I cup her face, leaning down so I can brush my mouth over hers, and whisper, "I love you today, tomorrow—"

"And for all the tomorrows that follow," she whispers back against my lips.

And then beneath the glowing sky with its green lights and its thousands of stars, in a country so far away from where I first laid eyes on her and knew, *I'm yours*, I kiss Savannah Rose Harvey, my wife, my best friend, the one woman I always want holding my hand—forever.

Thank you so much for reading Owen & Savannah's story!
I'm utterly in love with this world, so I wrote Georgie & Jean their own free short story! Be prepared for a few cameos of our favorite characters, including a certain cat named Pablo.
Download here: https://www.marialuis.org/kissing-the-gentleman

What To Read Next?

Did you fall just a little bit in love with Gage & Lizzie Harvey? I totally don't blame you! Their story can be found in Tempt Me With Forever, a standalone novel in the NOLA Heart series.

Have you already read all of the NOLA Heart books? Then start the Blades Hockey series with *Power Play!* You'll find a broody, delicious hero, a heroine determined to make it big (even if that means crossing paths with said broody, delicious hero), and hilarious bromances who weird hockey sticks for a living.

Swipe right for an exclusive excerpt!

POWER PLAY TEASER

Power Play is the first book in the Blades Hockey series, featuring a struggling journalist on the hunt for a scoop—and the one man who can either save or break her career.

TeaLicious is by far one of the most hipster-populated places I've ever visited. Think wine bar but with tea instead. It also happens to be Mel's favorite place in the Boston-metro area, and therefore it only made sense to kick off her last few weeks of Singledom by drinking one too many cups of Earl Grey.

What can I say? Some people prefer rum and coke; Mel James prefers orange-scented tea that spent a former lifetime as a jolly-rancher.

We give the party name to the hostess and she's quick to point us in the direction of the group of shrieking women at the back of the restaurant.

I purposely avoid making eye contact with Jenny as we sidle up to the group.

Mel spots us almost immediately, and she launches up from her chair to book it straight over, her arms outstretched. “You’re *here!*” she cries, cupping my face in her hands as she plants a smacking kiss on each of my cheeks. She does the same to Jenny, who squirms at the too-close contact.

Whereas Jenny carries hand-sanitizer everywhere she goes, Mel James—soon to be Mel Wellers—has no idea that some people require personal space.

“Charlie was running late again,” Jenny drawls, effectively throwing me under the bus.

I huff a little at that, even though it is sort of true. To Mel, I say, “I accidentally slept through my alarm. I didn’t go to bed until late last night.”

“Hot date?” Mel asks with a dash of hope in her expression.

I hate to disappoint her, seeing as how *my* love life is as silent as a graveyard, but . . .

“No, I was at work. You’d think that the boss man would want to head home early on a Friday night. Not the case. He decided at six p.m. on the dot that he wanted me to do research for a feature piece on Duke Harrison’s shit-tastic game from Thursday.”

Mel’s right eye twitches in that way it does when she’s hiding something. I pause, waiting for her to speak up like she always does when something is eating away at her.

She doesn’t, so I add, “I don’t get why everyone’s obsessed with Harrison. I mean, all right, he plays for the NHL. He’s quick with his hands, and he’s relatively good-looking—if you like that my-teeth-might-not-be-my-own appeal, which isn’t really my thing.”

“Sounds like someone’s got a crush,” Jenny snickers from beside me, and I promptly shoot her the bird. She mimes catching it, then ignites my offering in a pit of imaginary fire. Lovely.

"I don't have a crush," I mutter, tucking my crazy blonde hair behind one ear. You can dress me in fine clothes, but my hair is a beast of its own. There's no taming it. "All I'm saying," I stress slowly, "is that he should have retired by now. Just because he was a hotshot goalie for the last decade doesn't mean that he's adept at protecting the net anymore. He's weak."

"Thank you."

I flinch at the masculine voice behind me, my gaze immediately seeking help from my two best friends. Both Mel and Jenny look up at the ceiling, and I instantly kick them off of my short-but-sweet best friends list.

You see, there's the minute fact that I recognize that voice. I spent *six goddamn hours* listening to interviews on YouTube last night, and that husky baritone was featured in every single video I clicked.

I *really* don't want to turn around and face the music, and I can practically hear my bones creak in protest as I do so. My thoughts go something like this:

Ah, shit.

Why is this happening to me?

What karma did I accrue?

And, most importantly, *what the* hell *is Duke Harrison of the Boston Blades doing here?*

When I turn around, I have my answer.

Mel's cousin Gwen is suctioned to Duke Harrison's side like an octopus after its next meal. I'm not kidding. Her arm is wrapped around his back, her fingers stuffed into the front pocket of his jeans. Her bottle-dyed red hair cascades over his arm, she's that close to him. Unsurprisingly, she's shooting daggers at me with her eyes.

I blink back at her coolly, just to show that I won't be bullied.

Then I take my first look at Duke Harrison in the flesh and I'm surprised to find that I'm still standing.

I blink rapidly in an attempt to refresh my vision. My first glimpse of him has to be faulty, because there's no way that he is as hot as—

Holy baby Jesus. The camera does him no justice, no justice at all. He's huge, which is to be expected of a professional athlete of his caliber. Broad shoulders, encased in a black, fitted button-down shirt, taper into a fit waist. His jaw is cut from granite, which I understand makes no sense at all, but that doesn't even matter. A cleft punctures his chin. Honestly, I'm shocked by the handsomeness of his rugged features, not to mention his thick head of golden hair.

His overall attractiveness is almost unfair.

Blue eyes, the color of a bird's egg, narrow down at me. I ignore the obvious annoyance in his expression to continue my slow once-over of Boston's Hottest Bachelor Under 40.

Except, by the looks of things, he's not a bachelor any longer.

An engagement ring glitters on Gwen's left hand. It's huge. Probably the size of a toy poodle. If she punched someone with that thing, they'd be laid out cold in a heartbeat.

I inch back, just in case she gets any ideas. Gwen and *ideas* aren't commonly associated with one another, but you never really know. Once, when we were all in college, Gwen snatched a woman's hair at a club and ripped out a handful after the girl told Gwen that her dress was hideous.

I may not particularly like my hair—doesn't mean that I want to have any bald spots on my scalp.

"Charlie," Gwen says now, her voice a pitch lower than Death's. "This is Duke Harrison."

Mel makes a choking noise behind me. I feel no

remorse. Serves her right for not alerting me to the fact that *Duke* freakin' *Harrison* has been standing right behind me this whole time.

I force a smile, hoping that my red lipstick hasn't imprinted on my teeth from all of my recent gnashing, and blandly murmur, "How lovely."

I look up, up, up to Duke's face. I'm not exactly petite, but nor is he exactly average in height. Towering over me, he must be at least six-foot-something. He's still watching me, I notice, his full mouth twisted in a frown. It's sort of sexy now that I'm up close. His face, I mean, not the frown. Although the frown isn't too bad either. It's sulky, a little brooding. I find that I like it.

Gwen glowers and I realize that my greeting hasn't met her standard. For the sake of not throwing down at my best friend's bachelorette party, I try again. "It's so lovely to meet you, Duke. What made you decide to join our women-only tea party?"

Jenny joins the fake-choking train. My lips finally tug upward in a genuine smile.

Duke Harrison, goalie extraordinaire for the Boston Blades, does not return my smile. "Gwen encouraged me to come," is all he says.

"Ah."

It's all that needs to be said, really. What Gwen wants she generally gets—aside from Jenny's husband, that is. My gaze flicks down to Gwen's hand and the diamond ring sparkling under the soft, overhead lighting. "Maybe she wants you in the wedding planning mood," I say. "You know, to bring you up to snuff."

"We're not together."

Now I'm the one gasping for air. I pound my fist against my chest, rubbing in tight little circles. And, oh God, my eyes—they're stinging. Laughter, I think, not tears. Gwen's mouth opens and shuts, even as her gaze turns squinty.

"I was just *trying* it on my ring finger," she snaps. Yanking the diamond off her fourth finger, she fits it on her middle finger of the opposite hand. "Just to see how I feel about it. Duke likes to play hard to get."

"I'm not playing anything," he says evenly.

I can hear Gwen grinding her teeth from here. If she does so any harder, she'll turn them to dust. With her hand still wrapped around his arm, I nevertheless have the sneaking suspicion that while they might not be *together* they've probably swapped spit a few times. Crossed each other's hockey sticks, if you know what I mean—not that Gwen's got a penis. At least, I'm not aware of her having a penis.

Regardless, even if they *haven't* done the dirty, it's clear from the dog-in-heat expression on Gwen's face that she wants to get close and personal with Duke Harrison's twin pucks.

I glance over at Duke, expecting to see that same look of lust darkening his blue eyes. Instead, he appears bored. A little on edge, maybe, but there's no flare of desire in his expression when he attempts to pull away from Gwen's death grip.

Suddenly our gazes clash, hold, and I lift my brow, as if to say, *I wouldn't bother trying.*

He returns my brow-lift with one of his own, and I read his message loud and clear: *Get her off of me.*

My shoulders lift in a shrug—*not my problem*, it translates to—and I notice a pulse leap to his jaw.

"We have an event to go to after this," Gwen says, oblivious to the fact that the man beside her is on the verge of fleeing. "Duke agreed to be my date."

With a heavy sigh, Duke finally manages to detangle himself from the octopus otherwise known as Gwen James. "I'm not your date," he grumbles in overt frustration, "I'm your damn cl—"

Whatever he's about to say is cut off by Gwen's high-pitched voice: "It doesn't matter. *Tea*, Duke? Let's go grab some tea."

She doesn't wait to make any more small talk, not even with her bride-to-be cousin. Latching her hand around his wrist, she gives a quick tug and pulls him toward the table of women.

"Excuse me," Duke murmurs as he brushes past me. I objectively admire his butt as he walks away. It's a great butt, no doubt thanks to the fact that he's constantly squatting in the net. He moves like a lethal predator, and there's no shortage of female sighs as he settles into an empty chair at the end of the table. Gwen sits next to him, immediately turning to him with an accusing finger jab.

Trouble in paradise, it seems.

And then it hits me: I just met Duke "The Mountain" Harrison. *Holy crap.* This is . . . this is crazy. I cannot *wait* to tell Casey, my coworker, on Monday morning. Even if I do think he's overrated, there's still the fact that I am a sports journalist and I've been following his career for years. Since he was a rookie a decade ago.

But while I might be a sports journalist, I also happen to while away thirty-five hours per week at *The Cambridge Tribune.* To say that the newspaper is second-rate would be a stretch, and for one very good reason: my boss, Josh, doesn't believe in handing out press badges. No one takes us seriously because half of the city doesn't even know that we exist.

Who wants to read an online newspaper where the

quotes are regurgitated from other publications? No one knows who I am—this isn't a bad thing, necessarily—but my chances of even freelancing for a more reputable newsletter, like *The Boston Globe*, are slim to none.

Honestly, *I* wouldn't even hire me.

My clips are decent, but there's only so much that you can do with lackluster story material.

"I don't like that look on your face," Jenny says from beside me. "Whatever you're thinking, you stop that right now, Charlie Denton."

Bristling at her suspicious tone, I say, "I'm not thinking about anything."

"You are," Mel jumps in. "You so are."

They've got my calling card. I need a story—a story that will land on screens all over the Northeast—and Duke Harrison just became my muse.

Click here and binge Power Play!

The Blades Hockey series is available on all e-retailers.

DEAR FABULOUS READER

Hi there! I so hope you enjoyed *Love Me Tomorrow*, and if you are new to my books, welcome to the family!

In the back of all my books, I love to include a Dear Fabulous Reader section that talks about what locations from the book can be visited in real life or what sparked my inspiration for a particular plot point. (I like to think of it as the Extras on DVD's, LOL).

As always, we'll hit it up bullet-point style—enjoy!

- It started with me putting my foot in my mouth. There I was talking to a close friend of mine, who planned to visit Iceland with his wife, and he mentioned seeing the Northern Lights. Naturally, I became *very* excited (I've always wanted to go, myself) and started asking all these questions, to which he replied, quite drolly, "Maria, I'm going for her. I can't see them worth a damn." He'd told me in the past that he was colorblind and yet... and yet I had *forgotten*. Embarrassment swept in first, then the shame. For the rest of the night, I continued to think about that—him going with his wife to see the Northern Lights for *her*—and no matter what I did, I couldn't silence the questions. Unlike Savannah, when she discovers that Owen is colorblind, I pestered my friend. I wanted to know *everything*. To his credit, and because he's like an older brother to me, he answered my questions—and so, slowly, Owen began to form in my head . . .

- Naturally, that led to research online because I couldn't help but wonder, *are* there any colorblind tattoo artists? And the answer is *yes*: Joel "Swift" Springer hid his "secret" for a year, but that was only after he'd tried to get apprenticeships, by being honest about his color-blindness, and was promptly turned down from everyone. He taught himself. He built his own portfolio. He *thrived* and I became inspired, *so* inspired. Like Owen, Springer used various organizational skills to keep the colors sorted while he held on tight to his secret. And, like Owen, he defied the odds. Should you be interested in learning more about Springer—including seeing the moment he puts on colorblind correction glasses for the first time, you can do so here.
- Before we move on, I do want to share a source that I found absolutely invaluable throughout writing *Love Me Tomorrow*. While I used my friend's case of Deuteranopia (green-blind) for Owen, it was important for me to show that it's not as simple as Owen not being able to see greens or reds. His color-blindness affects *all*

shades and thanks to this online colorblind simulator, I found myself using it religiously. In every scene depicted from Owen's POV, I uploaded a matching photo with similar colors so I could describe his Deuteranopia as faithfully as possible. And, while colorblind correction glasses aren't always a guarantee, I'd like to think that they worked for Owen when he put them on.

- Did you know that the Edgar Rose Restaurant Group is based on a company here in New Orleans? It's true! In a city like the Crescent City, food is king. And family-owned restaurants are even more so. The Brennans, in particular, rule sovereign throughout the city. Their scandals have hit the newspapers; you can't throw a quarter without hitting at least of their establishments, they own so many; and I became so fascinated with that world—and the idea of these restaurant conglomerates that might as well be royalty—that I couldn't walk away from the idea. The Roses were born from that, and the rest, as you might say, is history! And, if you're keen to visit one of the Brennans' restaurants on your next visit to New Orleans, I highly recommend the Jazz brunch at Commander's Palace on Sundays. There are twenty-five-cent martinis and you can't go wrong - should you visit for dinner on any other night, be prepared to wear your finest. Like Rose & Thorn, Commander's is an elegant experience unto itself!
- But that's not all when it comes to New Orleans

cuisine from *Love Me Tomorrow*! If you recall the Hummingbird Room (and the wine cellar from Rose's), both were inspired by Antoine's Restaurant, which is the longest operating family-owned restaurant in the entire country. *cue mic drop* Like its Brennans counterpart, Antoine's is steeped in history, with over ten dining rooms—one of which directly influenced the Hummingbird Room. And, like Rose & Thorn, which survived Prohibition, Antoine's did the same! In one dining room, even, they put hay all over the floor, so if an officer showed up, patrons could simply pour their drink onto the floor without being caught. The food is delicious at this restaurant, but its history is even more amazing—if you visit, be sure to ask to see some of their old menus! And don't miss out on peeking into the massive wine "cellar" (it's street level) on Royal Street.

- What exactly does it mean to be Creole? Well, back in the eighteenth and nineteenth centuries, "Creole'" encompassed every person *born* in New Orleans. That's right, everyone was Creole. There were Irish Creole and Spanish Creole and African Creole. Slowly, however, the definition began to morph into what it is today: someone with blood of Spanish, French, African or Caribbean descent. Within New Orleans, there is still somewhat of an aristocracy—though without the fancy titles of dukes and ladies—and Creoles sit at the top. In fact, when I moved to New Orleans to attend university, I met my fair share of girls (and boys) who grew up exactly as

Savannah did: the fancy schools and the debutante expectations and the marriages that were expected to link the family to another high-standing Creole one. It fascinated me—especially as someone whose parents both immigrated to America and had, ahem, very little aristocratic pomp—and I couldn't resist bringing that high-class echelon of New Orleans society into *Love Me Tomorrow!*

- For those of you who are *The Bachelor/The Bachelorette* fans, then you may have an inkling as to the inspiration behind *Celebrity Tea Presents.* None other than *Reality Steve* himself. I don't know how the man does it—save for having potential spies rooted throughout the country—but he knows *everything*. In the course of writing the *Put A Ring On It* series, I've done my share of reading Steve's articles themselves. Confession: I'm a little terrified of how much I enjoyed writing *CTP's* chapters. Please don't hold it against me, LOL!
- Interested in going paddleboarding the next time you come to New Orleans? You can go exactly where Owen & Savannah did! City Park, and Bayou St. John, are absolutely real. Whenever I feel the need to get out into nature—or, as much nature as you can when living in a city—I head there to kayak. Each year, there's also a festival called Bayou Boogaloo, where everyone brings out kayaks and paddleboards to party it up on the bayou. Warning: there are alligators. Good news: you won't even notice after a drink or two!
- Barataria, Louisiana, is one of my absolute

favorite places. Though it's only a thirty-minute drive south of New Orleans, you truly get the feeling that you've entered a different world. Swamps line one half of the street in—and there is *only* one street in and out—and the other half is spotted with two-story houses overlooking the canals. A forty-minute boat ride south on the intercostal waterway would bring you straight into the Gulf of Mexico! It's beautiful and quaint and is actually where Mr Luis's dad lives. I couldn't resist adding it into the book, especially as Owen & Savannah's personal retreat from the city.

- Now, I can't be held responsible for the quality, *but* the astronaut-themed pet carrier that Pablo took a joyride in, is real! When writing that scene, I couldn't help but wonder, "If there are cat harnesses, are there cat backpacks?" Yes, yes there are, and Amazon has approximately a gazillion to choose from, including the space capsule one used by Pablo himself, LOL!
- And, lastly, if you've read *Tempt Me With Forever* (NOLA Heart, Book 4, and Gage & Lizzie's book) you may recall that there is a nightclub scene. Let's just say, Gage is an *exceptional* dancer. Lots of rhythm, if you know what I mean. That scene makes me hot, even thinking about t now—and call me evil, but I couldn't resist writing an echo of that scene into *Love Me Tomorrow*, but whereas Gage was all smooth moves, poor Owen is the absolute opposite. Let's hope that Savannah's toes have recovered!

As always, there are many more but here is just a sampling! If you're thinking . . . that seems rather fascinating and I want to know more, you are always so welcome to reach out! Pretty much, nothing makes me happier =)

Much love,

Maria

ACKNOWLEDGMENTS

Owen and Savannah have been a long time coming. Their romance, their chemistry, the finale of *Put A Ring On It*—and it wouldn't have been possible without the encouragement of every reader who wanted their story. Your emails and tags and posts have not gone unnoticed—and, truly, the biggest thank you of all goes to *you*. You waited almost two years for this couple, and you are single-handedly the reason that kept me going back to my computer to spill my soul into this book. Owen and Savannah deserved my everything, and so did you.

Najla—with every cover you send me, you blow my expectations out of the water, but this book, *this* cover, exceeded everything I could have ever dreamed of. Owen and Savannah are perfect and it wouldn't be possible without you!

Wander & Andrey—thank you so so much for working with me on the photography! It's because of you this wonderful image even exists. It has my heart, and I can't thank you both enough for bringing my vision to life.

Kathy—what can I say that isn't completely sappy?

Thank you, from the bottom of my heart, for pushing me to give more to these characters and this story. Your feedback is invaluable, and I'm so grateful to have you on this journey with me.

Brenda—I adore you! Thank you for always reading my words early, for giving me your feedback and supporting me—but, more than anything, thank you for your friendship.

Viper—your feedback means the world to me! I can't even put into words how much I love opening up a document from you because I know (just know) that you're going to give it to me straight. I promise, one of these days I'll remember *me* and *I* and which one goes where, LOL.

Ratula—I love, you lady! Thank you for pushing me to do better, to be more raw, and to give my characters everything they deserve. I couldn't do this without you, and I'm so happy you came into my life.

Dawn and Tandy—y'all are the reason my books sparkle as they do! Thank you for kicking the pesky typos off the island, and for being the awesome people that y'all are.

Dani—thank you for helping me to reach my dreams and for being a steady hand of support when I need it. You are the best partner-in-crime!

To my besties/family/awesome-sauce friends Tina, Sam, Jami, Amie, Jen, Jess, Joslyn, Stephanie, and to my girls in 30 Days to 60k, Indie AF, and Beach Retreat, I would absolutely be lost without you. I wouldn't want to take on this book world with anyone else but y'all at my side.

To my VIPers and to my family in BBA, just know that this book—this one is for you. Thank you for holding me up, for laughing at my ridiculous antics (cue, the Roomba story), for supporting me with every book and for being the best family a girl could ask for. I love you guys tons, and I'm so happy we found each other.

And, lastly, to you Dear Reader, for picking up this book and giving me a chance. Thank you for allowing me to live my dream—unapologetically and fearlessly—as a storyteller.

Much love,

Maria

ALSO BY MARIA LUIS

Nola Heart

Say You'll Be Mine

Take A Chance On Me

Dare You To Love Me

Tempt Me With Forever

Blades Hockey

Power Play

Sin Bin

Hat Trick

Body Check

Blood Duet

Sworn

Defied

Put A Ring On It

Hold Me Today

Kiss Me Tonight

Love Me Tomorrow

Broken Crown

Road To Fire

Kiss Me Tonight

Love Me Tomorrow

Freebies (available at www.marialuis.org)

Breathless (a Love Serial, #1)

Undeniable (a Love Serial, #2)

The First Fix

ABOUT THE AUTHOR

Maria Luis is the author of sexy contemporary romances.

Historian by day and romance novelist by night, Maria lives in New Orleans, and loves bringing the city's cultural flair into her books. When Maria isn't frantically typing with coffee in hand, she can be found binging on reality TV, going on adventures with her other half and two pups, or plotting her next flirty romance.

Stalk Maria in the Wild at the following!
Join Maria's Newsletter
Join Maria's Facebook Reader Group

Made in the USA
Monee, IL
13 July 2023